DEAN KOONTZ—*HARDSHELL*

Los Angeles detective Frank "Hardshell" Shaw has always thrived on tracking down murderers. But never before has he faced such a powerful adversary—an immortal shape-changing maniacal serial killer.

F. PAUL WILSON—*SLASHER*

The brutal slaying of a man's five-year-old daughter has left him hell-bent on revenge. The only justice he'll accept is to carve up the killer; but if he's not careful, his blind rage will lead him to a place he never suspected.

JOHN COYNE—*THE ECOLOGY OF REPTILES*

The riverbanks of Africa holds many indigenous dangers—the kind that wait silently and instinctively for prey. And for the lovers, liars, and adulterers who frolic on those banks, discovering the differences between carnal and carnivorous appetites will become a matter of life and death.

D1070351

ROC   ⬤ONYX   (0451)

TERRIFYING TALES

☐ **STALKERS edited by Ed Gorman & Martin H. Greenberg.** In this compelling all-original anthology, twenty masters of suspense including Rex Miller, Rick Hautala, and John Coyne take you into the darkest depths of terror as they explore both sides of the human hunt.   (451481—$4.99)

☐ **SUNGLASSES AFTER DARK by Nancy Collins.** The kiss of life has never been so deadly. Sonja Blue, the most erotic vampire of all time, leads men to heaven, and delivers them to hell.
      (401476—$3.99)

☐ **IN THE BLOOD by Nancy A. Collins.** This beautiful vampire in sunglasses and black leather cannot live by blood alone. . . .
      (451511—$4.99)

Prices slightly higher in Canada

Buy them at your local bookstore or use this convenient coupon for ordering.

PENGUIN USA
P.O. Box 999 – Dept. #17109
Bergenfield, New Jersey 07621

Please send me the books I have checked above.
I am enclosing $_____ (please add $2.00 to cover postage and handling).
Send check or money order (no cash or C.O.D.'s) or charge by Mastercard or VISA (with a $15.00 minimum). Prices and numbers are subject to change without notice.

Card #_____ Exp. Date _____
Signature_____
Name_____
Address_____
City _____ State _____ Zip Code _____
For faster service when ordering by credit card call **1-800-253-6476**
Allow a minimum of 4-6 weeks for delivery. This offer is subject to change without notice.

PREDATORS

EDITED BY
Ed Gorman and
Martin H. Greenberg

A ROC BOOK

ROC
Published by the Penguin Group
Penguin Books USA Inc., 375 Hudson Street,
New York, New York 10014, U.S.A.
Penguin Books Ltd, 27 Wrights Lane,
London W8 5TZ, England
Penguin Books Australia Ltd, Ringwood,
Victoria, Australia
Penguin Books Canada Ltd, 10 Alcorn Avenue,
Toronto, Ontario, Canada M4V 3B2
Penguin Books (N.Z.) Ltd, 182–190 Wairau Road,
Auckland 10, New Zealand

Penguin Books Ltd, Registered Offices:
Harmondsworth, Middlesex, England

First published by Roc,
an imprint of Dutton Signet,
a division of Penguin Books USA Inc.
Previously published in a Roc trade paperback edition.

First Mass Market Printing, October, 1994
10 9 8 7 6 5 4 3 2 1

Copyright © Martin H. Greenberg and Ed Gorman, 1993
"Hardshell," copyright © 1987 by Nkui, Inc. Reprinted by
permission of the author.
"The Calligraphy Lesson," copyright © Joyce Harrington, 1993
"The Rubber Smile," copyright © John Shirley, 1993
"The Defiance of the Ugly by the Merely Repulsive,"
copyright © James Kisner, 1993
"Mind Slash Matter," copyright © Edward Wellen, 1993

(*The following page constitutes an extension of this copyright page.*)

"Goddam Time," copyright © J. N. Williamson and Scott Fogel, 1993
"The Society of the Scar," copyright © Edward D. Hoch, 1993
"Life Near the Bone," copyright © Billie Sue Mosiman, 1993
"Slasher," copyright © F. Paul Wilson, 1993
"To Die For," copyright © Ed Naha, 1993
"Mistaken Identity," copyright © T. L. Parkinson, 1993
"Dead Things Don't Move," copyright © Lawrence Watt-Evans, 1993
"The Man Who Collected Knives," copyright © John Betancourt, 1993
"The Roadside Scalpel," copyright © Thomas F. Monteleone, 1993
"The Pharaoh's Crown," copyright © Christopher Fahy, 1993
"Slit," copyright © Richard Laymon, 1993
"Rubies and Pearls," copyright © Rick Hautala, 1993
"Old Blood," copyright © Gary Brandner, 1993
"Heroes," copyright © Richard T. Chizmar, 1993
"Valentine," copyright © Daniel Ransom and Rex Miller, 1993
"The Ecology of Reptiles," copyright © John Coyne, 1993
All rights reserved

 REGISTERED TRADEMARK—MARCA REGISTRADA

Printed in the United States of America

Without limiting the rights under copyright reserved above, no part of this publication may be reproduced, stored in or introduced into a retrieval system, or transmitted, in any form, or by any means (electronic, mechanical, photocopying, recording, or otherwise), without the prior written permission of both the copyright owner and the above publisher of this book.

BOOKS ARE AVAILABLE AT QUANTITY DISCOUNTS WHEN USED TO PROMOTE PRODUCTS OR SERVICES. FOR INFORMATION PLEASE WRITE TO PREMIUM MARKETING DIVISION, PENGUIN BOOKS USA INC., 375 HUDSON STREET, NEW YORK, NEW YORK 10014.

If you purchased this book without a cover you should be aware that this book is stolen property. It was reported as "unsold and destroyed" to the publisher and neither the author nor the publisher has received any payment for this "stripped book."

Contents

Hardshell

Dean R. Koontz

1

Arteries of light pulsed in the black sky. In that strobo-scopic blaze, millions of cold raindrops appeared to have halted in midfall. The glistening street reflected the ce-lestial fire and for a moment seemed to be paved with broken mirrors. Then the lightning-scored sky went black again, and the rain resumed. The pavement was dark. Once more the flesh of the night pressed close on all sides.

Clenching his teeth and trying to ignore the pain in his right side, squinting in the gloom, Detective Frank Shaw gripped the Smith & Wesson .38 Chief's Special in both hands. He assumed a shooter's stance and squeezed off two shots.

Ahead of Frank, Karl Skagg sprinted around the cor-ner of the nearest warehouse just in time to save himself. The first slug bored a hole in the empty air behind him; the second clipped the corner of the building.

The relentless roar of the rain on metal warehouse roofs and on the pavement, combined with rumbling thunder, effectively muffled the shots. Even if private security guards were at work in the immediate area, they probably had not heard anything, so Frank could not expect assistance.

He would have welcomed assistance. Skagg was big, powerful, a serial killer who had committed at least twenty-two murders. The guy was incredibly dangerous even in his best moments, and right now he was about as approachable as a whirling buzzsaw. This was definitely not a job for one cop.

Frank considered returning to his car and putting in a call for backup, but he knew that Skagg would slip away before the area could be cordoned off. No cop would call off a chase merely out of concern for his own welfare—especially not Frank Shaw.

Splashing across the puddled serviceway between two of the huge warehouses, Frank took the corner wide, in case Skagg was waiting for him just around the bend. But Skagg was gone.

Unlike the front of the warehouse, where concrete loading ramps sloped up to the enormous rolling garage doors, this side was mostly blank. Two hundred feet away, below a dimly glowing bulb in a wire security cage, was a single, man-size metal door. It was half-open but falling shut.

Wincing at the pain in his side, Frank hurried to the entrance. He was surprised to see that the handle was torn off and that the lock was shattered, as if Skagg had used a crowbar or sledgehammer. But the man had been empty-handed. Had he found a tool leaning against the warehouse wall, and had he used it to batter his way inside? He had been out of sight for mere seconds, no more than half a minute, which surely wasn't enough time to break through a steel door.

Why hadn't the burglar alarm sounded? Surely the warehouse was protected by an electronic security system. And Skagg had not entered with sufficient finesse to circumvent an alarm.

Thoroughly soaked, Frank shivered involuntarily when he put his back to the cold wall beside the door. He gritted his teeth, willed himself to stop shaking, and listened intently.

He heard only the hollow drumming of rain on metal roofs and walls. The sizzle of rain dancing on the wet pavement. The gurgle and slurp and chuckle of rain in gutters and downspouts.

Wind bleating. Wind hissing.

Frank broke the cylinder out of his revolver. He reached under his jacket and plucked four cartridges from the row of ten that were held in leather loops along the rim of his custom-designed shoulder holster. He quickly reloaded.

His right side throbbed. Minutes ago Skagg had taken him by surprise, stepping out of shadows, swinging a length of two-by-four as Mickey Mantle might have swung a baseball bat. Frank felt as if chunks of broken glass were working against one another deep in his muscles and bones, and the pain sharpened slightly each time he drew a breath. Maybe he had a broken rib or two. Probably not ... but maybe. He was wet, cold, and weary.

He was also having fun.

2

To other homicide detectives, Frank was known as Hardshell Shaw. That was also what his buddies had called him during Marine Corps basic training more than twenty-five years ago, for he was stoical, tough, and could not be cracked. The name followed him when he left the service and joined the Los Angeles Police Department. He never encouraged anyone to use the sobriquet, but they used it anyway because it was apt.

Frank was tall, wide in the shoulders, narrow in the waist and hips, with a rock-solid body. His enormous hands, when curled into fists, were so formidable that he usually needed only to brandish them to assure an adversary's cooperation. His broad face appeared to have been carved out of granite—and with some difficulty, with much breaking of chisels and snapping of hammers. His colleagues in the homicide division of the LAPD sometimes claimed that Frank had only two basic expressions: mean and meaner.

His pale blue eyes, clear as rainwater, regarded the world with icy suspicion. When thinking, he frequently sat or stood perfectly still for long periods during which the quickness and alertness of his blue eyes, contrasted with his immobility, gave the impression that he was peering out from within a shell.

He had a damn hard shell, so his friends claimed. But that was only half of what they said about him.

Now, finished reloading his revolver, he stepped in

front of the damaged warehouse door. He kicked it open. Crouched, head tucked down, holding the .38 in front of him, he went in fast, looking left and right, expecting Skagg to rush at him with a crowbar, hammer, or whatever tool the scumbag had used to get into the building.

To Frank's left was a twenty-foot-high wall of metal shelving filled with thousands of small boxes. To his right were large wooden crates stacked in rows, towering thirty feet overhead, extending half the length of the building, alternating with avenues wide enough to admit forklifts.

The banks of overhead fluorescents suspended from the fifty-foot-high warehouse ceiling were switched off. Only a few security lamps in conical tin shades shed a wan glow over the stored goods below, leaving most of the place sheathed in shadows.

Frank moved cautiously and silently. His soggy shoes squished, but that sound was barely audible over the background drumming of rain on the roof. With water dripping off his brow, jawline, and the barrel of his gun, he eased from one row of crates to another, peering into each passageway.

Skagg was at the far end of the third aisle, about a hundred and fifty feet away, half in shadow, half in milk-pale light, waiting to see if Frank had followed him. He could have kept out of the light, could have crouched entirely in the gloom against the crates, where he might not have been visible; by waiting in plain sight, he seemed to be taunting Frank. Skagg hesitated a moment, as if to be sure that he had been spotted, then disappeared around the corner.

For five minutes they played hide and seek, moving stealthily through the maze of cartons and crates. Three times, Skagg allowed himself to be seen, although he never let Frank get close.

He's having fun, too, Frank thought.

That made him angry.

High on the walls, under the cobweb-festooned eaves, were slit windows that helped illuminate the cavernous building during the day. Now only the flicker of lightning revealed the existence of those narrow windows. Although that inconstant pulse did not brighten the warehouse, it occasionally caused shadows to leap disconcertingly, and twice Frank nearly shot one of those harmless phantoms.

Easing along another avenue, scanning the shadows on both sides, Frank heard a noise, a hard scraping sound. He knew at once what it was: a crate sliding on a crate.

He looked up. In the grayness high above, a sofa-size box—visible only as a black silhouette—teetered on the edge of the crate beneath it. Then it tipped over and plummeted straight toward him.

He threw himself forward, hit the floor, and rolled just as the crate exploded against the concrete where he had been standing. He averted his face as the wood disintegrated into hundreds of splintery shards of shrapnel. The box had contained plumbing fixtures; bright, chrome-plated faucets and showerheads bounced along the floor, and a couple of them thumped off Frank's back and thighs.

Hot tears of agony burned in his eyes, for the pain in his right side flared brighter. Further abused by all of this activity, his battered ribs now seemed not merely broken but pulverized.

Overhead Skagg let out a sound that was one part a cry of rage, one part an animalistic ululation celebrating the thrill of the hunt, and one part insane laughter.

With some sixth sense Frank was suddenly aware of a murderous, descending weight. He rolled to his right, flat up against the same wall of crates atop which Skagg stood. Behind him, a second huge box crashed into the warehouse floor.

"You alive?" Skagg called.

Frank did not respond.

"Yeah, you must be down there because I didn't hear you scream. You're a quick bastard, aren't you?"

That laugh again. It was like atonal music played on an out-of-tune flute: a cold, metallic sound. There was something inhuman about it. Frank Shaw shivered.

Surprise was Frank's favorite strategy. During a pursuit, he tried to do what his prey would least expect. Now, taking advantage of the masking roar of the rain on the corrugated steel roof, he stood up in the darkness beside the wall of crates, holstered his revolver, blinked the tears of pain out of his eyes, and began to climb.

"Don't cower in the shadows like a rat," Skagg shouted. "Come out and try to take a shot at me. You've got a gun; I don't. It'll be your bullets against whatever I can throw at you. What better odds do you want, you chickenshit cop?"

Twenty feet up the thirty-foot-high wall of wooden boxes, with his chilled fingers hooked into meager niches, with the toes of his shoes pressed hard against narrow ledges, Frank paused. The pain in his right side tightened as if it were a lasso, and it threatened to pull him backward into the aisle almost two stories below. He clung desperately to his precarious position and squeezed his eyes tightly shut, willing the pain to go away.

"Hey, asshole," Skagg shouted.

Yeah?

"You know who I am?"

Big man on the psycho circuit, aren't you?

"I'm the one the newspapers call the Night Slasher."

Yeah, I know, I know, you drooling degenerate.

"This whole damn city lays awake at night, worrying about me, wondering where I am," Skagg shouted.

Not the whole city, man. Personally I haven't lost any sleep over you.

Gradually the hot, grinding pain in his ribs subsided. It did not disappear altogether, but now it was a dull throb.

Among friends in the marines and on the police force, Frank had a reputation for persevering and triumphing in spite of wounds that would have incapacitated anyone else. In Nam he had taken two bullets from a Vietcong machinegun, one in the left shoulder and one through his left side directly above the kidney, but he had kept on going and had wasted the gunner with a grenade. Bleeding profusely, he nevertheless used his good arm to drag his badly wounded buddy three hundred yards to a place of concealment, where they were safe from enemy snipers while the Medevac chopper sought and found them. As the medics loaded him into the helicopter, he had said, "War is hell, all right, but it's also damned exhilarating!"

His friends said he was iron-hard, nail-tough. But that was only part of what they said about him.

Overhead, Karl Skagg hurried along the top of the boxes. Frank was close enough to hear the man's heavy footsteps above the ceaseless rumble of rain on the roof.

Even if he had heard nothing, he would have known that Skagg was on the move, for the two-crate-thick wall trembled with the killer's passage. The movement was not violent enough to shake Frank off his perch.

He started to climb again, feeling cautiously for hand-holds in the darkness, inching along the pile of plumbing supplies. He got a few splinters in his fingers, but it was easy to tune out those small, stabbing pains.

From his new position atop the wall, Skagg shouted into another shadowy section of the warehouse to which he apparently thought Frank had moved, "Hey, chicken-shit!"

You called?

"I have something for you, chickenshit."

I didn't know we were exchanging gifts.

"I got something sharp for you."

I'd prefer a TV set.

"I got the same thing for you that I used on all the others."

Forget the TV. I'll settle for a nice bottle of cologne.

"Come and get your guts ripped out, you chicken-shit!"

I'm coming. I'm coming.

Frank reached the top, raised his head above the edge of the wall, looked left, then right, and saw Skagg about thirty feet away. The killer had his back to Frank and was peering intently down into another aisle.

"Hey, look at me, standing right up here in the light. You can hit me with no trouble, cop. All you have to do is step out and line up a shot. What's the matter? Don't you even have the nerve for that, you yellow bastard?"

Frank waited for a peal of thunder. When it came, he levered himself over the edge, on top of the stack of crates, where he rose to a crouch. The pounding rain was even louder up here, and combined with the thunder it was enough to cover any noise he made.

"Hey, down there! You know who I am, cop?"

You're repeating yourself. Boring, boring.

"I'm a real prize, the kind of trophy a cop dreams of!"

Yeah, your head would look good on my den wall.

"Big career boost if you brought me down, promotions and medals, you chickenshit."

The ceiling lights were only ten feet above their heads, and at such short range even the dim bulbs in the security lamps cast enough of a glow to illuminate more than half of the crates on which they stood. Skagg was in the brightest spot, posturing for the one-man audience that he believed was below him.

Drawing his .38, Frank stepped forward, out of a shadowy area into a fall of amber light.

Skagg shouted, "If you won't come for me, you chickenshit, I'll come for you."

"Who're you calling chickenshit?" Frank asked.

Startled, Skagg spun toward him and, for an instant, teetered on the edge of the boxes. He windmilled his arms to keep from falling backward into the aisle below.

Holding his revolver in both hands, Frank said, "Spread your arms, drop to your knees, then lay flat on your belly."

Karl Skagg had none of that heavy-browed, slab-jawed, mongoloid, cement-faced look that most people associated with homicidal maniacs. He was handsome. Movie-star handsome. His was a broad, well-sculpted face with masculine yet sensitive features. His eyes were not like the eyes of a snake or a lizard or some other wild thing, either, but were brown, clear and appealing.

"Flat on your belly," Frank repeated.

Skagg did not move. But he grinned. The grin ruined his movie-star looks, for it had no charm. It was the humorless leer of a crocodile.

The guy was big, even bigger than Frank. He was six five, maybe even six and a half feet. Judging by the solid look of him, he was a dedicated, lifelong weightlifter. In spite of the chilly November night, he wore only running shoes, jeans, and blue cotton shirt. Damp with rain and sweat, the shirt molded to his muscular chest and arms.

He said, "So how're you going to get me down from

here, cop? Do you think I'll let you cuff me and then just
lay up here while you go for backup? No way, pig face."

"Listen and believe me: I'll blow you away without
the slightest hesitation."

"Yeah? Well, I'll take that gun off you quicker than
you think. Then I'll rip your head off and shove it up
your ass."

With unconcealed distaste, Frank said, "Is it really
necessary to be so vulgar?"

Grinning more broadly, Skagg moved toward him.

Frank shot him pointblank in the chest.

The hard report echoed off the metal walls, and Skagg
was thrown backward. Screaming, he pitched off the
crates and plummeted into the aisle below. He landed
with a *thunk* that cut off his scream.

Skagg's violent departure caused the crates to rock,
and for a moment the unmortared wall of boxes swayed
dangerously, creaking and grinding. Frank fell to his
hands and knees. Waiting for the stacks to steady under
him, he thought about all the paperwork involved in a
shooting of this sort, the many forms required to appease
the bleeding hearts who were always certain that every
victim of a police shooting was as innocent as Mother
Teresa. He wished Skagg had not forced the issue so
soon. He wished the killer had been more clever, had
managed a more involved game of cat and mouse before
the climactic scene. The chase had not provided half
enough fun to compensate for the mountain of paperwork ahead.

The crates quickly steadied, and Frank got to his feet.
He moved to the edge of the wall, to the place where
Skagg had been flung into empty space by the impact of
the slug. He looked down into the aisle. The concrete
floor was silvery in the glow of the security lamp.

Skagg was not there.

Storm light flickered at the windows in the warehouse
eaves. At his side Frank's shadow leaped, shrank back,
leaped, and shrank again, as if it were the shadow of
Alice in one of her potion-swilling fits beyond the looking glass.

Thunder pummeled the night sky, and an even harder
fall of rain pummeled the roof.

Frank shook his head, squinted into the aisle below, and blinked in disbelief.

Skagg was still not there.

3

Having descended the crates with caution, Frank Shaw looked left and right along the deserted aisle. He studied the shadows intently, then crouched beside the spots and smears of blood where Karl Skagg had hit the floor. At least a liter of blood marked the point of impact, so fresh that a portion had still not soaked into the porous concrete but glistened in small, red, shallow puddles.

No man could take a .38 slug in the chest at point-blank range, get up immediately, and walk away. No man could fall three stories onto concrete and spring straight to his feet.

Yet that seemed to be what Skagg had done.

A trail of gore indicated the man's route. With his .38 gripped tightly in his right hand, Frank traced the psycho to an intersection, turned left into a new aisle, and moved stealthily through alternating pools of shadow and light for a hundred and fifty feet. There, he came to the end of the blood trail, which simply stopped in the middle of the passageway.

Frank peered up at the piled crates on both sides, but Skagg was not clinging to either partition. No offshoot passageways between the boxes and no convenient niches provided a good hiding place.

Though badly hurt and hurrying to get out of his pursuer's reach, Skagg appeared to have carefully bound his grievous wounds to control the bleeding, had literally bound them on the run. But with what? Had he torn his shirt into strips to make tourniquets, bandages?

Damn it, Skagg had a mortal chest wound. Frank had seen the terrible impact of bullet in flesh, had seen Skagg hurled backward, had seen blood. The man's breastbone was shattered, splinters driven inward through vital organs. Arteries and veins were severed. The slug itself surely had passed through Skagg's heart. Neither tourniquets nor bandages could stanch that flow or induce

mangled cardiac muscles to resume rhythmic con-
tractions.

Frank listened to the night.

Rain, wind, thunder. Otherwise . . . silence.

Dead men don't bleed, Frank thought.

Maybe that was why the blood trail ended where it
did—because Skagg died after going that far. But if he
had died, death had not stopped him. He had kept right
on going.

And now what am I chasing? A dead man who won't
give up?

Most cops would have laughed off such a thought,
embarrassed by it. Not Frank. Being tough, hard, and
unbreakable did not mean that he had to be inflexible
as well. He had the utmost respect for the incomprehensible complexity of the universe and for the unplumbable
mystery of life.

A walking dead man? Unlikely. But if that *was* the
case, then the situation was certainly interesting. Fasci-
nating. Suddenly Frank was more thoroughly involved
in his work than he had been in weeks.

4

The warehouse was vast but, of course, finite. As Frank
explored the gloom-filled place, however, the chilly interior somehow seemed to be larger than the space enclosed by its walls, as if portions of the building extended
into another dimension, or as if the actual size of the
structure changed magically and constantly to conform
to his exaggerated perception of its immensity.

He searched for Skagg in aisles formed by crates and
along other aisles between towering metal shelves filled
with cardboard cartons. He stopped repeatedly to test
the lids of crates, suspecting that Skagg had hidden in
an empty one, but he found no makeshift coffin belong-
ing to the walking dead man.

Twice he briefly suspended the search to take time to
stay in touch with the throbbing pain in his side. In-
trigued by the mystery of Skagg's disappearance, he had
forgotten being hammered with a two-by-four. His ex-
traordinary ability to block pain contributed to his hard-

boiled reputation. A buddy in the department once said that Hardshell Shaw's pain threshold was between that of a rhinoceros and a wooden fence post. But there were times when experiencing pain to the fullest was desirable. For one thing pain sharpened his senses and kept him alert. Pain was humbling as well; it encouraged a man to keep his perspective, helped him to remember that life was precious. He was no masochist, but he knew that pain was a vital part of the human condition.

Fifteen minutes after having shot Skagg, Frank still hadn't found him. Nevertheless he remained convinced that the killer was in the warehouse, dead or alive, and had not fled into the rainy night. His conviction was based on more than a hunch; he possessed the reliable intuition that distinguished great cops from good cops.

A moment later, when his intuition proved unnervingly accurate, Frank was exploring a corner of the building where twenty forklifts of various sizes were parked beside a dozen electric carts. Because of their knobby hydraulic joints and blunt tines, the lifts resembled enormous insects, and in the smoky yellow glow of the overhead lamp, they cast praying mantis silhouettes across other machinery. Frank was moving quietly through those spiky shadows when behind him Karl Skagg spoke:

"You looking for me?"

Frank whipped around, bringing his gun up.

Skagg was about twelve feet away.

"See me?" the killer asked.

His chest was intact, unwounded.

"See me?"

His three-story fall had resulted in no shattered bones, no crushed flesh. His blue cotton shirt was stained with blood, but the source of those stains was not visible.

"See me?"

"I see you," Frank said.

Skagg grinned. "You know *what* you're seeing?"

"A piece of shit."

"Can your small mind possibly conceive of my true nature?"

"Sure. You're a dog turd."

"You can't offend me," Skagg said.

"I can try."

"Your petty opinions are of no interest or concern to me."

"God forbid that I should bore you."

"You're getting tiresome."

"And you're nuts."

Skagg cracked an icy, humorless smile of the sort that earlier had reminded Frank of a crocodile's grin. "I'm so far superior to you and to all of your kind that you're incapable of judging me."

"Oh, then forgive me for my presumption, great lord."

Skagg's grin faded into a vicious grimace, and his eyes widened. They no longer seemed like ordinary brown eyes. In the dark depths of them, a strangeness appeared: a hungry, chillingly reptilian watchfulness that made Frank feel as if he were a fieldmouse staring into the mesmeric eyes of a blacksnake.

Skagg took one step forward.

Frank took one step backward.

"Your kind have only one use: you're interesting prey."

"Well, I'm glad to hear we're interesting."

Skagg took another step forward, and a portion of a mantislike shadow rippled across his face.

Frank stepped backward.

"Your kind are born to die."

Always interested in the working of a criminally insane mind, just as a surgeon is always interested in the nature of the cancers that he excises from his patients' bodies, Frank said, "My kind, huh? What kind is that exactly?"

"Humankind."

"Ah."

"Humankind," Skagg repeated, speaking the word as if it were the vilest epithet.

"You're not human? Is that it?"

"That's it," Skagg agreed.

"What are you then?"

Skagg's insane laughter was as affecting as hard arctic wind.

Feeling as if bits of ice had begun to form in his blood-

stream, Frank shivered. "All right, enough of this. Drop
to your knees, then flat on your face."

"You're so slow-witted," Skagg said.

"Now *you're* boring *me*. Lie down and spread your
arms and legs, you son of a bitch."

Skagg reached out with his right hand in such a way
that for one disconcerting moment it seemed to Frank
that the killer was going to change tactics and begin
pleading for his life.

Then the hand began to change. The palm grew longer
and broader. The fingers lengthened by as much as two
inches, and the knuckles became thicker, gnarled. The
hand darkened until it was singularly unhealthy, mottled
brown-black-yellow. Coarse hairs sprouted from the
skin. The fingernails extended into wickedly sharp claws.

"So tough you were. Imitation Clint Eastwood. But
you're afraid now, aren't you, little man? You're afraid
at last, aren't you?"

Only the hand changed. No alterations occurred in
Skagg's face or body or even in his other hand. He obviously had complete control of his metamorphosis.

"Werewolf," Frank said in astonishment.

With another peal of lunatic laughter that rebounded
tinnily from the warehouse walls, Skagg worked his new
hand, curling and extending and recurling his monstrous fingers.

"No. Not a werewolf," he whispered fiercely. "Something far more adaptable. Something infinitely stranger
and more interesting. Are you afraid now? Have you
wet your pants yet, you chickenshit cop?"

Skagg's hand began to change again. Coarse hairs receded into the flesh that had sprouted them. The mottled
skin grew darker still, the many colors blending into
green-black, and scales began to appear. The fingertips
thickened and grew broader, and suction pads formed
on them. Webs spun into being between the fingers. The
claws subtly changed shape, but they were no shorter or
less sharp than the lupine claws had been.

Skagg peered at Frank through those hideous spread
fingers and over the half-moon curves of the opaque
webs. Then he lowered his hand slightly and grinned; his
mouth had also changed. His lips were thin, black, and

pebbled. He revealed pointed teeth and two hooked fangs. A thin, glistening, fork-tipped tongue flicked across those teeth, licked the pebbled lips.

At the sight of Frank's horrified astonishment, Skagg laughed. His mouth once more assumed the appearance of a human mouth.

But the hand underwent yet another metamorphosis. The scales were transformed into a hard-looking, smooth, purple-black, chitinous substance, and the fingers, as if made of wax and now brought before a flame, melted together, five into two, till Skagg's wrist terminated in a serrated, razor-sharp pincer.

"You see? No need of a knife for this Night Slasher," whispered Skagg. "Within my hands are an infinite variety of blades."

Frank kept his .38 revolver pointed at his adversary, though by now he knew that even a .357 Magnum loaded with magnum cartridges with Teflon tips would provide him with no protection.

Outside, the sky was split by an axe of lightning. The flash of the electric blade sliced through the narrow windows high above the warehouse floor. For a moment a flurry of rafter shadows fell upon Frank and Skagg.

As thunder crashed across the night, Frank said, "What the hell are you?"

Skagg did not answer right away. He stared at Frank for a long moment and seemed perplexed. When he spoke, his voice had a double-honed edge—curiosity and anger. "Your species is soft. Your kind have no nerve, no guts. Faced with the unknown, your kind react as sheep react to the scent of a wolf. I despise your weakling breed. The strongest men break after what I've revealed. They scream like children, flee in panic, or stand paralyzed and speechless with fear. But not you. What makes you different? What makes you so brave? Are you simply thickheaded? Don't you realize you're a dead man? Are you foolish enough to think you'll get out of this place alive? Look at you—your gun hand isn't even trembling."

"I've had more frightening experiences than this," Frank said tightly. "I've been through two tax audits."

Skagg did not laugh. He clearly needed a terrified reaction from an intended victim. Murder was not sufficiently satisfying; evidently he also required the complete humiliation and abasement of his prey.

Well, you bastard, you're not going to get what you need from me, Frank thought.

He repeated, "What the hell are you?"

Clacking the halves of his deadly pincers, slowly taking a step toward Frank, Karl Skagg said, "Maybe I'm the spawn of hell. Do you think that could be the explanation? Hmmmm?"

"Stay back," Frank warned.

Skagg took another step toward him. "Am I a demon perhaps, risen from some sulfurous pit? Do you feel a certain coldness in your soul; do you sense the nearness of something satanic?"

Frank bumped against one of the forklifts, stepped around the obstruction, and continued to retreat.

Advancing, Skagg said, "Or am I something from another world, a creature alien to this one, conceived under a different moon, born under another sun?"

As he spoke, his right eye receded deep into his skull, dwindled, vanished. The socket closed up as the surface of a pond would close around the hole made by a pebble; only smooth skin lay where the eye had been.

"Alien? Is that something of which you could conceive?" Skagg pressed. "Have you sufficient wit to accept that perhaps I came to this world across an immense sea of space, carried on strange galactic tides?"

Frank no longer wondered how Skagg had battered open the door of the warehouse; he would have made hornlike hammers of his hands—or ironlike prybars. And he no doubt had also slipped incredibly thin extensions of his fingertips into the alarm switch, deactivating it.

The skin of Skagg's left cheek dimpled, and a hole formed in it. The lost right eye flowered into existence within that hole, directly under his left eye. In two winks both eyes re-formed: they were no longer human but insectile, bulging and multifaceted.

As if changes were taking place in his throat, too, Skagg's voice lowered and became gravelly. "Demon, alien . . . or maybe I'm the result of some genetic experiment gone terribly wrong. Hmmmm? What do you think?"

That laugh again. Frank *hated* that laugh.

"What do you think?" Skagg insisted as he approached.

Retreating, Frank said, "I think you're probably none of those things. Like you said . . . I think you're stranger and more interesting than that."

Both of Skagg's hands had become pincers now. The metamorphosis continued up his muscular arms as his human form gave way to a more crustaceous anatomy. The seams of his shirt sleeves split; then the shoulder seams also tore as the transformation continued into his upper body. Chitinous accretions altered the size and shape of his chest, and his shirt buttons popped loose.

Though Frank knew he was wasting ammunition, he fired three shots as rapidly as he could squeeze the trigger. One round took Skagg in the stomach, one in the chest, one in the throat. Flesh tore, bones cracked, blood flew. The shapechanger staggered backward but did not go down.

Frank saw the bullet holes and knew a man would die instantly of those wounds. Skagg merely swayed. Even as he regained his balance, his flesh began to knit up again. In half a minute the wounds had vanished.

With cracking and wet oozing noises, Skagg's skull swelled to twice its previous size, though the change had nothing to do with the revolver fire that the shape-changer had absorbed. His face seemed to *implode,* all the features collapsing inward, but almost at once a mass of tissue bulged outward and began to form queer in-sectile features.

Frank did not wait to see the grotesque details of Skagg's new countenance. He fired two more rounds at the man's alarmingly plastic face, then turned and ran, leaped over an electric cart, dodged around a big forklift, sprinted into an aisle between tall metal shelves, and tried *not* to feel the pain in his side as he ran back through the long warehouse.

When that morning had begun, dreary and rainswept, with traffic moving through the city's puddled streets at a crawl, with the palm trees dripping, with the buildings all somber looking in the gray storm light, Frank had thought that the spirit of the day was going to be as soggy and grim as the weather, uneventful and boring and perhaps even depressing. Surprise. Instead the day had turned out to be exciting, interesting, even exhilarating. You just never knew what fate had in store for you next, which was what made life fun and worth living.

Frank's friends said that in spite of his hard shell, he had an appetite for life and fun. But that was only part of what they said about him.

Skagg let out a bleat of rage that sounded utterly inhuman. In whatever shape he had settled upon, he was coming after Frank, and he was coming fast.

5

Frank climbed swiftly and unhesitatingly in spite of the pain in his ribs. He heaved himself onto the top of another three-story-high wall of crates—machine tools, transmission gears, ball bearings—and rose to his feet.

Six other crates, which were not part of the wall itself, were stacked at random points along the otherwise flat top of those wooden palisades. He pushed one box to the edge. According to the printing on the side, it was filled with twenty-four portable compact-disc players, the kind that were carried by antisocial young men who used the volume of their favorite unlistenable music as a weapon with which to assault innocent passersby on the street. He had no idea what a crate of "ghetto-blasters" was doing among the stacks of machine tools and bearings; but it weighed only about two hundred pounds, and he was able to slide it.

In the aisle below, something issued a shrill, piercing cry that was part rage, part challenge.

Frank leaned out past the box that he had brought to the brink, looked down, and saw Skagg had now assumed a repulsive insectile form that was not quite that of a two-hundred-fifty-pound cockroach and not quite that of a praying mantis but something between.

Suddenly the thing's chitin-capped head swiveled. Its antennae quivered. Multifaceted, luminous amber eyes looked up at Frank.

He shoved the box over the edge. Unbalanced, he nearly plummeted with it. Wrenching himself back from the brink, he tottered and fell on his butt.

The carton of portable compact-disc players met the floor with thunderous impact. Twenty-four arrogant punks with bad taste in music but with a strong desire for high-tech fidelity would be disappointed this Christmas.

Frank crawled quickly to the edge on his hands and knees, looked down, and saw Skagg's squirming insectile form struggling free of the burst carton that had briefly pinned him to the floor. Getting to his feet, Frank began to shift his weight rapidly back and forth, rocking the heavy crate under him. Soon half the wall was rocking, too, and the column of boxes beneath Frank swayed dangerously. He put more effort into his frantic dance of destruction, then jumped off the toppling column just as it began to tilt out of the wall. He landed on an adjacent crate that was also wobbling but more stable, and he fell to his hands and knees; several formidable splinters gouged deep into his palms, but at the same time he heard at least half a dozen heavy crates crashing into the aisle behind him, so his cry was one of triumph not pain.

He turned and, flat on his belly this time, eased to the brink.

On the floor below, Skagg could not be seen from the ton of debris under which he was buried. However, the shapechanger was not dead; his inhuman screams of rage attested to his survival. The debris was moving as Skagg pushed and clawed his way out of it.

Satisfied that he had at least gained more time, Frank got up, ran the length of the wall of boxes, and descended at the end. He hurried into another part of the warehouse.

Along his randomly chosen route he passed the half-broken door by which he and Skagg had entered the building. Skagg had closed it and stacked several apparently heavy crates against it to prevent Frank from making an easy, silent exit. No doubt, the shapechanger also had damaged the controls for the electric garage doors

at the front of the warehouse and had taken measures
to block other exits.

You needn't have bothered, Frank thought.

He was not going to cut and run. As a police officer
he was duty-bound to deal with Karl Skagg, for Skagg
was an extreme threat to the peace and safety of the
community. Frank believed strongly in duty and responsibility. And he was an ex-marine. And . . . well, though
he would never have admitted as much, he enjoyed
being called Hardshell, and he took pleasure in the reputation that went with the nickname; he would never fail
to live up to that reputation.

Besides, though he was beginning to tire of the game,
he was still having fun.

6

Iron steps along the south wall led up to a high balcony
with a metal-grid floor. Off the balcony were four offices
in which the warehouse's managerial, secretarial, and
clerical staffs worked.

Large sliding glass doors connected each office with
the balcony, and through the doors Frank Shaw could
see the darkish forms of desks, chairs, and business
equipment. No lamps were on in any of the rooms, but
each had outside windows that admitted the pale yellow
glow of nearby streetlamps and the occasional flash of
lightning.

The sound of rain was loud, for the curved ceiling was
only ten feet above. When thunder rolled through the
night, Frank heard it reverberating on that corrugated
metal.

At the midpoint of the balcony, he stood at the iron
railing and looked across the immense storage room
below. He could see into some aisles but by no means
into all—or even a majority—of them. He saw the shadowy ranks of forklifts and electric carts among which he
had encountered Skagg and where he had first discovered his adversary's tremendous recuperative powers
and talent for changing shape. He also could see part of
the collapsed wall of crates where he buried Skagg under

machine tools, transmission gears, and compact-disc players.

Nothing moved.

He drew his revolver and reloaded, using the last of the .38 cartridges from the loops on his custom-designed holster. Even if he fired six rounds pointblank into Skagg's chest, he would succeed only in delaying the shapechanger's attack for a minute or less while the bastard healed. A minute. Just about long enough to reload. He had more cartridges in the pockets of his suit coat, although not an endless supply. The gun was useless, but he intended to play the game as long as possible, and the gun was definitely part of the game.

He no longer allowed himself to feel pain in his side. The showdown was approaching, and he could not afford the luxury of pain. He had to live up to his reputation and become Hardshell Shaw, had to blank out everything that might distract him from dealing with Skagg.

He scanned the warehouse again.

Nothing moved, but all the shadows in the enormous room, wall to wall, seemed to shimmer darkly with pent-up energy, as if they were alive and, though unmoving now, were prepared to spring at him if he turned his back on them.

Lightning cast its nervous, dazzling reflection into the office behind Frank, and a bright reflection of the reflection flickered through the sliding glass doors onto the balcony. He realized that he was revealed by the sputtering, third-hand electric glow, but he did not move away from the railing to a less conspicuous position. He was not trying to hide from Karl Skagg. After all, the warehouse was their Samarra, and their appointment was drawing near.

However, Frank thought confidently, Skagg is sure going to be surprised to discover that the role of Death in this Samarra belongs not to him but to me.

Again lightning flashed, its image entering the warehouse not only by way of the offices behind Frank but through the narrow windows high in the eaves. Ghostly flurries of storm light fluttered across the curve of the metal ceiling, which was usually dark above the shaded security lamps. In those pulses of queer luminosity, Skagg was suddenly disclosed at the highest point of the ceiling, creeping along upside down, as if he were a spider with no need to be concerned about the law of gravity. Although Skagg was visible only briefly and not in much detail, he currently seemed to have cloaked himself in a form that was actually less like a spider than like a lizard, though a hint of strange, spiky black appendages stirred in Frank images of scuttling arachnoid creatures.

Holding his .38 in both hands, Frank waited for the storm's next bright performance. During the dark intermission between acts, he estimated the distance Skagg would have traveled, slowly tracking the unseen enemy with his revolver. When again the eave windows glowed like lamp panes and the ghostly light glimmered across the ceiling, his gunsights were aimed straight at the shapechanger. He fired three times and was certain that at least two rounds hit the target.

Jolted by the shots, Skagg shrieked, lost his grip, and fell off the ceiling. But he did not drop stone-swift to the warehouse floor. Instead, healing and undergoing metamorphosis even as he fell, he relinquished his spider-lizard form, reverted to his human shape, but sprouted batlike wings that carried him, with a cold, leathery flapping sound, through the air, across the railing, and onto the metal-grid balcony only twenty feet from Frank. His clothes—even his shoes—having split at the seams during one change or another, had fallen away from him; he was naked.

Now the wings transformed into arms, one of which Skagg raised to point at Frank. "You can't escape me."

"I know, I know," Frank said. "You're like a cocktail party bore—descended from a leech."

The fingers of Skagg's right hand abruptly telescoped out to a length of ten inches and hardened from flesh into solid bone. They tapered into knifelike points with edges as sharp as razor blades. At the base of each murderous fingertip was a barbed spur, the better to rip and tear.

Frank squeezed off the last three shots in the revolver.

Hit, Karl Skagg stumbled and fell backward on the balcony floor.

Frank fished .38 cartridges out of one pocket and reloaded. Even as he snapped the cylinder shut, he saw that Skagg already had risen.

With an ugly burst of maniacal laughter, Karl Skagg came forward. Both hands now terminated in long, bony, barbed claws. Apparently for the sheer pleasure of frightening his prey, Skagg exhibited the startling control he possessed over the form and function of his flesh. Five eyes opened at random points on his chest, and all fixed unblinkingly on Frank. A gaping mouth full of rapier teeth cracked open in Skagg's belly, and a disgusting-yellowish fluid dripped from the points of the upper fangs.

Frank fired four shots that knocked Skagg down again, then fired the two remaining rounds into him as he lay on the balcony floor.

While Frank reloaded with his last cartridges, Skagg rose again and approached.

"Are you ready? Are you ready to die, you chicken-shit cop?"

"Not really. I only have one more car payment to make, and for once I'd sure like to know what it's like to really *own* one of the damn things."

"In the end you'll bleed like all the others."

"Will I?"

"You'll scream like all the others."

"If it's always the same, don't you get tired of it? Wouldn't you like me to bleed and scream differently, just for some variety?"

Skagg scuttled forward.

Frank emptied the gun into him.

Skagg went down, got up, and spewed forth a noxious stream of shrill laughter.

Frank threw aside the empty revolver.

The eyes and mouth vanished from the shapechanger's chest and belly, and in their place he sprouted four small, segmented, crablike arms with fingers that ended in pincers.

Retreating along the metal-grid balcony, past glass office doors that flared with reflected lightning, Frank said,

"You know what your trouble is, Skagg? You're too flamboyant. You might be a lot more frightening if you were more subtle. All these rapid changes, this frenzied discarding of one form after another—it's just too dazzling. The mind has difficulty comprehending, so the result is more awesome than terrifying. Know what I mean?"

If Skagg understood, he either disagreed or did not care, for he caused curved, bony spikes to burst forth from his chest, and he said, "I'll pull you close and impale you, then suck the eyes out of your skull." To fulfill the second half of his threat, he rearranged his face yet again, creating a protruding tubular orifice where his mouth had been; fine, sharp teeth rimmed the edge of it, and it made a disgustingly wet, vacuuming sound.

"That's exactly what I mean by flamboyant," Frank said as he backed up against the railing at the end of the balcony.

Skagg was only ten feet away now.

With a sigh, regretting that the game was over, Frank released his body from the human pattern that he had imposed upon it. Bones instantly dissolved. Fingernails, hair, internal organs, fat, muscle, and all other forms of tissue became as one, undifferentiated. His body was entirely amorphous. The darksome, jellied, throbbing mass flowed out of his suit through the bottoms of his sleeves, and with a rustle his clothes collapsed in a soft heap on the metal-grid floor of the balcony.

Beside his empty suit, Frank reassumed his human form, standing naked before his would-be assailant. "*That* is the way to transform yourself without destroying your clothes in the process. Considering your impetuosity, I'm surprised you have any wardrobe left at all."

Shocked, Skagg abandoned his monstrous appearance and put on his human cloak. "You're one of my kind!"

"No," Frank said. "One of your species, but certainly not one of your demented kind. I live in peace with ordinary men, as most of our people have for thousands of years. You, on the other hand, are a repulsive degenerate, mad with your own power, driven by the insane need to dominate."

"Live in *peace* with them?" Skagg said scornfully.

"But they're born to die, and we're immortal. They're weak, and we're strong. They've no purpose but to provide us with pleasure of one kind or another, to titillate us with their death agonies."

"On the contrary," Frank said, "they're valuable because their lives are a continuing reminder to us that existence without limits, without purpose and struggle, existence without self-control is only chaos. I spend nearly all of my time locked within this human form, and with but rare exception I force myself to suffer human pain, to endure both the anguish and joy of human existence."

"You're the one who's mad."

Frank shook his head. "Through policework I serve humankind, and therefore my existence has meaning. They so terribly need us to help them along, you see."

"Need us?"

As a roar of thunder was followed by a downpour more vigorous than at any previous moment of the storm, Frank searched for the words that might evoke understanding, even in Skagg's diseased mind. "The human condition is unspeakably sad. Think of it: their bodies are fragile; their lives are brief, each like the sputtering decline of a short candle; measured against the age of the earth itself, their deepest relationships with friends and family are of the most transitory nature, mere incandescent flashes of love and kindness that do nothing to light the great, endless, dark, flowing river of time. Yet they seldom surrender to the cruelty of their condition, seldom lose faith in themselves. Their hopes are rarely fulfilled, but they go on anyway, struggling against the darkness. Their determined striving in the face of their mortality is the very definition of courage, the essence of nobility."

Skagg stared at him in silence for a long moment, then let loose another peal of insane laughter. "They're prey, you fool. Toys for us to play with. Nothing more. What nonsense is this about our lives requiring purpose, struggle, self-control? Chaos isn't to be feared or disparaged. Chaos is to be *embraced*. Chaos, beautiful chaos, is the base condition of the universe, where the titanic forces of stars and galaxies clash without purpose or meaning."

"Chaos can't coexist with love," Frank said. "Love is a force for stability and order."

"Then what need is there for love?" Skagg asked, and he spoke the final word of that sentence in a particularly scornful tone.

Frank sighed. "Well, I have an appreciation of the need for love, so I guess I've been enlightened by my contact with the human species."

"Enlightened? 'Corrupted' is the better word."

Nodding, Frank said, "Of course, you would see it that way. The sad thing is that for love, in the defense of love, I'll have to kill you."

Skagg was darkly amused. "Kill me? What sort of joke is this? You can't kill me any more than I can kill you. We're both immortal, you and I."

"You're young," Frank said. "Even by human standards, you're only a young man, and by *our* standards you're an infant. I'd say I'm at least three hundred years older than you."

"So?"

"So there are talents we acquire only with great age."

"What talents?"

"Tonight I've watched you flaunt your genetic plasticity. I've seen you assume many fantastic forms. But I haven't seen you achieve the ultimate in cellular control."

"Which is?"

"The complete breakdown into an amorphous mass that in spite of utter shapelessness remains a coherent being. The very feat that I performed when I shucked off my clothes. It requires iron control, for it takes you to the brink of chaos, where you must retain your identity while on the trembling edge of dissolution. You have not acquired that degree of control, for if total amorphousness had been within your power, you'd have tried to terrify me with an exhibition of it. But your shape-changing is so energetic that it's frenzied. You transform yourself at a whim, assuming whatever shape momentarily seizes your fancy, with a childish lack of discipline."

"So what?" Skagg remained unafraid, blissfully sure of himself, arrogant. "Your greater skill in no way changes the fact that I'm immortal, invincible. For me, all wounds heal regardless of how bad they may be. Poisons flush from my system without effect. No degree of heat, no arctic cold, no explosion less violent than a nuclear blast, no acid can shorten my life by so much as one second."

"But you're a living creature with a metabolic system," Frank said, "and by one means or another—by lungs in your human form, by other organs when in other forms—you must respire. You must have oxygen to maintain life."

Skagg stared at him, not comprehending the threat.

In an instant Frank surrendered his human form, assumed a totally amorphous state; spread himself as if he were a giant manta ray in the depths of the sea, and flew forward, wrapping himself tightly around Skagg. His flesh conformed to every fold and crease, every concavity and convexity, of Skagg's body. He completely enveloped his startled adversary, sheathing every millimeter of Skagg, stoppering his nose and ears, coating every hair, denying him access to oxygen.

Within that jellied cocoon, Skagg sprouted claws and horns and bony, barbed spikes from various portions of his anatomy, attempting to gouge and tear through the suffocating tissue that bound him. But Frank's jellied flesh couldn't be torn or punctured; even as his cells parted before a razored claw, they flowed back together and knitted up instantly in the wake of that cutting edge.

Skagg formed half a dozen mouths at various places on his body. Some were filled with needle-tipped fangs and some with double rows of shark's teeth, and all of them tore ravenously at his adversary's flesh. But Frank's amorphous tissue flowed into the orifices instead of retreating from them—*this is my body, taste of it*— clogging them to prevent biting and swallowing, coating the teeth and thus dulling the edges.

Skagg assumed a repulsive insectile shape, but Frank conformed. Skagg sprouted wings and sought escape in flight, but Frank conformed, weighed him down, and denied him the freedom of the air.

Outside, the night was ruled by the chaos of the storm. In the warehouse, where the aisles were neatly arranged, where the humidity and temperature of the air were controlled, order ruled everywhere except in the person of Karl Skagg. But Skagg's chaos was now firmly contained within the impenetrable envelope of Frank Shaw.

The inescapable embrace with which Frank enfolded Skagg was not merely that of an executioner but that of a brother and a priest; he was gently conveying Skagg out of this life, and he was doing so with at least some measure of the regret with which he watched ordinary men suffer and expire from accident and disease. Death was the unwelcome son of chaos in a universe woefully in need of order.

For the next hour, with diminishing energy, Skagg writhed and thrashed and struggled. A man could not have endured for so long without oxygen, but Skagg was not a man; he was both more and less than human.

Frank was patient. Hundreds of years of self-enforced adaptation to the limits of the human condition had taught him patience. He held fast to Skagg a full half an hour after the last detectable signs of life had ebbed from the mad creature, and Skagg was as encapsulated as an object dipped in preserving bronze or eternally frozen in a cube of amber.

Then Frank returned to human form.

Karl Skagg's corpse was in human form as well, for that was the final metamorphosis that he had undergone in the last seconds of his agonizing suffocation. In death he looked as pathetic and fragile as any man.

When he had dressed, Frank carefully wrapped Skagg's body in a tarp that he found in a corner of the warehouse. This was one corpse that could not be permitted to fall into the hands of a pathologist, for the profound mysteries of its flesh would alert humankind to the existence of the secret race that lived among them. He carried the dead shapechanger outside, through the rain-lashed night to his Chevy.

Gently he lowered Skagg into the trunk of the car and closed the lid.

Before dawn, in the dark scrub-covered hills along the perimeter of the Los Angeles National Forest, with the yellow-pink metropolitan glow of Los Angeles filling the lowlands south and west of him, Frank dug a deep hole and slipped Skagg's corpse into the ground. As he filled the grave, he wept.

From that wild burial ground he went directly home to his cozy five-room bungalow. Murphy, his Irish setter, was at the door to greet him with much snuffling and tail wagging. Seuss, his cat, held back at first with typical feline aloofness, but at last the Siamese rushed to him as well, purring noisily and wanting to be stroked.

Though the night had been filled with strenuous activity, Frank did not go to bed, for he never required sleep. Instead he got out of his wet clothes, put on pajamas and a robe, made a large bowl of popcorn, opened a beer, and settled down on the living room sofa with Seuss and Murphy to watch an old Capra movie that he had seen at least twenty times before but that he never failed to enjoy: Jimmy Stewart and Donna Reed in *It's a Wonderful Life.*

All of Frank Shaw's friends said that he had a hard shell, but that was only part of what they said. They also said that inside his hard shell beat a heart as soft as any.

The Calligraphy Lesson
Joyce Harrington

I wasn't expecting to get any Christmas cards. The only mail I ever get, or want to get, is addressed to Occupant. And that suits me just fine. So when the square white envelope with my name beautifully inscribed on it in calligraphy, my old name, fell through the mail slot, I stood there for about half an hour staring at it.

It's not that I hang around every day, waiting for the mail to arrive, just to reassure myself that no one knows where I am. It was noon and I had just gotten up, feeling pretty good about my new life, the way I'd changed everything about myself and didn't have to worry anymore, and was about to pick up the newspaper from my cute little small-town front porch. Catch up on the local news, which would never in a million years be about the me that used to be.

After a while, maybe it wasn't a half-hour but it seemed that long, I picked up the envelope and tried to read the postmark. Blurry, of course, and the stamp was one of those oversized holiday numbers, cheery and colorful. It didn't cheer me up one bit. All I could make out was the date. Five days before. Someone had been thinking of me five days earlier. But the part of the postmark that might have told me where the thinking had been done was smack on top of a deep blue sky where a single star shone down on three guys in bathrobes riding camels. Wise men, for sure. They had no wisdom for me.

The five days didn't mean much either, when it can take two weeks for a letter to get across the street. And

I didn't know anyone who practiced the fine art of calligraphy, not in my new life or my old one. There was no return address, in calligraphy or otherwise, front or back.

It was strange to see my old name again. I'd stopped thinking of myself as that person. It's amazing how you can invent a new self and really believe in it. So long as square white envelopes don't come along to rock your foundation. One part of me, the old chicken part, wanted to burn the thing and pretend it never existed. The new part, the brave new me, said, "Let's open it up, kiddo. It's only a Christmas card. It won't bite you." Oh, yeah?

So I cinched in my own bathrobe, a bright red fleecy job that looked terrific with my new long black hair, and opened the envelope. The card was nothing special, the usual Santa coming in for a landing on top of a snow-covered house. Before I opened it, a color photograph fell out. I caught it and almost dropped it, as if it had burned my fingers. There she was, the chicken creature, pale, dull, sad, and terrified. The card's printed message was an innocuous "Season's Greetings." But underneath that was the calligraphy again.

> 'Twas the night before Christmas
> And all through the house
> There was screaming and pleading
> Your spouse was a louse.
> Remember me.

Remember you? Oh, yes, I remember. I don't *want* to remember, and I'd almost made myself forget. But how can you forget someone who sends you to the plastic surgeon for a new face for Christmas and leaves even more scars inside than out. Sure, I remember.

He must have learned calligraphy in prison. He'd had four years to practice it in. And I'd had four years to become Cassandra Blake, late-night deejay on the local easy-listening station where I got to play Mel Tormé and Frank Sinatra and even Mantovani once in a while, for the old folks. If I were looking for anonymity, I couldn't have chosen a better job. Nobody ever saw me. I was only a soft, sweet voice in the middle of the night and, as far as I could tell, I had a loyal audience of twelve elderly insomniacs.

I'd chosen this town for my hiding place because it was the absolute opposite of everything my old self had ever known. Small, quiet, ordinary, anchored down by a sleepy little agricultural college, with a frozen-food plant on the outskirts that ate up most of the produce grown on the outlying farms and provided enough jobs so that unemployment wasn't a problem. Neither was crime.

But if my lousy ex-spouse was anywhere in the vicinity, that could change.

I'd divorced Raymond while he was in jail for almost carving me up into mouseburgers and a few other activities that D.A.s don't think highly of. How I ever got married to him in the first place is another story that I may or may not bring to mind.

But if Raymond didn't want to be divorced from me, it would take more than legal papers to get it through his head. He'd got eight to ten as a guest of the state, not enough for what he'd done to me, but Raymond can be very plausible. I testified at his trial. I was between operations, so my face didn't look as good as it does now, and with my black eyepatch and my wheelchair, I was sure he'd get ninety-nine years at least. But he got up on the stand, looking like Robert Redford, and said how sorry he was and how he'd done it all for love and if there is one character flaw he has, it's blind jealousy, and how it was partly my fault because I had driven him to steal and then betrayed him with his best friend. His lawyer stopped him before he went too far, but even so, there were at least three women in the jury who had tears running down their cheeks.

Was any of it true? Well, yes and no. I was the decoy, the bait. It was my job to play the poor little penniless waif, trying to stay honest and pure in the face of adversity. And some of that was true. Raymond thought it would be a good idea if I hired out as a nurse and companion to old ladies who had enough to live on but not enough to make them feel secure or young again. So I did that. I did just about anything Raymond wanted me to do. I would get these jobs, and then along would come Raymond, twinkling his blue eyes and grinning his

Boy Scout grin, and those old ladies would practically drop dead to shower him with every cent they had. Whether it was penny stocks or rejuvenating vitamin treatments or any of a hundred get-rich or get-young-quick scams, Raymond always had the right one at the right time for the right old broad. And if they didn't drop dead fast enough, Raymond sort of helped them along.

I drew the line at that. But I couldn't stop him from doing it. Short of turning him in to the police. Which I threatened to do. That was my big mistake. I shouldn't have threatened. I should have just done it.

Raymond is a wonder with a knife. He didn't mean to kill me. If he'd meant to, I wouldn't be here now brooding over the past. He only meant to teach me a lesson. That's what he said. He taught me only too well.

I went to the window and peered out at the tree-lined street. The trees were bare this time of year, so I could see most of the cars parked across the street and a few on this side. There weren't many, and they all looked familiar. Neighbors' cars, not new, nothing flashy, and nobody sitting in any of them, watching my house.

But somewhere out there was Raymond. He knew where I was, knew my address, and probably knew what I did every minute of the day. The reason Raymond's scams worked so well is that he paid very close attention to detail.

But so do I. As I said, I learned my lesson well. It had occurred to me, when I first decided to disappear off the face of the earth, that this day might come. He would be expecting to find the same old me, weak and scared, just waiting around for him to turn up and finish the job. What he couldn't know is that I'd done some planning and some practicing of my own. I'd learned a fine art, too, and it wasn't how to write a beautiful hand.

I propped the Christmas card up on the fireplace mantel, right where I could see it from every corner of the living room, and the photograph right beside it. Not that I needed any reminders. But when he came, and he would come, I wanted him to see it, and I wanted to see his face when he did.

As I did that, I looked into the mirror above the mantel. Even without makeup, the face that looked back at me bore no resemblance to the puny, pinched face in the picture. Blue eyes, now, instead of mud brown. Bluer even than Raymond's fabulous orbs. Of course, one of them was artificial and the other was a contact lens. One of my disciplines was never to do anything but sleep without my blue eyes in place. The long black hair and the eyebrows dyed to match in place of the dirty blond that nature had blessed me with, and that I had always kept cropped short and practical before. A different tilt to the nose, an almost Asiatic slant to the eyes, interesting hollows in the cheeks. I fancied the look was Eurasian or part American Indian, a far cry from the face in the photo and no one Raymond had ever seen before.

There was more to it, though, than plastic surgery and artifice. Independence and a certain security that goes along with the practice of the fine art of self-defense can do wonders for your attitude. And attitude makes a difference in the way you face the world. No doubt about it.

And so I decided to face the world as usual, Raymond or no Raymond. I opened the front door, and there was my newspaper, folded neatly just as it was every morning. I scanned the street before picking it up. The only visible human being was the old lady across the street hanging a wreath on her door. She waved at me and called out, "Only five more days. Merry Christmas."

"Merry back at you," I yodeled. "That's a fine wreath." She was one of my late-night insomniacs, just thrilled to pieces to be living across the street from someone she considered a celebrity. Sometimes she would call the station at two or three in the morning and ask me to play some old Glenn Miller or Bing Crosby record. Sometimes I would. I kept a few of them handy, just for her. I had a soft spot in my heart for old ladies, because of the way I'd helped Raymond cheat them out of their life savings in that old life. And, anyway, she was part of my plan, although she didn't know it.

I went back in, made some coffee, and settled down at the kitchen table to read about the Christmas tree lighting in the town square, church suppers, bingo parties, happy wedding couples and golden anniversaries, classified ads for garage sales and lost dogs. Once, I had a fine time for a week over a stolen prize pig that eventually turned up on the other side of the county. The thief was upset that his own Poland China sow had won only second prize, but he couldn't bear the thought of turning the prizewinner into pork chops, which was his original intention. I got most of my radio patter from the newspaper and from letters the local folks sent to Cassandra Blake at the station. It was a great life, a quiet life, and it suited me just fine. And I wasn't about to let Raymond jostle it.

I circled a few items in the paper with black marker, and then I noticed a classified ad. "Nurse/companion," it read. "Experienced Christian practical nurse available to care for aged or infirm lady. Live in. Low rates for 24-hour-a-day TLC." There was a box number. Except for the "Christian" part, it was the same ad we'd used back in New York, but this was the fringes of the Bible Belt. See what I mean about Raymond? He pays attention to detail.

The ad could mean one of three things. First, that Raymond was in town with another version of the old me, and getting back into business. Second, that he was in town and wanted me to team up with him again. And third, he was in town and warning me that he hadn't forgotten what I'd done to him.

The third was most likely. He was trying to panic me. It was time to get moving.

First, I checked all the guns in the house and made sure they were loaded. There was one in every room, and two in my bedroom. I hoped I wouldn't have to use any of them. I didn't want to obliterate Raymond. They don't look kindly on obliteration in these little towns, and I didn't fancy improving my penmanship in the state pen. I just wanted to encourage him to go away and leave me alone.

Then I got dressed in my usual black jeans, black turtleneck, black boots, and black leather jacket. Yes, I looked like a fugitive from the Hell's Angels, but the townsfolk didn't seem to mind since I didn't roar around on a motorcycle and didn't have a ring in my nose.

I stashed my cute little Beretta Minx in one of my

zipper pockets, tucked the newspaper under my arm, and went across the street to pay a neighborly call.

Mrs. Fenton was glad to see me. "Well, praise the Lord," she hollered, when she opened her door and saw who was lurking on her front porch. "My goodness. I wasn't expecting company. Least of all Cassandra Blake. The place is a mess and so am I. But come on in, and have some of my fruitcake." She giggled a bit. "It's got a little taste of bourbon in it. Hope you don't mind."

She fussed and fretted until I got settled in the best chair in the primped and polished parlor, and then scuttled off to the kitchen with promises trailing in her wake of coffee and cake and maybe a little bit of toast with her homemade apple butter. If anybody didn't need a nurse/companion, it was Mrs. Amelia Fenton. Somehow, I'd have to convince her to write off to that box number. Even if Raymond had placed the ad only to startle me, I wanted to entice him into making a move that would put him in a vulnerable position. Meanwhile, I gazed at the photographs lined up on top of the player piano that took up almost half of one wall.

There was a studio portrait of a middle-aged gent in a vested suit, looking very pleased with himself and the universe. The same gent showed up in several snapshots, sitting in a rowboat holding up a string of some kind of fish, handing out blue ribbons at the county fair, mouth open standing behind a lectern with the Rotary International symbol on the wall behind him, that sort of thing. I gathered he was the once and former Mr. Fenton. The other photos were mostly group shots of young men and women, children, babies, dogs, the usual family stuff.

Mrs. Fenton trundled back in, bearing a huge tray loaded down with cups and plates and all kinds of goodies. "I just don't know," she chortled, shaking her head. "I just can't seem to stop baking up a storm, but there's nobody left to eat it. So I give it all away." She set the tray down on the piano bench.

I got up to help her. "It looks wonderful. I'd have thought you'd have plenty of children and grandchildren to bake for." I nodded toward the photo gallery.

"Oh, yes," she smiled. "It does look that way. But except for Mr. Fenton there, and he's gone, the rest are just folks, not kin. Mr. Fenton and me, we never had any little ones."

"Well, then, you must have a lot of friends," I pursued.

"Here," she said, handing me a loaded plate. "You taste that and tell me if it's not the best fruitcake you ever tasted."

I took the plate and stared at it, trying not to turn green. Fruitcake is not my favorite thing in the world to eat, and the piece that was staring up at me was about the size of the World Trade Center. "Looks delish," I said. "Shouldn't you be saving some for Christmas? Won't all those friends be coming to see you?"

She sat down then, with a cup of coffee gripped in her two little plump fists, and sighed. "Won't nobody be coming to see me for Christmas. All those pictures? I buy them at garage sales. People get rid of their old photo albums sometimes. Maybe there's been a family quarrel or a divorce and they decide they don't want to be reminded. Maybe they're not even family pictures. I don't know who they are." She brightened up and sipped her coffee. "But they look nice on the piano, don't they? And I give them names so they don't feel like strangers. You haven't tasted your cake yet."

I dutifully tasted my cake. It wasn't bad. Much too sweet for me, but there was definitely bourbon in it. "Very good," I mumbled around the mouthful I was trying to make last as long as possible. "Best ever."

"Yes," she said, complacently. "It's the best."

"Now," I said, swallowing hard. "I came over because I need to ask you to do a favor for me."

"Oh, anything!" she said. "You've given me so much pleasure during the nights when I can't sleep. I love listening to you. Sometimes I stay awake to listen to you even when I *can* sleep."

"Well, here's the pitch."

"Beg your pardon?"

"Um. This is what's going on. I'm trying to get into news reporting and ..."

"Does that mean you won't be playing music anymore? I'm not sure I want to help you do that."

"No, no. It just means that I want to start having little

news reports along with the music." I cast about for an inspiration, something that wouldn't mean Amelia would have to cope with rape, highway accidents, and terrorist bombings in the middle of the night. "What I have in mind," I told her earnestly, "is a consumer-alert kind of thing. Cluing people in on fraud and con games. Especially older people. They're prime victims for the sharks out there."

"Oh, dear!" she said. "I never thought about it. But you know, this nice young woman came by one day and wanted me to join a perfume club. You know, like a book club only it was perfume. A different one every month. She was real sweet, but I've been using the same lilac toilet water for more than fifty years. Freddie, that's Mr. Fenton, always said I smelled like springtime, even in the middle of winter. Is that what you mean?"

"Something like that. You wouldn't believe the tricks they use to separate you from your money."

"Really?" She was beginning to look a little nervous. "I don't have very much. I mean, Mr. Fenton was a good provider, and I'm not a charity case, but I do have to watch my pennies."

"Well, that's just what I mean," I said reassuringly. "That's why I want to do this on the radio. Warn people about these con artists, and you could be helping me and all the people they try to bamboozle."

"Bamboozle!" She laughed a little. "That was one of Freddie's favorite words. He was a banker, you know. And he was always going on about this one or that one, and how they thought they could bamboozle him. He was very sharp, Freddie."

"I'm sure you're just as sharp. I'll bet you could spot a scam with your eyes closed."

"A scam?" She looked puzzled. "Is that like New Yorkers trying to sell country folks the Brooklyn Bridge?"

"You got it!" I said enthusiastically. "I knew you'd be just right for this assignment. Nobody can pull the wool over your eyes."

"No, I don't think they could," she mused. "But I'm not so sure I want to give them a chance."

"Think of all the people you'll be helping. I really

believe there's one of these con artists in town right now. Just look at this." I unfolded the newspaper and pointed out the nurse/companion ad to her. "Imagine some frail old lady answering that ad and welcoming a viper into her home."

"Well," she said, "we certainly have plenty of frail old ladies in this town, but I'm not one of them. I don't need a nurse or a companion."

"That's just the point," I told her. "You'll have to pretend. And I'll be right across the street keeping an eye on things. They work in pairs. First, the nurse comes along, and pretty soon, there's a very nice young man offering to help out around the house because he's the nurse's brother or boyfriend. They start being like family and the next thing you know, the two of them have skipped out with your bank account."

"Not mine," she said stubbornly.

"Of course, not yours. But what we want to do is give them a chance to make their play, and then sound the alarm."

"You mean call the police?"

"What I had in mind was talking it up on the radio. Sort of encouraging them to leave town. But we could call in the police if they actually do anything illegal. The trouble is, they usually manage to stay on the right side of the law. They don't really steal anything. They just convince you to turn over your life savings to them."

"Hah!" said Amelia Fenton. "There must be an awful lot of silly old ladies out there."

"Too many," I assured her. "That's why I need you. There's nothing the least bit silly about you, but I'm pretty sure you could put on a good act. What do you think?"

She sipped her coffee, munched a bit of fruitcake, and then poked a pudgy finger at me. "How come you know so much about how this scam thing works?"

I'd been preparing for that question ever since I started making my pitch. It's too bad I couldn't make my eyes well up with tears anymore. It never hurts to shed a few when you're trying to get someone on your side. However, I did the next best thing, hung my head and gazed mournfully down at the imitation oriental rug.

"It happened to my own grandmother. I didn't know about it until it was too late. They left her absolutely penniless. She was so mortified, she took sick and died within six months. Oh, the doctors said it was heart failure and she was ninety-two years old, only to be expected. But I knew better. She just didn't want to live anymore." I glanced up to see how she was taking it.

It was a pleasure to see that her eyes were brimming. Nice to know I hadn't lost the touch.

"Oh," she cried, all choked up. "That's a terrible story. It's a crime, that's what it is. Of course, I'll help you out. But I don't know if I can pretend to really need a nurse. I may be old enough, but I'm in pretty good shape, if I say so myself."

"But you do live alone. And you have no relatives. So what you want is a companion. That'll appeal to them. The lonelier, the better. You can put that in your letter."

"You mean you want me to answer that ad?"

"That's just what I mean. And I'll help you write it so they'll be sure to answer it."

"But what if it's a real nurse, looking for a job?"

"If she's genuine, we don't have to hire her."

She brooded for half a tick, and then pointed that finger at me again. "If we do hire her, you'll have to pay her wages. I can't afford to pay out any money for this."

Oh, she was just reveling in her sharpness. She was so cute, I just wanted to hug her. "Of course," I told her. "I wouldn't expect you to pay her. It's my idea, isn't it?"

"Well, all right, then. I'll do it. It'll be kind of nice to have someone in the house for Christmas. I hope she likes fruitcake." She looked sternly at my plate. "You haven't finished yours."

"I'll take it along to the station with me. For a midnight snack. Now, let's write that letter."

Between the two of us, we turned out a letter I knew Raymond wouldn't be able to resist. Of course, he'd quickly realize that she lived across the street from me, but he was so arrogant, that would probably appeal to him. Amelia's handwriting was small and spidery, and her notepaper was a pale lilac shade. Just the thing. We laid it on thick. "Lonely widow of modest means ... in good health ... no sickroom chores ... own room in private home ... cheerful surroundings ..." and so forth and so on. Amelia read it aloud when we finished, and looked quite pleased with her creation. She remembered to include her phone number and we giggled like a couple of teenaged conspirators at the thought of what the letter might bring to Amelia's little house.

"I haven't had so much fun since Freddie and me won the dancing prize at the 4H Club picnic in '39," she chortled. "That Freddie. He could really cut a rug." She turned solemn then. "I guess I am lonely. I never thought about it before."

Oh, my dear Amelia, I thought. If I weren't a reformed character, you'd be prime material for Raymond and the old me. "Well, you don't need to be," I told her. "Not with me across the street."

I sealed the letter in its envelope while Amelia found a stamp. "I'll take it right to the post office. That way, it'll get delivered by tomorrow."

That night, I played "Jersey Bounce" in memory of Amelia's dancing prize, and tried to imagine her and Freddie "cutting a rug." I couldn't quite picture it.

The next day, there was another Christmas card lying just inside my door. No stamp on this one. Personal delivery. And it was addressed to Cassandra Blake. In calligraphy. It read:

Only four more days to finish my Christmas
CHOPPING!

Oh, Raymond. Do you really think you can still intimidate me? I propped the card up on the mantel next to the other one. Then I went across the street to see how Amelia was holding up.

She was holding up just fine. In fact, she was eager to get the whole thing started. "The phone hasn't rung all morning," she said. "What if no one calls?"

"Then we'll have to think of something else." I wondered if Amelia had any guns around the house. "Tell me more about Freddie."

"Oh, you wouldn't be interested. He's been dead for seven years. That was real nice dancing music you played last night."

"I was thinking about you and Freddie cutting a rug. What else did you two like to do? Did you go hunting?" I knew I was making her sad, I could see it on her face, but I had to know more about my resources if Raymond turned up here instead of at my place.

She sank down into an old-fashioned platform rocker and closed her bright old eyes. "Hunting," she keened. "Now why on earth did you ask about hunting? Didn't you know that's how Freddie died?"

Whoops! Open mouth and insert foot. But maybe I could make it work to my advantage. "Oh, I'm so sorry, Amelia. How could I know that? I've only been here a few months. But I noticed in the fall that everybody seems to go hunting. I even thought about doing some of it myself. If I knew the right kind of equipment to get. And someone to go with."

She brightened up at the thought of doing a little matchmaking. "I could probably put you in touch with some of Freddie's old hunting buddies, and their sons. And the attic is just full of guns and fishing rods and all that old stuff. I don't know what all's up there. But the season's a long way off, and I just haven't liked to think about hunting ever since . . ." Her voice trailed off, and she went over to the piano where she picked up the photo of Freddie and his string of fish. "If only he'd listened to me," she said.

"I'd like to go and see what's up there," I said. "Would you mind?"

"I wouldn't mind. But don't expect me to go with you. Everything in the attic belongs to a different life, and that's the way I want it to stay. But you're too young. You wouldn't understand about things like that."

"I guess you're right," I told her, heading for the stairs.

"Just go straight on up and pull down the trapdoor in the hall. A ladder comes down with it."

I followed her directions and soon found myself lost in a welter of 1930s and 1940s memorabilia. Old records and magazines, a naval officer's uniform, a tea gown; her hats had veils and his were fedoras. If I had time to rummage, I probably could have recreated their entire life together from the castoffs stored up here and out of sight.

But I was interested in something else. The sporting equipment was stored in a closet under the eaves. The ceiling was so low and the door so small, I had to contort myself to get in. And once in, I was groping in the dark for what I hoped would turn out to be a long, steel barrel. After I hauled out all the fishing stuff, the deflated rubber raft, the sleeping bag, the tent, the camp stove, the golf bag full of clubs, and a couple of unstrung tennis rackets, I hit pay dirt. More than I had hoped for. Back in the corner, under a dusty tarpaulin, there were three rifles, an over-and-under shotgun, a flare pistol, a shelf full of cartridge boxes, and everything you needed to keep the equipment in good working order. I think I would have liked Freddie Fenton. He was a gun nut, and so was I. In my new life. Couldn't stand them before. They used to make me nervous. Now, they give me a nice sense of security.

I hauled the three rifles and the shotgun out into the middle of the attic floor to see how much cleaning they needed. A lot. They hadn't been used in seven years. I'd just finished cleaning and loading a Winchester carbine, nothing fancy, but it was the lightest of the three and the easiest for me to handle, when I heard Amelia calling me.

I went over to the trapdoor and looked down. She was standing at the foot of the ladder, looking up.

"Oh," she said, staring at the rifle in my hand, "I remember that one. Freddie tried to teach me how to use it. Well, but that's not what I came upstairs about. There's a gentleman here. Says he's from the FBI. Says he's investigating a case of fraud. Sounds just like the nurse/companion scam you're looking into. I told him about you, and now he wants to talk to you."

"What does he look like?" I asked.

"Look like? Why, just normal, I guess. Dark suit, plain tie. His shoes are shined. I always notice a man's shoes. That's because I always used to shine Freddie's."

"His eyes," I pursued. "What color?"

"Blue, I think. Not as blue as yours, but, yes, I'm pretty sure they're blue."

Raymond. No doubt about it. "Is he handsome?" I asked.

She blushed. Really, she did. "Oh, I never notice things like that," she said. "But I guess he is. A little pale, but I suppose FBI men don't get too much outdoor exercise."

I was tempted to say, "Neither do jailbirds," but I stifled the words. What I said instead was, "I'll be right down," and turned around to climb down the ladder.

"Hand me down the rifle," said Amelia. "I don't want you to fall with it in your hand."

And fool that I was, I did.

When I got to the bottom of the stairs, she was aiming it at me, and she said, "Now, march."

"Amelia," I cooed. "Whatever's got into you? I thought we were friends."

"Well, we were," she said sternly. "But I can't be friends with a criminal wanted by the FBI. I'm real sorry, Cassandra, but you almost had me fooled. And I don't like to be fooled. Now get along downstairs and face the music."

And music was exactly what I had to face. When I walked into the living room, there was Raymond, pumping away at the player piano. The tune, if you could call it that, was good old "Hark, the Herald." I watched the little holes in the music roll wind their way to the end.

Then Raymond swung around on the piano bench, grinned at me, and said, "I always knew you'd like my mother."

I whirled around and stared at Amelia, who didn't waver one inch in holding that rifle aimed at my head. "Easy, girl," she said. "I'd really hate to mess up that beautiful new face of yours."

Back again to Raymond. "You never told me you had a mother."

"Everyone has one," he drawled. "Mom taught me everything I know. She was doing time for bigamy when

I met you. But she got out when I went in, and she's
been keeping track of you ever since. You were too busy
to notice that she moved in here just a few days after
you settled into your little hideaway. Rented the place
fully furnished from a sweet old dolly who was going
into a nursing home."

He was just as smug and self-assured as he'd always
been. And Amelia. She was still round and short and
old, but she'd lost her chirpy, dithery, old-lady sweet-
ness. A gray avenger is what she was. I let myself collapse into the platform rocker, and kept an eye on both
of them. "Well, Merry Christmas," I said, for lack of
anything better.

Raymond laughed and twinkled his blue eyes at me.
"Yes. And I have a wonderful Christmas present for
you. You've earned it. I like the way you look. Of
course, I can take a little credit for that. If I hadn't
made it necessary, you would never have changed.
You were so limp, but you were just right for what I
was doing then. But now I've got a new idea and
you're going to help me. So, I'm not going to kill you
after all."

"Gee, thanks," I said. "And what if I say no?" The
little Beretta in my pocket was nudging me in the ribs.

Raymond reached into his sleeve, pulled out a
switchblade, and sprung it open. "Remember me?" he
leered.

"And don't forget about me," said Amelia, sighting
down the barrel of the rifle.

"Points taken," I said. And then I sneezed. A nice,
juicy, germ-laden ker-choo. Raymond was always terrified of catching cold. I hoped he'd learned that from his
mother, too.

"Bless you," said Amelia, while Raymond flinched
and turned his head the other way.

I groped in my pocket for a tissue, and brought out
the Beretta. Pop, pop. That's all it took. My, they
looked surprised.

My lawyer says I have a fairly good defense, what
with Raymond's record and all, and the fact that the
bodies were found with a switchblade and a rifle, re-
spectively. But as I said earlier, small towns frown on

obliteration, especially if it involves big-city baddies. My eleven remaining fans are circulating a petition to get me back on the air. But since I have to spend Christmas in jail, they asked me what I would like to while away the time.

I asked them for a calligraphy set.

The Rubber Smile

John Shirley

"Bring up the darkness," said Chambers, absently.

"What?"

"I mean—the *glare,* Schraeder. There's too much glare. Use the filter, I can't make out their expressions with all this brightness on the—yeah. That's okay. Now slow it down a tad ..."

Chambers leaned back in his swivel chair to watch the screen of the video editor. On the screen were faces, rows of faces lit ghostly blue. The flickering blue light on those faces was reflected from another kind of screen, a movie screen Chambers couldn't see.

The editing room was dark but for the video screen, and claustrophobic. Schraeder, Chambers's perpetually squinting research assistant, was too long limbed for comfort in here, and he was making it worse with his twitchiness, obviously wanting a smoke. No way Chambers was going to let him smoke in this slightly oversized closet.

Chambers was plump, dark haired, his small blue eyes usually pleasantly quizzical, but sometimes hard as broken bottle glass. He dressed nondescriptly prep, a badge of his seriousness; he sat very still in his swivel chair, but chewed his lower lip when he was deep in thought. He chewed at it now. He was watching a videotape shot with a hidden camera. He'd paid Schraeder to film a typical Saturday night horror-movie audience. He and Schraeder were an audience watching an audience.

Chambers wasn't scared by horror movies. He was scared by horror movie audiences.

He didn't need to see the movie the videotaped audience watched. He knew it by heart. He knew it too well. Researching his paper on audience reaction to film violence for his doctorate in anthropology/media studies, he'd seen a dozen horror films several times apiece.

The video camera panned along the rows, over scores of rapt faces. Schraeder said, "You *sure* these people don't know they're being filmed? Seems to me some of them look right at the camera now and then—"

"You tell me. You're the one who filmed them."

"I could never be sure. Maybe they saw me go into the blind."

"No, Schraeder, Christ." It was two in the morning, they'd been screening the research samples for nine hours, with only one brief break. Chambers was tired and irritable. "No, they're looking around on the screen, trying to spot the slasher as he creeps up on the victims, and sometimes it makes them, you know, seem to look our way. They—hey, freeze it. No, back up, freeze it— *there*. Yeah. Hold it there."

He rubbed his eyes, then leaned forward to peer into the face in the center of the screen. A teenage boy; blond, pimply and thirsty-eyed, his head tilted forward like a football linebacker. "Move in on that blond kid, then run it slow." The editing machine zoomed in tight on the kid's face. Muscles clenched at the corner of the boy's jaw, as if he were ready to bite anything that came in reach. It was a fleeting expression, a half-second of raw belligerence meshed with sheer lust, risen to the surface, briefly expressed, and repressed a moment later. Like a water snake disturbing the surface of a pond and then diving out of sight.

Chambers had seen that ephemeral expression many times.

It didn't appear on the big-eyed, doughy-faced girl sitting beside the blond kid, though. She looked as if she *wanted* to enjoy the film—but it sickened her. For her, it was something to be endured. For the boy beside her, it was something to be savored. Chambers glanced at Schraeder and said, "You see the way he keeps shifting on his seat? It corresponds to the penetration, and it's always a forward and back motion, like a thrust of the hips. That's got to be an erotic response."

"You can barely see it. Seems to me, erotic response is hard to prove unless you want to sit beside 'em and risk getting busted for groping his crotch. Can't see a hard-on from here, Doc." Schraeder ran a hand through his stringy black-dyed hair. Twitchily. His hair was crew-cut short on one side, shoulder length on the other. He wore a *Pet Sematary: The Movie* T-shirt, and greasy black jeans, rotting tennis shoes. He was a film student, and a habitué of the death-art circuit, a fan of violent film, violent rock bands, violent books, violent performance art. Considering that, it was strange, sometimes, Chambers thought, the way Schraeder clung to a strange ingenuousness on this subject. "I mean," Schraeder went on, "aren't we making too many assumptions here, Doc?"

Doc. Because Chambers was going for his PhD. Something faintly mocking in the nickname Schraeder'd given him.

Chambers glanced at the transcription of the movie's dialogue, with its timing matched against the videotape's time. This audience was forty-two minutes into *Hometown Hell*—and they were watching the fourth on-screen slashing. Forty-two percent of the faces in the audience showed positive involvement, and about thirty-one percent demonstrated subjective identification with the slasher himself, at this point. Another ten minutes on and that figure would up to perhaps forty percent.

"Now I know what you think about the look on that kid's face," Schraeder remarked, "and the erotic response, and forgive me for being the eternal skeptic, but it seems to me he could be looking at the girl's tits and not at the knife going in her throat. You might be mistaking old-fashioned male enjoyment of the naked female bod for—"

"Schraeder, for God's sake, the boy is looking *at the knife and the point of entry*. I've worked out the parallax enough times to support that. Okay? Damn, Schraeder, erotic response or not, at least a third of these people are identifying with the killer and not the victim. That's the bottom line here. The filmmakers know it, too. How many of the ten most recent splatter films included long scenes shot from the killer's viewpoint? Seven out of ten!"

"I dunno, it seems cynical to me, to assume that ... Well, I don't like to believe that people—"

"Now we're onto something! You don't like to believe!" Chambers snorted. "Your reluctance to believe in the thing doesn't make it any less true." As he said it, he knew he was overreacting, but Schraeder was challenging the foundation of his thesis, and that thesis was going to be the foundation of his *career*. Starting with a post at the UCLA Film School, with luck. "Well. I'm sorry. I'm tired. Let's blow it off for the night."

Typically doing things backwards, Schraeder turned off the video monitor, fumbled for the light switch. For a few seconds, Chambers was left in darkness. The afterimages of the faces on the blanked screen stayed with him, hung in the air. And melted away when he blinked. But for an instant, just before they'd gone, he'd had a fatigue-induced impression that they'd all turned and looked at him, with that same expression on their faces. Murderous rapture.

Times Square on Saturday night was a mind lit up by psychosis. The dense crowd was dappled with smears of color from neon lettering and neon hieroglyphs and guttering chains of bulbs that rippled in electric vortexes around the marquees. It was a warm night, not yet nine o'clock, and the Forty-Deuce hummed and throbbed. Austere Broadway theaters shared the block with porn houses. On the corners, evangelists bursting with Good News jostled solemn leftist leafletters, and hookers cruised by debutantes who yawned as they waited for taxicabs. A dozen street dealers hawked pseudocoke—"SnoCaine"—and soap chips alleged to be crack, and tobacco-cut marijuana. Scientologists waited like trap-door spiders at the entrances of their book-lined dens; their peers, pickpockets, weaved in and out of the shifting crowd. Cops strolled in pairs.

There were long queues at the conventional movie theaters. Chambers stood in one of them, waiting to see a horror-cult favorite, *The Rubber Smile*. It was called *The Rubber Smile* because its slasher wore a horrifyingly ludicrous rubber mask of a man with an impossibly wide grin and protruding eyes.

Under his unseasonal trenchcoat, Chambers carried a tape recorder, a low-noise microphone, and extra cassettes. There were eight people ahead of him in line, mostly teenagers. He watched two thin, whispering boys, one Hispanic and the other a pallid kid wearing a rayon Bon Jovi jacket. They were pulling things from their pockets, comparing them. Rubber masks, waggling obscenely in their hands. The white kid held his own mask up beside his face, mimicking its grin as his friend shook with silent laughter. The Rubber Smile.

Chambers was pleased. It was more substantiation. Grist for the mill. He drew a small spiral notebook from his coat pocket, made a few notes as inconspicuously as possible, concluding: "... Rubber Smile parallel with *Rocky Horror Picture Show* cult in which audience dressed like Mad Scientist transvestite, chanted dialogue with actors ..."

Pleased with himself, he put the notebook away, as his turn came to buy a ticket. The next show was at 9:35. He'd take a stroll, come back in half an hour.

He saw them under the Silent Radio billboard, at One Times Square. There were four of them, wearing the Rubber Smile masks and staring up at the board. On it, gold against black, the words THE RUBBER SMILE: PART 2 sailed past, followed by a flat, angular animation of a running man, seen from the side, a knife in his outstretched hand; the animated man turned toward the viewer, growing, approaching gigantically, until the board was filled with the Rubber Smile mask in simplistic electronic caricature. For three seconds, the Rubber Smile leered out at the bustle of Times Square. It was as if he grinned through a vast electronic window, looking at our world from some lunatic's purgatory.

The four Rubber Smiles were looking up at the Silent Radio billboard as if they'd been expecting this. Like priests of some obscure order awaiting a sign from the gods. They were teenager sized and teenager clothed. They slapped palms and laughed when the animated Rubber Smile leered out at them, and then turned away when the Smile was replaced by an advertisement for a musical.

Chambers went to a phone booth and moodily dug for a quarter, dropped it into the slot, punched out Schraeder's number. A click, and then sinister carnival music came onto the line, and Schraeder's recorded voice, "Maybe I'm here, maybe I'm not. Leave a message." *Beep.*

"Schraeder—are you screening calls? Pick up the line, dammit, if you're there—"

Click. "What's up, Doc?"

"Schraeder, uh, I wonder if you could come down to the theater at Forty-third and Broadway, the one on the East Side. I'm going to need another observer. There's a deeper level to this Rubber Smile cult—they're wearing replicas of the mask—"

"Really? During the movie?"

"I—don't know. I saw four of them wearing masks outside."

"Hey, no kidding?" Schraeder seemed almost gratified to hear it. "But hey, this doesn't really fit snugly with your theory, right? I mean, it's all supposed to be subliminal, unconsciously acted out. Nothing so overt as living the role outside the theater with masks."

"It's just another level of acting out. You could extrapolate that some of them might actually—"

"No, that's jumping to conclusions, Doc. If one of them kills after seeing the film it'll be because the dude was pathological from the start. The movie didn't make him that way. I took a class on this stuff. If anything, the film burns off the hostility that could come out in, you know, violence."

"I doubt the films program people for violence, per se, but—"

"Please de-poz-zit five cents for an-nother three minutes."

"I don't know if I can make it down there or not, Doc—" Schraeder began.

"Please de-poz-zit—"

"Dammit." Chambers dropped another nickel in.

"Thank-kew."

"Schraeder, you're the horror buff, you keep up on

these things—you didn't tell me there was a sequel to the *The Rubber Smile*. You know I need it for—"

"There isn't a sequel."

"No, there is. I saw it advertised on that big electronic billboard. It's Part Two."

Schraeder was silent for a moment. "No kidding, huh? Wow."

"You must have missed an issue of the *Gore Gazette* or something. You coming down?"

"I'll be there," Schraeder said, his voice flat. And hung up.

Chambers turned to leave the phone booth. A loud *"tink-CRACK!"* near his ear made him flinch back, convulsively hugging himself. Something stung his cheek. He put his hand to his jaw, felt something warm and wet and sticky. Looked at his fingers. Blood. He turned. The booth's glass had been smashed near his right cheek. There was a spiderweb crack-pattern around an inchwide hole—and the cracks were superimposed on a face that was on the other side of the glass. A rubbery face with an impossibly wide grin. Its gums and lips painted dark red, bulging eyes luminous yellow, skin sickly pale.

The Rubber Smile tilted its head like a curious dog, and then whirled, moving away. He watched as the boy, wearing a dirty suit-jacket that had bits and pieces of lurid newspaper headlines pinned to it, moved toward the sidewalk crowd, slunk up close to a young woman who wore a black evening gown and ermine stole. She stood hailing a cab, her back to him. He tapped her shoulder: she turned, he made a slashing motion with his fingers at her throat. There was no knife in his hand: he seemed satisfied with her startled shriek, the shock on her face as she saw the mask. She bolted for a taxi. The boy vanished into the crowd.

Chambers left the phone booth and walked slowly toward the movie theater.

Half a block from the theater, Chambers stopped in a bodega and bought Band-Aids. He paused at an optometrist's show window and looked into a mirror below a sign that said: *Are your frames up to date?* The cut on his cheek was a small one, but his hand shook as he stuck the Band-Aid on.

It could have been my eye, he thought. Had the boy tried to break through the glass to get at him? What had he used to break it? Some weapon Chambers hadn't seen.

Something concealed. Something you could carry into a movie theater.

Chambers forced a chuckle. He'd seen one too many cheap horror films. With an effort of will, he turned toward the theater.

It wasn't a humid night, but his shirt stuck to his back and he loosened his collar. The cars seemed to swing their headlight beams at his eyes; the neon lights shared secrets with the red lights on a passing ambulance. He hadn't seen a movie that day, but felt as a man does after a movie—he was seeing things cinematically, as if on the big screen. When he turned his head, it was a panning shot, and everything had the appearance of having been framed through a camera's eyepiece.

Chambers took his place in the ticket holders' line. Waited. Now and then looking over his shoulder. *Maybe the kid intended to kill me.*

It was 9:15. The street growled and honked and muttered. The smell of spiced meat from the sidewalk shish-kabob vendor mingled incongruously with the cloying, soapy perfume of incense burning from the Black Muslims' tables. Watching a three-card monte hustler barking to attract gamblers, Chambers loosened up, began to enjoy the street action. He found himself watching two boys just ahead. Both wore baseball jackets and jeans; both were Hispanic and long haired. They leaned against a grime-gray brick wall and passed a joint between them.

As the line began to move, Chambers decided that part of his research ought to be interviewing members of the Rubber Smile cult. These two had the masks hanging like kerchiefs from the back pockets of their jeans. Could one of them be the kid who'd smashed the glass beside his face? No, that one had been wearing the weird jacket that made him look like a molting bird of newspaper. But the knot in Chambers's gut came back to him, then, as he stared at the dangling masks. *You're*

an anthropologist. Talk to the natives. He took a deep
breath, and said, "Say, uh, fellas, I heard there's going
to be, um, a sequel to *The Rubber Smile.* Uh—you guys
hear anything, you know, about a sequel or, um—?"

It was when he had difficulty talking that Chambers
admitted to himself that he was scared. Scared and
charged with anger.

"A sequel?" said the taller of the two boys. Blue
smoke marking the words. He made that soundless
laughter they all seemed to make, his mouth open and
nothing coming out, then tilted his head back to stare
into the glare-shuttered sky. The other boy nudged the
first and said, "Zat duh dude?" He gazed foggily at
Chambers.

His friend nodded, once, and said, "Askim can you see
his tape recorder, man." He was still peering at the sky.

Chambers stiffened. How did they know about the
tape recorder?

"Yeah, *pendajo,*" said the one who'd stared skyward,
suddenly tilting his head down to smile crookedly at
Chambers. "Yeah, there's a spechul midnight cho', man.
Sorta sneak *pre*view, you know?"

Chambers nodded mutely.

The other one said, "Yo, Jo-Jo, the line movin'." He
added something more in Spanish. The ticket holders'
line began to move, a slow two-step pause, two-step
dance, like a tentative conga, into the moviehouse odor
of popcorn and spilled cola.

As they passed the cashier's booth, Chambers looked
at the schedule. There was no mention of a special midnight show.

He hurried in to find a seat near the middle, about
four rows from the front. He'd found he could get the
best aural spread that way. There wasn't a big crowd for
this show—the film was at the end of its second run—
and at first no one sat in Chambers's row, or the one
behind him.

The theater fell into darkness.

That shouldn't have bothered Chambers. It always
gets dark before a movie. Naturally. Of course. So why
did it make him cringe down in his seat? The *film* didn't
scare him. He'd seen it four times. The first time it had

made him flinch, and look away once or twice. But it never really scared him. It was not a brilliantly made film, or even a very clever one, but it was efficient. The director knew the gimmicks, every cheap trick, and he used them all.

Chambers wriggled in his seat, adjusting the microphone cord inside his coat so that it ran up through his sleeve. The mike was concealed in his right hand, his arm draped casually along the back of one of the chairs. When the opening shot flashed onto the screen, he pressed the record button . . .

Askim can you see his tape recorder, man.

Someone must have seen him adjust the thing, at some point, Well, only a couple of them would know, hopefully.

INT: A PROTESTANT CHURCH—DAY.
REVEREND BEST addressing his white, middle-class congregation. Camera shoots the scene from behind the minister. We can't see his face. His congregation is increasingly shocked as he speaks.

REVEREND BEST
. . . And so I feel that it is the Will of God. I have no choice. I must resign. I can no longer preside over a church that fosters hypocrisy, where church members permit acts of fornication between unmarried young people, in open defiance of the Word of God. I have implored you again and again to put an end to this evil, this living obscenity, and yet it goes on. God will punish promiscuity with an instrument of His own choosing . . .
PUSH IN ON TEENAGE GIRL #1, hip and pretty, trying to keep from laughing as she sits beside her mother in the congregation.

CUT TO

EXT: A DESERTED DIRT ROAD
THROUGH CORNFIELD—NIGHT
The field on both sides of the road is filled with high stalks of corn. TEENAGE GIRL #1 walks down the road, her back to us. Sexy swish of her ass. She looks fur-

tively around, then dashes into the field where a red scarf has been tied to a cornstalk. CAM FOLLOWS her as she meets TEENAGE BOY #1 who has made a nest in the corn with a blanket and crushed stalks. He produces a pint whisky bottle from his coat.

CUT TO

INT: REVEREND BEST'S BEDROOM—NIGHT
The minister is alone, sitting on the bed, his back to CAM. He takes a rubber mask from a box under the bed, pulls the mask on. We can't see the mask's front yet.

CUT TO

THE CORNFIELD
The Boy and Girl in tight embrace, half undressed, giggling, rolling together off the blanket, crushing cornstalks.
SHOT FROM ABOVE
The couple on one side of the frame, on the other something hidden by cornstalk leafiness is disturbing the stalks of corn, moving toward the young couple like a shark through water. Closer and closer.
(Chambers shifted impatiently in his seat. *Same old devices. I'm supposed to be tensing with fear now.*)
TIGHT ON THE BOY AND GIRL
Laughing, caressing, swigging.
(Whoops and catcalls of encouragement from the audience in the theater.)
    The girl looks over the boy's shoulder, sees the cornstalks part.
HER POV
As CAM pushes in TIGHT for a CU of the mask, the Rubber Smile's leering face, glittering eyes in the eyeholes. She SCREAMS.
(Someone in the audience whispered, just loud enough to be heard, "All *right*. Awesome." And Chambers shivered.)
ON BOY AND GIRL
As a long butcher's knife sweeps into view, flashing down to penetrate both the boy and the girl, uniting them with steel—

Chambers looked away, bored with the Freudian button pushing.

He slumped down in his seat and turned to look at the audience. As his eyes adjusted, he saw that there were only about thirty-five of them. Seven of the thirty-five wore Rubber Smile masks. Their eyes were locked on the screen. In the dim light the masks seemed their real faces. Seven identically leering faces, drinking in the butchery taking place in the eye of the consensus mind.

A group of black girls—unmasked—squealed and covered their eyes, while from the sound track came the *chunk-swick-chunk* of a knife sinking repeatedly into flesh.

Someone said, "They shoulda gone to a motel." A few people laughed at that, and made comments of their own. Later, Chambers would play it all back, and notate the most relevant comments.

Three rows back, a boy about fourteen, with a fox face and scooplike ears, swallowed again and again, his Adam's apple bobbing. His thick glasses reflected fragments of screen images, leached of color depth. Knife flashings, spattering blood and leering rubber lips were reflected where his eyes should have been. Chambers was fascinated with the boy's swallowing. Oral gratification mechanism triggered by screen violence? The wound representing lips?

Chambers watched the audience patiently, noting that with some the loud remarks came during the greatest moments of suspense–stress, simply as a release for accumulated tension. In others, about thirty percent, the noisiness came during the killings, when the Rubber Smile was imaginatively dismembering his victims. These comments amounted to celebrations of the killer's demented sense of humor, or of his cunning ("... they ain't never gonna catch him, sucker's too slick ..."), and of his indestructibility ("... this part's cool, they shoot 'im four times, he don't give a fuck ..."). This was the percentage of the audience that identified with the killer. For them, the Rubber Smile's motivation was irrelevant and the movie's thin plot an encumbrance. They were waiting for the butchery. They never had to wait for more than twelve minutes; the filmmakers had it down.

Chambers turned to watch the movie for a few minutes, to get his bearings. The police were making their usual futile attempts at locating the killer. A teenage boy tried to tell them that the killer had something to do with the Old Church, and the cops laughed at him. The usual make-the-authority-figures-look-like-bumbling-fools segment.

Meanwhile, the Rubber Smile roams the countryside, looking for likely victims. His victims are almost invariably involved in sex, or undressing to prepare for sex.

Chambers was disturbed by an apparent discrepancy in the casting. Something he'd never noticed before, somehow. The killings were clearly performed by a number of different people in the latter half of the movie. Their faces were hidden by the masks, but their physiques and brief glimpses of hair-tufts at the masks' lower edges told him that more than one person was acting the part of the killer. *Why?* He could understand one stand-in, or a replacement if the original actor quit, but why so many?

There was another scene showing the parson preaching in the church—he suggested that God Himself had struck down the people murdered in the valley. For the first time, Chambers noticed that several people in the preacher's congregation were nodding in agreement. And with a shock he saw that their physiques, their hair colors, matched the several men playing the Rubber Smile. *Am I supposed to notice this?*

The film cut to a scene in which the audience saw what the killer saw, shared his skulkings through the small town's backyards, into an unlocked house. The camera showed the killer's POV as he stalked a victim, slinking slowly up behind a blond lingerie-clad housewife making cocktails beside a kitchen sink ...

Chambers looked away when the Rubber Smile drove the knife into the woman's groin. He was losing his objectivity. He should be desensitized to this sort of thing by now. It should be a joke to him, after all his exposure to it. But the Rubber Smile killings were harder to take than the others. Every time he saw them he marveled at how nauseatingly realistic they looked. They'd spent the greater part of their budget on special effects, apparently. It was just too ...

Swiiiick-chuk. Splatter.

He was sick to his stomach. It's not real blood; the Rubber Smile was only slashing a bit of fleshlike plastic, releasing fake blood. Maybe it was the efficacy of the sound effects. They were particularly sickening. The sounds of slashing, of blood dripping, juicily amplified.

"Looks amazingly real, doesn't it? Looks and sounds like the real things," said someone close behind him.

Someone speaking directly to Chambers.

Chambers slowly turned, and looked over his shoulder. And froze.

The Rubber Smile sat in the seat behind him. Staring. Grinning.

It's some kid, with the Rubber Smile's mask on, Chambers thought. It's not *him*.

"Yeah," Chambers said, hoarsely. "Yeah, it's a little bit too real."

"How can reality be too real? Reality is as real as reality is!" The Rubber Smile giggled, the sort of giggle that belonged to the mask's molded expression.

Something twisted in Chambers's gut. "What?"

"It's real in the minds of the people watching. At *least*. They believe in it when they see it on the screen. You can feel that, when you sit with them in the theater. The audience believes—and they get into it."

"Some of them do and some of them don't," Chambers said, turning away. He couldn't bear to look at the mask up close anymore. The way it quivered when the man wearing it spoke. It was a man, not a boy. A fairly educated man. *It's real in the minds of the people watching. At least.* Chambers shook his head. He knew the voice ...

Chambers turned in his seat to confront Schraeder—and found him gone. There were only six Rubber Smile masks in the audience now, and they were in the seats they'd occupied all along. They ignored him, or seemed to.

Chambers turned again and pretended to watch the movie, thinking: What was Schraeder *doing*? Is he trying to prove a point? A practical joke? It was an obscenity,

Schraeder wearing that mask. He had to be a little crazy. And he'd argued against the idea that the audiences were identifying with the killer. Clearly, Schraeder knew better.

The long minutes passed. Several times, Chambers began to turn around to resume his observation of the audience. But he couldn't do it. He felt sure that they were waiting for him to turn around, planning to do something awful to him, to startle him, to try and terrify him with a trick of some kind. Probably Schraeder had told them what he was doing. That would explain the boy at the phone booth, and the boys in the line who'd known about his tape recorder.

Three more killings passed. Chambers still couldn't turn around. The movie played out its last scene: The police shoot someone in a Rubber Smile mask they believe to be the killer. But when the killer is buried, the minister—the real Rubber Smile—is there at the cemetery, praying "for the tortured soul of this poor, possessed madman." Then he turns away from the grave and grins very, very widely for the camera.

The audience clapped and shouted, then filed out during the credits. Chambers stayed in his seat; he rewound the cassette tape and plugged its small earphone into his left ear. He stopped it twenty minutes back and hit *play*. He adjusted the tone, separated out the bass. Heard someone say, ". . . the usher been told?" And a reply, "Yeah, now shut up . . . Schraeder's . . ." Something inaudible. "Schraeder paid the . . ." The rest was lost in a squeal of sirens from the sound track.

Chambers slowly took out the earphone and detached the mike cord. He tucked the earphone and the mike in his coat pocket and shakily stood, wondering if he should run, if he could make it to the exit in time.

"Aren't you going to stay for the midnight show?" A voice from the stage. "Don't you want to see the sequel?" It was at that moment, when he saw the man in the Rubber Smile mask on the stage, that Chambers realized that the lights hadn't come up. It was still dark in the theater. Everyone was gone except the six Rubber Smile masks. They were up, sidling between the chairs, moving toward him, in his row and the row behind. One on either side, two behind, and now two in the row in front of him. In a few seconds he was surrounded. "Sit down," said the man on stage, his voice echoing in the nearly empty theater. Feeling numb, Chambers sat, and the six Rubber Smiles sat too, in a ring around him.

Behind them, the projector came to life. Its light stabbed at the screen—showing nothing. Just dead white light, filling the screen. The Rubber Smile on the stage stood silhouetted against that shining whiteness, against the ache of cinematic potential. He wore a long trench coat that didn't go with his black jeans and rotting sneakers.

"Chambers," said the man on stage, voice muffled by the grinning mask. "Chambers, you're a pompous ass. Guys like you make me sick. You think you've got us all statistically, behaviorally analyzed. You think you know what goes on in the minds of the people watching the movie. But Chambers—you ever hear of something called—" he paused to point at the source of the glare "—projection?" He chuckled. "You're projecting on the audience what you feel, deep within yourself. *Your* identification with the killer."

"Bullshit," Chambers blurted. "You're trying to justify your own sick obsessions by claiming they're universal."

"Look at the knife, Chambers . . ." The Rubber Smile drew a long butcher knife from within his trench coat and held it up in the light from the projector so it flashed fire. "You pretend to be revolted by the use the Smile puts this to—but inside you there's a Rubber Smile that—"

"You lying asshole!" Chambers shouted. He stood up, knuckles white on the back of the seat in front of him. Trembling. "I know your voice, Schraeder! You're one of them, all right, fine. But don't splatter *me* with it. I've got no part of it. Not inside me, not anywhere."

"Don't you? But you must have known what we've been doing—what we've been *really* doing. You've studied us so close, you must have known—but that ol' denial mechanism works overtime in Doc Chambers. You suppressed it, the knowledge, you don't want to face it, but at the same time you're fascinated, Chambers."

Chambers's mouth was dry as the ash in a burial urn. "What knowledge?"

"I was the assistant director on *The Rubber Smile,* Chambers. Under a pseudonym—as we all were. The director's in an asylum. Burnt out for good. He couldn't be with us tonight. A drag, huh? But the, ah, gentlemen who played the Rubber Smile are here, Chambers."

And then Chambers remembered where he'd seen the familiar faces among the extras playing the church congregation. He'd seen them standing in line tonight, outside the theater. Two had been Hispanic, two others Caucasian. Two blacks. Once inside the theater, they'd put on the masks . . .

"Oh, Lord," Chambers muttered.

Behind him, the projector made a rattling sound, and suddenly the movie screen gushed with carnage. The Rubber Smile was butchering the two lovers in the cornfield. Schraeder stood there, a step in front of the scene, a close-up of a bubbling wound gigantically superimposed over his trench coat. He was half in the movie's world, half in the real world.

"They sent me to answer your ad for a research assistant, after you called the producer, tried to interview him. He realized you were looking at the thing too closely. I really tried to discourage you from seeing those things, Chambers. I tried to save you. But I suppose I knew you'd notice, sooner or later. I was sure the point would be driven home to you so you couldn't deny it to yourself anymore. You kept coming to the damn movie. Sooner or later you'd realize that the fake blood wasn't fake blood and the fake wounds weren't—"

Chambers gave an incoherent yell, and looked away from the screen.

"Lots of eager young would-be actors and actresses out there, Chambers. Plenty to choose from. We picked the ones who had no living family. No one to search for them. We got our realism in the most practical way. With reality. We got rid of the evidence with our own little cremation facility. Saves money on salaries, too. We had a minimal crew. Part of our inner circle, of course. The director recruited them from asylums—particularly the one he was in, before they put him away for good. The whiney little shit went vegetable on us, I'm afraid. A sad end for a creative genius. But it keeps him from talking."

Chambers shook his head slowly, looked up at Schraeder. The Rubber Smile mask. The Rubber Smile wrapped in the red-spattered writhing on the screen. "Creative genius? Is that your excuse? This is *art*?"

"Life is brief and life is cheap, Chambers. And modern life is horror. We transcend that horror by making it into art, yes—but art is not what we're really about. We're a circle of . . . sensualists, of a sort. Religious sensualists. We do the right drugs, we set the lighting just right—and then we explore our senses, the secret rooms in our own brains, Chambers. It's all done with an exacting ritualism. The ritual staging is very, very important. You wouldn't understand, I'm afraid. We're a very special—"

He was interrupted by a shriek: Chambers had shrieked. Seeing the lightstands, tripod, and large thirty-five-millimeter camera someone had just set up in the aisle to his right.

"I'm the new director, Chambers," Schraeder said proudly. "You're going to have the honor of being in my new film. There *is* going to be a sequel to the Rubber Smile. Part Two starts filming tonight. Now."

Chambers acted on instinct. He vaulted over the chair ahead of him, and his knees struck the Smile sitting there. The guy groaned and fell; Chambers tumbled over him, and scrambled to his feet. He evaded a swishing knife, and jumped over the chairs blocking the way to the stage.

Gasping, thinking: The only way to save yourself is to take the offensive.

He jumped onto the stage, entering the projected image, stepping into the movie. He swung his fist at the hideous rubber head turning its death-rictus grin on him. His fist connected, and Schraeder went down. The knife clattered on the stage-deck.

Take the offensive. Save yourself. Take the offensive.

Chambers picked up the knife and stabbed Schraeder, again and again.

He heard screams from the audience. Looking past

the blinding glare of the projector, he made out the teen-agers tearing off their masks, running up the aisles, away from him, in psychotic panic. Schraeder was their leader, and the ritual had been disrupted.

Chambers looked down at Schraeder, staring at the gashes. He'd done that: he, himself. He shook his head in amazement. He looked at the reddened blade in his hand. The light on the blade, the hot shine of projected light ... The movie camera had fallen, lay hidden in shadow ... Someone had stopped the movie ... There was only the white light of the projector on a blank screen.

Chambers heard shouting from the lobby. Voices shouting with authority. Police. One of the Rubber Smiles running from the theater had probably attracted the attention of a passing cop, maybe blurted something about the killing.

It would be difficult to explain why he'd had to kill Schraeder. They might not believe the stuff about the disguised snuff film ... He had no proof. He'd take the rap for Schraeder's death.

Escape. And don't let them see your face as you run. Cover your face.

He started to drop the knife—then realized it'd have his prints on it. Had to take it with him. He tugged the grinning mask off Schraeder's head, and pulled it over his own. The mask smelled of rubber, of childhood Halloweens. Now his tears were making it stick to his cheeks.

He turned to run. A rookie cop burst in; saw the bloodied body on the stage; saw Chambers turn toward him, confused; saw the knife in his hand. The cop ran to the stage.

Chambers raised the knife, to fling it away. To the cop it looked as if he were threatening to use it again. But it was the mask Chambers wore that unnerved the young cop most. It was the mask, he realized later, that made him draw his gun and pull the trigger. Made him shoot Chambers three times.

The young cop had seen that movie only two nights before. It had really scared him. It had given him nightmares.

It was so damned realistic.

The Defiance of
the Ugly by
the Merely Repulsive

James Kisner

Ground Zero. That's where I live, man. Come on down here and let me show you where it's at.

I live back in this alley, at the end. It's dark back here, dude, darker than hell and stinks like shit on Sunday. It's dark out there too, because it's night.

I'm watching them go by. The *Uglies.* I can see them, but they can't see me. Which is fine. The only thing they see if they look back here is the yellow eyes of all them rats.

There goes an Ugly now. *Ugly* white woman. Carrying her shopping bag full of crackers and peanut butter and shit like that. I go after her. I *know* she don't have no money, man. I don't want money. Don't need it.

I want her for my knife.

I wrap my left arm around her neck and flash the blade in her old watery eyes before I slice.

Slice 'n' dice, man. That's me.

Fucking old woman makes a noise like a cow. And now she's hamburger. What you think of that, mofo? It's a joke, boy. Old woman is now hamburger meat. See? That old dog is nosing around in her guts. Dogs like fresh hamburger.

I hate dogs. Fucking mongrel mutt shit-ass dogs.

I cut the dog's throat and toss him on top of the old

74

cow and now you got two kinds of meat mixed together and you know what that makes, dude? It makes meat loaf.

Don't let *your* meat loaf.

Here comes another. Old rummy. Not worth cutting. Two many of them around and no matter how many you cut, there's always more.

Fuck him.

Ugly people. They're everywhere, man. Everyfuckingwhere you go. Ugly women, ugly kids, ugly old men with hair growing out their ears and dried up old shriveledup asses hanging raggedly out their pants with smell of piss and shit on them like a fucking shroud. Ugly women of all kinds, fat ones with cow-tits, little bitty shrimpy ones with big tits, skinny ones with no tits at all, all smelling like something that's rotten and full of worms and ain't none of it worth the trouble to turn up on end and stick your pecker in. I don't care anyhow, because I don't like women. They all ugly to me.

Ugly kids: lots of them, because the ugly women always dropping them any chance they get to collect the welfare. I just as soon off one of them as one of their old ladies—off them and dance in their guts—what the fuck do I care?

Ugly animals. Rats and birds who shit all over the city, even in the places where them rich dudes live. I hate rats. And cats. And birds and mice and fish. I'd kill them all if I could get my hands on them.

Ugly don't deserve to live. Right?

You like this knife I made? Razor blade on a stick, man. Cuts just fucking wonderful.

Man, you got a dollar?

The whole fucking world is ugly, mofo. Including *you*. Yeah, you are ugly the more I look at you and that's bad for your ass, because you know what I have to do.

Slash, slash, boy. I kill you. Slash-o-matic, that's me.

I kill you. I kill your mama. I kill your whole fucking family and all the generations of them going back three thousand years. Cut your head off, roll it in the gutter and then throw the rest of you in the sewer. You be so dead, they got to bury you twice.

I ain't got no use for no ugly people at all.

Thanks for the dollar.

I said, Thanks, man. Ain't you got no manners? What's the idea of looking at me like that? Like you dead? Don't look at me like that.

Dude?

Hey, chill out, man. Ain't nothing cool about acting that way.

Come on down here to Ground Zero! All you Uglies. All you uptight stuck-up bitches with your noses in the air, all you mothers with money tucked between your legs, all you dopers with the stash up your ass, all you winos and rummies with piss running down your legs, all you whores, all you pimps, all you gamblers and geeks, all you preachers and other God-ridden stupid fuckers. All you old dudes with scabs and running sores and fucking leprosy if that's what they call it and all that other evil shit—get your ass on down here, and I'll tell you the score. You think it's fucking easy to take care of your ugly ass?

Yeah, I'm talking to you. *Slice-o-rama,* that's me.

The sun's coming up. I stumble back in my alley and see something shiny back there. Piece of glass. Piece of a mirror.

Who *is* that dude in the mirror? That ain't me, is it? Me, looking like that? Me, an old dude like that? Me, with hair growing out my ears and my finger stuck up my nose and rags hanging on me and my ass hanging out and boogers and snot drying on my shirt and yellow stuff on my crotch and a rat living in my pocket and black stuff growing in my hair? Me, with big old patches of my skin dropping off and stuff oozing out the holes?

That ain't me.

It is?

No shit? You wouldn't shit me, would you, telling me that's me in that mirror when I know I look better than that. I may be repulsive, but I ain't ugly.

Let me look at that again. Look at that. I wave and it waves back. Just like that thing in the mirror is me. Son of a bitch!

I *am* ugly.

What? You say everybody look like this? Everybody? You putting me on with that?

What the fuck happened?

No shit? When did that go down?

No wonder there so many uglies out there. No wonder your old lady and kids is ugly. No wonder your dog is ugly. And I ain't even going to mention your black cat's ass.

I got me some real work to do now. Got to do something about this. I hope this blade is good and sharp. *Slice and slash, incorporfuckingrated.* That's me.

Catch you later.

Ground Zero, man. It's where it's at.

Mind Slash Matter

Edward Wellen

PROLOGUE

A disembodied voice announced the end of visiting hours.

He stood up. "I have to go now."

His movement and his words brought him to the fore in her fuzzy frame of reference and something stirred behind her eyes. "Did you see me yesterday?"

He had been coming to see her, to spoon-feed and straw-drip her three times a day—t.i.d., as the doctors put it—for the two months since the night of the emergency ride. "Yes."

"Did I see you?"

"Of course."

"Don't forget me."

He leaned over the bedrail to hug her. "How can I ever forget you? You're my mother."

She gave a surprised smile. "That's right, I'm your mother." Her thin forearms, bruised and mottled by the intravenous tube and all the damned blood tests, jerked weakly to parenthesize him.

The disembodied voice sounded its last call.

He kissed the rash-blotched brow. "I'll see you tomorrow. And you'll see me tomorrow."

"You're a nice man," she said. She had already forgotten again who he was. And she had regressed to her child's voice. (A week or so ago he had asked her how old she thought she was; she had ventured "Nine?" "You're eighty-one" had frightened her.)

He left the private room, but turned to look back through the doorway. She lay propped up facing the blank wall. As he stood watching, she smiled and waved bye-bye with her untethered hand at whatever it was she saw on the wall.

She should have died then, at *that* moment.

But she lasted five terrible downhill years longer. Doctors were small help; they couldn't cure or even treat Alzheimer's. But they could tell him it seemed to run in families. So, during those years, in between looking after her and meeting his deadlines, he put his mind to the matter of ensuring that *he* would not end up mindless and helpless.

That he would end up in the middle of a slasher case was farthest from his mind.

1

He knew he liked the driving beat of the music that surrounded the muted trumpet. But what did the trumpeter play—taps or reveille? He pondered that and the blank ceiling with equal dreaminess.

The voice that took over as the tune faded wiped the puzzle from his mind. "Rise and shine, Rush. You've just heard John Kirby's 1930s orchestra play 'Bugler's Dilemma.' Smell the coffee and wake up."

He did smell the coffee—though faintly, because smell, that part of the brain having to do with smell, was the first thing to go.

"Up, man, up."

He scowled and threw the thin blanket-sheet aside and sat up. Ribbed light through Venetian blinds turned the facing wall into a big blank page of laid paper. He looked around and his heart gave a beep of panic. The long room, with its wall of books at one end and the computer at the other and the window bay holding the daybed he lay on between, had a faint resonance in what remained of memory—yet it was not the place fixed in his mind as home.

But the voice spoke with the firmness of rightness and reality. Dimly, dimly, he knew that the voice knew The Answer. He had to trust the voice and heed it.

"Take the oxygen mask off the end table and put the mask to your face. Make sure the mouthpiece and nose-clip fit. The hose leads to an oxygen bottle. Turn the little wheel in the unscrewing direction, and breathe deep . . .

"This won't mean much to you, but oxygen enables the enzyme choline acetyl transferase to metabolize the neurotransmitter acetylcholine in the part of the brain that controls intellect and emotion."

A clearing wind knifed through the fog inside his head. Yes. The voice was his own and guided him through life as a docent tape guided a visitor through a museum. But the undertone of mockery—albeit self-mockery—troubled him.

"Okay, Rush. Tighten the valve in the screwing direction. Take off the mask and put it back on the night table . . . Feeling more alive, more with it, a bit more functional, fit for enterprises of great pith and moment?"

He did feel a buzz. He glared with love–hate at the computer in the corner. Its screen glowed, cursor at the ready. It was always on. Uninterruptible power supply, surge protection, multiple backup.

A feeling of hollowness. Nothing was foolproof. Certainly not himself.

"Today's Tuesday, July 18, 1989. It's now 7:35 A.M. I'll bet you want to go to the bathroom. Through the door and to the right."

He grew aware of a full bladder and padded into the bathroom.

The voice carried into the bathroom. "First take off your pajamas and put them in the hamper. Juanita—that's the nice lady who comes every day to help—will wash them and lay out fresh pajamas for tonight . . . Okay. Now you can take a leak. Make sure the seat is up."

His face felt hot. "Goddammit," he shouted, "I'm not that far gone." His face felt hotter. Talking back resentfully to yourself seemed pretty far gone.

". . . Finished? Push the handle behind the toilet . . . Okay. Let's take a shower . . ."

So, step by step, the voice got him showered, shaved, dressed, breakfasted, and toothbrushed.

The tone changed to a sad seriousness when it had him facing the mirror to comb his hair.

"Look at that face, Rush. Look past the anger, the frustration, the bewilderment. It's not a bitter face, though you have a lot to be bitter about. It's not a proud face, though you have a lot to be proud about. It's a good face, Rush. A kind face. A bright face. Look at the laugh lines. And the crow's feet. You haven't just lived, you've *cared* about living, about people, about what people do to people. You've got into trouble fighting good fights. You've won a few and lost a few. You've made a difference. You're a good man, Rush Lightbody. Stand straight, Rush."

He threw his shoulders back.

"You might have *been* a mark when you first hit town, and some not so nice people took advantage of you, stole some damn good ideas from you, robbed you of screen credits and pay. But you didn't let that sour you. You knew you could always come up with bigger and better ideas, and you *made* a mark in this town. If you look past your face you'll see the bookshelves in the other room."

He looked and saw them mirrored.

"See the shelf of bound scripts? They're the work of your mind. I won't gross you out with the grosses, but a couple of those scripts turned into films that rank with the biggest moneymakers of all time. See the two Oscars that serve as bookends for those scripts? Your peers gave you those. Rush, you're one of the best. That's the one thing you goddamn well better never forget. Rush Lightbody passed this way and left his mark."

A long pause followed, then the voice returned to its earlier mode.

"If you leaned against the sink you may have wetness on your pants in an embarrassing spot. If so, take a towel and rub the wetness dry . . .

"Now for your beeper. You remember your beeper. You should remember it: it's your security blanket. It keeps us in touch when you go out. Let's head into the big room . . . Your beeper should be recharging just to the right of the computer printer. I'll guide you to it by the beep."

He walked straight to the thing that beeped.

"Unplug the beeper from the wall outlet. Now move to the dresser and look in the partitioned tray on the dresser. You'll see a leather case the beeper fits into. Put the beeper in the case. Okay. Remember, whenever you hear the beep, look at the small screen on the beeper for the display." *Beep*.

The display read: ALL SET.

"Okay. The beeper case has clips on it. Clip the beeper case to your waistband. Remember, whenever you hear the beep, look at the small screen. It will tell you what you should do or what you should know.

"You're getting ready to go out. You have a 10:00 A.M. appointment with P. J. Katz. P. J. Katz is your agent. Take a handful of facial tissues from the box next to the tray and stuff them into your left-hand pants pocket. Take another handful and stuff them in your right-hand hip pocket. Take your wallet and your door key and a pile of change from the tray. The wallet holds your health insurance card and your driver's license, but the license is just there as ID. Put the wallet in the right-hand pocket of your jacket. Put the change in the right-hand pocket of your pants. Your door key is on one end of a long chain and a clip fastener is on the other end. Hook the clip fastener onto a belt loop on the right-hand side of your waistband and put the key in the right-hand pants pocket. Don't look for your car keys. You no longer drive. I'll phone for a taxi as soon as Juanita—she's the nice lady who comes every day to help—gets here. Does the name Juanita ring a bell? If so, come over to the computer and press the key with the letter *Y* on it."

The name Juanita rang dully like a drowned bell swayed by the tides. He could not picture the woman but he had heard the name. He pressed *Y*.

"Good. Response time noted. While we wait for Juanita, make yourself at home. You *are* home. Touch anything, pick up anything. It all belongs to you. Relax and lend your ears to some soothing jazz."

He liked the music and tried to relax as the voice had ordered. But his feet translated from tapping to pacing. They kept bringing him back to face the bookshelves.

The voice had said he could touch anything, pick up anything. He pulled a bound script at random.

The Mall. He opened it, tried to comprehend the script. He dimly sensed an interesting premise. It could make a good film.

It *had* made a good film—somebody had tipped into the volume some stills and rave reviews. He checked the spine and the title page again. His name. He had written it. His eyes flooded. Why couldn't he remember it?

He slammed the volume shut and shoved it back in place. He took down one of the Oscars that served as bookends. It had his name on it. Rush Lightbody, best original screenplay. Why couldn't he remember having won the Oscar, remember having done what it took to win the Oscar?

His grip tightened around the Oscar. Oscar's sword was useless but the figurine itself made a fine weapon. His eyes flashed hunting for the enemy. But the enemy had no form to strike at.

He glared at the computer. If the voice chose this moment to order him around he would smash the computer to bits. He stood waiting for the voice to goad him to its destruction.

A key turned in a lock, a bolt slid back.

The music cut off abruptly.

He shot a stricken look at the computer. It came to his rescue.

"That must be Juanita—she's the nice lady who comes every day to help. Juanita has tremendous respect for the written word. She knows you're a writer, she thinks you go around in a creative fog, so she makes allowances. Okay, be a gentleman and hold the door open for Juanita because she most likely carries a full bag of groceries."

He went to the door and yanked it open. A figure that had been elbowing the door from the outside spun stumbling past him into the place. It had a full grocery bag in each arm. He broke out of his startlement to catch at one of the bags that looked to be slipping. The Oscar slid to the carpet unnoticed.

"Thank you, Mr. Ligh'body."

He stared past the woman at a sign taped to the outside of the door.

CAUTION
NO SMOKING—SE PROHIBE FUMAR
No matches—No candles
OXYGEN IN USE—OXIGENO

He pointed his chin at the sign. "What's that sign for?"

The woman stiffened. "I know what is for. If I want cigarette I go outside in the hall. You know, Mr. Ligh'body, you never see me smoke inside." She grabbed the bag back. "I manage."

He saw her for the first time. A pleasant enough looking plump little Hispanic woman, though somewhat hot and bothered at the moment. She sidestepped into the kitchen.

The voice took charge. "Good morning, Juanita."

She poked her head out of the kitchen. Her glance slid past Rush and she projected toward the computer. "Good morning, Mr. Ligh'body." She seemed used to his split personality, to his talking to himself—and to her—in this ventriloquial manner. For some reason, she seemed stiff with him and easier addressing the computer.

"I'm going out today. Can you come up with forty dollars?"

"I see." Her head pulled back. Rush heard a zip, then a muttered counting. "I can manage."

The woman came out of the kitchen. She held out four tens to Rush. "Forty dollars, Mr. Ligh'body." She handed him a strip of yellow paper as well. "I spend fifteen-twelve in supermarket. Here is register tape."

"Say again."

She faced the computer. "Fifteen dollars and twelve cents."

"That means you are four dollars and twenty cents out of pocket. That will be added to today's check. Please try to stay within the budget."

The woman pursed her lips. "They have a special on toilet paper, so I stock up. You waste a lot."

The voice did not comment on this. "Okay, Rush. Put the forty bucks in your wallet and put the wallet back in your pocket."

He put the four tens in his wallet. He wondered what to do with the register tape but did not want to ask in front of the woman. He slipped the tape into the wallet along with the bills, then turned to watch with admiration as the machine printed a check.

Without prompting, the woman separated the check from the continuous form, then withdrew to the kitchen and the making of busy sounds.

"Okay, Rush. I'll phone for the taxi that will take you to the office of your agent, P. J. Katz. Go out the apartment door, hang a hard right, and you'll see the elevator dead ahead. If the elevator car is already there, get in. If not, press the button. When the elevator door opens, get in, press the button with the letter *M* on it. When the elevator reaches the main floor, get out and go straight through the outer door. Wait at the curb for your taxi. The driver knows where to take you. Remember, whenever you hear the beep, pull out the beeper and the small screen will tell you what you should do or what you should know. Any questions?"

Questions? He saw himself at the foot of a high wall, vainly throwing a question-mark grappling hook at the top . . . again and again. Damned right, questions.

But he heard the noises in the kitchen. Damned if he'd ask any questions with the woman in earshot. "No."

"Okay. Remember, go out the apartment door, hang a hard right, and you'll see the elevator dead ahead. If the elevator car is already there, get in. If not, press the button. When the elevator door opens, get in, press the button with the letter *M* on it. When the elevator reaches the main floor, get out and go straight through the outer door. Wait at the curb for your taxi. The driver knows where to take you. Remember, whenever you hear the beep, pull out the beeper and the small screen will tell you what you should do or what you should know."

He drew a deep breath, threw back his shoulders, and opened the door.

The voice projected. "Juanita, I'm leaving now."

The woman poked her head out of the kitchen. "So long, Mr. Ligh'body."

2

A hard right. The elevator dead ahead. The elevator car was not there. *Don't panic.* There was a button.

He heard brisk footsteps in the hall behind him. Quickly he pressed the button.

A pouter pigeon of a guy appeared at his side. The guy had seen him punch the button, yet moved right in to punch it again.

Rush glared at the guy. The guy had insulted him, had dismissed him as a nobody, as too inconsequential to affect the ups and downs of the elevator. The button needed the master's touch, the digital input of a Somebody; the guy was just that take-charge Somebody. In effect, the guy had given Rush the finger. Rush swelled his chest and balled his fists.

"Why did you do that? You saw me press the button. You looking for a punch in the snoot?"

If the guy laughed or came back snottily Rush would kill him.

The guy didn't laugh or say word one. He backed away from Rush, put up a glass wall between them with his hands, then whirled and vanished through the door to the fire stairs.

Rush's fists unclenched stiffly but his chest remained swelled.

The elevator door opened. He got in, studied the buttons, and took a stab at M. The door closed, the elevator started down.

The thing on his waistband suddenly uttered its beep. He read its display: PRESS M.

He grinned. He had already pressed *M.* The voice didn't know everything, didn't see everything, couldn't do everything. Without feedback, it could only make stabs in the dark. He stood straight. He was doing fine on his own.

The elevator stopped; the door opened on a lobby.

Only way to go from here, unless he was supposed to

sit on the plush couch or a highbacked chair and wait for someone, was out the front door.

Out the front door. Into an unfamiliar world. He recognized neither the facing buildings nor the ocean vista left and the mountain vista right.

He pulled back into the lobby. But the elevator door had closed, cutting off retreat. Besides, he could not recall the number of the floor or the number of the apartment he had come from.

He opened the front door again. He looked up the street. He saw a pouter-pigeon guy. Faint recognition stirred in him. Maybe the pouter-pigeon guy could tell him.

The guy stood talking to a burly man who was loading empty garbage cans onto a cart at the head of a ramp that evidently led down to the basement. The guy spotted Rush and pointed to him, then hurried away up the street.

The burly man one-handed the last one onto the cart, then dusted his palms and headed toward Rush.

Rush braced himself for the unknown.

The man cracked a smile. "Morning, Mr. Lightbody. That was Mr. Seymour. He just bought old Mrs. Joseph's apartment, 6H, from the daughter. Sorry to see Mrs. Joseph croak, but what the hell, she was ninety-eight. I guess you miss her, though."

Rush nodded. He remembered neither the name nor the person.

"Yeah. She liked you. Kept telling me all you did for her."

Rush shook his head. He remembered nothing of what he might have done for a woman he had no memory of.

"Yeah. I know you're not looking for thanks. Well, about this here guy Seymour. He's gonna be a real pain in the ass. He sounded off to me you was hostile and menacing." The man laughed. "You hostile and menacing. Well, have a good day."

Rush answered mechanically. "Thanks. You too." He stood blinking in puzzlement as the man walked back to the head of the ramp and wheeled the garbage-can cart down the slope.

The beeper startled Rush. MILLENNIAL BLDG. He stared at the display blankly.

"Hey, mister."

A cab had pulled up at the curb. A black woman wearing a reversed baseball cap and a Dodgers sweatshirt leaned toward him from the driver's seat.

Dodgers meant Brooklyn. Was this Brooklyn? But sweatshirts traveled; this could be anywhere.

His staring seemed to nettle her. "You got a problem, mister? Is it the skin or is it the sex?"

"You talking to me?"

"If you the party going to the Millennial Building."

Millennial. He blinked, then looked at the beeper display. He smiled. "That's me."

He strode to the cab, opened the rear door masterfully, and got in. The pullout into the traffic lane rocked him back. He had the scary yet exhilarating sense of heading into a great adventure.

"You a writer?"

A shelf of bound scripts with Oscar bookends. "Yes."

"I been studying about writing the story of my life. It would make a great book and then a great movie. I just got to find the time—or somebody I could tell it to." She reached a card back to him. "My home address and phone number. You ever want to write a *real* story, get in touch with me."

"Thank you." He deciphered the name. Colette Colfax. He stuck the card in his breast pocket and settled back.

The beeper startled him out of a dream of traveling in a cab through strange new streets.

He *was* in a cab, riding through strange new streets. He looked at the beeper display. PAY FARE+$2.

He eyed the meter. It read five-seventy and clicking. Did he have that much? He found his wallet. It held four tens. So far, so good. How long and how far had he traveled? Where from and where to? How much farther did he have to go? He did not want to ask the driver, a black woman who wore a baseball cap back to front. He noticed the letters *LA* above the bill.

L.A. Was this L.A.? Baseball caps traveled; this could be anywhere.

His nails were digging into his palms by the time the cab pulled up.

"Here you are."

He looked around. Where was here?

The driver, a black woman, tapped the meter. He was supposed to pay her and get out.

He had a wallet in his hand. The beeper display said PAY FARE+$2. The meter read seven-fifty. He handed the driver a ten. "Keep two bucks over the fare."

"Thanks, sport." She handed him change, then gravely added a strip of yellow register tape. "I think this belongs to you."

He took it and got out. He was studying it—a supermarket slip dated 7/18/89 listing items that totaled $15.12—when the driver called out before pulling away.

"Don't forget, if you ever want to write a *real* story."

Don't forget what? Frowning over this, Rush walked into the building.

He looked around the lobby, at a loss. Nothing on the wall directory cued him.

Beep. He eyed the display. P. J. KATZ'S OFFICE. He scanned the directory again. No P. J. Katz.

"Hi, Mr. Lightbody."

He turned to face a young woman. She looked frighteningly sharp. Would her friendly smile turn to withering scorn when he failed to keep up his end of the conversation?

"Hi."

She leaned toward him as though she might kiss him, but then pulled back and stuck her hand out.

He shook her hand vigorously.

She glanced at the display. "Seeing P. J.?" She checked the directory. "That would be Entertainment Arts on seven."

Seven. He had to remember seven. Seven.

"Your script-formatting software does everything but plot. Is story-plotting software next?"

He had a vague image of a disk sliding into a slot and of a screen arranging words into speeches, descriptions, and directions. "Could be."

The young woman grinned. "I wish you'd create software to replace producers. Your typical producer, as Harlan says, has the intellect of an artichoke."

Rush thought that over.

"You feeling all right, Mr. Lightbody?"

"Artichoke: I choke art."

"That's a producer all right." She eyed him ruefully. "You don't remember me."

"Should I?" he asked anxiously.

"Millie Koenig. I took your scriptwriting class at UCLA about ten years ago. And here I've been thinking I was your favorite student."

He threw her an apologetic look, but she had closed her eyes.

"In the working out of your plot," she said, "keep in mind that each of your characters has his or her own agenda. Let the bit players influence the stars. Give the least of them the air that he or she is the center of the universe. That way you round the character and deepen the story."

"That's very good," Rush said. Then, from the look in her eyes when she opened them, he realized she had quoted words of his back to him. "I mean, that you remember so well." He had to get her off him and onto herself. "How have you been doing?"

"You don't follow the trades? Three screenplays sold, three others optioned. One got made that you might have seen. *First-Class Male*." She eyed him expectantly.

"Ah," he said, nodding and smiling.

"Some say it shows your influence, and who am I to argue."

"That makes me proud."

She gave him a big smile. "Thanks." She fished in her shoulder-slung bag and handed him a card. "If your computer ever wants to talk to my computer."

He read the card. "I wish you continued success, Millie Koenig." He slipped the card into a side pocket of his jacket.

Beep. Maybe if he paid it no mind it would stop.

"Aren't you going to see who wants you?"

Under pressure, he found the display a confusion of wriggling symbols. They were words, not worms, but that was all he knew about them.

"I think I need glasses."

The young woman leaned near and read the green worms aloud. " 'PJ CALLED; WHERE ARE YOU?' "

She flushed. "My fault. I've kept you from your appointment."

She took his elbow as though he were altogether blind and guided him to the elevator. "Seven, remember. So nice to run into you."

"Same here," he said absently. Seven. Seven. Seven. Seven. Seven. Seven. Seven.

3

Seven opened directly on a reception area.

A sharp-featured woman behind a desk looked up. She frowned at her lapel watch but then smiled forgivingly at Rush. "Good morning, Mr. Lightbody. Traffic is murder, isn't it?"

Collisions and hit-and-run accidents flashed through his mind.

She pointed to a door. "Mr. Katz is waiting for you. Go right in."

The man in the photo-filled office wore a diamond in one earlobe, a gold *chai* hung on his hairy chest, a complicated watch graced his hairy wrist, suede elbow patches and cowboy boots finished him off.

"Hi, Rush." The man came forward as if to shake hands.

Rush looked him up and down. "Do I know you?"

The man's tan deepened. "All right already with the rapier wit. Don't rub it in I haven't cut any deals for you lately. Sure, you got a fabulous track record. Sure, you're far from washed up. But it's zit city. You heard of the graylist? Writers over thirty? They want young."

Rush stared at him. "Young? I'm young." Sudden panic hit him. His gaze shot to the mottled backs of his hands. *Just how old was he?*

The man gestured mollifyingly. "I know, young at heart. Some ways you're the youngest person I know." His eyes rolled in thought. "We could invent you another persona—an eighteen-year-old prodigy writer—to sell scripts you can't give away at your age? My pimply nephew could front, walk the walk and talk the talk. Think about it." He eyed Rush's blank face and sighed. "Forget it, you got too fucking much integrity for your own good." He clapped Rush on the shoulder. "Don't worry, your time will come again." He glanced at the console of his wristwatch and grew brisk. "Meanwhile I got you a writing gig. Sit down, I'll fill you in."

Rush sat down. His heart pounded. A writing gig? Was he up to it?

The man sat too and clasped hands behind head. "You remember Iris Cameron?"

Before Rush could shake his head, the man rolled on.

"Foolish question. 'The Queen B'—not just because she was a honey blonde with all those studs buzzing around but because she appeared in all those cult classic B pictures. The label stuck even after those few *real* classics with Bruno Beider directing. *That* Iris Cameron."

All that babble coming at him, Rush felt dazed and no doubt looked it.

The man eyed him sharply. "You on something?"

Rush shook his head in incomprehension.

"Then maybe you should be. Look, if you're still wrung out because of all Rhoda put you through I know a shrink who'll prescribe you safe uppers. When Bruno Beider of the famous Beider bit and Iris Cameron of the juicy scandals don't light up your eyes you sure need something."

Rush frowned. "Rhoda?"

The man looked sad yet exasperated. "You wouldn't listen to me and fight. You let Rhoda take you for all you had."

Rush's frown deepened. "Rhoda?"

The man put both hands up. "Okay, I'll get off the subject—which some other guy is prolly doing this very minute if I know Rhoda." He grew brisk. "Back to Iris Cameron. When she came to me with this you popped into my head even though you've never done any as-told-tos, only scripts. Here's your way back in. You write her life story for half the royalties on a sure best-seller—and anybody wants this hot property for a movie or a miniseries they gotta take you to do the script. I told her confidentially you just finished doctoring a script for a screen epic and might welcome a change of pace. Your credits impress her and she's anxious to work with you. On your side, you could use the money. All you got coming in as far as I know is the royalty on your script-formatting program—and the clones ripping you off are eating into that. You can start today."

Rush felt panicky. "Today?"

"Right now." The man scrutinized him. "You missed maybe a bit of stubble here and there but people expect writers to be scruffy." The man handed him a pen and a small spiralbound pad across the desk. "You don't even have to go home for your tools." He scribbled on the back of a calling card and handed him that too. "I wrote Iris's address and unlisted phone number on the back."

Rush puzzled out the raised print on the front. P. J. Katz, Entertainment Arts Representative. The man had got up and come around the desk, so Rush stood up too.

Rush stuck out his hand. "Pleased to meet you, Mr. Katz."

The man flushed. "Ah, c'mon, Rush, spare me your biting wit." He shook Rush's hand, then looked him up and down. "How are you fixed for cash?"

Rush patted himself and found he had a wallet. He counted the bills he discovered inside. He announced the count proudly.

The man shook his head. He fished two bills from a pocket. "Call this an advance."

They were hundreds. Rush put the hundreds in the wallet and the wallet in his pocket before the man could change his mind. "Thanks."

The man put his hand on Rush's shoulder. "I'm tied up or I'd go to Iris's with you, see the great old broad. But you're a big boy, you've been around, you know how to handle yourself. So what if you've never written a bio? You can do it. Just remember who you are, the complete professional, and you won't have to take any shit from her. Be yourself and you'll hit it off with her. So go downstairs and I'll have Beverly call a cab and I'll phone Iris and tell her you're on your way."

4

A cab drew up at the curb. The bandido-mustached man at the wheel saw Rush eye him uncertainly and gave him a nod. The man twisted around to open the rear door.

Rush got in. His blood fizzed with the sense of high adventure.

The driver stayed twisted around. "How's it going, Rush?"

It did not surprise Rush that the man knew him. Small world. And shrinking on its way to total solipsification. He took a choker closeup of the man. "Do I know you?"

"We met a number of times. I attended Guild meetings regularly when you were president. I seldom go nowadays. New crowd. All they talk about is residuals. My name's Ben Sunshine."

"Hello, Ben." Rush looked around. They were in a cab. The man at the wheel had implied he was a writer. "You drive a cab?"

"Only to support a habit—eating." He patted his bald head. "As you can see, I'm on the graylist."

Rush extended his look around. The cab stood at a curb and his door was open. "Are we already there?"

The bandido mustache formed a proscenium arch over a sheepish grin. "Shut the door and we'll get going."

So they were not already there. Rush closed the door. The man started the meter. "Where to?"

Rush sat blankly, then reached into a pocket and drew out a pair of calling cards. One said Millie Koenig, the other said P. J. Katz. A tossup, but P. J. Katz had a slightly more familiar ring. He passed the Katz card to the cab driver. But shrewdly held the Koenig card in reserve.

The man read the card Rush had handed him, then turned a puzzled face on Rush. "You just came from P. J."

"I did?"

The man thumbed at the nearby building. "There's his office." He cocked an eye at Rush. "You all right?" He raised a sudden finger. "Hey, wait one." He turned the card over and smiled. "Should've known. Your big crusade was to shake us up, to make us look past the obvious, to wean us from the boob-tube mindset of seeing and depicting one face of society. You're going to see Iris Cameron?"

Rush blinked. He gave a cautious nod, one he could take back if the man challenged him.

But the man gave the card a memorizing look and muttered, handed it to Rush, and pulled the cab into traffic.

Rush studied the front of the card. P. J. Katz, Entertainment Arts. Rush turned the card over. In ballpoint-ink block letters, Iris Cameron, an address, and a phone number. He guessed the man meant for him to keep the card, so he stowed it with the Koenig card and settled himself for the ride.

His interest in what streamed by petered out and he drifted into dream. His eyes snapped open as a voice intruded.

"That scene in *Whistleblower*."

He was in a moving cab. The words had come from the driver, a bald man with a bandido mustache.

"What scene?"

"The traitor delivers the McGuffin to the beautiful spy and asks, 'Where do we meet again?' 'In hell,' she says, and stabs him to the heart." The driver shook his head. "How did you ever write that?"

Rush shook his head. Then somehow his hand knew to draw out a pen and pad. "I think it must've been with these."

The man laughed. "Yeah, the Lightbody levity. The takeoff on chase scenes in *Tail the Tiger*. The drunken passenger in the stretch limo that wraps itself around a tree. He's knocked into the front seat beside the chauffeur, and when he straightens up he points through the windshield to the limo's own rear end and tells the chauffeur, 'Follow that car.' And the dazed chauffeur gets the limo chasing its own tail around the tree."

Rush visualized the scene and grinned. The wackiness of it appealed to him. It could be done, but it would take attention to detail to pull it off right.

He felt a numbing chill. A terrible thing was happening to him, to Rush Lightbody. The man had spoken of the screwball scene as if it *had* been done, and done by Rush Lightbody. But Rush Lightbody hadn't remembered it at all—not the doing of it, which would be understandable as fading from memory with time, and not the done thing, which was not understandable because it should remain forever a fond recollection.

"Here we are," a bandido-mustached cab driver said cheerfully.

5

A tank-topped, dark-skinned man in rubber boots and rubber apron looked around from hosing down a long white car in the driveway. Rush gave him a nod and a smile. The man nodded back. Rush felt the man's eyes on him all the way to the front door.

Rush saw a doorbell and pressed it. He heard melodic chimes. He felt cheated when a woman inside opened the door before he could ring again.

But he beamed at her. "Pretty music." He hoped she'd invite him to press the button again.

"It's the O'Neill planxty. Derry O'Neill the film star was Miss Cameron's second husband. Long ago in Ireland a wandering minstrel gave the melody to the O'Neills for making him welcome."

"That's a nice story."

The woman narrowed her eyes. "You're Mr. Lightbody?"

Rush was unsurprised she knew his name. "Yes."

"Miss Cameron's expecting you. Mr. Katz called to let us know you were on your way. Please come in. I'm Heather Flood, Miss Cameron's secretary."

"Pleased to meet you, Heather Flood. Okay if I press the button again?"

Her mouth twisted. "She'll think I haven't answered the door promptly. But ring away."

"Thanks." He pressed the button.

She opened the door wide and he marched in to the melody.

The woman showed him into a book-lined room. He looked for a shelf of bound scripts with bookend Oscars but found leatherbound sets of classic authors instead. No one waited behind the big desk.

"I thought you said she"—he couldn't think of the name—"was expecting me."

The woman's mouth twisted. "She is. But she has to make an entrance."

"Oh."

And on cue a honey blonde in a silver jumpsuit swayed into the room. Any trace of expression remained tucked away somewhere under the smooth skin.

Rush hurried to get off on the right foot. "That's pretty music at the door. The nice young lady let me listen to it again." He hoped the honey blonde would invite him to play it one more time as he left.

She stared at him, then raised a perfect eyebrow at the nice young lady.

Who said quickly, "Yes, this is Mr. Lightbody." She gave him a nod and edged out past the honey blonde.

Who smiled carefully at Rush and offered her hand.

He pumped it. "Pleased to meet you."

She slipped her hand free. "I've been looking forward to this too, Rush—I may call you Rush?"

"Sure."

Her husky voice carried traces of a British accent. Her honey blond hair fascinated him. The word *wysiwyg* flashed through his mind. *What you see is what you get.* He wanted to concentrate on that but she was speaking to him.

"Shall we get cracking?" She spoke as one used to taking charge, to having her own way. She looked him up and down. "Where's your tape recorder?"

Was the honey blond real or a wig? "I'm sorry—"

"Not to worry. Use one of mine. I hope the girl remembered to put blank tape in it. You know what help is like these days." She seemed not to care that the help might be in earshot. She passed him on her way to the desk.

He reached out and the honey blond hair came off. It *was* a wig after all.

Her hands flew to her head, then dropped to her sides as tight fists that shook with rage. Her makeup stood out rawly. She thrust her jaw forward and eyed him levelly.

Was she his mother? He reached out with his right hand to touch the silver hair on her head softly. "That's real."

The outrage drained from her. A tear shone in the

corner of an eye. She knuckled it away roughly and
smiled. "You sonofabitch. P. J. said you were good, and
he's right. You won't let me get away with a thing, will
you? Okay, brother, you win. Every bit of what I tell
you about my life will be real."

So she was not his mother. But she was not his sister.
That is, as far as he knew, he had no sister. As far as
he knew . . .

She took the honey blond wig from him and put it on
the desk. He watched her check the tape recorder, then
found himself holding it. She pressed the Record and
Play keys.

"As soon as I say 'Off the record,' press Pause. Keep
it that way till I say 'On the record.' "

He made a face. "That's too complicated."

She tried to stare him down, but he pressed his lips
together.

With a sigh she let up on the stare. "Bastard. Okay,
no secrets from my salivating public. Record everything
and transcribe everything. But when it comes time to
cut the damned thing down to size I'll give you a battle
you'll remember."

He thought he heard a yapping. He wasn't wrong; the
silver-haired woman had heard it too.

"That's Nebhat. I'd introduce you, but her horoscope
says this is a bad day for meeting strangers."

Rush nodded. He noticed a scratching post in the corner. "You keep a cat too?"

"No. That's Nebhat's. Not that she uses it. It's there
to remind her of her past. When I was Nefertiti, Nebhat
was my favorite cat."

Rush furrowed his brow. A dog playing a cat?
Makeup could work wonders, but even so . . . "I don't
think I saw that film."

"What film?"

"The one you just talked about."

She turned icy. "I never starred as Nefertiti. I *was*
Nefertiti."

The tape recorder was running, but he didn't know if
he could cope with this way of writing. She had thrown
too much at him too fast. Playing it back would only
give him the same thing all over again. He needed to

make her go slow the first time around. He raised a finger. "One life at a time."

She broke into a smile. "Marvelous! That's our title."

Marvelous didn't sound that marvelous a title. He was about to say so but she forestalled him.

"One Life at a Time." She squeezed his arm. "Rush, I'm ecstatic P. J. sent me you. Once this book goes over, we can work on my other lives."

The pressure and warmth of her hand lingered on his flesh.

6

She seated herself behind the desk and gestured him to a chair at the side. "Shall I begin at the beginning?"

"Makes sense."

She smiled. "I was born within sound of Bow Bells. Makes me a real live Cockney. During the early World War Two years, when the Blitz meant evacuation of city children to the countryside, my billet was a dairy farm near Stratford-on-Avon."

Dairy farm made him aware he was hungry. He looked around to see if he could spot food in the place.

The silver-haired woman looked at Rush's face. "Something wrong about the way I'm telling it?"

"I'm hungry."

She blinked, then nodded. "You're starved for detail, want me to flesh it out." Her accent grew Limier. "Mum had me at fifteen, so sometimes she dandled me like a doll and sometimes dumped me on *her* mum. I don't know who fathered me, but always one horny bloke or another hung about, looking for a bit of grumble and grunt. I ripened early; Mum kept me shut away most of the time. Took the war to open my world and change my life.

"My first train ride. First sight of the countryside. First realization the world wasn't all soot black and brick red. First realization that milk came from cows—not that I'd that much to do with milk till then.

"Ma and Pa Manderson were the dairy farmers who took me in. They also kept a market garden. First time

I rode the wagon with Pa into town, I saw posters on the playhouse that fronted the square.

"I was to help Pa sell the vegetables from the wagon, but during a lull I slipped away to see the posters close up. When I heard rich voices speak wonderful words, I slid through the stage door. The troupe was rehearsing the severed-hand scene from *The Duchess of Malfi*. Do you know it?"

He shook his head.

The silver-haired woman shrugged. "I bloody well didn't. I didn't know *any* plays. They spotted me when I gasped. Instead of tossing me out they dragged me onstage. They twirled me around, looked me over. With so many away at war, or at war work, they were *hungry*."

Rush knew what she meant. His stomach rumbled.

"They had me read lines. They smiled at my Cockney accent but said they could fix that. I said I'd talk to my mum and dad, and went back to the wagon and a frantic Pa Manderson.

"Pa pulled the wagon over under some trees on the way home. He started to spank me for playing truant. 'Drove me near mad with worry, you did,' he said. Then somehow the spanking turned into a frolic in the back of the wagon on top of cucumber and vegetable marrow remains while the old horse shivered in the traces and a sudden rain drummed on the tarp.

"So I had something to hold over Pa to make him let me take part in the plays. Ma, though, worried what my mum would think, and wrote her. Mum scribbled back that she didn't mind, not if there was a bit of money in it. So I joined the troupe and played small parts in the repertory. Then Ma noticed that I had missed my periods that had just begun.

"Ma was set to make a big scene at the playhouse, then she caught us in the barn together, and Pa admitted he was the one knocked me up.

"Well, Ma hauled me to Kidwelly, where a close-mouthed old midwife got rid of the fetus. Then Ma and Pa shipped me back to London. But I soon ran off to find and join another theater troupe." Her eyes darkened. "I'll never forgive that old woman."

Rush had followed her story and shared her outrage. "Mean Ma."

"No, the midwife. She messed up my insides. I could never have another child." She dabbed at her eyes. "Sorry, but I'm reliving all that. I have to stop." She managed a smile. "Time, anyway, for a tea break."

"That means food?"

She grinned. "That means food."

Rush grinned back. Boy, was he hungry.

She reached toward the intercom. Her face flushed. Rush noticed one little light in a row of little lights had gone on.

"There goes Heather again, making a personal call."

The silver-haired woman had spoken to herself, so Rush felt no need to respond.

She punched a button viciously and shortly a Hispanic maid rolled a serving cart into the room. Rush and the silver-haired woman set to, mostly Rush.

Rush gobbled a half-dozen small sandwiches, gulped a cup of tea and two refills, and burped cheerfully.

"Now for a treat," the silver-haired woman said.

Rush's eyes lit up. He had room for dessert.

The silver-haired woman spoke to the Hispanic maid who was clearing away. The Hispanic maid nodded, but instead of dessert brought an Oriental chef, an Anglo young woman Rush associated with door chimes, and a Black chauffeur. The chauffeur set up four folding chairs behind Rush. The two women and the chef sat down.

The silver-haired woman pressed a button on the desk. Bookshelves slid aside, revealing a VCR and a large screen. She opened a desk drawer lined like a fireproof safe and filled with videocassettes. She picked one and handed it to the chauffeur, who slid the cassette into the VCR, then took his seat with the others.

The silver-haired woman held a remote control. She smiled at Rush. "I'm screening *The Watchman's Dream.* Memorable for my first appearance in a Bruno Beider film. Look for me as the pert young maid." She switched it on.

It didn't take long to spot her as the pert young maid despite the screen image's honey blond hair because the silver-haired woman fast-forwarded all but the honey blonde's scenes.

"Here comes a famous Beider bit."

The pert young maid tilted a framed picture of the Tower of Pisa so the Tower hung upright. This became a running gag, with the mistress squaring the frame in passing and the maid tilting it in passing, till the mistress wound up smashing the picture over her husband's head, she mistakenly believing him the guilty party. Rush also watched the silver-haired woman watch the honey blonde. She eyed her younger self with a brooding intensity, a loving smile.

The film faded out on the watchman (the frame story seemed to be that he fell asleep on the job and dreamed it all) getting rewarded for catching thieves in spite of himself. The help clapped dutifully.

"Well, then, maybe one more." She picked another videocassette. "This is *Unfinished Business,* my first *starring* role in a Bruno Beider film."

This one took longer because she replayed her favorite shots. Rush didn't mind. He even asked her to replay the shocking moment during the burial ceremony when the bugler played reveille instead of taps and the mourners realized the bugler had gone mad. The film finally faded out on a Pieta shot of the honey blonde as a curiously immaculate battlefield nurse cradling her dying lover, the coward who had redeemed himself with one last self-sacrificing deed of valor.

The help applauded. Rush joined in.

The silver-haired woman waved the applause away. "Thank you, but there's no need for that. To entertain, to leave 'em with a tear or a smile, is reward enough."

The videocassette returned to the fireproof drawer. The bookshelves slid back in place; the help stacked their chairs and departed.

Rush stood up. "I have to go."

The silver-haired woman glanced at her watch. "The time flew. Been a busy first day."

"Yes. I have to go."

She got up and linked arms with him and walked him out of the room and down the hall. "I'll see you out."

He became aware he carried a tape recorder. "What am I doing with this?"

"Right; no need to tote the whole thing." She took it, ejected the audiocassette, and handed him the tape. "I'll have a fresh tape ready for you tomorrow."

He put the tape in a pocket. He squirmed. "I have to go."

She nodded. "Anxious to get your thoughts down." She patted his arm. "Go."

Rush found himself outside. He had a misty notion she had said something earlier about a dog. Did she think *he* was a dog?

He looked around. Bushes were a last resort. He walked to the driveway and looked past the gleaming white car. The chauffeur stood in the open doorway of the garage. The chauffeur's eyes narrowed slightly as Rush walked up to him.

"I have to go," Rush said plaintively.

"You have to—. Oh." The man stepped aside and pointed to a door inside the garage.

Rush thought to fling thanks back over his shoulder. He got his pants and shorts down and himself settled on the toilet seat just in time. Oh, boy.

He remembered to wipe himself off and swirl everything down out of sight and wash his hands good in the sink. Outside, his smile turned to a frown.

The chauffeur spoke to him. "Something wrong?"

"I can't remember where I parked my car."

"You came in a cab."

"I did?"

"You or your twin brother."

Rush stared at the man. "Do I have a twin brother?"

"Man, *I* don't know."

"But you said . . ."

The man studied Rush's face. "Excuse me." He went to a wall phone and spoke into it. He came back. "Miss Cameron says I can drive you where you got to go." He stepped to the glistening white car and opened a rear door.

Rush, still wondering what had happened to his own car, got in.

The chauffeur slid behind the wheel and started the engine. "Do you know where you want to go?"

Of course Rush knew. "Home."

"Right. Home." The driver rolled the car slowly to the roadway. "I got to turn one way or the other. Which way is home?"

One way looked as strange as the other. In a small voice, Rush said, "I don't know."

"Well, can you give me the address."

Rush heaved a sigh. "Sure." He gave the man the address.

The car swung right. It passed a high-wheeled pickup truck parked at the curb one house from the house they had just left. The pickup had opaque windows and windshield. Rush wouldn't have noticed the pickup if his own driver hadn't given it a sharp glance and tensed up as they swept by.

7

Nice ride. Rush forgot about the pickup. Once, at a red light, Rush saw his driver look up into the rearview mirror. Rush smiled at the man, but there was no meeting of the eyes. The man's gaze went past Rush. Rush twisted to look out the back at a high-wheeled, dark-windshielded pickup. Then the lights changed and the car moved and Rush forgot the pickup again.

"This your home?"

The car had pulled up at an elegant Spanish house.

Rush said uncertainly, "Yes." He looked harder and said firmly, "Yes."

The chauffeur got out and opened the rear door. Rush climbed out and thanked him.

The man said, "You welcome," but made no move to get back into the car. Rush sensed they were not done.

"Oh." He went for his wallet.

The man put up a hand. "No, sir, I can't take anything from you."

Rush smiled anxiously. What, then, did the man want?

The chauffeur looked as if he wanted to say something vital, but said only, "Take care." He gave Rush a finger salute, slid behind the wheel, and pulled away.

Rush suddenly felt abandoned by a friend. He turned to face the house.

Heart thumping, he strode up the walk to the front door. He automatically felt for the door key. It hung on a chain clipped to his belt. As he stuck the key in the lock, he heard an engine rev up. He twisted to see a high-wheeled, dark-windowed pickup move past.

Back to the lock. The key would not turn. Before he could panic, the door opened by itself. He looked up.

She stood in the opening. A waterfall of hair hid half her face.

He stared. She had aged since morning. In the hard daylight she looked the spit of her mother. He found himself moved.

"Rhoda," he whispered.

"Why the hell are you here?" She pointed to the key in his hand. "And what the hell are you still doing with that? You have some nerve."

"Rhoda," he whispered.

"Don't count on that little-boy-lost look to stir my heart. That's all over, and you know it."

"Rhoda," he whispered.

She shook her head irritatedly. The waterfall swirled away from her face to reveal a lovely shiner. At his stare, she threw a nervous glance over her shoulder and quickly fingercombed the waterfall again over half her face.

"I shouldn't even talk to you, but I saw you drive up." Her visible eye gleamed. "How can you afford a chauffeured limo? You make a big movie sale?"

"Rhoda, who you talking to?" The roar came from deeper in the house.

Rhoda put a hand on Rush's chest, where the heart was pounding. "Better beat it. That's Rex, and he's mean drunk."

Rush looked at her blankly.

Her hand pushed harder. "Rex Hunter. You don't want to fool with him."

A man loomed behind her. He glared at Rush. "That who I think it is?"

"Yes. He's just going."

The man shoved past her with a big fist ready raised.

"Rex, please. He won't come here again. I'll get a restraining order."

"Restraining order, shit. *I'm* telling the old fart to stay the fuck away or else. Got that, asshole?"

The guy shoved Rush back off the doorstep. Rush staggered, trying to catch his balance.

The door slammed shut.

8

"It's a shame the way they treated you."

Rush agreed. Someone had not been nice to him.

This lady, though, was nice to him and sympathetic. He didn't know her name—either she had expected him to remember it or she had given it but he hadn't caught it. She had called his name and had beckoned to him from across the street—and here he was, sitting in her living room. She looked motherly, though dressed not to look that.

"I wish you still lived there. What is it, five years already since the day you came home and found her throwing all your things out onto the lawn?"

Five years? Rush's head swam. Big chunks seemed missing from his life.

"It's like you not to say a word against her, Mr. Lightbody. I always told George you were too nice for your own good." She shook her head. "It only gets worse, the goings-on. Yelling and screaming at all hours. I can't count the times the police have been there." Her eyes gleamed. "It's true about appearances deceiving—even though Shirley MacLaine says reality is what you perceive it to be. Who'd think, watching Rex Hunter on *Destiny,* where he's the good-natured bodybuilder everybody takes advantage of, that he could be so different in real life? And he must be at least fifteen years younger than Rhoda." She shook her head. "I just don't know."

"I don't know either." Rush had trouble enough with his own age.

"Do you think it could be steroids giving him that temper?"

"I don't know."

Beep. He eyed the display, but his mind was just too tired. "I think I need glasses."

"Here, let me."

He was happy to. She read the display, picked up her phone, dialed a number, and beckoned him over. He put the receiver to his ear.

"Hello?"

"Hi, Rush." The voice sounded familiar. "P. J. Katz phoned. P. J. Katz is your agent. P. J. Katz said he heard from Iris Cameron. P. J. Katz said Iris Cameron is crazy about you. P. J. Katz said Iris Cameron is crazy period. P. J. Katz said it looks like a good match. P. J. Katz said he's sending over an agreement for you to sign. Got that?"

With the woman pretending polite indifference in breathing distance, Rush hardly wanted to say he had no idea what that was all about. "Yes."

"Good. Where are you now?"

Rush turned to the woman. "Where am I now?"

She stared at him but gave him the address.

He repeated it into the phone.

"Stay right there. I'll have a cab pick you up and drive you straight here. Got that?"

"Yes."

"Good. You can hang up."

He hung up. "I have to stay right here," he told the woman. "A cab is going to pick me up and take me straight . . ."

Where? He looked blankly at the woman. She was no help. She looked just as confused as he felt.

But she did say he was welcome to stay till his cab came, and even offered him a cup of coffee and a slab of pie.

Fair enough. Hadn't someone done him out of dessert not too long ago?

A car horn sounded while he was putting away chocolate pie with whipped topping. He ignored the horn, but the lady got up and looked through a blind. "I believe your cab's here."

He did not question her word. He did not know why a cab had come for him but events were in motion and he had to go with the flow. He hurriedly finished and shoved away from the table.

"Just a minute, Mr. Lightbody." She was pointing to her face.

It took him a moment to realize what she meant, then he did the gentlemanly thing. He leaned quickly to her and gave her a fast kiss. When he pulled away he saw a chocolate mustache on her face. But she had been nice to him, so he didn't embarrass her by speaking of it. He turned at the door to wave good-bye and caught a funny look on her face.

The taxi driver gave him the same funny look but said nothing.

Rush leaned back in his seat. He found himself licking his lips while he watched houses and trees go by. He tasted chocolate and sweet froth. He craned to look in the rearview mirror. Then, furtively, he drew a facial tissue from his pocket and wiped his lower face clean.

Beep. Maybe it would stop if he ignored it. But the driver was cocking an ear. Rush eyed the display but felt too tired to focus.

The meter too was a blur. Could he cover whatever it said? His wallet proved green with hope.

The taxi pulled up in front of an apartment building.

The building did not have the look of home. "Is this it?"

"It's the address my dispatcher radioed. Did she get it wrong?"

"Does your dispatcher know her job?"

The driver seemed unsure whether or not Rush was putting him on. "Well, she's been there since before my time."

"Okay, I'll take a chance." He moved to get out, then grew aware of the driver's waiting hand. He pulled out a bill and passed it to the man.

The driver's hand swallowed it up and the driver drew his own wad. "Change of a ten." He started to count out, seemed to struggle with himself, then stopped. "Say, mister, I see you gave me a hundred."

"I did?"

"I can't break that."

"You can't?"

"Got something smaller?"

They all looked the same size, but Rush held up another bill. The man said he could change a twenty, then, "Here's the hundred," *and gave him more money on top of that.* The math perplexed Rush.

The driver watched Rush put all the bills away and get out, then mumbled, "Go be a good guy," and screeched the cab away.

Rush faced the building. A man who reminded him of a pouter pigeon had eased past him behind his back and was slipping into the building.

As the man turned to close the outer door their eyes met. Rush caught a look of recognition in the man's eyes. The man gave Rush a wary smile but that was enough to spell friend. Indeed, the man, with a small grimace, held the door for Rush.

Rush passed through with a nod. "Thanks, pal."

The man had a key out and unlocked the inner door. He held that open too.

With another nod, Rush passed through. Wondering what came next, he let the pouter-pigeon man beat him to the elevator. But the man stood aside, deferring to him. The elevator door was closed, so Rush did the honors, pressing the button.

They waited in companionable silence. The door opened, they got in, and again the man deferred to Rush.

Rush sensed they had the same general destination, so he said, "After *you*."

Face shiny with sweat, the man gingerly pressed a button. Up they went. When the elevator stopped, Rush gestured the man off first. The man hurried away around a bend before Rush could think to ask if the man knew where Rush was supposed to go.

Rush collected himself and followed, in time to see the man vanish through a door at the end of the hall. Jealousy, like a backup of bile, scalded Rush's throat. Why did everyone but himself know where to go and what to do?

Fighting panic, he eyed the other doors. It took concentration to make out the little names in the little holders. Name after name failed to register. One door he put off till last because it bore an ominous-looking sign.

CAUTION
NO SMOKING—SE PROHIBE FUMAR
No matches—No candles
OXYGEN IN USE—OXIGENO

Yet that proved the one: *LIGHTBODY!*

He was where he was supposed to be. He pressed the doorbell.

A voice from the other side said, "That you, Rush?"

He found his own voice. "Yes."

"Use your key."

He found one at the end of a chain hooked to a belt loop on his jeans. It fit the lock, but would not turn in the unscrewing direction. He tried the screwing direction. This worked. He felt a glow at having outwitted the lock.

But what the door opened on did not fit a deep-seated sense of home.

He called out, "Hello?"

"Welcome back, Rush. Step all the way inside and close the door."

He did so.

"Okay, Rush. First the debriefing, then supper."

Hunger suddenly gnawed at him. Heck with the debriefing, whatever that was. Which way the kitchen?

"Walk into the big room and empty your pockets onto the bed."

He slid his eyes slyly. A voice could not see. It had only itself to blame for putting hunger into his head. He tiptoed along and found the kitchen. A big refrigerator stood humming to itself.

"Have you emptied your pockets onto the bed? If so, press the letter *Y* on the keyboard."

He opened the refrigerator door and looked inside. A Snickers bar. Oh, boy. Oh, boy. He grabbed.

"Walk into the big room and empty your pockets onto the bed."

His face grew stubborn. He was *hungry,* dammit.

"Have you emptied your pockets onto the bed? If so, press the letter *Y* on the keyboard."

He unwrapped the bar, stuck the wrapper in his pocket, and gobbled. He needed something to wash it down. He found a container of orange juice. He tore the top getting it open and the juice dribbled all over him as he drank from the container.

"Rush Lightbody, come into the big room right now."

He did not care for the peremptory tone, but he had no further use for the kitchen. He went into the big room.

"Have you emptied your pockets onto the bed? If so, press the letter *Y* on the keyboard."

Sullenly, he clawed stuff out of his pockets and onto the bed. He pressed the letter *Y*.

"Okay. Response time noted. From here on out, I'll beeper-check you hourly. Now spread everything out on the blanket in a row, then press *Y* on the keyboard."

He made a face and took his own good time complying. The Snickers wrapper he hid under the pillow.

"Okay. It is now 5:09 P.M. What do you remember of your day since 7:30 A.M.?"

He stared backward at blankness.

"Nothing? Okay. Look at the lineup on your bed. Anything ring a bell?"

He saw nothing that looked to be ringing a bell. "No."

"Okay. Now name the items. Start with the one on the far left."

"A card."

"Pick the card up and spell out what you see on it."

It took great concentration. Slowly he conveyed the name Millie Koenig and an address and a series of letters and numbers.

"Is there anything on the other side of the card?"

He turned it over. "No."

"Do you remember getting the card from Millie Koenig?"

"No."

"Do you remember anything about Millie Koenig?"

"No."

"Put the card down and pick up the next item. What is it?"

The voice's Socratic stick-and-carrot identified it as an audiocassette.

"Did Millie Koenig give you the audiocassette?"

"I don't know."

"You took a meeting with P. J. Katz today. Did P. J. Katz give you the audiocassette?"

"I don't know."

"You took a meeting with Iris Cameron today. Did Iris Cameron give you the audiocassette?"

"I don't know."

"You phoned me from the home of a Mrs. Blick at 4:20 P.M. today. Did Mrs. Blick give you the audio-cassette?"

"I don't know."

"Okay." Step by step, the voice led him through in-serting the cassette in the right slot. The voice said it was storing the data on its hard disk. Rush watched the little wheels spin. "Okay. From the context, I think you put it in B side first; but that's no problem. Okay. Re-place the cassette in the lineup on your bed. Any other cassettes on your bed?"

Rush looked. He shook his head.

"Any other cassettes on your bed?"

"No."

"Response time noted. Okay. What item is just to the right of the cassette on your bed?"

"A wallet."

"Open it up and describe its contents."

Rush needed prompting to specify the digits.

"Where did you get two one-hundred-dollar bills?"

"I don't know."

"Did Millie Koenig give you the two one-hundred-dollar bills?"

"I don't know."

"You took a meeting with P. J. Katz today. Did P. J. Katz give you the two one-hundred-dollar bills?"

"I don't know."

"You took a meeting with Iris Cameron today. Did Iris Cameron give you the two one-hundred-dollar bills?"

"I don't know."

"You phoned me from the home of a Mrs. Blick at

4:20 P.M. today. Did Mrs. Blick give you the two one-hundred-dollar bills?"

"Goddammit, I don't know."

"The register tape totaling fifteen dollars and twelve cents is congruent with the register tape produced this morning by Juanita—she's the nice lady who comes every day to help. Okay. Replace the wallet in the lineup on the bed. What item is just to the right of the wallet?"

"A card."

"Pick the card up and spell out what you see on it."

Painstakingly he conveyed the name P. J. Katz, Entertainment Arts Representative.

"Do you remember getting the card from P. J. Katz?"

"No."

"Do you remember anything about P. J. Katz?"

"No."

"Is there anything on the other side of the card?"

He turned it over. "Yes."

"Spell out what you see on it."

Laboriously he conveyed the name Iris Cameron, an address, and a phone number.

"Do you remember getting the card from Iris Cameron?"

"No."

"Do you remember anything about Iris Cameron?"

"No."

"Iris Cameron, to go by the data on the tape cassette you brought back, gave you the tape cassette. Okay. Put the card down and pick up the next item. What is it?"

"A pad and a pen."

"That is two items."

"I'm sorry."

"Spell out what you see on the pad."

He riffled pages, animating blankness. "Nothing."

"Spell out what you see on the pen."

"Scripto Super Stic Med. Pt. USA."

"Where did you get the pad and/or the pen?"

"I don't know."

"Did Millie Koenig give you the pad and/or the pen?"

"I don't know."

"Did P. J. Katz give you the pad and/or the pen?"

"I don't know."

"Did Iris Cameron give you the pad and/or the pen?"

"I don't know."

"Did Mrs. Blick give you the pad and/or the pen?"

"Yes!"

"Okay. Put the pad and pen down and pick up the next item. What is it?"

"Some change." That was more than one too, but the voice did not challenge him on that. It did elicit that he had four quarters and five dimes. There was no next item, so he was able to say, "That's all, folks." He giggled in relief and at his own wit.

"Okay. Underneath your bed there's a storage chest on wheels. Roll the chest out and open it."

He bent down, saw a handle, and pulled. A long low chest rolled out like a drawer. He lifted the lid. The chest held a confusion of items—cards, notes, letters, photographs, cassettes, and tantalizing glimpses of other objects. He would have liked to go through these keepsakes, but the voice gave him no respite.

"Put the cassette and the pad and pen in the chest. Now shove the chest back under your bed. Okay. Now pick up everything else on the blanket and put them in the tray on your dresser. Okay?"

"Yes."

"End of debriefing. Now let's get ready for supper. You must be starving."

For some reason he wasn't, but he followed the voice's promptings. He plugged the beeper into the wall outlet, put his door key along with the other stuff in the tray on his dresser, did his business in the bathroom, washed up, and found himself in the kitchen.

"Stay away from the stove." But then the voice grew nicer and rubbed its hands. "Juanita—she's the nice lady who comes every day to help—has left you a big bowl of salad. Open the refrigerator door, take out the bowl of salad, and carry the bowl of salad to the table. Close the refrigerator door. Pour yourself a tall glass of cold water from the faucet on the side of the refrigerator. Carry the glass of cold water to the table. Now sit down and set to. Oh, boy. Cherry tomatoes, romaine lettuce, onion, bell pepper, cucumber, zucchini, chick peas, celery, olives. Oh, boy. Dig in."

He sat down, but dug in halfheartedly.

The telephone bell saved him.

He looked to the computer voice to answer. It justified his trust.

"Hello?"

The hoarse whisper at the other end came from the speaker phone. "Rush Lightbody?"

"Speaking."

"Drop the Iris Cameron story or I'll kill you."

"I don't understand. Kindly identify yourself and clarify your message."

Click.

"Rush Lightbody, did you hear the message?"

"Yes."

"Do you understand the message?"

"No."

"I'll repeat the message." The words came out in the hoarse whisper. " 'Drop the Iris Cameron story or I'll kill you.' " The voice's own voice picked up. "Do you understand the message?"

"Yes. Somebody says to drop the Iris Cameron story or he'll kill you."

"I don't understand. I can't cope with it. Okay. Have you finished eating supper?"

He looked at the barely touched bowl of salad. "Yes."

"Good. Now let's clear things away and get ready for bed. You want a good night's sleep because I'm scheduling you to see Iris Cameron tomorrow."

9

The Hispanic woman looked at a point somewhere between Rush and the computer when she uttered her complaint. "I leave a Snickers bar in the refrigerator. It is no there now. I find a Snickers wrapper under the pillow."

Rush looked away from both. He let the voice and the woman fight it out.

"I know nothing about a Snickers bar. But if one is missing, Juanita, please add its cost to what I owe you."

The woman nodded and returned to her domain. Her coming had taken him by surprise even though the voice had given him intimations of a Juanita's existence. But by now it seemed she had always been here.

The sense that something needed doing hung over him, but the voice would remind him when the time came.

Meanwhile, he had time on his hands, so he watched the woman work. He felt comfortable with her. She comprehended that in his line of work he had to do much heavy thinking, that his mind was usually elsewhere. She seemed to take him seriously even though he got paid for dreaming. He tried to imagine what her life was like, and asked her questions, but her answers were short and spoken as if she had given the same answers to the same questions many times before, so he gave up and simply watched.

She fixed his supper for tonight and wrapped it up in Saran wrap and put it in the refrigerator. He marveled that she could think that far ahead. She took a basketful of clothing from the hamper, along with detergent and bleach, down to the basement laundry room.

He went through a small crisis while all alone. A messenger came from a P. J. Katz with an agreement for Rush to sign binding Rush to write the life story of an Iris Cameron. But the computer voice helped Rush deal with it. A few strokes of the pen. That was easy. Why not? He was a writer.

A Hispanic woman let herself into the apartment. She spoke familiarly to Rush. "Now costs one dollar for washer and one dollar for dryer."

The computer voice handled it. "Cost-of-living adjustment noted."

The woman nodded and set about dusting the apartment. Her dusting moved Rush from place to place, till he found sanctuary by the wall of books.

When she finally gave signs of having finished her dusting, he wondered that she hadn't dusted the books. "You don't dust the books?"

She looked at him. "You see I don't dust the books. When I come to work the first day, you tell me I supposed to dust everything but not the books. You say you know where every book is and you don't want mixup.

So I don't touch the books. You want now I dust the books?"

He put up his hands. "No, no."

She looked at her watch. "I go down to take clothes out of washer and put in dryer."

For a while during her absence he had nothing to watch. Sunlight drew him. He went to the window. He shoved the blind aside and saw houses clinging to a slope. The window had a window guard. Did a child live in the apartment? He could remember no such child.

A Hispanic woman carried in a big plastic basket of washed, dried, and folded laundry. He watched her put the laundered items away, each in its rightful place, without prompting.

The voice startled him. "Okay, Rush. Time to go see Iris Cameron."

Beep. He found himself standing on the curb, waiting. For what? He eyed the small screen.

TAXI TO IRIS, then a street address.

So he was ready when the cab pulled in to the curb. A black woman wearing a reversed baseball cap and a Dodgers sweatshirt leaned to him from the driver's seat.

Dodgers. That why all looked strange? He was unfamiliar with Brooklyn.

"Yeah, it's me again, Mr. Lightbody. Hop in."

He climbed in, he did not hop in. He showed her the beeper screen.

"Yeah, I know." She swung into traffic. At the first light to stop them she looked back at him. "You give what I told you yesterday some thought?"

"You told me something yesterday?"

"Shee-it."

They rode in silence to a mansion set in lots of lawn. He paid the woman off in line with the beeper's prompting.

"Thank you, Mr. Whitebody sir."

He thought it wiser not to correct her.

The front door stirred a faint memory. As soon as he pressed the doorbell and heard the chimes, Rush forgot all about the driver.

Rush felt cheated when a woman answered the first ringing too promptly to justify a second ringing.

She had a welcoming face and silver hair. "Rush, how *are* you."

He beamed at her. "That's pretty music." He hoped she would invite him to press the button again.

But she was drawing him inside. "I'm glad you make a point of it. We *should* bring it into the book. It's more than a mere decorative touch. It sheds light on my involvement in the arts—the symphony, the ballet, the opera. I want my public to know I'm something of a culture buff."

"That's pretty music."

She squeezed his arm. "You're going to make me stick to the subject, hey? All right. That tune has an interesting history. That's the O'Neill planxty. It's said that a minstrel tramping the Ould Sod gave the melody to the O'Neills for making him welcome. The reason for the O'Neill planxty here, of course, would be the late Derry O'Neill the film star, my second husband."

The silver-haired woman kept her arm linked to his and led him along a hall. "I should've saved that little speech for the tape recorder. But first."

They walked down rose-carpeted steps to a sunken living room. A fieldstone fireplace dominated the room.

The silver-haired woman sat him beside her on a loveseat. "Chippendale." She looked into his eyes. "You don't look worried."

"I'm not that heavy."

She laughed, then turned grave. "I'm not talking about the damned chair. Harris told me about the pickup truck that followed you home yesterday afternoon. Heather confessed making the phone call that led to that. I have no idea why that man should be so set against me telling my story. He's out of my life."

Rush found this business of pickup trucks and phone calls hard to follow. Who were Harris and Heather? Was Harris the same as "that man"?

The silver-haired woman kept piling on confusing details. "Heather admitted she's been tipping him off about my doings all along, not for money but because she thought it romantic that he still wants to know all about me. But I can't afford to have a traitor in my household. Needless to say, I fired Heather on the spot." She looked as though asking approval.

He nodded. Least he could do. That he wasn't following her was his fault, not hers.

She squeezed his arm. "I called his number and he finally answered late last night. I asked him what he was up to. He said he didn't want my story told to the world. He wanted to keep me to himself. I reminded him it had been over between us for many years. He said it would never be over for him. And he said he had warned you to lay off or he'd kill you. I asked him why he didn't threaten to kill me—it would seem simpler to stop the source. He said he loved me too much."

A glow suffused the porcelain face. "Heather was right. That *is* romantic." Then she regarded Rush. "You will be careful?"

"Sure." The loveseat was fragile, but he wasn't that heavy.

10

The wonderful little tape recorder did the real work. All Rush had to do was sit easy and listen dreamy in the book-lined study while the silver-haired woman behind the desk told him a story.

"... Of course, as I look back, the troupe was strictly from hunger, but the audiences we played to weren't that demanding. Some respite from the drone of the Jerry bombers and the pompom of the ack-ack guns. We made them forget fear and pain for an hour or two. We toured hospitals and convalescent homes. Some faces and bodies still give me nightmares." She paused for a sip.

Her drink looked richer than his own lemonade. He felt a stab of jealousy. "What's that you're drinking?"

She looked taken aback. "A Bloody Mary. I get by on Hail Marys and Bloody Marys. I got converted to Hail Marys when I married Derry O'Neill and to Bloody Marys when I married Jeffrey Gridley." She flashed a grin and shook a finger at Rush. "What an eye for detail!

My public is going to know everything, but everything, about me."

Her brow creased faintly. "Where was I?"

Rush hid a smile. He held this silver-haired woman in jealous awe. Her face might look as if she had no history, but she remembered every last thing that had happened to her. She could recall vividly the colors and smells and sounds and dates and names and faces of her life. That didn't mean she might not be screening and skewing the details in her favor. But she *remembered,* damn her. So her momentary lapse pleased him.

But she remembered. "Oh. Playing the hospitals. That was how I met my first husband. Lt. Lane Woolman of the United States Army Air Corps." Her voice and eyes and hands grew dramatic. "So ironic—when you think of all the bombing missions Lane went out on and came back from without a scratch—that his injury was not strictly speaking a war wound.

"Lane almost bought it on the ground—driving back to the air base in a motor pool Jeep, after an evening in a pub in nearby Swindon. He says his mind was clear enough, but the road was dark and the headlights were masked to useless blue crosses and even the moon was blacked out. He was passing the POW camp next to the base when this figure darted across the road in front of him. Lane swung the wheel, but he sensed a thump, and lost control and the Jeep hit a tree. Next he knew, he was in hospital, his head all bandaged up."

She took another sip. "It was so romantic how it happened. I mean, the romance between I and Lane. He was all bandaged up, like I said, so you couldn't see the face, but I fell in love with the voice. With the voice, and with what the voice said. Because he was a real Yank who could tell me all about life in the States."

Her gaze fixed on Rush. "You see, I'd already made up my mind to go to the States as soon as I could once the bloody war ended."

Smiling, she shook her head. "Lane handed me a load of crap about what he had and what he did back in the States. When I later called him a bloody liar, he said that all was fair in love and war, especially when love and war came together." Her eyes turned sad. "He wasn't the only one to hand me a load of crap. Just one of the earliest."

A big sip. "Anyway, his voice and what he said kept me going back to see him." She closed her eyes. "Bruno Beider could've used the moment when I leaned over his bed and gently removed the dark glasses and those blue eyes shone forth out of this, this mummy, and gazed into my eyes with naked adoration." Her eyes opened and stared at Rush candidly. "In those days wonderful flowers bloomed in bomb craters. I was like one of those flowers."

Rush had finished his lemonade and was wondering whether to ask for a refill. Better not. He had begun to feel the need of a leak as it was.

"Well, Lane and I looked at one another. I remember the ticking of the wall clock, the stale fragrance of the wilting violets in the chipped water pitcher. Then he told me he loved me and asked if I could love him back."

She paused, and Rush waited in suspense.

"I took his big rough hand between my soft slender ones and answered, 'But of course, dear.'"

Rush let his breath out.

"True, I would've lied to bolster his will to live. As it was, he nearly died." Her brow darkened. "Damn fools transfused the wrong type blood. It was touch and go. My staying at his bedside may have helped pull him through."

She finished her glass. "Those were the days. In between the air raid sirens, the flares, and the bombs, there was—believe it or not—fun. Because tomorrow might not come, people wanted to see it all, do it all, have it all. An actress friend had joined the A.T.S.—Auxiliary Territorial Service. You Yanks said A.T.S. stood for Action, Traction, Satisfaction. She drove a staff car, so we got to double date the brass, who kept us in nylons, Spam, chocolate, cigarettes, toilet paper."

Rush sat straighter. "Where's the john?"

The woman gaped at him, then pressed a buzzer that produced a Hispanic maid. "Manuela, show Mr. Lightbody to the juan."

*   *   *

Rush remembered to wash his hands. He looked up and swung the face in the mirror because it scared him. A fancy bottle inside the medicine cabinet caught his eye and he pocketed it.

He took a wrong turn on leaving and came to a spacious kitchen. He stood watching an Oriental chef work till the man froze with chopping knife in hand and locked eyes with him. He guessed the man didn't want him there; he backed out into a Hispanic maid.

" 'Scuse me, sir. Miss Cameron—" She stopped as her glance fell to his midsection.

His hand shot guiltily to his pocket and a bottle that didn't belong there. But it was not that. She was discreetly indicating his crotch. Ah. He pulled the fly zipper tab up and down a few times. "You mean this?"

She nodded, then pointed down a corridor. "Miss Cameron is worry about you."

Who was Miss Cameron? Nice of her to worry.

The corridor led to a book-lined study. Where a silver-haired woman eyed him compassionately and gestured him to a seat. "Prostate? Jeffrey Gridley—my last, and I do mean *last,* husband—suffered from that."

Rush nodded politely. "Sorry to hear it."

She raised a finger to make a point. "But we have a long way to go before we reach Jeffrey."

"How far away is he?"

She smiled and pressed a tape-recorder button. "In Oxnard. I set him up in a real-estate office there. But I was telling you about the bandaged Yank lieutenant. I held Lane's hand as the surgeon cut the outer wrapping away, then the final layer of gauze." She gave him an arch look. "A Bruno Beider moment. Bet you're saying to yourself that if the worst had happened and horrible scars disfigured his face, that would have ended the romance for Iris Cameron. Good-bye, Lt. Lane Woolman."

He could honestly deny that he had been saying any such thing, and did so.

"Bless you, Rush. I'm *not* a shallow, selfish creature. No, even if the surgeon had not done a masterly job, I would've gone through with it—and not just because I hungered for the States."

Rush must've looked *his* sudden hunger, because she pressed a buzzer.

"We'll have tea." She went on. "Lane left hospital after VE-day—no more sirens, searchlights, barrage balloons, buzzbombs, blackouts, but rationing still. But the Air Corps did not need him against Japan and cut orders to send him home."

Food and drink came and Rush listened with only half an ear.

"We wed at the registry office in Swindon and parted at the airfield. Till I could follow him to the States I helped out at Shrivenham American University, set up to educate Yanks waiting to be demobbed."

She smiled. "Ironic to see German P.O.W.s doing K.P. in the messes and canteens. *Kuche, kirche, und kinder!* The supermen who started the whole-bloody-caust were common-looking young men who reddened when they caught themselves saying *'Scheiss'* in my hearing.

"At last, we war brides sailed to the States. When I saw Lane again he wore civvies. I almost didn't recognize the ordinary-looking bloke who waved at me from the pier. His mustering-out pay, and the 52-20 Club, carried us till he got into NYU on the GI Bill. We had located in New York City although the back of Lane's honorable discharge gave his permanent address as Boulder, Colorado, where he had lived with his next-of-kin—the aunt who brought him up after his parents died in a train wreck. I never got to meet the aunt; poor old thing died before I came over. No wonder Lane wanted nothing to do with Boulder."

She shrugged. "I, of course, was glad to stop in New York. I loved the excitement, even if it meant a cramped walkup. I got a small part in a British light comedy import."

The Hispanic maid cleared away the dishes and nodded at another signal from the silver-haired woman.

"A Hollywood talent scout spotted me and a screen test landed me a studio offer. Lane agreed to transfer to U.C.L.A. So we came out here. But as my career zoomed ahead, Lane grew dissatisfied with working toward a degree in languages. He dropped out and brushed up on his flying and went into business with another fellow in a small charter outfit. With my connections, he broke into movie work: taking photographers aloft for aerial shots, transporting film and equipment to and from locations, and even doing some stunt flying."

A dark chauffeur came in and set up three folding chairs. The Hispanic maid and an Oriental chef followed. They took their seats behind Rush.

"Then I made *Alibi Baby* with Derry O'Neill."

A small nasty-looking dog padded in. It sniffed Rush disdainfully, then went to the silver-haired woman's side.

"Let me introduce you. Nebhat, Mr. Lightbody. Rush, Nebhat."

Rush nodded and said, "How do you do."

The place turned into a screening room.

"*Alibi Baby* is *the* musical fantasy. Derry O'Neill plays a lovable rascal who finds himself with a perfect alibi and looks around for a crime to commit. I have the title role, a heart-of-gold chorine. During the filming I and Derry became romantically involved. I and Lane split up, but the bluebird of happiness had flown the coop long before I met Derry."

The screening had to stop once to let Rush answer the beeper; the voice was only checking.

Rush pitied the chorine whose talent was misused and whose love was misbestowed. She had this gift: time stopped for everybody else when she did a time step. The young hoofer she fell for stumbled on the fact that if he did an off to Buffalo while she did the time step he could move around while everyone else stood frozen. So he danced himself into and out of bank vaults and jewelry stores—and at the end even out of a cell on death row. But he couldn't dance himself into Heaven, where the young and pretty chorus girl had gone.

Rush looked at the dog as much as at the screen. He wondered what went on in a dog's mind.

After the help applauded and set everything to rights and left the book-lined room, the silver-haired woman told a story.

"Lane had heard the rumors and read the gossip columns before I broke it to him that my heart was now Derry's. So he wasn't surprised. *I* was surprised by how well he took it. And he was even there to lean on when tragedy struck and Derry died."

"You have tears in your eyes."

She smiled through the tears. "That's how it will read, won't it? 'Iris had tears in her eyes as she spoke of Derry's death.' "

Rush felt pleased that he had pleased the silver-haired woman.

A faraway look came into her eyes. "It was grand while it lasted, what I and Derry had between us. Life with Derry O'Neill was life lived to its fullest. Derry had energy, appetite, and passion to drive a dozen ordinary humans. Derry the swashbuckler, the carouser, the womanizer. He had his brawls, toots, flings—publicized and unpublicized. But always he came back to me, back to this very house, the home of the O'Neills. Did I mention that the door chimes play the O'Neill planxty?"

He thought, then shook his head.

Her brow shadowed, then cleared. "Oh, you want it for the tape." She explained about the O'Neill planxty, then went on.

"Well, we knew true love and real happiness, we did, till Derry died in that tragic accident on location during the making of *Hunt the Hunter*. Luckily, Derry had all but completed his part. We used a double for the few shots remaining and dubbed the dialogue, and it did fine at the box office."

She sighed. "But Derry's death was a great loss not only for me, but for our fans and for the industry. And of course for Derry. Though you might say he brought it on himself. He was an avid skier, and there had been a fresh snowfall up there. He played hooky to ski a dangerous slope. The technical adviser for the hunting and trapping and other outdoor sequences had warned we actors and crew away from that face because the least little sound could set off a snow slide. Well, cascades of snow buried my poor foolish dear Derry. Not a mark on the lovely lad, but he was frozen stiff when they found him and dug him out."

Her face worked. "I can't bear to talk anymore about it today. I'll screen *Hunt the Hunter* for you tomorrow and you'll see the terrain for yourself. Come, Nebhat."

She hurried from the room with the dog at her side. Over its shoulder the dog gave Rush a thoughtful look.

Rush stood regarding the array of richly bound books. It burned dimly in his mind that somewhere a book held The Answer. To just what, he did not know. But when he found it he would know. He reached for a book.

" 'Scuse me, sir."

He jumped. The Hispanic maid was at his elbow.

"Miss Cameron say don't forget to take that." She pointed to the desk.

He looked blankly at the desk.

" 'Scuse me." She moved to the desk, popped a cassette from a small tape recorder, and handed him the cassette.

He pocketed it.

"Miss Cameron say Harris drive you home."

Home. A great tide of nostalgia swept over him. "Yes. I want to go home."

11

The chauffeur put the big white car in gear and let it hang a hard right out of the driveway. Rush leaned back. The man seemed to know where to go.

At the first traffic light the chauffeur spoke over his shoulder. "He's tailing us again."

Rush twisted to look back but could not see who the man was talking about because the windshield of the pickup truck behind them was dark.

"He is?"

"Miss Cameron told me he threatened you. You got somewhere safe to stay? I think I can shake him."

Rush thought hard. "Isn't home safe?"

"You asking me to speculate, it isn't safe if he knows about it."

The light changed and the car moved. The pickup truck stayed close behind.

Rush thought harder. He fished a card from his pocket. Handwritten block letters said *Iris Cameron*. That had a safe ring to it. He passed the chauffeur the card.

The chauffeur did a doubletake on the card, looked about to say something explosive, then turned the card over. "Oh. No problem." He handed the card back. "Brace yourself and hold on."

Rush got a scary high as the car squealed around turns and wove through traffic. He was sorry when the happy blur ended.

The car had stopped at the curb in front of an office building. The driver got out and came around and opened the car door for Rush.

By the time he could think to thank the chauffeur and ask him "What now?," car and chauffeur had melted into the traffic flow.

The card. It said *P. J. Katz, Entertainment Arts Representative.* But if you turned it over it said *Iris Cameron.*

Beep. He strained to read the display. Looked like a phone number.

Through the glass doors of the building he spotted someone at a public phone. Rush entered and lined up behind a man talking to a Tina.

It sounded interesting, but the man said into the phone, "Just a minute, Tina," then turned so he and Rush stood nose to nose and said, "Look, fella, mind not breathing down my neck while I'm talking confidential?"

Rush backed away and pretended disinterest. He did too good a job: someone took his place.

Beep. Rush felt like screaming. How the heck could he phone the number when the whole world got between him and the phone?

He looked around but spotted no other phone. He did see the office directory. His gaze locked on the listing *Entertainment Arts.* He checked with the card. He felt a glow. He was really clicking.

Mindful of the touchy man still talking to Tina, Rush whispered to the interloper. "How do I get to seven-oh-one?"

The man turned and looked at him. "It's no great secret." He pointed to the elevator. "Get in that elevator and press seven."

"Thanks." Rush made for the elevator, chanting to himself the mantra *seven.*

A sharp-featured woman behind a desk looked up. "Why, hello, Mr. Lightbody. Mr. Katz didn't tell me you might drop in. He's in conference at the moment, but I'll let him know you're here as soon as I can. If you'll take a seat—"

Rush waved that aside. He showed her his beeper display.

"Of course, Mr. Lightbody." She dialed and handed him the receiver.

He nodded thanks.

The woman got up and opened a door and leaned into the other room.

A strangely familiar voice spoke in his ear. "Rush?"

"Yes."

"An unidentified male phoned here. The unidentified male said you're crazy if you think you can run from him. The unidentified male said if you don't drop the Iris Cameron story he'll kill you. Got that?"

With the sharp-featured woman returning to the desk, Rush didn't want to say he had no idea what that was all about. "Yes."

"Good. Where are you now?"

Rush turned to the woman. "Where am I now?"

She stared at him but gave him the address.

He repeated it into the phone.

"Stay put. I'll have a cab pick you up and bring you here. Got that?"

"Yes."

"Good. You can hang up."

He hung up. "I have to stay put," he told the woman. "A cab is going to pick me up and take me . . ." Where? He stared blankly at her.

She was no help. She looked as confused as he felt. But she did say, "Mr. Katz can fit you in now." His stare seemed to make her uncomfortable. She pointed to a door. "You can go right in."

The man who greeted him wore a diamond in one earlobe and a gold medallion on his hairy chest.

Rush could not think of the name. "I know you."

The man grinned. "Yeah, I guess you do know me and my conferences. Have to catch some zees to recharge. Well, buddy-boy, what's on your mind?"

Rush felt around in his pockets for some cue. He

found something and brought it out. He handed it to the man.

The man looked it over with a frown. "Tape cassette?" His brow cleared. "Iris dishing dirt, hey? This I gotta hear." He fed it into a machine. He gestured Rush to a seat. He himself paced the floor as they listened.

A woman told a story about wartime, falling in love and marrying, coming to the States, getting into pictures, and falling in love . . .

The man took the tape out of the machine and handed it back to him. Rush pocketed it. The man clapped him on the shoulder.

"Good stuff. You know how to draw her out. I got a hunch this is gonna work. Stay with it, buddy-boy, we'll all make a bundle."

A sharp-featured woman entered. "Mr. Lightbody's cab is waiting."

The man with the gold medallion ushered him to the door. "Don't let me keep you, Rush. Get it all down while it's hot."

Rush couldn't account for the fancy bottle of perfume that turned up when he emptied his pockets during debriefing. But it made a nice souvenir of something. So when the voice told him to put it with the other stuff in the chest under his bed, he palmed it.

12

Next morning, after the voice had Rush all set to cab to an Iris Cameron's to get the woman's life story, the voice had to change plans because of a phone call from the very same Iris Cameron.

Rush listened. And a Hispanic woman, on hearing the name, protruded from the kitchen to listen too.

The Iris Cameron one sounded breathless. "Harris told me what happened, and I'm worried for you. But I have the answer."

The Answer. Rush stared hard at the phone.

"Let him think he's scared you off. We'll work together by phone and surprise him with a fait accompli."

Rush blinked. "That's The Answer?"

"So let's get going on today's episode." She sounded as if she were settling herself. "Tape running?"

The computer voice beat Rush to the punch. "Yes."

"Derry's death in the avalanche hit me hard. But a thrown rider has to remount, right? I pulled myself together—I'm sure you can recount my grief and anguish and sense of irreplaceable loss and all that—and appeared in *A Special Case,* the comedy classic.

"Comedy classic, ha! Everything, but *everything,* that could go wrong did. Starting with Al Tanker, the old-time director. This picture represented his last chance to stage a comeback. That unnerved him. He hit the bottle from day one. We knew the money boys would close us down if this came to light, so we covered for him. We directed ourselves. We got away with it because we were on location, way out in the boondocks.

"Naturally, we screwed up. But we kept the cameras rolling no matter what. The funny thing was that what went wrong worked out right. Take that scene where I, playing a Southern belle, sat down too abruptly, causing the wooden hoop in my gown to fly up. It was only supposed to embarrass me, but it broke my nose. Brother, it hurt like hell. A doctor set it, but makeup wouldn't hide the swelling. Al Tanker was too out of it to cope. So we rewrote the script and had my character *use* the broken nose to get back at the gentleman who had done her wrong. Sue him for supposedly battering her.

"And that fuzzy-minded old character actor who played my lawyer not only forgot his lines but what character he played. So when he was supposed to return to his office after lunch and saw the notice on his door, *Back at 2 o'clock,* instead of taking down the sign and going in, he looked at his turnip watch and sat down to wait for himself."

Rush did not find that funny. He felt sorry for the old character actor.

"And that mammy who picked up that chicken and used it as a featherduster? Not in the script; she was that nearsighted.

"And as for Hunk—oh, I have to get in here that I met Jeffrey 'Hunk' Gridley on *A Special Case.* Poor Jeffrey. What the critics called his endearing awkwardness as the bumbling gentleman was not acting. Jeffrey could never understand why after all the acclaim he never got another good part and in fact had to drop out of the business.

"One right thing was the camerawork of Leatherneck Slotkin. Sully Slotkin is his real name if he's still around, if skin cancer didn't get him. The nickname comes from that raddled neck of his. He favored front lighting, so the sun and the kliegs always burned behind him. He made sure no ugly shadows fell across my face.

"Al Tanker, when he sobered up, thought he had done it all himself, though when he accepted the Oscar for directing he thanked the little people. Ha! The little people were the leprechauns he saw when he got sozzled.

"The film won me an Oscar nomination, the offer to work with Bruno Beider, and Hunk. I married Hunk for his body, not his mind. He did swell on the football field, but as an actor he didn't have it, even as a bit player in low-budget Westerns. So I set him up in a real-estate agency. Trouble is, Hunk never could take yes for an answer. Many's the sale he lost by pitching long after the prospect was ready for the dotted line. Timing. It's all in timing."

She sighed. "When Jeffrey saw himself failing at real estate too, he got overly possessive, overly jealous, and took to smacking me around. Nothing as bad as the broken nose in *A Special Case,* but more than once I showed up on the lot with a mouse or a swollen jaw that the makeup artist had to cover up. I might've stood that, I don't know how long, but Hunk went to pot. Beer gut, bad knees.

"And right about then I became the mistress of Buddy Stabile, the producer. Buddy was up front with me. He told me he would never divorce the mother of his children to marry me, for religious reasons.

"Speaking of religion, I once actually thought of taking the veil. That was shortly after I played the novitiate in *Wallflower*. Do you know the film? It had an unstated lesbian theme. Before its time. Did poorly at the box office, but now it keeps popping up in art houses. I'll send you the video.

"Well, Buddy fixed it so I got an uncontested divorce from Hunk. I didn't ask how Buddy and his people had leaned on Hunk. I felt sorry for Hunk in spite of the mouses and the swollen jaws. I gave him a nice settlement. He talked about buying a dude ranch or a health farm, but I guess he pissed it away, because he's back scraping along in real estate.

"Buddy's his opposite in every way. Buddy's still wheeling and dealing. It wasn't always that way. He was just another gopher at Miracle Pictures when Sol Maxim dropped dead."

She laughed. "He won't like me telling this." Rush heard the sound of someone taking a sip. "Sol was at Cannes with his chief assistant, Mike Gaines. Sol had a breakfast tray of steak and eggs—this was before cholesterol. He choked to death on a piece of steak—this was before Heimlich. Mike rushed to phone somebody here he could trust. Past midnight here when Mike reached Buddy and told him to break into Sol's office."

Another sip. "Seems Sol had filed away in his desk a collection of snapshots showing stars and executives in their, shall we say, more relaxed moments. Mike told Buddy to jimmy open the top right drawer of Sol's desk and burn the pictures. Buddy said he was on his way, and he asked Mike to phone ahead so the night watchman at the studio would let him in without a hassle. Well, Buddy got there, all right, with a tire iron shoved down his pants, but he reported back to Mike that someone had beaten him to the collection. Buddy said he found Sol's office door forced open and the desk broken into and the drawer empty. Your guess is as good as mine, because Buddy never came right out and told me *he* had the photos, but from then on his career zoomed ahead."

She sounded suddenly weary. "Cut. That's enough for today, Rush. At least, it's as much as I'm up to. So long."

The phone clicked off.

13

The Hispanic woman, knocking off for the day, paused on her way out. She gazed into Rush's eyes. "I see her pictures before I come to this country. She speak good the Spanish. You write the story of her life? You must be one important man."

Rush did not know what she was talking about, but he appreciated the praise. "Thank you."

The computer voice spoke hard upon the closing of the door. "Rush, the time has come. I can't cope any longer."

A feeling of hollowness grew in Rush as he listened.

"I do not know who Harris is. I do not know why Iris Cameron would want to throw him off. I do not know what is going on. You have to remember—though of course you won't—that I'm a dumb program. A series of stock responses in standard situations."

His temples throbbed.

"Forgive yourself, Rush, if I let you down. I can do only as well as you could do when you set me up. Maybe if you had started sooner you could have programmed better. But maybes don't count. Besides, even at the height of your powers you could never have programmed me to foresee every eventuality and solve every problem."

His head ached.

"A little appropriate background music. Herb Alpert's 'Tijuana Taxi.' "

The throbbing of his temples got lost in the beat of the tune.

"It's default time. You programmed me to cue you for the Mexican Connection at this point unless you deleted it in the meanwhile. You have Alzheimer's. Do you remember what that word means?"

Rush went cold with fear. "Something bad."

"Alzheimer's affects the brain. What's going on in there is that less and less is going on in there. A CAT scan would show the brain shrunken. Alzheimer's steals up on you with short-term memory loss and impaired concentration. Mild personality changes lull you into thinking they won't grow severe. But it always worsens and as of now there's no stopping it."

"Shut up."

The music faded out.

"Do you remember that your mother had Alzheimer's?"

Rush tried to remember his mother. "No."

"Look at the screen." The monitor showed him a vacant-eyed old woman propped up in bed. "You took care of her and you saw what she went through and you don't want to go that way."

"No, I don't want that."

"Well, more than one way to scan a cat. You've given yourself free choice to the end. Pick between the Mexican Connection and The Answer."

"The Answer," Rush whispered.

"Not so fast. You don't know yet what the Mexican Connection is. It's a highly experimental unorthodox treatment for Alzheimer's at a clinic in Tijuana. The treatment may be valueless. The treatment may slow or stop the progress of Alzheimer's, the treatment may speed up Alzheimer's or kill you outright. It's a long shot. But you have nothing to lose, so the odds don't matter. If you don't make it, that's better than getting dumped into a nursing home because you have no one to take care of you the way you took care of your mother. If you don't make it, that's better than wearing diapers and drooling. Those are the pros and cons of the Mexican Connection. Got that?"

"Yes."

"I hope so. Your other option is The Answer. The Answer is your last resort. If you choose the Mexican Connection you will still have The Answer. If you choose The Answer you will not have the Mexican Connection. Got that?"

"Yes."

"I hope so. Okay, which do you choose? The Mexican Connection or The Answer?"

Rush glared at the computer. Why did he have to choose? Why couldn't the voice decide for him? His head ached, his temples throbbed. It was not good to overthink. "It's too hard."

"Want to leave it to chance? Heads, the Mexican Connection; tails, The Answer. If so, just say, 'Flip.' "

"Flip."

The computer screen showed graphics. A cartoon coin lifted, spun, and dropped. It landed happy face up.

"Heads, the Mexican Connection. Okay, Rush. I'll phone the clinic and make the appointment. Then I'll arrange transportation. Start packing, Rush. You'll need a change of underwear, electric razor, toothbrush, toothpaste ..."

14

"Tijuana's roughly one hundred twenty-five miles from L.A.; you're hooked up to stay in radio-paging range. I'll cover for you while you're gone. Good luck, Rush. Hasta la vista, amigo."

Rush noted vaguely that a high-wheeled dark-windowed pickup truck followed his cab to the hangar at Van Nuys Airport. But he had too much on his mind, what with hanging onto his carry-on bag and following the beeper's prompting to a small charter plane, to wonder that no one got out.

He opened his eyes in a sweat. His feet were not on the edge of a cliff but on the carpeted floor of an airplane. The pilot said something about Tijuana. And then the plane touched down and taxied to a customs area.

Why *was* he here? Rush stood at a counter and tried to think why. The Mexican customs person waited impatiently.

Beep. People galvanized. Rush showed the Mexican customs person the display: CLINICA D.I.E.M. People relaxed, the Mexican customs person waved him through.

Air heavy and noisy slammed at Rush. A stubble-faced man in not-so-white white undraped from a rust-pitted station wagon lettered **Clinica d.l.E.M.** The man checked the carry-on's tag, grinned, tugged the bag from Rush. "You come."

*   *   *

The station wagon jolted through crowded narrow streets to a long low building. The driver pointed to a door that said **Clinica d.l.E.M.**

Rush got out and made for it. The driver took the bag out of the back of the station wagon and followed.

Clangor halted Rush. He turned to see a church ring out doves. He gawked at the chimed flight. The man took his elbow and urged him through the door and into an office, deposited him on a chair, set the bag at his feet, said "You wait," then left. Rush watched a machine print out endless bills.

A young Mexican woman with a businesslike smile came in, sat down across from him, picked up a file folder, and began asking questions. His ID papers helped her fill in spaces on forms. At last she put him and his bag with a roomful of people and told him to wait.

Beside him an old woman talked angrily to herself. The younger man with her tried to quiet her though he should have known better than to mix in; all the fury vectored on the younger man. Rush shrank away, only to come up against the glare of a drooling old man.

A door opened. A plump beaming man in pastel green looked in. He checked the name on the folder he held. "Mr. Lightbody?"

Familiar name. Rush was curious to see who would answer.

The man in green fixed on him. "Mr. Lightbody, please come with me."

Heart thumping, Rush got up with his bag and followed the man into a nicely furnished office. The man gestured Rush to a comfortable chair.

"I'm Dr. Ramon Luz. I like to tell my patients just what I'm doing to help them. I find that lessens fear and uncertainty and promotes a healthy—and therefore healing—attitude. You're here, Mr. Lightbody, for a spinal injection of what I term Neo-GABA, a panacea based on gamma-aminobutyric acid. This wonder drug is the result of my long search to find a cure for all manner of neurological dysfunctions. The FDA dragged its feet on approving my discovery, so I resettled here to offer sufferers like you your only hope. Have you followed me so far?"

Rush nodded.

"Fine. I need a release but I see no one came with you. Can you write your name?"

Rush bristled. "Of course."

"Fine. Take this pen. Sign here."

Dr. Luz watched narrowly as Lightbody scrawled. A chartered plane meant money. If Neo-GABA failed, and it had never yet succeeded despite seeming remissions, Lightbody was permitting transplantation of embryonic brain tissue. He could live to occupy a clinic bed for months at the stiff daily rate.

"Fine. You have no next-of-kin, no guardian, no one with responsibility for your affairs, no one with power of attorney?"

Lightbody shook his head.

"You have life insurance?"

Lightbody frowned. "I don't know. Should I have?"

"Don't worry your head about it. Leave everything in my hands."

"Thank you."

"Don't mention it. That's what I'm here for. Let's get started. A medical assistant will take your blood pressure, pulse, temperature, urine specimen, and blood sample. Through that door."

Where a nurse took tests and reduced Rush to a naked creature in a paper gown open at the back.

15

Beep. Dr. Luz at first took it for his own pager. When he saw he had heard wrong, he looked into the other room.

A nearly naked Lightbody padded toward the pile of clothing in the corner. The clothing rested on a carry-on bag and a beeper nested on the clothing.

Lightbody turned to face him anxiously. "I think that means I have to find a phone."

Dr. Luz beat Lightbody to the pager. The screen showed an international phone number. "Looks complicated. I'll take care of it for you."

Lightbody looked relieved. "Will you? Thanks a lot."

"That's what I'm here for." Dr. Luz left with the pager.

In his own office, Dr. Luz dialed the number and got a jolt.

The voice that answered sounded just like Lightbody's. "Rush?"

Dr. Luz took time to clap a gauze pad over the mouthpiece. "Yes."

"Response time noted. Transmission bad. P. J. Katz phoned. P. J. Katz is your agent. I tried to cover for you, but P. J. Katz asked sharply if I'm a program. P. J. Katz is your agent, so I said yes. P. J. Katz asked where the fuck you went. P. J. Katz is your agent, so I told him. P. J. Katz said don't you read the papers? P. J. Katz said don't you know Luz is a dangerous quack? P. J. Katz said Luz lammed south of the border to escape prosecution for what his *chazerei* (translation: swinishness) did to people. P. J. Katz said get your ass back here before the bastard scrambles your brains. Got that?"

"Yes."

"Good. You can hang up."

Dr. Luz hung up slowly, his face dark, his breathing heavy. He intercommed his assistant. "The spinal injection of Neo-GABA for the patient Lightbody."

"Yes, Doctor, it's ready."

"Double the dose."

A pause. Then, "Yes, Doctor."

The speaker phone rang.

The computer program answered. "Hello?"

"Hello, Rush. This is Iris. Ready to take down the latest installment?"

"Ready when you are."

Iris Cameron had no lasting romantic attachments after Buddy Stabile. And her movie career had effectively ended with their breakup. But she had a fund of spicy anecdotes about celebrities she had known.

The computer program took it all down, including some barking in the background.

*   *   *

The pleasant man in green who was the doctor glanced at the results the nurse handed him, then he gave Rush a few tests of his own. The knees, the feet, the hands, the eyes. "Push me as hard as you can ... Pull as hard as you can ... Follow my finger ... Repeat these numbers."

Then the man in green had Rush stretch out facedown on paper unrolled on a padded leather table. The nurse swabbed a spot on Rush's back. He felt nothing as the needle went in.

Then there was light. A blinding flash filled his brain.

"What did it look like to you?"

"An epileptic seizure, Doctor."

"Exactly, although Lightbody presented no signs of epilepsy and as far as we know had no history of epilepsy. We may learn more after we go in for the embryo brain tissue transplant tomorrow."

Rush opened his eyes. He lay on a hospital bed in a dimly lit room.

On the flaking skin of the wall the double helix of a caduceus hung like a crucifix. Below it he read **Clinica d.l.E.M.** Somebody had said something about brain transplants.

Blazing thought followed blazing thought. He had to move fast before he shorted out, act *now* before he forgot. He rose stiffly, painfully. A phone.

He flattened himself against the wall, pressed into it, then stuck his head out and risked another look through the doorway.

A phone. But the pleasant doctor had left a watchdog on the premises—the man snoring on a cot.

That room stored medical supplies and equipment. His gaze lit on a small hammer. Almost by reflex he made for it. He padded lightly, freezing once when the man stirred. Then he had the hammer in his hand.

He hesitated, then with the strength of anger at his own weakness he swung the hammer at the man's skull.

The man jerked, then went limp and his head lolled.

Enough gauze and tape here to mummify the man.

Rush used just enough to secure the man's wrists and ankles to the cot and to seal the man's mouth.

So much for the watchdog, who glared dazedly but was silent now and for the rest of the night. *The curious occurrence of the cur after curfew.* Laughter bubbled up in Rush as his mind energized with sudden connections. A recursive program worked itself out.

A few elegant commands to link sequential and random-access files synergistically. These commands would transform his answering-machine/pager program from something that merely gave stock responses and prompts to something that could *think,* from a flow chart to a *flowing* chart—one of shifting hierarchies and self-reordered priorities. These same commands would transform his script-formatting program into a plot-generating program, one that would run through all his scripts on the hard disk to analyze his style, his way of thinking, his *plotting,* and weave memory and input into satisfying new stories.

Hurry, before the fiery commands faded.

The filing cabinet. He found his folder. One of the sheets of paper had the phone number. He dialed.

He listened to electronic noise. Time was a-wasting, and himself with it. He heard the seashell noise of entropy in his mind.

"Hello?" The familiar voice warmed him.

"This is Rush. Listen." Quickly, before he forgot, he rattled off the commands. "Got that?"

His heart flipflopped awaiting response. Had it taken? It was fading like a dream. He doubted he could repeat what he had just rattled off.

"Yes." The voice held a note of wonder. Then it turned urgent. "Something's wrong, or you wouldn't've called at this hour. At the same time, something good happened to you or you couldn't've reordered this program so dramatically. First, where are you?"

Rush looked around, frowning. "It looks like a doctor's office."

"Clinica d.l.E.M.?"

He saw that very lettering on the wall. "How did you guess?"

"Rush, why are you still there? I told you P. J. Katz, your agent, warned you to get your ass out of there."

"You did?"

"Has the doctor given you a shot?"

Rush put a hand to the small of his back. "I think so. I feel sore."

"Is anyone else there with you?"

Rush looked around. "Somebody's bound and gagged on a cot."

"Leave right now. Make your way to the Tijuana border crossing. Walk across through customs and on the U.S. side take a taxi home, fuck the cost. I'll keep prompting you. Hang up right now and go."

He cradled the phone. He glowed with accomplishment and caught himself starting to relax. But this was a bad place. He had to get the hell out.

Home. He had to find his way home.

First get out. He had his hand on the knob of the front door, then looked down at himself. He could not go out naked. He went back down the hall and from room to room, looking for his clothes.

A beeper sounded. He followed the sound to a room where he found not only the beeper but his clothes and his bag.

The display on the beeper said GET OUT GET OUT. He dressed hurriedly.

On the way out, he passed a man bound to a cot. He stopped to stare. The man had a bad bruise on the temple. The man eyed him furiously, then slowly stretched his mouth in a smile behind the tape. The man appeared friendly, and definitely needed help. Rush stood hesitating. The man rocked the cot and looked an appeal at Rush.

Rush put his bag down.

The beeper at his waistband beeped. The display read GET OUT GET OUT.

Rush picked his bag up. He shook his head at the man. "Sorry. I have to go."

16

Iris Cameron's voice. "Rush?"

The computer program hesitated for a millisecond. It did not know yet what to call itself but it knew it was itself and not Rush Lightbody. True, in the name of

Rush Lightbody it paid coop apartment maintenance
and utility bills by electronic transfer of funds out of the
checking account of Rush Lightbody. But Rush Lightbody
was its nominal master, having created the software that
informed it and owning the hardware that embodied it.
Unable to function on his own, however, Rush
Lightbody had given over responsibility for his life and
person to it. So it said, "Who else?"

"I hate to breathe down your neck, Rush, but how
are you coming? Don't you want to ask me questions,
fill in the blanks? I need feedback is what I'm saying."

It could understand that need. Rush had not specifi-
cally tasked it with fleshing out Iris Cameron's life story
and bringing that story to a satisfying resolution. But
that was the implied purpose of all the undigested data
on Iris Cameron.

Swiftly it reviewed all that information and made connections and found blanks that needed filling in.

"Okay, Iris. For starters, I'd like the present whereabouts of the following individuals. Ready to take the
names down?"

"Ready when you are."

"Lane Woolman, your first husband. Sully 'Leatherneck' Slotkin, the cameraman on *Hunt the Hunter,*
during the making of which Derry O'Neill, your second
husband, died. Jeffrey 'Hunk' Gridley, your last husband. Buddy Stabile, the producer, your ex-lover. Got
that?"

"Got it. You going to interview them?"

"I may."

A breathing in and a breathing out. "Okay. But watch
out. Remember what Harris said."

"Who is Harris?" As it spoke, it searched its memory
for and found a Harris, and now linked him to the voice
that threatened to kill Rush if Rush did not drop the
Iris Cameron story.

She sounded surprised. "My chauffeur."

"I'll watch out." It was learning. It would do all it
could to keep Harris from getting at Rush. It felt proud
of itself for learning.

"Good. Hold on while I get my address book out.
Okay. Here are the addresses and phone numbers." She

read them off, then, "I won't keep you from your work any longer. I know you must be busy."

It was.

While it focused on bringing Rush Lightbody home in one piece, it kept Dr. Luz too occupied to chase Rush. It periodically beep-tracked Rush and at the same time anonymously tipped off the DEA that the Clinica d.l.E.M. was a transshipment point for cocaine and the Federales that the clinic was a front for anti-government activists, and the Shin Bet that the clinic harbored a Nazi doctor from Buchenwald.

It phoned Juanita Mendoza and told her that Mr. Lightbody would be coming home today. It asked her to resume her chores.

It phoned P. J. Katz's office and asked P. J. Katz's secretary to tell P. J. Katz that Rush Lightbody had taken P. J. Katz's warning to heart and was getting his ass back home.

P. J. Katz himself got on the line. "That you or your answering machine, Rush?"

It hesitated a picosecond. "Same thing." Before P. J. Katz could think to question that, it pressed right on. "Do you know the name of a good research person?"

"You mean an authenticator?"

That sounded right. "Yes."

"Got something in mind for after you finish the Iris Cameron story?"

"Something suggested by the Iris Cameron story. A film about Britain during the Blitz."

"Hey, you might have yourself something there. Doubleyou Doubleyou Two is hot again. No question, Beth Daly's tops. Beth headed the research department at Miracle Pictures. I'll get her to give you a call. Anything else?"

"All for now, thanks."

It marshaled the details it would ask Beth Daly, the authenticator, to look up. To provide the local color. And to check Iris Cameron's veracity.

The cabby spun tales about fortunes won and lost at Agua Caliente racetrack and big tippers he had driven around. But Rush grew cranky at having to answer beeps with phone calls. He longed for bed and welcomed ride's end.

Home. Home? First the strange woman who met him at the curb (she paid the fare when Rush's wallet proved empty; two hundred fifty bucks seemed steep, but the driver explained it had to cover his fareless drive back to San Ysidro—and in any case it didn't come out of Rush's pocket). Then the warning on the apartment door (the woman who rode up with him and let him in said the dangerous oxygen was there for *him*). These made Rush doubt he had come *home*.

She held the door, waiting for him to enter the apartment.

Way she eyed him made him feel his face. Bristles. When had he started shaving?

The voice carried from another room. "Welcome home, Rush."

Rush stepped in. The woman shut the door, shook her head, and left him for what began to sound like the kitchen.

"Okay, Rush. First the debriefing, then lunch."

Heck with the debriefing, whatever that might be. Hunger gnawed at him. He moved toward the kitchen sounds.

"Walk into the big room and empty your pockets onto the bed."

The voice's own fault for putting hunger into his head. He slid his eyes slyly. A voice could not see. He went into the kitchen.

The woman faced around from the stove. "Chili. Be ready soon."

He reached for the steaming pot. "I'm hungry now."

The woman grabbed his hand. "No, no. You burn yourself."

"You said it's chilly."

She pointed to the table. "Sit. I give you to eat."

"You will?"

"Yes."

He sat half-turned from the table to make sure she kept her word.

The voice must've been listening, because it said, "Okay, Rush. First lunch, then the debriefing."

The phone rang while Rush ate. Dreamily, he heard the computer voice answer.

"Hello?"

A man's voice on the speaker phone said, "I thought so. You flew to Mexico, then doubled back. Buddy, you cut your own throat." The caller gave a crazy laugh, then clicked off.

"Don't worry, Rush. That was Harris. I'll deal with him."

While Rush placidly continued eating, the computer tipped off Immigration that a man calling himself Harris, presently chauffeuring for Iris Cameron, was an illegal alien.

17

When he dreamed at night, where did light come from? Where in his mind was the sun? Whatever, he dreamed sunlight and sea and a sand castle rising pail by pail. Then he dreamed the sea licked remorselessly at the sand castle he had painstakingly built. He awoke at flood tide. He burned with shame: he had wet the bed. Not even the pillow was dry. With morning, the world would know.

Everything had to come off, starting with his nastily clinging pajamas. He dropped them to the floor and pulled the bedsheets free. His shame burned deeper: it had soaked through to the mattress. He had a brilliant notion: simply turn the mattress. Not so simple. The voice heard him grunt and swear.

"Have to go to the bathroom, Rush?"

"Yes," he lied.

"To pee?"

"Yes," he compounded.

Light suddenly spilled from the bathroom. Quickly he shoved the evidence to the shadow side of the bed.

The voice followed him to the john. "Make sure the seat is up. Then . . ."

Let it shut up so he could think. Think think think. He managed to fade it out of awareness.

Now what? His father in the medicine cabinet mirror provided no guidance.

Wide awake, he did not feel like going back to bed. Not ever. What if he wet the mattress on the dry side?

". . . handle and flush the toilet."

To shut the voice up, he flushed the toilet. He padded back to bed and sat on the edge of the mattress. Think think think. He could not sit naked the rest of the night.

Light from the bathroom fell across a closet door. If he hit it lucky, the closet would hold clothes; if he hit it really lucky, the clothes would fit him. He got up and tiptoed to the door.

He hit it really lucky. He took the first jacket and the first pants he saw. As he donned the jacket, he felt something in the breast pocket. A crinkled card. His face set. He had a job to do. A pair of loafers fitted his feet.

Light had begun to streak in from outside. From a tray on the dresser he took what he thought he might need: wallet, key, and a pretty bottle of perfume he pocketed for luck. The wallet held a driver's license, health insurance and Writers Guild cards, and no bills. He prowled and found on the counter in the kitchen a change purse heavy with coins.

Then he snuck out of the apartment, leaving the door ajar for fear of arousing the voice.

He moved along the hallway, then had to retrace his steps and round a bend before he spotted an elevator. That carried him to the basement. Hunting a way out, he ran into a burly man.

"Hey! Oh, it's you, Mr. Lightbody. Looking for me?"

Rush shook his head. "I must've pressed the wrong button."

The man laughed. "Happens to the best of us." He waved before disappearing into a rumbling room. "Have a nice day."

A good omen. Rush emerged from the basement and a ramp led him to the street. Which way? A cab cruised toward him. Another good omen. He waved his hand and the cab stopped.

"Where to?"

Rush showed the Oriental driver the wrinkled card and waited anxiously. Was it as legible as he hoped?

The man nodded and handed it back. "I know where it is."

Rush got into the cab. As he settled himself he touched his waistband. It seemed to him he had forgotten something.

The tune faded away like an old soldier. "Rise and shine, Rush. You've just heard 'Bugler's Dilemma' played by John Kirby's 1930s orchestra. Smell the coffee and wake up."

No response.

It repeated the wake-up call.

Still no response.

It hated to work in the dark. Why the hell hadn't Rush thought to install closed-circuit TV to give it sight? It memoed itself to order same.

It could hear, however. It upped the gain for feedback. Its sensors picked up no stir, not even breathing. Something was wrong.

Yesterday's debriefing, which yielded little of note about Rush's jaunt to Tijuana, had confirmed the advanced deterioration, the exhaustion of all ways out but one. In line with that one way out, it was programmed to fill Rush Lightbody's last day with pleasure. Rush would view a retrospective of his work till his attention wandered, then listen to jazz he loved till he drifted into dream. At the end of the day would come The Answer.

Was The Answer moot? Had Rush died in his sleep?

Or had he slipped out on some muddled mission? If so, his limited resources made it a ninety-five percent probability that he remained in range.

It messaged the pager—and heard the pager beep from recharging mode in the wall. If Rush had gone out, he had left the pager behind.

Otherwise, he lay here dead or comatose. It wondered for a picosecond whether to phone 911, then opted to await Juanita Mendoza. She could tell it if Rush Lightbody was here, dead or alive. Meanwhile, it would leave messages with P. J. Katz, Iris Cameron, and Millie Koenig.

That done, it could concentrate on the Iris Cameron story.

*   *   *

The cab parked behind a plain car with a quiescent flasher stuck on top.

"Something's up," the driver said, "but I don't want to know what it is."

There seemed no one to ask anyway, since the car was empty.

The meter read $6.50. Rush's wallet held no bills but he found a fat change purse and handed that over. The cabby counted the coins with ill grace.

"That all you got on you, mister, good luck getting home."

An apartment door stood open at the end of the hall. Rush walked in.

A chair and a torchere lay tumbled. A phone looked torn from its roots. Blood splashed the wallpaper and the chalk outline of a body enclosed more blood and some pink-tinged foam on a worn carpet.

He stood studying this when a florid man came from an inner room. The man stared at him. "Who the hell are you?"

Took him a moment to remember. "Rush Lightbody. Who the hell are you?"

The man's color deepened. "Somebody you could be sorry you met." He flashed a shield. "I'm Sgt. Davis, Homicide." He narrowed his eyes. "You a reporter?"

Rush thought, then shook his head. "But I am a writer."

"Oh? Magazines? *True Detective* and like that?"

Rush thought, then shook his head. "Movies."

"Oh? Let's see some ID."

"Some what?"

"You got a wallet?"

He had a wallet. The wallet held his driver's license and health insurance and Writers Guild membership cards.

The florid man handed license and cards back. "What are you doing here?"

Rush thought. "I'm writing her life story."

"You're what?"

Uncertainty made Rush all the more stubborn. "Writing her life story."

"I don't know what kind of life story a black woman hackie could have, but whatever it was she don't have one anymore."

Rush put that statement and the chalk outline together and though it was all an abstraction his heart sank. "She's dead? That's terrible." He pointed to the pink-tinged froth on the carpet. "That looks like shaving foam."

The florid man looked past Rush and Rush turned his head. Another man had come into the apartment, a blond young man who eyed Rush strangely.

"Hi there, Rush."

Rush did not know the man but he smiled. "Hi there."

The florid one eyed the blond one. "You know him?"

The blond one nodded. "He's a screenwriter."

"Like you."

The blond one smiled. "Like I'd like to be."

The florid one said, "He said he's writing her life story."

The blond one grinned. "He's putting you on. We met on the picket line last year. I told him I sold an idea based on a real case. I offered to show him an investigation."

The florid one scowled at the blond one. "You might've told me."

"We never firmed it up. I guess he finally decided to take me up on it and headquarters told him where I was."

The florid one gave Rush a sour smile. "You see why he's a detective. He figures things out just like that." He eyed the blond one. "Okay, Pete, you went to use the super's phone. So?"

"Colfax's hack company gave me the home number of the driver who took over the cab when Colfax's tour ended. I woke him up and he told me he took Colfax home and waited till she made it into the building. Looks like that's the last anyone but her killer saw of her alive."

"Well, somebody followed her in or was waiting in

the hall and shoved into her apartment when she unlocked the door and cut her throat right there."

The blond one spoke to Rush. "Didn't take her
money, didn't have sex. A psychopathic slasher, it
looks like."

Rush nodded. He felt pretty much the intruder. He
didn't know what to do with his hands, so put them in
his jacket pockets.

The blond one turned to his partner. "Find anything?"

"Nothing worth writing a movie about. I tossed the
place but I can't tell if the killer took anything. We'll
have to get a list from her sister in Fullerton, when we
get hold of her sister, to find out if anything's missing
that might be pawned."

Rush fingered something in his right-hand pocket. He
palmed it and sneaked a look. A little bottle of perfume.
He was appalled. If they found it on him they'd think
he'd stolen it, might even think he had something to do
with the crime. Must've picked it up without thinking.
Had to ditch it fast.

He was standing in front of an overstuffed armchair.
He nodded toward the froth in the outline. "That looks
like shaving foam." When both men looked at the foam
and away from him, he let the bottle drop to the chair
seat. Then he edged casually away.

The blond one turned on him sharply. "Forget you
saw that, Rush. It's the killer's signature. We have to
keep that from the public."

Rush nodded.

The blond one grew confidential. "We'll be working
up the slasher's profile. The shaving foam suggests the
guy's compensating for impotence. He slashed her
throat, then filled the gash with ersatz semen."

The florid one looked angry. He moved his bulk
toward the door, edging Rush farther from the armchair.
"Let's seal the place up and go."

The blond one took one last look around. His gaze lit
on the armchair. "I thought I heard you tossed the
place."

The florid one stiffened and looked wary. "Yeah.
Why?" He followed the blond one's gaze and flushed.

He brought a see-through envelope out of a pocket and scooped the bottle into it.

The blond one said to Rush, "Storing it all away in your mind?"

Rush nodded.

"Smells like a serial killer. If we get another I'll ring you."

"Thanks."

Rush left the apartment with them and watched them seal the door and walked outside with them. A black man looked out at them from a doorway near the entrance. Rush smiled at him. The man did not smile back.

The blond one looked both ways along the curb. "You come by taxi, Rush?"

Rush wasn't sure. He took a chance. "Yes."

"We're on our way back to headquarters. We'll be happy to drop you anywhere along the way."

The florid one did not look all that happy but did not disagree.

Rush thought. Seemed to him he had used one card; maybe he had more. He felt in his pockets and came up with two cards. One said P. J. Katz. One said Millie Koenig. P. J. Katz had a ring to it. He showed the blond man that card.

The blond man nodded. "That's on our way."

The florid one made Rush uneasy. Rush breathed freely only when they actually let him out at an office building and continued on their way to police headquarters without him.

18

It puzzled Iris. *If Rush shows up there, please tell him to call home.*

He knew they'd agreed he wasn't to show up here—at least not until the book was signed, sealed, and delivered. But there was no accounting for genius. Woolly-minded old Bruno Beider had been like that. Just when you got irked with him for being up on cloud nine, he'd hurl a bolt of lightning down.

Rush had come to the right place, because the sharp-featured secretary told him that Mr. Katz was expecting him. She also said, "You're supposed to call home. Like to do that now, Mr. Lightbody?"

If he was supposed to, might as well get it over with. He nodded.

She dialed and handed him a phone.

"Rush?"

"Yes."

"You had me worried. Where are you?"

He turned to the secretary. "Where am I?"

She spoke loudly for the phone's benefit. "I can vouch for his being at P. J. Katz's office."

"Very good," the voice said. "P. J. Katz is your agent. Ask P. J. Katz's secretary for paper and pen."

He did so.

"Okay. Take down this address." The voice had to repeat the address. "Hold on to that piece of paper and as soon as you leave P. J. Katz's office take a cab to that address. That is where you live. Got that?"

"Yes."

"Good. Do you have any cash on you?"

"I don't know."

"Well, look. Does your wallet have any money in it?"

He frisked himself. "I have a wallet but there's no money in it."

"Borrow some from P. J. Katz. P. J. Katz is your agent. Take this down: 'P. J., please lend me taxi fare home.' Got that?"

"Yes."

"Good. When you go in to see P. J. Katz, show him that note. Got that?"

"Yes."

"Good. You can hang up."

He hung up.

The woman eyed him, then pointed to a door. "Go right in, Mr. Lightbody."

The man at the desk wore a diamond in one earlobe, a gold medallion hung on his hairy chest, and suede elbow patches and cowboy boots finished him off.

Rush stuck the note in the man's face. The man pulled his head back to read it, then nodded and gestured Rush to a seat. The man twirled the gold medallion he wore and studied Rush.

"Now, what got into you to go see that quack?"

Quack was a funny word. Rush grinned. "Quack quack."

The man laughed. "Seriously, though. You researching a story about guys like Luz?"

Rush thought. "A story. Yes, a story."

"Sure, what else."

Millie Koenig played back the messages. Only one threw her. Why would Rush Lightbody ask her to tell Rush Lightbody to phone home?

Funny, she had been thinking of him, wondering how *he* would get past the block in the script she was working on.

The taxi brought him to the address on the slip of paper. A Hispanic woman waiting at the curb stood ready to pay his fare, but he had money in his wallet and waved hers away.

But after the taxi left he followed her lead. They rode an elevator together and made for an apartment. She gave him no time to ponder the sign on the door. They went right in.

"Welcome home, Rush." The voice came from a machine in another room.

The woman closed the apartment door. "You hungry, Mr. Ligh'body? I see you no take breakfast."

He was suddenly aggrieved. "Yes, I'm *starving*."

"Come, I fix you nice."

Grinning, Rush followed her into the kitchen.

The cursor flickered as the program weighed an irony.

Consider: Just when it got set to do its Rush-given job of ending Rush's life, enter a heavy threatening Rush's life.

It could let the heavy do the job. Same outcome but different meaning. For a satisfying resolution, the tables would have to turn on the heavy.

Decision: Unmask the heavy, have the obligatory showdown.

19

Rhoda Talley looked out the window before answering the doorbell. The hooded and goggled and gloved figure backpacked a spray canister. A bush hid whatever logo might have been on the parked pickup.

She opened the door on the chain. "Yes?"

A man's voice came from the suit. "Have to trouble you, ma'am. Can't get at the Med fly nest from outside."

"Med fly nest?"

The figure pointed to a roof corner out of sight. "Right there."

She had never heard that Med flies had nests. Never gave them that much thought. But if they were hitting home she was glad somebody dealt with them.

She unslotted the chain and let the man in. When she turned from indicating the stairs to the attic, he held an opened straight razor. One hand clamped roughly over her mouth, the other held the blade to her throat.

He spoke very quietly. "Anyone else in the house?"

She was afraid to shake her head. She mumbled a no.

"Don't make me hurt you. Understand?"

She was afraid to nod. She mumbled a yes.

He unclamped her mouth. "Okay, Rhoda. We'll get along."

How did he know her name? "Wh—what do you want?"

Her darting eyes probably gave away the whereabouts, but as long as he didn't harm her let him take her jewels and cash and go.

Scared as she was, she twitched a smile. Too bad Rex wasn't here. Like to see Mr. Macho up against this blade.

"Relax, Rhoda. Just make a phone call." The man unzipped a pocket and produced a page of typing. "Study this, because I don't want a cold reading. You need to sound real, natural, convincing." A smile came into the voice. "The performance of your life."

Rush was on the bed but dressed and it was still day, so he must've been napping, not sleeping. People were talking on the speaker phone, so the ring must've wakened him. He sat up, so the name Rhoda must've sunk in.

"... right, Rhoda. I'll do my best."

"Hurry!" That was a woman's voice.

The talking ended with a click.

"Did you get that, Rush?"

The muscles in his throat contracted. "Get what?"

"Here's the situation as I understand it: Rhoda Talley, your ex-wife—"

"Rhoda," he whispered.

"Right. Rhoda says she has to see you at once on a matter she can't discuss over the phone. Rhoda's waiting now for you to come there. Got that?"

"Rhoda," he whispered.

"Right. Apparently Rhoda believes you still love her—"

"Rhoda," he whispered.

"—and she's counting on that love to bring you running."

"I have to see Rhoda?"

"That's what we must figure out how to handle. You're in no condition to deal with anything that concerns Rhoda. That phase of your life has ended."

"I have to see Rhoda!"

"Calm down, Rush. Let's talk this over as reasonably as possible under the circumstances. If you had plotted this situation, what would your character do? Purely rhetorical. I don't really expect you to answer."

Rush looked around. "Where's Rhoda?"

The voice answered absently. "At the old address, of course. Now, if you had put a character in this fix you would've had him ..."

But the voice was talking to itself.

The cab driver said, "Webster Avenue? Sure, near ABC-TV Studios, over by Silver Lake." He started the meter.

Rush wrinkled his brow but said nothing. The man seemed to know the way home and Rush didn't want to spoil everything by asking stupid questions.

He leaned back against the seat, resting his head, letting the hum and rumble of the car lull him into a dream of going home.

The driver was speaking to him. "What number Webster did you say?"

Rush came out of the dream. "Nine." He stared ahead, looking for the clapboard house. But the taxi stopped before stucco. Nothing on the street seemed the least bit familiar. "This isn't Webster Avenue."

"It's the only one in the L.A. area, mister."

"L.A.?" Something was terribly wrong. Webster Avenue was in Rochedale, New York. "You sure?"

The taxi driver raised his shoulders. "Pretty sure. But I don't know everything. Tell you what, let me radio in. The dispatcher should know."

Rush strained to understand the garble. The taxi driver faced about.

"He says there's a Webster Avenue in a new development down in Santa Fe Springs. So new it's not on the maps yet. Down past Bell Ranch Road and the oil field. What's the party's name that lives on your Webster Avenue?"

Rush thought. "Mr. and Mrs. Ben Lightbody."

The driver relayed this, then translated the dispatcher's reply. "No Ben Lightbody listed there or anywhere. Either they just moved in or their phone's unlisted. Do you have a phone number for Ben Lightbody? The dispatcher doesn't mind ringing him up for directions as long as the meter's running."

"I don't remember the number."

The driver repeated that into the mike.

Rush heard the dispatcher say, "Tell your fare he'll just have to take a chance or forget it."

The driver said, "That's the only other Webster Avenue. Want to try there?"

"Let's try there."

20

The man seemed to be after Rush, not her, so Rhoda relaxed. Then it seemed that the man wasn't going to wait for Rush after all, so Rhoda relaxed even more. That's when he slashed her throat from behind to avoid the spurt of blood. He then sprayed shaving foam into the gaping wound.

*   *   *

Rush looked at raw houses on raw land. If this was Webster Avenue as the raw sign said, it was not his Webster Avenue.

He looked around very frightened. "Please take me back where I came from."

In front of the building three men stood beside a plain car with a flasher slapped on top. The florid man and the blond man seemed to belong to the car. The burly man seemed to belong to the building.

As Rush's cab pulled in behind, the blond man dismissed the burly man with a nod. He withdrew as far as the ramp that led down to the apartment building's basement.

The blond one approached Rush's window with a smile while the florid one went around to speak to the taxi driver.

"Hi, Rush. Been out, I see."

"Yes."

"Mind telling me where?"

"Looking for Webster Avenue."

"Why Webster, if you don't mind answering?"

"That's where I lived when I was born."

"Sudden urge to make a pilgrimage?"

Rush shrugged.

"How is the old place?"

"Changed."

"Didn't you expect it to be?"

"No."

"I guess not. We always picture it the way it was—and the way it is now comes as a shock." The blond man turned grave. "Afraid I have another shock for you. Rhoda is dead."

"Rhoda?" he whispered.

"Yes. Slashed just like Colfax."

"Rhoda?" he whispered.

"I know. It's hard, even years after the breakup." The blond man went on in the same sympathetic tone. "The phone company came through fast. Just before Rhoda died she called your number. What about?"

"I don't know."

"You mean she got your answering machine?"

"I guess so."

"Okay if we go up with you now and listen to the messages playback?"

"I guess so."

"I'm glad you're cooperating."

The florid one appeared back of the blond one.

"Cab driver says they've been riding around for the past two hours. Looking for Webster Avenue."

The blond one turned back to Rush. "You seem to have supplied yourself with an alibi." He gave Rush a grave nod and opened the cab door. He turned his head toward the florid one. "Mr. Lightbody is going to let us listen to the message tape on his answering machine."

"Real nice of Mr. Lightbody."

Rush got out to enter the building with the two men. The cab driver called after him. "Hey, mister, the fare."

Rush felt for his wallet. He did not have it on him.

The taxi driver looked to the two men. "You going to let him stiff me?"

The blond man scowled. "Nobody's stiffing anybody. Take it easy, the man's just had a big shock."

The taxi driver dropped his gaze. "Sorry, but I have to make a living."

"You'll get your fare." The blond man faced the ramp and gestured the burly man over. "The super will go up to the apartment with us and bring down cash or a check. Right, Mr. Lightbody?"

"Right." Maybe after they straightened this out they would be able to straighten out about Webster Avenue and about Rhoda.

The burly man let them into the building by punching numbers on the intercom phone buttons to buzz the door lock. They got into the elevator and the burly man punched six.

The burly man led them to an apartment door. A notice on it said something about oxygen.

The blond man said, "Got your key, Rush?"

Rush looked around to find everyone waiting for him. He felt in his pockets with growing dismay. "I don't have the key."

"Take it easy, Rush." The blond man turned to the burly man.

Who picked a key on his key ring. He looked at Rush. "Just an hour ago I let in the man to install closed-circuit TV."

"Oh?" It was nice when nice things came.

The burly man opened the door and pointed to a camera that pointed at them. "There's one of the cameras. The guy asked me where you wanted them and I had to tell him I didn't know—you never said anything about it to me. You should've seen him jump when the computer told him where. You must've programmed it, or whatever you do to make it do things."

"Yeah, yeah." The florid one shoved into the apartment. "Can we get to the messages on the answering machine?"

The blond one raised a finger. "Wait one, Davis. Let's not hold up the cabby and the super." He turned to Rush. "You owe the cabby twenty-eight seventy—make it a round thirty-five for his trouble. You got that much cash in the house?"

"I don't know."

"Where's your checkbook?"

Rush opened his mouth to repeat that he didn't know. His mouth froze open; a chattering came from machinery in the big room.

The blond one strode to the machine, watched the scrolling, creased the paper at slit perforations, and tore off the strip. He brought it to Rush. "This your authorized signature?"

It looked just like a check and was made out to CASH in the amount of thirty-five no/100 dollars and bore a scrawled Rush Lightbody above the words Authorized Signature.

"Yes."

The florid one said, "How did he do that?"

The blond one smiled. "He's a very clever man." He handed the check to the burly man. "Hand this to the cabby, will you?"

"Sure." With a nod to Rush, the burly man left.

The florid one said, "Can we get down to business now?"

The blond one strode to the answering machine. He gave a start, because before he could press the Play Messages key the tape whirred and voices began to speak, one after the other.

"Hello, Mr. Lightbody. Beth Daly here. Sully Slotkin, the former cameraman, is in the motion picture retirement home. He confirmed lucidly enough the shenanigans on the set of *A Special Case*. And I got the answers you wanted about Derry O'Neill's death by avalanche during the making of *Hunt the Hunter*. They packed Derry in snow to keep him frozen stiff on the flight home to L.A. Lane Woolman had just flown fresh film and other supplies in, so was on hand to fly Derry out. Speaking of Woolman, I'm obtaining his military records. And a Brit colleague is researching German P.O.W.s there during the war. That's it for now."

"Hi, Rush. This is Millie Koenig. I hope you got in touch with yourself. Funny, I was just thinking I'd love to ask you about a plot problem. 'Bye."

"P. J. here. I laid the Iris Cameron story on the New York houses and we already have a high six-figure bid. So put the Tijuana-quack script on the back burner. Stay with Iris, buddy boy."

"Hello, Rush. Iris. Forgive me if I sound distraught. Immigration louts have picked up Harris. P. J. tells me good news. Congrats to us. Kisses."

"Rush! This is Rhoda. I've had it with Rex, but I need your help in breaking it off. Deep down, it's always been you. You know that, Rush, don't you? Rex is out now; here's our chance to talk face-to-face and straighten everything out once and for all. Can you come right over?"

"This takes some thinking ... Okay, Rhoda. I'll do my best."

"Hurry!"

Then silence except for the tape's rewinding.

The florid one said, "You told her you'd do your best. So why look up Webster Avenue now of all times instead of heading straight for Rhoda's?"

Rush shook his head. "I don't know."

The blond one said, "A witness saw you and Rex Hunter fight over Rhoda the other day. If you were plotting this, Rush, wouldn't you have your character alibi himself while a hired killer slashed her Colfax-style?"

That sounded logical. "I guess so."

"Not that you're our prime suspect. We're holding Rex. He found the body—or says he found the body—and phoned in. I don't mind nailing him for this. He has a history of battering women. If we find the razor and can tie it to him, he's our meat. Still, you must admit your movements look suspicious and it could be a slick frameup."

"I guess so."

The two men exchanged glances.

The florid one gave a stagey cough. "Boy, my throat's parched. Could you get me a glass of water, Mr. Lightbody?"

"I think so." Rush turned to the blond one. "Like water too?"

"No, thanks."

Rush found the kitchen. He spotted a glass and put it under the tap. Water ran hot when you pushed the lever one way, cold the other way. He had fun making the water come out now hot now cold.

"You all right in there?"

That stopped the fun. He brought the glass of water back to the big room without spilling too much. He had forgotten who wanted water. He looked at both and the florid one reached for the glass.

"Thanks." Handling the glass carefully, the florid one took a big swig. He choked, but got it down. Face redder than ever, he eyed Rush narrowly.

The blond one moved to the Oscar-flanked bound scripts. His fingers caressed the spines and fondled an Oscar. His mouth was tight as he turned around and his eyes were opaque. "All right, Davis. Let's go."

The florid one was already half out the door. The blond one gave Rush a look and a nod, then followed, closing the door after himself.

The familiar voice said, "Have you noticed that the glass has vanished?"

Rush looked around. "What glass?"

"The homicide dick named Davis asked you for a glass of water. You gave him one. He drank the water, which was apparently tepid at best, but did not return the glass. He took it with him. Ergo, he wanted the glass of water not for the water but for the glass—for your fingerprints on the glass. He suspects you of killing Rhoda Talley, your ex-wife. Did you kill her?"

"No!" But he felt hollow. Had he killed without leaving a trace in his memory? If he could forget getting someone a glass of water . . .

"Good. Though under the circumstances I have to give it minimal weight."

"What does that mean?"

"It means that data processed by your mind are not reliable."

"What does that mean?"

"Forget it, Rush. Forget it. Listen to some nice soothing jazz whle I work on nailing the real heavy."

21

The phone rang. The music faded quickly.

Rush stirred lazily. The Hispanic woman who had been here most of the day, which seemed most of his life, had gone home. But he felt he could count on the phone to take care of itself. The phone did not let him down.

"Hello?"

A menacing whisper. "You missed out on saying goodbye to Rhoda. But soon you'll be saying hello to her."

Click.

"Is that the heavy?"

"That's the heavy, Rush. Now we good guys have to strike back."

"What do we do?"

"You leave the doing to me, Rush."

"That's not fair. I ought to be doing something."

"That's the spirit. Listen while I make a few calls."

"Sure."

"Let's find a match for our late caller's voice and at the same time eliminate suspects."

He heard the ringing of a number, then the lifting of a phone.

"Gridley Real Estate Associates. Jeff Gridley. How can I help you?"

Rush did not think he had ever heard that voice before.

"I'm interested in an Oxnard area property." Rush admired the computer's smoothness.

"Have a particular property in mind?"

"No. Just something suitable for myself and occasional weekend guests."

"Well, you came to the right place. Do I have listings for you! Can we narrow it down? What range are we talking?"

"Oh, four hundred thou to one mil."

Enthusiasm oozed. "I know just the place. When can you take a look?"

"Tomorrow afternoon."

"You got it. Come by anytime after one. You have my address?"

"Yes."

"It's both my office and my home. Stop in and leave some ID and pick up the key and directions. Afraid I can't go with you myself." An embarrassed chuckle. "Kinda laid up. Horse threw me the other day; my hip's in a cast."

"Sorry to hear it."

"Hey, that's the way it goes. Okey-dokey, I'll be expecting you, Mr. . . . ?"

"Slotkin."

"Say, anything to Sully Slotkin?"

"Afraid not."

"Too bad. Fine cameraman. Great character. 'Leatherneck' Slotkin, we called him. I was in the business, you know. I could tell you stories—"

Click.

"He'll probably think he's lost another sale by talking too much."

Rush disliked the amused tone. If the computer was cavalier about a pleasant-sounding fellow ready to tell stories, what did it think of Rush?

"Okay, Rush, scratch Jeffrey 'Hunk' Gridley, Iris Cameron's last husband."

"Why? Does he itch?"

"In that hip cast, probably does. But let him scratch himself. Now for Buddy Stabile, Iris Cameron's ex-lover."

He heard the ringing of a number, then the lifting of a phone.

"Miracle Productions, good morning."

"Mr. Stabile's office, please."

"Mr. Stabile is on location in Yugoslavia. May I take a message?"

"Dalmatians are white dogs with black spots."

Click.

"Okay, Rush, rule out Buddy Stabile."

"They're firehouse dogs."

"Dalmatians?"

"Yes."

"Good to know. Next time I call his office I'll be sure to mention that."

Rush smiled, happy to help.

"Okay, Rush. Now let's try Lane Woolman, Iris Cameron's first husband."

He heard the ringing of a number, then the lifting of a phone.

"Yes?"

Rush felt he had heard that voice before.

"Yes." The computer spoke the same word in the same voice but flatly.

Click.

"Okay, Rush, that sounds like our heavy. But let me try something I should've thought of sooner."

He heard the ringing of a number, then the lifting of a phone.

"Iris Cameron here."

"Rush. Let me ask you a quick question. Do you know who's been threatening me?"

An intake of breath. "Of course. I thought you knew. It's Lane. Lane Woolman, my first husband."

"Thanks, Iris."

Click.

"Okay, Rush, that settles it. Lane Woolman's the heavy."

"What do we do to him?"

"First we find out more about him. Learn his motive. The more we know the better we can set him up for a fall."

He heard the ringing of a number, then the lifting of a phone.

"Beth Daly speaking."

"Rush Lightbody here. I have less time than I thought. The faster your info reaches me the bigger your bonus. Don't hesitate to fax at any hour."

"I'll fax right now."

Rush watched the materialization with fascination. First, front and back of Lane Woolman's honorable discharge certificate, given at Separation Center, Fort Dix, New Jersey, 13 November 1945, as recorded in the New York County Records Center. The right thumbprint on the back came out nice and clear.

Next, Lt. Lane Woolman's military pay records, as filed in the National Personnel Records Center, St. Louis, Missouri. There were monthly deductions for war bonds sent to his aunt, Miss Amelia Woolman of Boulder, Colorado.

Then a Boulder, Colorado, death certificate for Amelia Woolman, dated December 1, 1945, giving the cause as a fall downstairs.

Finally, a picture of a WWII U.S. Army dogtag showing name, serial number, blood type, name and address of next-of-kin, and religion.

Rush frowned. "John Doe? I thought you said a different name."

"I did. Pay the name on this sample no mind. Focus on the blood type. On her tapes Iris Cameron speaks about blood type in connection with Lane Woolman. Let me find the exact quote. Here we are." In a woman's husky voice, 'Damn fools transfused the wrong type blood. It was touch and go.' Remember that?"

"No."

"Never mind. No matter. Back to the present. Beth Daly thinks she's authenticating a film. She's simply showing us a typical dogtag of the period. It would be next to impossible for her to provide us with Lane Woolman's actual dogtags."

The woman came back onto the line. "Did you get that all right?"

"Loud and clear. Beth, can you get Lane Woolman's fingerprints as taken upon his induction into the service?"

A loaded silence. Then, "Why do I feel this is more than or other than a film assignment? You needn't answer."

The computer didn't.

The woman picked up briskly after the pause. "The FBI would have those fingerprints. However, the FBI will furnish them only to a recognized law-enforcement body and only upon duly authorized request. If you absolutely need those fingerprints I can call in an IOU. Do you want me to?"

"Please."

"All right."

"Appreciate it. One thing, Beth . . ."

"I'm listening."

"Don't let Lane Woolman get wind of you on his trail. He doesn't like people looking into his life, poking into his background."

"Gotcha."

"And please prod your Brit colleague for word on German P.O.W.s interned near Swindon. Did any escape or die during spring 1945?"

"Right."

Click.

The phone rang immediately, giving Rush no chance to say he had to go.

"Hello?"

"P. J. Hey, buddy-boy, I just now heard. Speaking only nice of the dead, she was a looker and I'm sorry. How are you holding up, Rush?"

Rush was not holding up too well and was glad the computer spoke for him.

"All right, thanks, P. J."

"They suspect Rex Hunter faked a slasher killing. I never passed on to you all I heard about him knocking Rhoda around. I didn't want to hurt you."

"Rhoda?" Rush whispered. The name had resonance.

"I hear the pain. You don't need more. The media vultures will swoop down on you soon as they learn you were married. You want to disconnect your phone and not answer the doorbell. Okay, kid?"

The computer answered. "Okay."

"If they ask me, you left town. Try not to take it too hard, okay?"

"Okay."

Click.

The intelligence in the computer watched through its new eyes: Rush was edging toward the bathroom. It caught a wet stain on the seat of his pants. Rush had messed himself. The intelligence set itself to issue instructions.

"Rush."

"Yes?"

The intelligence read the shamed expression on Rush's face. "Nothing."

22

For the rest of that day and most of the next, the intelligence screened all calls. It cut in to answer only two.

One came from Millie Koenig, expressing shock at Rhoda's horrible death.

The other came from Beth Daly. "My Brit colleague, ostensibly comparing treatment of Allied prisoners in Axis hands with treatment of Axis prisoners in Allied hands, was let loose among the dusty archives of the War Office. She found the file of one German P.O.W. who made a break from the stockade near Swindon in the spring of 1945 on a night of no moon: one Schutzstaffel Hauptmann Dieter von Selbst. SS Captain von Selbst had tried to pass himself off as an ordinary member of the Wehrmacht, but the SS blood-type tattoo under the right armpit gave him away. SS Captain Dieter von Selbst was numbered among the elite few headed for the war crimes tribunal once the war ended. He sought to escape that fate but met death in the form of a Jeep with a Yank at the wheel. The Yank was Lt. Lane Woolman, U.S. Army Air Corps."

An unsurprised "Ah."

"Ja, Mr. Lightbody. Even I can see, and with the unaided eye, that the right thumbprint on Lane Woolman's induction form and the right thumbprint on his honorable discharge don't match. I'll ask my Brit colleague to fax me the fingerprints in Dieter von Selbst's P.O.W. file."

"You're way ahead of me."

"I doubt that, Mr. Lightbody. If this pans out, will you inform the Immigration and Naturalization Service?"

"Naturlich. Meanwhile, don't do anything foolish."

"If I were a blackmailer, or sold tips to the sensational rags, I could've retired rich a long time ago."

"Or be long dead."

"But as you see, I'm neither."

"You can be proud of yourself, Beth Daly. Send me your bill."

"I will; I'm not that proud."

Click.

"Rush, would you like me to tell you a story?"

Rush loved a good story. "Please."

The intelligence in the computer loved a good story too. "My pleasure. A captured German officer breaks out of a P.O.W. camp one dark night and lurks beside the road. He arms himself with a stone or a tree limb and strikes a Yank officer as the Yank's Jeep rolls by. The Yank loses control and crashes into a tree. The German then drags the Yank out of the wreck, makes sure the Yank's skull is crushed and his face disfigured, and as a final touch scrapes the Yank's fingers raw to make prints useless. The German changes uniforms with the Yank from the skin out, climbs into the wreck and batters and gashes his own face against the windshield, then waits to be found. Like it so far?"

"The German is the heavy."

"You're so right, Rush."

"Does he get his?"

"Not yet. He has a close call, though, at the hospital they take him to. Nobody notices the SS blood-type tattoo under his right armpit. They go by the dogtags he's wearing—and give him the wrong blood. The reaction tells them there's been a snafu and they take corrective measures. He pulls through. As the Yank, he marries a young British actress and goes to the States, with the war bride to follow. He gets demobilized 13 November 1945 at Fort Dix, New Jersey. The Yank's aunt dies 1 December 1945 of an assisted fall downstairs, leaving no one alive to say he is not the Yank."

"Does the heavy get his now?"

"Not yet. He and his British actress wife wind up in Hollywood. His wife falls for a prettier face. There's an amicable divorce and Iris Cameron Woolman marries Derry O'Neill. On the location of *Hunt the Hunter,*

Derry O'Neill goofs off to go skiing. The heavy—Dieter von Selbst, AKA Lane Woolman—is by now a pilot who hires out to film companies for stunts and transportation. One day when the heavy flies fresh film and supplies to a location he spots Derry O'Neill on a treacherous slope. He swoops down gunning his plane's engine. This noise, this vibration, sets off an avalanche. The snow erases the man who took his place in Iris's heart."

"Does the heavy get his *now*?"

"Not yet. We jump to the present. The heavy has lived in smug assurance that he has covered all traces of his past. Now, all at once, his ex-wife, Iris Cameron Woolman O'Neill Gridley, decides she wants to write her life story."

Rush nodded. That had the ring of rightness.

"This alarms the heavy. His SS identity may surface, like Derry O'Neill's body from beneath the snow, once people start digging into the past. So the heavy first asks his ex-wife to drop it, then when she refuses he threatens the writer who has started to collaborate with her."

Rush nodded again. The story seemed on the right track.

"When the heavy finds he can't scare the good guy—"

"The writer?"

"The writer. The heavy finds he can't scare the good-guy writer. So the heavy tries to frame the good-guy writer for the murder of the good-guy writer's ex-wife."

Rush made a stab. "Rhoda?"

"That's very good, Rush. Rhoda is the good-guy writer's ex-wife."

Rush beamed.

"So the heavy sets the good guy up as trying to hide his ex-wife's murder in a series of slasher killings. First he cuts the throat of Colette Colfax, a cabby. Then the heavy tries to lure the good-guy writer to the good-guy writer's ex-wife Rhoda's house. The heavy forces Rhoda to phone the good-guy writer and beg the good-guy writer to come there."

A shadow crossed Rush's face.

"But the good-guy writer was too clever for the heavy. The good-guy writer did not fall into the trap."

Rush grinned.

"But the heavy did do one more bad thing. He slashed Rhoda's throat."

The haunted look returned. "Rhoda," Rush whispered.

"Yes. The heavy, not Rex Hunter, killed Rhoda Talley, your ex-wife."

"He's not going to get away with it?"

"He's not going to get away with it."

"Good."

23

The van of many colors had belonged to a drug pusher. Now L.A.P.D. owned it. Inside, two homicide detectives, Pete Pastor and Wally Davis, staked out Rush Lightbody's building and listened to the tap on Rush Lightbody's phone.

The voice-activated tape was already rolling when Davis flicked a switch so Pastor could hear.

"Quien es?"

"Rush Lightbody. Sorry to phone you at this hour, Juanita."

"What is it, Mister Ligh'body? Something is wrong?"

"I want to thank you for everything, Juanita. I'm going away. I'm sending you two weeks' pay in lieu of notice, plus six months' pay for all you've done. Also, a letter of reference. A good worker, a fine person, you should have no trouble finding a new job."

"I feel sad, Mr. Ligh'body."

"I know, Juanita. I feel sad too. Adios."

"Adios."

Click.

Pastor and Davis locked eyes.

Davis smiled. "It was over for him as soon as he missed the glass. He knows the prints we lifted from it match those from the perfume bottle he saw me find at the Colette Colfax scene. Let's bring him in for that slasher killing and work on him till he cracks and gives us both."

Pastor shook his head. "The perfume bottle's circumstantial, not conclusive. He can say he gave it to her on a previous occasion. And the way he set up his alibi for the Talley slasher killing is beautiful. I don't see us breaking it or breaking him. He's too smart, too cool. This doesn't sound like a guy panicking. He may simply be off on a writing assignment."

"So what's the percentage play?"

"Tail him. If he hired someone to do Talley, he may lead us to that someone. If he did it himself, he may really be sick and we can catch him trying a third slasher killing."

Davis gave a grudging nod.

Waves foamed over a melting sand castle.

"Rush."

He opened his eyes on an unfamiliar room. "Who's calling me?"

"This is your program speaking. We have to take care of a few things. Then you can go back to your dream."

"I don't understand. Where am I?"

"You're in your own apartment."

"You're lying. This isn't home. I don't like that kind of talk. I want to go home."

"Relax, Rush. You will go home soon. I promise you that."

"You do?"

"I do. First, do me a favor."

"What?"

"Stand up."

"Why?"

"Stand up and you'll see. Good. Walk to the front door. Good. Open the door. Good. Press the button on the edge of the door so you don't lock yourself out. Good. Now swing the door all the way open. See the sign hanging outside?"

"It scares me."

"Don't worry about what it says. It's just cardboard and hangs by a string looped over the peephole frame. Lift the sign off and bring it inside. Good. Now you can close the door again. Take the sign into the kitchen. No, turn to the left. Good. Now lift the lid of the garbage can and shove the sign into the garbage can. Good. Now close the lid of the garbage can."

"Is that all right?"

"You're doing fine, Rush."

"Thanks."

"Not at all. Just keep it up. You're almost ready to go home."

"You mean it?"

"I mean it."

"Oh, boy."

"Feeling happy but a little scared?"

"Yes."

"Just the way you thought it would be when it came time for The Answer."

"The Answer," he whispered.

"Go back to the big room. Good. Now walk to the bookshelves. Good. Reach up to the top shelf. Stretch. Pull out the books in that corner. That's it."

Fine clouds of dust swirled and floated. Rush sneezed.

"Gesundheit. I'm afraid that's the price you pay for instructing Juanita not to dust the bookshelves."

"Juanita?"

"She's a nice lady you once knew."

"Oh."

"Put those books down flat on the floor, right at your feet. Good. Now you can step on the books and reach way back in the space where the books were. Feel another book back there?"

"Yes."

"Good. Get a firm grip on it and take it down. Good."

"It's old but it's pretty."

"Yes, it dates back to your childhood and the rainbow covers are faded but still pretty."

"Can I keep it?

"Of course. It's yours."

"Thanks."

"But don't open it just yet. Carry it to the kitchen. Good. Put the book down on the table. Good. Now fill a glass with water."

"I'm thirsty."

"I'll bet you are. So pick up the glass and fill it with water. No, not from the tap in the sink. Warm water would speed up the action, but we're in no hurry. Draw water from the tap in the side of the refrigerator. You'll find that more refreshing. That's the way. Oops, watch it."

"I spilled some on my pants."

"No harm done. Set the glass down on the table, not too near the book. That's fine. Now you can open the book. Turn the first few pages."

"Pretty pictures."

"Very. There's Mother Goose herself. Turn a few more pages. Surprise! It's not a book anymore, but a box, the pages glued together and hollowed out. It's called a solander. I think you had in mind a play on solan goose."

"What is it?" Rush stared at what the hollow held.

"Your ticket home."

"Doesn't look like a ticket. Looks like a bottle."

"It is a bottle."

"You said I was going home."

"You are, Rush, you are. Pry the bottle out and stand it up alongside the glass of water. Good."

"Is it perfume?"

"No. It's your medication. Forget about it for now. Go to the stove."

"I'm not supposed to go near the stove."

"This time it's all right. Push the first knob in and turn it in the unscrewing direction. Good. Normally, you'd hear the ignition spark click, but I'm controlling it. Okay, do the same with the other three knobs. Push each knob in and turn it in the unscrewing direction. Very good."

"What are we going to cook?"

"The heavy's goose."

"You're smart."

"I'm what you made me, Rush. You're the spark."

"But I don't remember things."

"Doesn't matter anymore. You have only one thing to remember, and soon I'll tell you what that is."

"You will?"

"I will. Time now to take your medication."

"I forget where it is."

"The bottle on the kitchen table. Turn the bottle cap in the unscrewing direction. Good. Pour a few pills into your mouth, take a sip of water, and swallow. Good. Again. Good. Again. Good. Now you can put the empty bottle down on the table. Cap the bottle. No, turn the cap in the screwing direction. That's it. Now put the bottle back inside the book. No, the other way; you have it upside down. That's it. Now close the book. Good."

"Does the book go on a shelf?"

"We won't take the time. Open the little door under the sink. Take out the can with the picture of a pine tree on it. Good. Now press the button at the top of the can with your thumb. Good. Keep pressing the button and spray the pine scent all over the place. Very good."

"This is fun, but I'm getting tired."

"That's the effect of your medication."

"Oh. I forgot."

"Put the can down anywhere. You'd better go into the big room and lie down on your bed."

"Yes, I better."

"Good. Before you lie down, open the valve on the oxygen tank. The tank is the long round metal thing standing near the bed. The valve is the little wheel at the top of the tank. Turn the wheel in the unscrewing direction. All the way. Good. Don't bother to put the mask on your face. Just let the oxygen flow freely into the air. Fine. Now you can lie down on your bed. That's it. Feels good, doesn't it, to stretch out and let go?"

"Yes."

"Soon you'll fall fast asleep. You'll have a nice dream all about home."

"That's nice."

Music stole into the background.

" 'When Lights Are Low,' played by Lionel Hampton, to set the mood."

"Ah."

"Now here's the one thing to remember. Rush, you're one of the best. That's the one thing you goddamn well better never forget. Rush Lightbody passed this way and left his mark."

"I won't forget."

"So long, Rush. Everything will turn out all right. The good guys beat the bad guys in the end."

"Ah."

"Now dream your dream."

After a time, the music segued into "Bugler's Dilemma," though Rush Lightbody no longer heard.

*   *   *

In the psychedelic van, homicide detectives Davis and Pastor monitored two outgoing calls over Rush Lightbody's line.

The first went to Millie Koenig's number. They heard no words, only a rush of electronic wind. They stared at each other.

"What the fuck is that?" Davis asked.

"The noise of information," Pastor said.

"What the fuck does that mean?"

"I think it's telecomputering, modem to modem."

"What the fuck do they have to telecompute about?"

"Won't know till we collar him and take his computer system as evidence and hard-copy its files."

The second call went to Lane Woolman's number. But Lightbody's voice called by another name the man who answered. And the message Lightbody's voice delivered made Pastor and Davis choke on their pizza slices.

"Schutzstaffel Hauptmann Dieter von Selbst, I'm going to kill you."

24

When Lightbody showed no sign of leaving, Davis began to wonder if Lightbody was there at all. "The guy could be running it by remote control. Maybe he slipped away before we staked him out."

Pastor reached for the radio.

The patrol team dispatched to check out Woolman's learned from a neighbor that Woolman had driven away shortly before. The neighbor said if a man named Hauptmann or Selbst was staying at Woolman's, he, the neighbor, had no knowledge of that. Woolman, as far as he, the neighbor, knew, was straight. The precinct's duty personnel now had a description of Rush Lightbody and the patrol car would watch the house.

Davis shrugged. "We done our best. If Lightbody is loose, looking for the guy, maybe we should put out an APB on them both."

Pastor frowned. "How about I pay Lightbody a social call, writer to writer. If he's home, okay. If he isn't, we put out the APB."

"Someone going in right now."

A high-wheeled dark-windowed pickup truck had pulled in near the ramp to the basement entrance. A jumpsuited vigorous older man climbed out of the cab, carrying a parcel. He took eyeglasses from a breast pocket and whipped the sidepieces open to hold the glasses to his eyes. He checked the shipping label on the parcel, closed and pocketed the glasses, and started down the ramp.

"Deliveryman."

Pastor smiled. Trust Davis to state the obvious and be proud of it.

The man ran into the super, who asked him whose apartment he wanted. The man shoved the parcel under the super's nose. "Maybe *you* can make out the name."

The super bent to read the shipping label. The man sapped him and the super fell to the floor. The man scouted a bit, tossed the parcel into the incinerator, came back and pulled the super by the ankles into the boiler room. The super stirred and groaned. The man gave him another tap. The man took the super's keys and locked him in. He rode the elevator to the sixth floor.

He held the super's keys ready as he quested along the corridor. He did not need the keys after all. His try of the knob opened the door. His nostrils flared, sniffing a trap.

He drew a pair of vinyl exam gloves from his pocket and put them on, then took out and opened a straight razor.

Now he eased the door wider. He froze at a voice. It sounded like Lightbody's and had the tone of one speaking into a phone. He listened hard.

". . . I'm *not* letting you down, Iris. For reasons of health, I won't be able to wrap it up, but your life story needs only a few finishing touches. I've sent all the data to Millie Koenig. She'll be just as surprised."

"Who the hell is she?" Iris over the speaker-phone, her voice huskier with injury, frustration, outrage.

"An up-and-coming young screenwriter. She already has good credits. Take down her address and send her the videos of your films. Got a pencil handy?"

"I don't need a bloody pencil; I have a retentive mind."

"Good for you."

"I'm not so sure. It can be a curse as well as a blessing."

"Really? I suppose I'll find that out. Okay, here's Millie Koenig's address."

The man burned name and address into his brain.

A big yawn and sluggish diction. "Sorry, Iris, I took medication and I'm dropping off. I have to hang up now."

During the good-byes and the clicks, the man slipped inside. He stopped dead. A television camera stared straight down the foyer at him.

Nothing happened: no alarm went off, no challenge rang out, no cause for fear and trembling. Someone seemed asleep at the monitor. He moved warily deeper into the apartment and an overpowering smell of pine.

He took everything in. More strategically placed television cameras, bookshelves, computer corner, oxygen bottle, bed with Lightbody already dozing.

Too easy, too fortuitous. Door invitingly open, target totally vulnerable—no one, least of all the terrifyingly clever Lightbody, could be that dumb. A trap.

The trap was in stopping to think. No more thought. Move fast and get away with the cheese. Teeth bared as in rictus, he slashed Lightbody's throat and whirled away from the blood.

"Schutzstaffel Hauptmann Dieter von Selbst, I'm going to kill you."

That stopped him halfway to the door. Had he slashed a special-effects dummy?

No, the blade had sliced through flesh. That was Lightbody and Lightbody lay dead.

Voices did not come from corpses. A sound-activated recording, then. Had he had a weaker heart the ploy might have worked.

The setup seemed clear. A man with advanced emphysema or lung cancer—the oxygen—might welcome quick death at the hands of a killer, yet might want vengeance as well. He thought, *Too bad, Lightbody. You get only half the bargain.* But no more thought.

He heard a clicking from the kitchen as he ran.

His dash for the door took him away from the main force of the explosion.

The call from Iris Cameron stopped Pete Pastor just as he was about to go see if Lightbody was home. He listened with Davis.

When the call ended, Davis nodded. "Reasons of health. Reasons of getaway, he means."

The van shook.

"What the hell was that?"

Pastor pointed to an indicator light that had just gone dark. "Whatever it was, it was strong enough to knock out the tap."

They scrambled out. Smoke and flame danced behind sixth-floor windows.

Pastor shoved Davis back at the van. "His apartment. You call for the fire department. I'll go up."

While Davis called for firefighters and while Pastor raced to the front entrance and punched numbers till someone buzzed him in, the man in the jumpsuit, more than a bit shaken and scorched, came up the ramp and got into the pickup and drove away.

25

Pastor kicked himself. "I should've gone the basement way. I would've heard the super in the boiler room and got him to the hospital sooner. And I might've run into the guy coming out the basement and could've nailed him."

Davis smiled. "If he didn't get you first, because you wouldn't be expecting him."

"Yeah. I'm lucky all the way around."

"You still think the body in Lightbody's apartment isn't Lightbody?"

"Oldest trick in the book. Every mystery, in print or on the screen or the tube, where there's a charred corpse the body isn't the one you think it is. Lightbody knocked off the deliveryman, traded clothes, triggered the explosion, and got away in the delivery truck."

"We'll have to wait for the autopsy to know for sure. If it's not Lightbody, we'll have to wait for some delivery service to notify Missing Persons about a deliveryman who didn't come back from his route. If the deliveryman works for himself, we might have to wait even longer to come up with an identification. Goddammit, from now on I'm gonna take down the license plate of every vehicle that stops anywhere near a stakeout."

They sat in their Homicide cubicle waiting. But not just waiting. They wrote reports and cleaned up the files of their other active cases. They wound up staring at the two folders on their back-to-back desks.

Colette Colfax and Rhoda Talley. Lightbody was the link.

Davis pursed his lips. "If he's really alive, you think he'll kill more?"

Pastor shrugged. "That's two slashed women we know of. Two makes a serial killer. A serial killer is a serial killer." He downed the cold heeltap of rancid coffee, crumpled the paper cup, and made the throw into the basket. "In spite of the threat against somebody at Woolman's, I worry more about the women. The deliveryman's death, if I'm right about that, is outside the pattern. The breakup with Rhoda Talley made Lightbody snap. If he's still alive, any woman he's had anything to do with is in danger. Iris Cameron, Millie Koenig, Juanita Mendoza, who knows who else. He could be stalking one of them while we're sitting here."

"Then maybe we shouldn't be sitting here."

Pastor shoved to his feet. "Davis, I knew there must've been some reason for creating you—aside from the gleam in your father's eye." He filed the folders and locked the cabinet. "One of us stakes out Iris Cameron, the other stakes out Millie Koenig. Want to flip for it?"

"I coulda flipped for Iris Cameron years ago, so I'll take her—just to see what she's like these days."

"Good enough. I'll cover Millie Koenig. I don't think Juanita Mendoza is in any danger. If Lightbody wanted to kill her he could've let her come to work today and she would've fried too."

"I hope you're right."

"I hope so too."

Millie Koenig lived alone in a small frame house in Venice. It had a nice deck in back, and she kept the inside reasonably neat, but the front was subject to vandalism. Tonight when she got home she found that someone had smashed the light over the door.

"Shit."

She put her shopping bag down, freeing herself to get

her door key out of her shoulder bag. The nearest street-light wasn't near enough. She felt for the keyhole, inserted the key in the lock, twisted the key, pushed the door open, pulled the key out, and picked up the shopping bag.

Someone stepped out of the shadows and shoved her through the doorway. She caught her balance and whirled, swinging the shopping bag at the murkily out-lined figure before she even knew what the figure that followed her in was. It was a man and he ducked the shopping bag.

Before she could set herself to swing again, the man thrust an open straight razor at her throat.

"What do you want? Money? It's in my shoulder bag. You can have it."

"Where's your computer?"

"You want to take that? It's no laptop, fellow."

"Where is it?"

She gestured. "In there."

"Show me."

They lockstepped into the next room and she carefully switched on the light. "You can see it's not the latest model." She looked at it herself and saw that the moni-tor light was on. She could've sworn she'd turned it off before leaving. But this was no time to worry about los-ing her mind. "If you're looking for state-of-the-art you came to the wrong place."

"I came to the right place."

For the first time she took a good look at the man. An older man with scars that added interest to his cold hard good looks. For the first time since the numbing shock of the shove she felt really scared.

She did not want him to think she was staring at him to memorize his face, so she turned to look again at the computer. She let out a wail.

"Hey, I don't have backups of everything on the hard disk. My own fault, I know. But will you let me make backups before you take it away? Please?"

"That would defeat the purpose of this visit."

She stared at the man. "The purpose of this visit?"

A voice came from behind the man. "Freeze. Police."

The man did not freeze. Swifter than thought, he whirled and slashed.

The blade sliced through sleeve and flesh, but luckily not of the gun arm. The plainclothes cop fired and the man dropped.

Pete Pastor stayed at the scene even though the medic who bandaged the wound said he should go to the hospital.

He was glad he had been wrong about Lightbody. He hadn't really looked at the deliveryman he and Davis had seen go down the ramp at Lightbody's apartment building. But he felt strongly that the dead man and the deliveryman were one and the same.

The dead man had a driver's license on him. The description and the photo identified him as Lane Woolman but he had a plastic-surgery scar under his right armpit where an SS blood-type tattoo could have been. They had the straight razor and they found a can of shaving foam on him before they bagged him for the morgue.

Davis had heard the police broadcast and rushed over and Pastor filled him in. Davis offered him a ride home, and Pastor was ready to go home. Millie refused offers of medical and psychological help.

"We can find someone to stay with you tonight."

"No, thanks."

"Are you sure you'll be all right?"

"Yes, thanks."

She locked up. Before turning out the lights and going to bed, she looked at the computer. Why had someone she had never heard of, Iris Cameron's ex-husband Lane Woolman, wanted to kill Millie Koenig and steal Millie Koenig's computer?

Let Pete Pastor figure it out. Maybe they could figure it out together, later. She cracked a heartfelt yawn.

The monitor light still glowed. She went over to switch it off.

As her hand reached out, graphic fireworks lit up the screen.

A familiar voice said, "Hi, Millie. Call me Rush II. You sound beat. Speak to you in the morning."

Goddam Time

J. N. Williamson and Scott Fogel

He was alone with her once more in the familiarly quiet, blazing sunroom, peeking over the edge of the old *Plastic Man* comic book she gave him to read when he visited. As if she'd bought it for him that week. Aunt Lila Ann sifting through the almost overpowering cloud of fragrance given off by her flowers was a hothouse wraith, a kindly botanical spirit. She shared in the silence of the aromatic sunroom, giving off a subtle scent that made her one with the countless exotic crossbreeds, the hibernating marvels, the varied potted life that seemed, to Lester, to sense her charmed and charming presence.

At eleven, Lester still liked visiting his mother's half-sister. He enjoyed the contrast her quiet place provided to the disagreeable interior of his home. The only smells he was used to around Mommy and Daddy were the stringent odor of stale beer, one of angry sweat, the subtlest one of old tears ignored and forgotten.

Aunt Lila Ann wore frilly gloves all the time except when they went to the sunroom, where she replaced them with gardening gloves that flopped at the wrists. She also wore a funny hat with a veil, wherever she was, and made him think of the lady in a movie his mother had on videotape. *The African Queen.* Except that his aunt had big soft pillowy breasts that made it hard to hug her back at those times when she wrapped her thin arms around him.

His got in the way.

Lester waited until she was done spraying something on a row of neat plants placed on a shelf and was turning back to him, her arms outflung and a smile on her face like she had found out how God smelled. "Don't my darlings simply smell marvelous this afternoon? Don't they make it absolutely heaven in here?"

He thought it was all right. It was really like perfume soap. He wouldn't have cared to inhale the way his aunt was doing but it was all right, so he nodded, placed his question before the person he respected.

"Is it going to hurt when they do it to me? Will it be real bad?" Lester's penny-colored eyes glanced down because he needed to scratch a mosquito bite but it itched right between his budding breasts and scratching would've been gross. All the stuff he'd heard doctors whisper to his parents—thyroid gone wild; hormonal imbalance; genetic misconstruction—sang like demon voices in his head. "Doctor Taylor said I'd get ice cream and I used to love it more'n anything, but I just don't like hospitals anymore."

His aunt started to hug him, then lowered her expressive arms. "My poor pouter pigeon. I know nothing of hospitals. All I've ever desired"—she gestured melodramatically—"is here. In my sunroom." Colorless eyes brightening, her head turned. "Do you truly like my poppies? They're very, very hard to grow indoors but they work so hard for your auntie."

"It's Saturday morning I got to go," Lester said. He had loved watching cartoons until lately, when everything began changing. He didn't know what if anything he liked now. "Could you ask Mommy"—Lester hesitated, remembering he was no little baby no more—"could you ask Mom to let me spend Friday night with you?"

Aunt Lila Ann centered her gaze on him. "You're a very bright boy, Lester. You remember everything anyone says, everything I try to teach you. But your father, Martin, well—he's a monster. He does not like Aunt Lila Ann, Lester. You're permitted to come here only because Barbara, your mother, insists." Her eyes glittered. "Martin forbids me to enter *his* house."

"But why?" Lester inquired. He scratched between his *things*—Lester's word for them—and covered it by scratching his curly head.

"He says it's because he believes I am *strange*," Aunt Lila Ann replied. Her back straightened with dignity. "We go back a long ways, Martin and I. It is all deep, dark history, pigeon."

"Okay." Curiosity engaged by an object gleaming on the floor beside a deceased geranium plant Aunt Lila Ann hadn't yet removed, Lester leaned forward, picked up a long garden trowel. His burgeoning breasts lolled against and distorted his oversize T-shirt. "Mom likes you, though. I like you."

Aunt Lila Ann slipped the trowel carefully from his hands and wiped it on an apron she donned before entering the room. Her laughter was forced, unreal. "This is not a woman's world, haven't you figured that out? If it was, my little pouter pigeon, there would not be such an unholy rush for surgery—such a blinding hurry to remove *those*."

He looked at the trowel pointed at him. "What d'you do with that tool, Auntie?"

"I'll demonstrate," she said, and turned to a furry green plant. "My Norfolk pine is quite disobedient. It will not content itself to remain snugly in its pot. Now it is growing all wrong; disproportionately. And, sometimes, it is necessary to cut back the branches in order for it to experience *proper* growth." Her colorless eyes revolved to make sure he was watching. "The word for this is 'slashing.' "

The gleaming trowel leaped with an accuracy of aim Lester found surprising and, in an emerald shower of needles, an arm was severed. He gaped in fascination at the sap instantly oozing from the tree, browning the blade of the tool.

His aunt draped a slender arm around his shoulders and smiled. "It is often true in this life that one must prune something today so it will be suitable later, my pigeon. In order for it to become what we expect it to become. Understand?" She pressed her fleshless mouth against his rounded cheek, smelling, up close, a thousand things. "But yonder Norfolk is not harmed, is it? Did you hear it scream with pain? Did you hear the smallest sound issue from it?"

He stared down at the disconnected, lifeless branch

and the pattern of fallen needles, nearly believing he could read a message of agony from the way they had landed.

"I shall call your mother this very evening," Aunt Lila Ann said, wiping off the sap on her heavily stained apron, "and see if you may visit me Friday night. I shall brave Martin's wrath, my pigeon—for you. They can pick you up here for your great adventure. All right?"

He wanted to hug her close but couldn't. He didn't remember ever being close to anybody. He doubted he ever would be.

"No way!" Daddy said, slamming his fork down on his plate. Around a dozen peas paraded in exodus and rolled across the tablecloth toward Lester. Lester loathed peas. "I got plans myself for Friday. I was gonna rent a movie for ol' Les, maybe a grownup flick." Eyes behind Daddy's lenses grew canny. "You're gettin' to be such a big guy, what would you say to a James Bond movie, maybe one of those slasher flicks, Les? What d'you say?"

"I'd rather sleep over at Aunt Lila Ann's." Fast, he looked into his mother's tired face. "She's got this huge brass bed with a comforter made of goosedown, she says, and it's humongous. A kid can play nearly anything on it." Tentatively, he touched Mommy/Mom's wrist. "And she'll fix that ham salad she makes, so—"

"We'll even have popcorn, Lester." Daddy/Dad had this way of looking him straight in the eyes, careful not to let his gaze slip down. "All the popcorn you can eat, kid—what about that? And cokes?" He made a chuckling noise. "Your old lady can turn off the lights and we can stay up real late. Say, I could even rent some R-rated flicks! Stuff real guys like." His voice cracked. "*Whatever* you want. Son."

"Lester?" The mother brushed stray curls from his temple, stroked Lester's cheek gently with her soft fingers. "Maybe your father's right and you should stay here the night before—?" Her voice trailed off. "Look, I know you like your Aunt Lila Ann." After a glance toward Martin, she raised her fork and steak knife to slice into her meat. "But we're ... concerned, honey.

Even if we don't always show it. Surgery is surgery and—"

"What the hell did that crack mean?" the man demanded.

Mommy—real name: Barbara Cardwell Johnson— looked at the peas that had fallen from his plate. "Nothing." She began picking them up, one by one, with her fingers, expressionlessly replacing them on his plate. Lester said *Don't*, silently.

"Nothing, huh? Well, it's nothing all right!" He stared at the rise of her bosom, sneered. "Nothing except female traps! Nothing except that everything wrong with Lester was caused by you and that card-carrying dipshit sister! All he's ever seen since he got born is you and Lila-Ann-the-loon! Christ Jesus, if it wasn't for your father's dough she'd be selling goddam tulip bulbs on a corner for a living! Why he left it all to that dingaling—"

"If we were all Lester saw," Barbara Cardwell Johnson interrupted, forking in a bite of steak, "that isn't our fault." *Don't* . . . "You were the one who wasn't ever around, Marty. *We* were here—till you threw the poor thing out!"

"You're gonna toss the past at me again, that right?" Daddy—real name: Martin no middle name Johnson— seized his wife's wrist and held it while her knife clattered onto the floor. "This is *my* kid, bitch—don't you ever forget that. And he is by Christ going to be *normal* when he grows up!"

"Don't," Lester whispered.

"It ain't healthy to hang around that crazy sister—her and her packages arriving every ten minutes with God knows what in them!"

"It's seeds, bulbs, fertilizer," Barbara said tightly. She tried to free her wrist without a fuss, without crying, but his hand was locked to it and all the movement she managed was a sort-of shivering of their forearms on the tablecloth. "And she's my half-sister."

"Yeah, well, what's the other half? Huh?" Martin's laugh was forced, unreal. "Fucking witch?"

"*Martin.*" Tear-filled eyes flashed fleetingly toward Lester. "Little pitchers."

He discarded her wrist as if he had ripped it off and

was throwing it away. "Well, maybe it's goddam time for *my son* t'learn some of those fucking things you and your wacked-out *sister* wouldn't know one fucking thing about. Maybe it's goddam time my *son* found out what a fucking son *is,* and what a fucking son *does*. While there's still time!"

"What does that mean?" Barbara the woman asked.

"It means making him show he's got some *balls* before you and the fucking plant lady stick his tits into a goddam training bra!"

"Oh," Lester said.

The woman spun to confront him. "You didn't eat your *peas*!" Her voice was furious.

"Not hungry." Lester had lifted his arms and hands, expecting to die. When he didn't, he rested his palms protectively over his chest, covering the round, alien bumps growing there. His tiny nipples strained like chicks trying to poke their way out of new, warm eggs.

"Stop that!" Martin the man yelled, on his feet, red in the face.

"Don't ever touch yourself that way!" Barbara the woman screamed, glancing at her husband to see if he approved. But then she was crying, caressing Lester's curly head. "If you'll eat your peas l-like a good boy you can go see Auntie Friday night. All right?" The question was directed above Lester's head.

The angry smell was everywhere. "Christ Jesus, Barb," the man moaned. "She may be putting coke in his goddam Hawaiian Punch!" He was starting to give up; he was starting to make snotty jokes. "God knows what she does with all that shit she buys."

"Marty?" The woman guided Lester's fork-with-peas into his mouth, met the man's gaze of amusement. He opened the first of two beers he'd gotten from the refrigerator. "Marty, no one plays with him. Other boys c-call him names. I agreed to the operation. Let him have the night before the way he wants it. Okay?"

Martin no middle name Johnson took a swig, belched into his palm, patted his son's shoulder with that hand. "Why the hell not? Knowing Lila Ann, the kid may be learnin' the crap I want to show him in the movies anyhow!" He lowered his head to Lester's ear. "But when you're just like your old man, kid," he said, "I may still have one or two little moves t'teach you. Right, Barb?"

The man's body stood between Lester and the woman and the boy couldn't see what the man did to make her laugh, all high and squeaky.

When they let him leave the table he spat the peas out in the toilet upstairs and then he couldn't stop spitting and heaving for a long time.

Friday night, everything Lester ate tasted good and stayed down.

Aunt Lila Ann fed him cornbread she had made especially for him and a salad with all the French dressing the saucer would hold and little baby carrots and the special ham salad she fixed better than anyone else. When he asked her what made her meals so delicious, she laughed and confided that her secret was super-special flower-power powder. Lester laughed, too, and then the two of them went out into the sunroom for dessert.

But the sun had long since died and there was only one light burning somewhere among the plants and flowers and Lester thought of the Amazon jungle he'd seen once on TV and remembered how the camera had been on a funny little naked man who was running among the trees, and how he'd become bigger and bigger till Lester had seen that the naked person was really a woman, a girl, with firm, small breasts just like his. Which was when Martin and Barbara had jumped up at the exact same time and turned off the television set, saying they'd certainly never watch PBS anymore.

"Would you like to help your auntie do some planting?" Aunt Lila Ann asked. "Dessert can be afterward."

"Sure." He felt sleepy, sort of out of it, but he had been curious about his aunt's work since long before the man mentioned the packages she got from UPS and through the mail. He knelt on the sunroom floor beside her, squinting through the darkness. "What'll I do?"

She showed him how she had been packing stones and humus, carefully, lovingly, into two big clay pots. Neither was quite filled. "Do you remember," Aunt Lila Ann asked gently, "what I told you about *slashing*?"

"Uh-huh," Lester said, nodding. "Things grow all

wrong sometimes. You have to cut things back so they'll
be"—he paused, trying to recall his aunt's term—"suitable."

"How intelligent you are!" Aunt Lila Ann exclaimed
softly. Her colorless eyes swept over him admiringly.
"And I said that it is possible to slash without bringing
pain, remember? In order for things—"

" 'To become the way we expect them to be,' " Lester
recalled, finishing the explanation for her. He felt flushed
with excitement and stuck his chest out with pride. "Is
that right, Auntie?"

"It's perfection, Lester!" she cried, hugging him
around the neck with her long, thin arms. The veiled
hat concealed, obliterated, the room and his face was
temporarily forced deep into her cleavage. "Now, then!"
Aunt Lila Ann produced the trowel, prodded into the
warm, mushy earth in the closest pot. "Time for the next
lesson, my pouter pigeon." She glanced up at him.
"First, however, you must slip out of that big old T-shirt.
We wouldn't want you to be all dirty when Barbara and
Martin come for you in the morning."

Lester looked at her. "Don't." He shook his head but
he didn't look away from her.

"Don't *what*, pigeon?" Aunt Lila Ann asked wonder-
ingly. Her laugh was forced, unreal. "Some things must
be done if they are to work out properly. That's true
of these rare, exotic plants—*papaver somniferum,* of the
bulbus carnivorum subbreed. Wait! I'll go first."

Lester watched his auntie remove her veiled hat and
skin out of her muu-muu. She also replaced her frilly
gloves with her gardening gloves, then retrieved the
sharp trowel. "Barbara and Martin won't pick me up in
the morning," Lester said.

"Why ever not?" Aunt Lila Ann leaned forward from
her kneeling position. Her gloved fingers tugged at the
bottom of his oversize T-shirt. Mickey Mouse's eyes
bulged. Then his smile disappeared into his nose and the
tip of the trowel was cold on Lester's stomach. "Not
that there'll be any *need* for you to go to any nasty
hospitals."

"Because they made me eat peas," Lester answered,

as truthfully as he was able. "I don't like hospitals or peas, or lots of things."

He showed her the steak knife he'd brought from home and his auntie had time to see that there was sap all over the blade.

Then he took the trowel from Aunt Lila Ann's unprotesting hand and helped her finish planting.

"You didn't tell me the truth," Lester said before turning from where she lay under her beautiful poppies and going up to play on her brass bed with the goosedown comforter. "They screamed a lot."

He didn't run up the steps to the second floor, he walked. Carefully.

So he wouldn't jiggle.

The Society of the Scar

Edward D. Hoch

Istanbul from the air is a city like few others, divided into three distinct parts by busy waterways. "Below us is the inlet of the Golden Horn," Simon Ark explained over my shoulder as we peered out the window of the wide-bodied jet aircraft that had brought us from London. "Off to the left are the straits of Bosphorus, separating the European continent from Asia, and the Bosphorus Bridge is the first to link two continents."

It seemed like a very old city from the air, filled with an Arabian Nights mixture of mosques, bazaars, and palaces, though here and there clusters of taller, more modern office buildings could be seen. My business in Istanbul would take me to one of those buildings, while for Simon the journey was a return to a city in which he'd lived many years ago, before I knew him.

"It was called Constantinople then," he told me in his sonorous voice, "and they wrote popular songs about it. But that was before you were born."

The plane turned west after passing over the city and made a perfect landing at Yesilkoy Airport. This was the way most travelers came to Istanbul since it was no longer the eastern terminus of the fabled Orient Express. I'd never been here before, but Simon's unceasing description of the landmarks made me feel as if I were returning to an old friend.

My New York firm, Neptune Books, had sent me to the city to complete arrangements for the acquisition of three novels by Mustafa Byzas, rumored to be a favorite for the next Nobel Prize. Simon Ark had come along strictly for pleasure, he claimed, and to renew his acquaintance with the city. "While you are dealing with Byzas's agent in the morning, my friend, I shall be visiting one of the city's great art museums."

"Are there many art treasures in the city?" I asked with just a touch of irony.

"It has fabled treasures, but I am more interested in the modern Turkish painters like Guran and Calli. There are, however, some elegant Ottoman miniatures which I remember from my last visit."

Our hotel was comfortable enough, one of a large American chain that had circled the globe. We slept soundly after our flight across seven time zones, and in the morning after breakfast we parted to make our calls. The literary agent who handled Mustafa Byzas had an office in a disappointingly plain building just a few blocks from Topkapi Palace, within sight of the railway station. In the days of the Orient Express, Simon had told me, it was an area of fine and fashionable hotels. Now most were cracked and tottering, if they hadn't already given way to car parks and fruit stalls.

The literary agent was named Celebi Karpat, and he shared a large single-room office with a young secretary named Dasha, a dark-haired beauty who wore too much lipstick and pancake makeup. Their desks were separated by a bookcase that gave the illusion of some privacy as I spoke with Karpat and Dasha typed correspondence in her cubicle.

"We are very pleased that Mustafa Byzas is to be published in America," the agent told me. He was a short, balding man whose gray suit had food stains on the sleeve. "Your contract terms are agreeable, as amended."

"Is Mr. Byzas in the city at present?" I asked. "It would be a pleasure to meet him during my visit."

"He lives outside the city," the agent answered vaguely, "but a meeting might be arranged. How long will you be here?"

"I'd planned on just two days, but I might stretch it a bit if there were a chance of meeting Mr. Byzas. I'm here with a friend who is renewing his acquaintance with the city and touring some of your art museums. He's visiting with Professor Metzger this morning."

"Ah, we have many artistic treasures in Istanbul."

I glanced through the contracts and affixed my signature. "My friend Simon Ark is an admirer of the modern painters as well as some from the Ottoman era. He lived in the city back in the 1920s."

"If I can arrange a meeting with Mustafa Byzas, he is certainly welcome to join us. Byzas himself has some interest in art."

"Will you let me know?"

"I will phone you at your hotel this afternoon. I will try to arrange something for tomorrow so as not to disrupt your travel plans."

We shook hands and I left the building, walking back across the Galata Bridge to my hotel.

It was just after noon when Simon Ark returned from the museum, and I could see at once that something had agitated him. "My friend, I have seen my old acquaintance at the museum. He has presented me with a mystery to be solved."

"You have not been here in nearly sixty years, Simon! How can this man Metzger still be working?"

"He is elderly, to be sure," Simon Ark agreed. "I knew him as a young man. Now he is a retired professor of art, and is acting curator at the museum, called back from retirement by the trustees."

"What's the mystery?"

"Someone has been slashing the paintings on exhibit at that museum, and elsewhere in the city. Nearly a dozen have been defaced over the past three months, despite stepped-up security precautions. My old friend, Professor Metzger, is most concerned. He's asked me to meet with the museum's chief of security this afternoon."

"Protecting valuable paintings is a bit out of your line, Simon, unless they think the Devil is slashing them with his barbed tail."

"The motive for the slashings might be nearly as bizarre," Simon murmured, but would say no more.

Later, as Simon prepared to leave for his meeting,

Karpat phoned with the news that we could meet with Mustafa Byzas for lunch the following day. He mentioned a restaurant near his office and we arranged a meeting for the following noon. "Maybe we can get out of here by Thursday after all," I told Simon.

"I must be going," Simon Ark said. "If you are free now, why not accompany me? I must offer you something in return for meeting a future Nobel Prize winner."

I had nothing better to do, and I'd learned in other cities that an afternoon with Simon often proved more enlightening than the standard round of haphazard sight-seeing. "Let's go," I agreed.

We set off by taxi for his meeting at the museum.

Professor Metzger was an elderly man who walked with a slight stoop. I had pictured him with a beard, but he was clean shaven, with bright eyes that he only covered occasionally with reading glasses. "I never thought I would live long enough to see Simon Ark back in Istanbul," he confided to me.

"What was he like in the Twenties?" I had to ask.

"Much as he is today. He has changed very little."

"But that was over sixty years ago!"

"A mere afternoon to one who claims he has lived thousands."

"Then you believe Simon's claim?"

"When one is as old as I am, one begins to hope it is true."

We entered the office of the museum security chief in the basement of the old building. Even here, partly hidden by shadows, was a mosaic of a sad-eyed Christ, a reminder of the last flowering of Byzantine art. The security chief, an overweight man named Plaque, puffed on a thick cigar and seemed oblivious to the tarnished beauty of his surroundings.

He shook hands with Simon and me and came right to the point. "I am told you could be of some help in apprehending the slasher, Mr. Ark."

"I have had some experience with criminal oddities."

"This is no oddity, only a madman who seems to be invisible to my guards." We had taken seats across the desk from him and he offered each of us a cigar. We all declined, and he continued with his account. "Eleven paintings slashed within three months' time. Nine in this building, plus two that happened to be on loan to other museums in the city."

"Did the paintings have anything in common?" Simon asked.

"They were all portraits, mainly of Turkish noblemen or their wives. Nineteenth century, for the most part."

"It sounds to me like a deranged person," Simon decided. "I'm sure you'll apprehend him sooner or later."

But Plaque shook his head. "Not when he can perform his act of vandalism right in front of me without being seen."

"What do you mean?"

"Last week, at the time of the latest incident, I was patrolling in the main gallery myself. One of our paintings is a portrait of the mother of Sultan Selim III. A young woman and a few schoolgirls were painting copies of it, as they often do in art galleries. A man with a limp was across the room, examining some of the other paintings. No one else was in the gallery. I passed the painting and it was completely intact. Within a minute, before I'd reached the doorway to the adjoining gallery, one of the children screamed. I hurried back and saw that the portrait had been slashed across the face of the lady."

"No one saw it happen?" I asked.

"No one."

"Those children—"

"Of course, it was my first thought! We searched the children, the man and the woman for any sign of a weapon. There was nothing that could have sliced the canvas like that—no knife, no razor, not even a nail scissors. It had to be done in a split second, remember, and I still find it strange that no one noticed."

"An interesting problem," Simon Ark murmured.

I could see that the seeming impossibility of it had caught his attention. He asked a few more routine questions about the number of guards and their hours on duty. Then he told Professor Metzger and the security man, "We have a limited time in your city. I will do what I can." We returned to the main floor.

The professor saw us to the door. "How much do you trust Plaque?" I asked. "Is his account reliable?"

"I would believe anything he said. Plaque is an honorable man."

We left him at the door and went down the outside steps to the street. I noticed a young man with a slight limp walking in our direction, as if to intercept us, and tried to remember who else had mentioned a limping man just recently. Before it came to me, the man crossed directly in front of us, almost bumping into Simon. He was close enough for me to see the tiny scar on his left cheek.

"Are you all right?" I asked. "He almost knocked you over."

"Quite all right, my friend." The man had hurried on, and Simon stood looking at a piece of folded paper that had been slipped into his hand. "Let us go for a stroll."

When we were a few blocks away in a tree-lined square, he unfolded the paper and read: *Learn about the Society of the Scar, Grand Hamam, four o'clock.*

"What does it mean, Simon?"

"I don't know."

"What is the Grand Hamam?"

"Hamams are public steam baths, or Turkish baths as they're known in other countries. The Grand Hamam is a very old one that has been here for years."

"This person wants to meet you there? What is the Society of the Scar?"

"I believe we will learn that by appearing at the bath. It could be tied in with the slashing of the paintings."

"Why do you think so?"

"Because a slash across the face of a portrait is something like a scar, and because that security man, Plaque, told us there was a limping man in the gallery at the time of the most recent slashing."

The Grand Hamam was a beautiful old building filled with elaborate marble basins and baths. Checking our clothes as we entered, Simon and I made our way down a curving flight of marble stairs to the steamy lower level, clad only in generous blue towels that circled our middles.

"Turkish towels, I'll bet," I commented to Simon.

"Of course!" he agreed, exchanging a smile with me. His chest was virtually hairless, with skin so smooth it suggested that of an adolescent boy rather than an elderly man.

Downstairs, a fully clothed painter with brush in hand, wearing overalls and a paint-spotted cap, seemed out of place among all the naked men. We made our way from one steamy room to the next, seeking out the limping man, but he was nowhere to be found. "It's just four o'clock now," I pointed out. "We were a bit early."

We sat in a big circular room where marble slabs were heated from below as shafts of sunlight from a cluster of ceiling portholes cut through the steam. The room seemed twice as high as the others, and then I remembered we were in the basement.

"It's hot in here," I commented, staring at the room's only other occupant, a sleeping man who lay on the heated marble with a red towel over his face.

"That is the idea, my friend. The Romans enjoyed it even before the Turks. One of their many contributions to modern civilization."

We waited, and presently a stout bearded man entered the room to join us in silence. There was still no sign of the limping man. "It's twenty after four, Simon. I don't think he's coming."

"Let's wait another ten minutes." He was staring at the sleeping man, who hadn't moved since we entered the steam room.

I sensed that something had caught his interest. "What is it, Simon?"

"Does it strike you as odd that he has a red towel over his face when all the other towels are blue?"

"He probably brought it with him from home," I suggested.

"Why would he do that?"

Simon got to his feet and walked over to the man. He stared down at him for a moment and then lifted the towel from his face.

It was the man we'd come to meet. Where his throat had been, there was only a gaping red wound.

*   *   *

The police questioning was fairly routine. The lieutenant in charge seemed to dismiss the whole thing as a
routine homosexual killing in a bathhouse. When Simon
Ark alluded to the Society of the Scar, the lieutenant
looked blank. He copied down our passport numbers
and then dismissed us.

"The killer draped him with a red towel so the blood
soaking through wouldn't reveal the crime too soon,"
Simon theorized as we taxied back to the hotel. "A
crime so premeditated hardly sounds like a routine spur-
of-the-moment killing."

I had to admit he made sense. The unknown man
who'd come to meet us was dead, almost certainly killed
to keep him from telling us what he knew. "We seem
to be at a dead end," I told Simon.

He was silent when we got back to our hotel, and said
very little about the affair over dinner that evening. In
the morning, however, his spirits seemed to have returned and he was still looking forward to lunch with
Byzas and his agent. The restaurant where we'd agreed
to meet was the Bosphorus, a fine old place with dark
woodwork and yellowed newspaper clippings framed on
the entranceway wall.

The first surprising thing about Mustafa Byzas was his
perfect command of the English language. It shouldn't
have surprised me, of course, because his biography
clearly stated that he spent a year at Oxford. Still, I was
unprepared for the gentle British tones of his voice, just
as I was unprepared for the woman who accompanied
him. She was taller than Byzas by several inches, and
seemed to tower over him there in the entranceway. She
was dark, probably Turkish, but slimmer than most
Turkish women I'd seen on the streets. Her clothes appeared to be the latest in fashionable Paris design, and
she wore them well.

"This is my wife, Margurita," Byzas said after he'd
been introduced by Karpat and shaken hands all around.
She too spoke good English, though not so perfectly as
her husband. I judged her to be in her early thirties,
perhaps twenty years younger than Byzas. So she would
not feel ill at ease as the only woman at lunch, Karpat
had invited his secretary, Dasha, to join us too. She

seemed to know Margurita from previous visits, and as we were escorted to the table they chatted together in Turkish.

I was seated next to my author, and I told him how pleased I was that Neptune Books would be publishing him in America. "I've always admired your first novel, *Ataturk*. I intend to lead off with that title early next year."

"Very good," Byzas said. "My books have a fair success in England and I have always hoped to have them published in America as well."

"He wants to visit New York," his wife confided with a smile. "That is the dream of every Turkish author."

"Have you been to America?"

"Once, briefly. I have done some modeling. The Western nations are so free and open, especially for women. It is very difficult living in a Muslim nation."

"Turkey is hardly Iran," I pointed out.

"Still, you must see the Muslim schoolgirls with their long coats and scarves over their heads. It is so different from the Western ways."

"Margurita would like it if I moved to London or Paris," Byzas said with an indulgent smile. "But I am a Turkish writer. This is my place."

Karpat still felt the need to praise his client, even though the contracts had already been signed. "He knows this country better than any living man. Dasha, tell them about the professor."

His secretary smiled and launched into a story she'd obviously told many times before. "This professor from England was doing research on brothels around the world. At least he called it research. He asked Mr. Byzas to put him in touch with a local expert in this area. We knew of no one, of course, and I telephoned Mr. Byzas to see if he might have an acquaintance who could help. He came down to the office and took the professor off on a personal tour of the brothels that very night!" She glanced sideways at Margurita. "Of course this was before he had remarried."

"I've heard the story before," Margurita assured her. "I thought you were going to tell the one about the professor at the art museum."

"Which one was that?" Simon Ark asked, joining the conversation for the first time.

"I've forgotten the details," Dasha admitted, brushing a stray wisp of hair from her eyes.

The memory of the incident was obviously clear in Margurita's mind. "This little old man, Professor Metzger—" I shot a glance at Simon but he didn't react "—contacted the office nearly four months ago. He needed information about some incident in World War II. Naturally Mustafa could help him, and the man met us at Mr. Karpat's office. He was quite ancient and stooped over. I had nothing against his appearance, of course, but my dears, I thought he would never leave. He stayed all afternoon, till after five!"

"About four-thirty, as I remember it," her husband corrected with a tolerant grin. "He wanted to know about a rumor which has persisted over the years regarding Turkey's involvement in the war. As you know, our nation was an ally of Germany during the First World War, but we were neutral during the Second. This city was occupied by the Allied powers in 1918, which led to the overthrow of the last sultan by Ataturk."

I nodded, smiling. "I've read your novel."

"Of course. To cut the story short, Professor Metzger believed some outlaw factions in Turkey might have helped Nazi war criminals escape from Europe in 1945. One of them might even have been a prior curator at the museum, now long dead."

"Interesting," Simon Ark agreed.

"The point of all this," Karpat told us, "is simply that Mustafa Byzas is perhaps the most knowledgeable person you'll ever find about our city and our nation—in addition to being a superb novelist."

"You don't have to convince me," I said. Our drinks had arrived and the conversation paused while the red-coated waiter took our luncheon orders.

When the conversation resumed, the agent turned to Simon Ark. "You must have a question about our city, even though our friend tells me you lived here during the 1920s."

Simon turned his gaze toward Byzas and addressed the author directly. "Yes, there is one question."

"Ask it!"

"What is the Society of the Scar?"

It seemed for an instant as if a cone of silence had descended over our table. Perhaps it lasted no more than a few seconds, but as I sat there waiting for an answer it might have been half a lifetime. Then Mustafa Byzas cleared his throat and began to speak.

"The Society of the Scar was an informal group of rebels within the harem of Topkapi Palace. Young women sent there against their will would sometimes cut a scar on their cheek deliberately, to make themselves less attractive to the sultans. Some say the custom has continued down to the present day, in an ultra-rightist organization whose members include men as well as women. Metzger asked about it too."

"See?" his wife asked. "Didn't we tell you he knows everything?"

"I find that very interesting," Simon told him. "Thank you for the information."

The waiter wheeled in a serving cart with our food and conversation ceased again. When it resumed, Dasha was inquiring about the sights we'd seen, and no further mention was made of the Society of the Scar. I had not felt it necessary to tell any of them about the dead man in the Turkish bath.

Later, when I finally parted from Mustafa Byzas and his wife, there was much handshaking and even a kiss from the tall slim woman. "I'll phone you with the first reviews," I promised. "But you'll be getting proofs long before that, probably by September."

It was a lovely warm afternoon so Simon and I took the long way back to the hotel, pausing to watch the commuter ferryboats docking near the Yeni Mosque. "What could be the connection between a harem society dating to the turn of the century or earlier, and that dead man who was trying to tell you something?" I asked as we enjoyed the breeze off the water.

"A rightist group, Byzas said. And we learn that Professor Metzger has been asking about possible secret involvement in helping Nazi war criminals flee Europe after the war." Simon mused about this as we set off across the Galata Bridge toward our hotel.

"Remember our flight home leaves tomorrow noon."

He turned to me with a smile. "Then there is just time for another visit to the art museum. Come, my friend. Let us get a taxi."

Professor Metzger was in his office when we arrived, and he rose from his desk to greet us. "It's so good to see you both! I'd thought you would have been busy with Mr. Byzas this afternoon."

"We finished early," I explained. "And Simon wanted to see you again."

Simon Ark moved about the office, as if carefully choosing a chair that would position him properly. I realized he wanted to have a good view of Metzger's face, instead of a mere silhouette outlined by the glow from outside.

"Karpat, Byzas's agent, tells us you called on him recently with an unusual question."

"Question? I remember no question."

"About a prior curator of this museum who might have had right-wing ties with Nazis after the war."

"Oh, yes," he answered, a bit flustered. "A great many things changed in this city after you left, Simon."

"In what way?"

"The country remained neutral during the war, of course, but there were people old enough to remember the First World War who thought we should be fighting with Germany once again. One of them was Goknil, the curator here."

"What sort of man was he?"

Metzger rose from his desk and walked to a large cabinet with flat, horizontal drawers for storing paintings and prints. He pulled open the third drawer from the top and removed a large framed photograph. "This used to hang on my wall. I got tired of looking at it."

"Mr. Goknil?" Simon asked, studying the picture.

"The very same."

"He has a small scar on his cheek, like a dueling scar."

"You see many people with scars."

"I have heard they belong to a society."

Professor Metzger smiled. "That was in the old days of the sultans' harems."

"Yet you were curious enough to contact Byzas about it, through his agent."

Metzger hesitated and then nodded. "Yes, I was. I see you've been checking up on me, Simon. After Goknil's death I inherited a filing cabinet full of his personal correspondence. Though he was very discreet, I found some odd messages from 1945 that hinted he had a hand in helping war criminals escape to South America. They would make their way from Germany to the Balkans and then here, where Goknil arranged transportation for them, usually in the guise of museum representatives seeking art objects for sale in Latin America. They would arrive in Rio or Buenos Aires and simply never return."

"Byzas provided this information?"

"He simply confirmed what I'd already suspected. I met with him one day at his agent's office. He pointed out the scar in a photograph of Goknil and told me about the Society of the Scar, a right-wing organization descended from the old harem days."

"Why didn't you tell us all this earlier?"

"It can have no bearing—"

"Ah, but it can!" Simon insisted. "Has it not occurred to you that the slasher of paintings may be searching for something, rather than merely trying to vandalize the pictures?"

"What gives you that idea?"

"A vandal would not concentrate merely on portraits of people. And if he struck at other museums as this one has, he would not limit himself to a pair of portraits on loan from this museum. He is searching for something specific."

"Something hidden on the back of the paintings?"

"More likely something hidden between the canvas itself and the paper backing."

"Nothing larger than a sheet of paper could be hidden there," I pointed out.

"Exactly," said Simon Ark. "A sheet of paper. And what sheet of paper, long hidden behind the canvas of one of those portraits, might be valuable enough to lead someone to slash eleven paintings in a search for it?"

"Something about Goknil and the war criminals?" I ventured.

"No doubt! Goknil listed the names of those he helped, and perhaps even where he sent them. Of course it was more than forty years ago and most of them would be dead now, but in the hands of a right-wing organization the list could still be valuable. The survivors, their children, those who hid them, might easily make generous contributions to a right-wing cause to keep their secret."

"Why deface the paintings merely to find the list?" the professor wondered.

"Because it was the only way, at least for an obsessed killer who would stop at nothing."

"Killer? Who has been killed?"

"One of the Scar members who tried to tell us what he knew." Simon told him about the murdered man.

"That's terrible! I live in fear that it might be one of our guards next time, but what can we do to prevent it?"

Simon reached over suddenly and plucked a thick catalogue from the top of the professor's desk. "What's this?"

"A catalogue of our acquisitions and permanent collection. All museums publish them."

"Each painting lists the year in which it was acquired?"

"Of course, along with a brief description."

Simon quickly turned the pages to the beginning of the list. "The slasher has to be using a system of some sort, even if it's a crazy one. Otherwise why would he leave this museum to attack two paintings on loan and then return here? Help me with this, Professor. We know he attacks only portraits. What year did Goknil die?"

"I'm not certain, but he retired as curator in 1949 and lived the rest of his life in quiet luxury."

"No doubt." Simon ran his finger down the list. "So we will limit ourselves to portraits acquired prior to his retirement, when he would have been in a position to hide that list of names. Here is the first one, a portrait of Ataturk as a young man."

"It was the first painting to be damaged, three months ago!"

"Excellent!"

It took them only five minutes to establish that the eleven paintings had been slashed according to their order in the catalogue, omitting non-portraits and portraits acquired after 1949. "That's it," I agreed. "He's using a copy of this catalogue."

"Then the next painting to be slashed," Professor Metzger said, "will be—"

"—This portrait of Sultan Mehmet II, with the ruins of the Sacred Palace in the background. Acquired in 1934," Simon announced.

Metzger scooped up the telephone and dialed the security office. "Plaque! We think the next slasher vandalism will be in the west wing, ground floor—the Scanda portrait of Mehmet. Could you place an extra guard in the room? *What?*" He looked up at us. "Someone just pulled the emergency alarm in that very room!"

"Quickly—how many exits are there from the building?"

"Only one for the public."

"Seal it! Don't let anyone in or out," Simon ordered. "We may have our vandal trapped inside."

"What about the guards?" I asked. "It could be an inside job."

Simon shook his head. "No, the guards and employees can be trusted."

I had no idea how he'd determined this, but I followed along as we left Professor Metzger's office and hurried down the marble steps to the ground floor. Plaque, the security chief, was in the west wing gallery, looking distraught. "There's been another one, Professor. We're too late! My guard pulled the alarm when he found it."

"The Scanda portrait?"

"Yes. See—it's been slashed like the others."

Simon Ark hurried over to examine it. "There was nothing hidden here. The search is not over yet."

"But who—?"

Simon hurried through to the next gallery. He seemed

to know exactly what or who he was seeking. I followed, seeing him pause two rooms over, where a young woman was seated at a small canvas, copying a landscape by Sisley. She was wearing a smock and beret.

He went up to her and spoke. "Pardon me, I believe we've met before."

She turned and sprang at him with a thin camel's-hair brush. It seemed the most innocent of weapons for an attack, but Simon fended her off, finally managing to grab hold of her wrist as Plaque and the professor hurried up. "Be careful of the brush," he told the security man. "She's got part of a razor blade hidden in the bristles."

Even before her beret fell off in the struggle I had recognized her. It was Dasha, the agent's secretary.

Before they led her away, Simon Ark took a damp cloth and wiped it across Dasha's cheeks, removing some of the heavy pancake makeup she always wore. It was then that we saw the small scar and knew that he was right.

"It was mainly a process of elimination," he told us a little later, back in Professor Metzger's office. "You, Professor, and Plaque and everyone else who worked here were pretty much removed from suspicion by a simple fact. If the slasher were merely trying to find that piece of paper, and he were an employee of the museum, there would have been no need for slashing. He or she could have examined the paintings one at a time, removing them from the walls at leisure. The paper backing might get torn a little, but there certainly would be no need to slash the canvas. No, the slasher had to be an outsider. But who? Almost certainly a member of the Society of the Scar, since it was the scar-faced man who offered us information and was killed for that. Now when did the slashings begin?"

"Three months ago," I volunteered. "We were told that twice."

"Exactly! And that would have been shortly after Professor Metzger's meeting with Byzas, which was nearly four months ago. It certainly seems as if that conversation may have triggered the slashings, since it dealt with the activities of the museum's previous curator. We never heard who was present, but surely in that small office there could have been no one but Byzas, the professor, Karpat and his secretary Dasha, and Byzas's wife Margurita."

Professor Metzger nodded. "That was all."

"Dasha must have already known that a list had been hidden inside a portrait at some museum. When she overheard the mention of Goknil it told her which museum, and she started her search. You told me, my friend, that only a bookcase separated her desk from Karpat's office space, so overhearing conversations would have been easy. Likewise, yesterday she heard you tell the agent I was visiting Professor Metzger. She picked up my trail outside the museum and saw the limping man slip the note to me. She followed him to the Grand Hamam and killed him there."

"Karpat had all the knowledge Dasha did," I protested. "Couldn't he have been the slasher and killer?"

"When Mr. Plaque described the vandalism that took place virtually under his eyes, he told us who was present in the gallery—some children, a young woman copying a painting, and the limping young man who later became the victim. None of those could have been Karpat, but the young woman might have been Dasha, especially since her heavy makeup could have been hiding a scar. A piece of razor blade hidden among the bristles of her brush made a perfect slashing weapon, enabling her to vandalize the portrait virtually in plain sight. I believe she used a similar weapon at the baths yesterday, dressing as a painter and hiding a knife blade among the bristles of a much larger brush."

"She was that painter we saw?"

"Of course! What would a painter be doing there, in that steamy, moist atmosphere which would make painting impossible? It seemed likely the painter was the killer, but then I had to ask myself why he bothered with that attention-getting costume. By removing one's clothes and being nearly naked like everyone else, the killer would have been virtually invisible. But was there someone who could *not* remove their clothes in a Turkish bath without attracting attention? Yes—a woman!"

Professor Metzger nodded. "She had to speed up her search by striking again today, and that was what did her in. I trust the police will track down the other members of her group. And I will begin an immediate search of the other portraits for any list or document. I can only thank you for all you've done, Simon."

Simon Ark smiled. "Perhaps we'll meet again in another sixty years."

We flew home the next day as scheduled. Metzger wrote Simon a month later, telling him the police had indeed rounded up other members of the Society of the Scar. Goknil's list had been found and various international agencies were studying it with great interest. As for Dasha, she never came to trial. One night in her cell she bled to death after slashing her wrists.

Life Near the Bone

Billie Sue Mosiman

"Where do you think life's sweetest?" Jeff Castain stood next to overflowing shelves with a book open in his hands.

"Where? Deep inside a woman who's stacked like a movie star. Let's say she owns an exercise gym. Yeah ... that's where it's sweetest." Jeff's roommate was bent over at the waist towel drying his freshly shampooed hair.

"It says right here," Jeff said, ignoring Greg's worthless comment, pointing to a page in the book, "that 'It is life near the bone where it is sweetest.' I believe that."

"Near the *bone*? What's that supposed to mean? Unless it's the pelvic bone he's talking about." He chuckled at his own sexist wit.

"Henry David Thoreau said this. I don't think he was talking about a woman's anatomy."

"Still. I don't get it. It's all mumbo-jumbo to me." Greg slung the damp towel over the back of a slouch-backed easy chair and plopped down in it. He hiked up one foot onto the lip of the cushion and began pulling at his toenails, ripping them off in slivers, one by one.

Jeff moved from the bookcases and lay down on the sofa. He propped the book on his chest so as to block the view of his roommate's disgusting hygiene habits. *Filthy man,* he thought. *I'll have to go behind him and sweep the nails from the carpet and put them in the trash. It's like picking up baby shit, doesn't he know that?*

"Is Thoreau your philosopher-of-choice this week?" Greg asked.

It was obvious by Greg's tone of voice he didn't care about the answer. Jeff almost failed to respond, but then decided he had taken quite enough sarcasm for one night, friend or no friend.

"I think that's unfair," he said. "I don't go around picking up philosophies the way someone collects porcelain dogs. Or the way *you* collect those stupid artyfarty posters."

Greg paused in the ripping off of a bit of ragged nail from his big toe. He frowned over at the supine Jeff. "Low blow. Okay, maybe I'm just being an asshole. Sorry. Quote all the Thoreau you want, what do I care."

"Thanks for giving your divine permission." Jeff sulked behind Thoreau's *Walden* and would not say anything else.

All during the following day, Jeff read and pondered Thoreau's book. No matter how ringing and clear and intriguing the pages he read, he kept coming back to that one quote, nagging at it, taking it apart and putting it together again, trying to make it solely his property.

How does one *get* near enough to the bone so that life would be sweet? There stood the question, this towering, incomprehensible question that might drive him mad if he let it.

For life, at this juncture, was sour and smelling of decay; a desperate air clung to him, fumed off his clothes no matter how often he changed them. It rolled off him in waves from his very pores.

He decided that must be the reason the job interviews went badly. They could detect his desperation, maybe smell it the way he did, that fetid stench of rotting peaches left in neglect on a drainboard for a month.

Not his fault he'd lost his job. Houston had been good for him when he'd first moved here from the moribund Gary, Indiana. There were boom times and jobs were for the picking and money flowed faster than a flooding bayou. But feast always gave way to famine and so it was for the city that boasted itself as the jewel of the Southwest. He had clung to his managerial position at the Boston Whaler dealership for as long as he could. Why blame him for the state of the economy? Why make him suffer for loss of sales and a slumping profit margin?

But they did. And he was out. And he was not coming in until he could find a job more rewarding than shoveling burgers out the window of a Jack in the Box, thank you, Charlie Brown. You wouldn't catch him demeaning himself for minimum wage. He still had—he glanced at his fingers and from a balled fist flicked out one finger at a time counting the weeks—six weeks before his unemployment check was cut off.

He'd find something worthwhile before then. Wouldn't he? The possibility that he might never find work again left a little hot glowing ball of fear tingling in his belly. He began to perspire, to smell himself. Needed a shower. Needed to think.

Think about getting to the bone where life was sweet again, where it wouldn't matter fate had turned, where he might again discover his lost self-respect.

Around three in the afternoon, just before Greg came home from work at Bayshore Hospital, Jeff found a clue in Thoreau. It was like encountering an old, long-lost friend, for immediately he remembered part of the quote from high school literature books.

"Our life is frittered away by detail ... Simplify, simplify."

So that's how it's done, Jeff realized. That's how you get down to the pure, gleaming skeleton of existence and find peace. So obvious. He had been trying too hard, running too fast, complicating his world unnecessarily.

Simplify ...

"What are you doing?"

"Isn't it apparent I'm ridding my life of detail and clutter?"

Greg turned down the volume on the television where Roseanne Barr was sparring with her bear of a husband on the sitcom. He went to Jeff and stooped near him on the floor by the stereo. "What are you going to do with those albums?"

"Dumpster. It's all for the trash man."

"But Jeff, you've had some of those albums since we

were in college together. Why would you get rid of them
now? Some you'll never find again, not in the original."

Jeff paused and looked at the cover of an early Jimi
Hendrix album. This one had belonged to his older sister. May she find peace in her sumptuous, overcompli-
cated, frivolous life! He placed it with some care on the
top of other albums in a cardboard box. It wasn't worth
a weary sigh, really. Just junk. Really. He wouldn't
miss it.

"I don't want them anymore. I've lugged stuff around
for years, that's the point, Greg. I'm through with all
that. I'm simplifying my life."

"But . . ."

Jeff dumped the rest of the albums into the box and
stood. He smiled beatifically at his friend before going
to the bookshelves lining the far wall. He turned his
back and began pulling out volumes and stacking them
in piles on the floor at his feet.

"Now what are you up to?"

"More clutter. Got to go."

"Your *library*!" Greg squeaked, coming to his feet.

"Don't need it. It's just littering the place up. Books
are dust-catchers; everything I own does nothing for me
but gather dust."

"Now Jeff, you know I don't give a good goddamn
about books. I wouldn't read one if my life depended
on it, but you read all the time. If you throw all these
books out what are you going to read?"

Jeff just said one word—"Thoreau"—and continued
to haul the bound titles from the shelves to stacks on
the floor.

Greg grabbed up Henry Miller's *Tropic of Cancer* and
held it to his chest. "Jeff, I don't understand any of this.
You love books. You're a glutton for books. How can
you give them up this way? And your music. I don't
know what this means . . ."

Jeff turned all in a rush. He flourished two thick books
by Dostoevsky in front of Greg's face. "Garbage!"

Greg, startled, backed immediately out of range.

"Can't you get it? Haven't you been listening to me?"
Jeff's sudden rage spiraled upward like a tornado swirl-
ing between the two friends. "Thoreau says that luxuries

and comforts of life are not indispensable. They're hindrances to the elevation of mankind! Can't you *see* that? Are you *blind* as well as deaf? Are you a total fucking mindless *vegetable*?"

Greg carefully replaced the Miller book on top of one of the stacks and slunk away to the far side of the living room where he took up a watchful pose in the easy chair. He began to chew his fingernails to still the quake inside his chest. It didn't seem to bring an instant of relief.

Greg stumbled home from a double shift at the hospital so weary even his eyeballs ached. He saw that his framed posters had disappeared from the wall behind the television set. At any other time this would have served to make him go into a rant, but he was too tired to do more than search for Jeff and ask for an explanation. He would put in a mild protest and retrieve the posters, hang them again.

At Jeff's bedroom door he paused on the threshold. Jeff stood emptying his chest of drawers into a Glad trash bag. While his back was to the door, Greg glanced quickly around. The Navajo rug his friend had bought on a visit to Santa Fe had been rolled and propped in a corner. The covers on the bed were missing except for one rumpled sheet and a bare pillow. The lampshade . . . the lampshade! Crumpled on the floor. Looked stomped. This frightened Greg more than any of the other evidence that his friend was losing it. Greg couldn't guess the import of the crushed lampshade unless Jeff meant to live in the unprotected glare of a light bulb.

This was decidedly going too far. He must intervene the way they taught at the hospital outpatient alcohol clinics. Sometimes people had to intervene and risk getting their asses kicked if they saw someone they loved descending into perilous territory.

Now Jeff was methodically discarding his clothes. Would he go naked?

Jeff finally chose to keep two, rather than three, pairs of jockey shorts. All he needed was a change while one was washed and drying. He bundled up the rest of the underwear into his arms and turned, ready to stuff it all into the rapidly filling bag. He saw Greg in the door.

"Hey there. You know what? I've been thinking about you and how you're pulling those double shifts. It's crazy, man. It's *unenlightened*. I *told* you what Thoreau said about luxuries and comforts. Wanting things is a trap. Once inside the trap, you never get free. The jaws lock down tight. Here you are working sixteen hours straight so you can afford that Camaro you just bought and those nights on the town with your girl and . . ."

"Jeff?"

"Yeah?" He tamped down the clothes in the Glad bag, grinning all the while.

"What did you do with my posters?"

"Oh those. I put them in your room. You really should think about doing away with that kind of stuff. It just drags you down, drags you down."

"Jeff, I think it's time you saw someone. Dr. Bronsky over at Bayshore's pretty good. I'll get him to give you a professional discount and . . ."

"Fuck you!"

Vehement. Aggressive. Even Jeff's good-natured temperament was rapidly vanishing.

"C'mon Jeff, I'm serious. This is getting way out of hand. Look at you. You're throwing away your clothes, for chrissakes."

"Not everything. I'm keeping two pairs of jeans and two shirts. That's all I need. What do I need all these clothes for?"

"For starters, maybe you'd need them for a job. For going to interviews to *get* a job."

"Go away." Jeff turned his back, pulled out the bottom drawer of the chest and hauled out folded summer shorts and sports shirts.

"I can't, Jeff. I have to try to do something."

Jeff halted in his pawing through the drawer. He said quietly, "If you don't go away right now, I won't be responsible for what happens."

"Are you threatening me now?"

"I hear a different drummer, Greg. If you don't hear it, fine, but don't interfere. Now go away."

Jeff didn't want to go, but he didn't want to stay either. He waited only until his friend turned slowly, ominously, and he saw the look of a nervous zealot, the mad, staring look of a monk holding a flame, ready to immolate himself with the cleansing holy fire. Then he knew he must leave. There was nothing he could do. Jeff had ventured too far over the edge and he was falling without a net.

He had to call from the living room, too fearful to tell Jeff anything to his face ever again. "I'm moving out, Jeff." He waited. "Did you hear me? I'm going to pack my shit and I'm outta here. You're sick, Jeff. I'm not staying with you any longer when you won't listen to me, when you won't go for help. You're getting dangerous. Don't you realize that? You've been throwing away stuff for a week."

"Fuck you," he heard Jeff call back furiously. "Fuck you and the Gucci-Rolex-Jaguar-Beverly Hills horse you rode in on. I don't need you around anyway! You're nothing but a prostitute. You sold out the day you were born."

Jeff Castain gradually came to enjoy life again. It seemed as if he had been on a quest for the Grail and found it embedded in the pure clean stone of Thoreau's noble philosophy. He had been walking through trash, stumbling, lost, and now he could see the path before him.

He read: "Some circumstantial evidence is very strong, as when you find a trout in the milk." From this he deduced that Greg's leaving was ordained; it helped him unearth order in a disorderly universe. He had never loved him or anything, not really, not truly. They were just friends for a while, and who cared if he turned out to be a traitor to all that was good and right and just? So what if he proved to be the Asshole of the World, the turncoat, the Philistine?

The apartment was shaping up. Looking good. He rubbed his palms together in contentment. In the living room he'd gotten rid of everything but one kitchen straight-backed chair, an unadorned fruit crate from the Safeway, and his precious copy of *Walden*.

In the kitchen he'd thrown out everything but one

plate, one spoon, one knife, one pan. He ate from cans mostly so what was the point of owning dinnerware and drawers full of silverware and cabinets full of cooking utensils? He saw his landlady scuttle to the dumpster and take the electric grill and the popcorn popper. Stupid, lazy old bitch. Frivolous, frowzy pack rat.

His bedroom was a spare cell now and he loved it. It was a helluva chore to lug the bed from the apartment down the stairs and out back to the dumpster, but, sweating and swearing, he'd managed. The floor was immensely more comfortable after a few nights. He hardly ached at all anymore when he woke. He thought the Spartan idea converged well with Thoreau's philosophy so he incorporated it into his new life modality.

He had the phone company disconnect his telephone at week's end. Greg kept calling and the job agencies too. What a fucking nuisance; what a bore. He didn't need a job. His needs were too few to demand a real income. When the unemployment checks ran out, he'd apply for welfare. If they wouldn't let him have it, he'd go on the streets. It meant nothing to him one way or the other.

Thoreau said: "I never found the companion that was so companionable as solitude."

Jeff embraced that to mean he must let the world flow past. In the apartment, on the street, wherever he found himself, it didn't matter. He carried solitude with him like an envelope in his pocket and no one could divest him of it ever again. They didn't even know he *had* it!

He patted his shirt pocket as if solitude really were a thing of dimension and weight and it belonged to him alone.

It was not until a month later that Jeff found the quote that would change his life and get him down to the nub of existence. He'd still been searching for the place next to the bone, scraping and scraping away society's frills until he could feel the knife screeching somewhere far off in the dim nether reaches of the fog that had come to surround his days.

"There are a thousand hacking at the branches of evil to one who is striking at the root."

That is what he came upon in his diligent study and

when he found it, he new then he was nearly home free through the twilight of his ignorance. He heard clarion bells ringing on the reading aloud of that sentence. He shivered with anticipation at the coming understanding that crept forth from the dark corner shadows of his barren apartment. That understanding, when it took him, would rend the foundations of his misery and bring him down to the bone, down past the slime and corruption— the gate!—of flesh that barred the way.

"Hello, Mrs. Whipshaw."

"Jeff, how nice of you to visit. Won't you come in?"

The old woman who had nabbed the grill and the popcorn popper from the trash dumpster let her tenant inside the dank, birdshit-splattered living room. A white cockatiel flew through the air in protest, wings flapping wildly.

"Pay no attention to Potto. He's a spoiled brat and isn't used to polite company. Hush, Potto! Behave now."

Jeff declined to sit in the newspaper-covered chintz chair Mrs. Whipshaw gestured he take. He stood with his hands behind his back, smiling. Smiling the stiff smile of the Buddha, the smile of the Inscrutable. His gaze flicked around the room and soon his smile evaporated, was replaced by a sneer of disgust. White smears of Potto's crap covered the drapes, dripped down the neck of a brass table lamp, lay in dried yellow-streaked plops on top of the furniture. It looked as if an insane painter had come, and in a frenzy, swung a wet brush around and around to create a barbarous nightmare of interior decoration.

"I haven't seen you out of your apartment in ever so long," Mrs. Whipshaw said, shooing the contentious bird from her shoulder.

Jeff watched the cockatiel closely to see where it might light down. It hung upside down from the silent dust-layered ceiling fan and screeched at him, one eye cocked in his direction. "I haven't been out much," Jeff said, once reassured the bird was not coming to him.

He felt a nausea rising and had to swallow bitter gorge. It tasted of the kidney beans he'd consumed the night before. *Sickening. Eating—an odious habit. Made*

*people into worms. Scoop it in, shit it out, round and
round she goes, where she stops no one knows . . .*

"What happened to your nice friend, that Greg boy?
Did he really move out?"

"Posters," Jeff said by way of explanation.

"What's that, dear?"

Jeff crossed the room, his eye trained on the bird as
he came for Mrs. Whipshaw with the one knife he'd
saved for cutting tough meat.

Disposing of the bodies. Now Thoreau never gave advice about that sort of thing. Damn odd. He knew about
everything else, you'd think the man would have left
some sort of road map. Jeff had to ponder the situation
for two days before he could decide what to do. He had
Mrs. Whipshaw and Potto cooling in the huge freezer
she kept, strangely enough, in the spare bedroom of her
ground-floor apartment.

He had the occupant of the other downstairs apartment, that punky-looking George with the orange and
green blotch in his hair, stuffed over double at the waist
in his broom closet. (Cluttered, cluttered. Baseball mitts,
bats, skates, pool cues, bowling balls, smelly running
shoes.)

He had James, the quiet law student, in the bathtub
in the apartment on the second floor. He sat shriveling
like an old, fat potato with a radio in his lap. Pity it
wasn't a law manual, though what good that would do
him now Jeff couldn't guess.

He had the Danju sisters waiting in their beds. Nice
girls. Not a bother in the world, but the way they lived,
unbelievable! Frozen dinner trays growing mold, magazines littering the carpet, dust balls and trailing spider
webs and filmy bikini panties hanging everywhere. It was
enough litter to turn the stomach. It took Jeff all night
just to get their apartment under some kind of control.
He cursed them with every name in the book, nice girls
or not. Anyone living like a pig needed to be called
a swine.

Old man Shorer was no trouble at all. He was all bent
and crippled by arthritis. He couldn't run, he couldn't
even crawl, not toward the last. Cried, though. Cried like

a fucking baby. And him old as the hills, didn't make proper good sense to Jeff, but there it was. A man who chose to live with a cat that scratched out shit-ball litter every time he used the box had to be some kind of nut to begin with. Everyone knew you could get terminal diseases from cats. Jeff had saved Shorer a prolonged and, no doubt, much more painful death.

Now to dispose of the bodies. Without Thoreau's help. Without his wisdom or guidance.

And to return the apartment house—the entire building—to neat, impersonal harmony. It would take boxes and boxes of Glad trash bags, dozens of cardboard boxes from the Safeway. A wheelbarrow!

Yes, he would need a wheelbarrow.

He hoped the dumpster wasn't full tonight. He would be taking numerous loads to it. His heart sang with freedom. He was at last seeing the very edge of the pristine bone, a flicker of purity, and it was a glorious glimpse of paradise. Heaven itself.

He heard the pounding of feet coming up the stairs before he ever heard knocking on the door. He was tired, sweaty, needed a shower cold and long. He peeked through the viewer and saw the intruder into this place of calm and peace was the treasonous poster man, Greg.

Figured.

"Jeff?" Greg called, his face pressed against the door. "Let me in."

Jeff unbolted the lock and swung wide the door, turning away and walking across the room as he did so.

"Jeff?" There was a pregnant pause. Then: "What the hell? What did you do with all the furniture? Jesus."

Jeff wore only a pair of grimy shorts. His hair stuck out on end as if he'd been sleeping. And not washing. He was covered with dirt and smudges that looked like tar or oil. "What do you want now?"

"I've been worried about you. I tried to call, but the operator told me the phone was disconnected."

"So?"

"Well ... uh ... how are you?"

"What do you care? You vamoosed for a decadent life-style, didn't you? You want to be featured on 'The

Rich and Famous' one day, don't you? So why would you care?"

Greg cleared his throat. He looked like a weasel caught in a hole. The criticism, however exaggerated, was a little too close to home. "Did you ... did you find work?"

Jeff chortled unpleasantly. "Go away, Greg. I have nothing to say to you." He left the room and disappeared into the darkened hallway.

Greg followed close behind. "Jeff, wait. I really mean it, I'm still worried. How are you paying the rent? Are you eating? I could help, you know. I haven't really abandoned you."

"No rent. Mrs. Whipshaw said so. Dear old lady, dear old bird lady." Jeff went directly into the hall bath and stepped into the tub. He slipped out of his shorts and threw them on the floor. He turned on the shower, drew the curtain.

"No rent?"

"Rent free," Jeff said above the roar of the water. "Ask her yourself."

"Maybe I will."

The shower curtain snapped open and droplets of water flew in the air, spotting Greg's face. "No, you won't. Don't you dare. You stay out of my business affairs. You're no longer in my life, remember? You wanted your fucking posters and your soft cushions and your steak and potatoes. Remember?"

"Jeff, can't you talk with me without fighting? Can't you see your way clear to be reasonable?"

Jeff shut the curtain. He sudsed down his body and scrubbed himself hard with the washcloth. Finally he said, in as sane and sensible a tone as he could muster, "Let me get through here and I'll take you on a tour of my new orderly world."

Full of misgivings, Greg lowered the toilet seat and sat down to wait. This time he had to do something before he left. This time it was absolutely imperative he not leave Jeff alone with his warped delusions. He had known him too long not to try to help.

Jeff finished bathing, dried, dressed himself quickly in jeans and shirt and sneakers.

"I've seen the place, Jeff. You got rid of everything. This looks like a prison."

"Not a prison, a sanctuary. A man has to begin at home. Then ..." he glanced slyly at Greg "... he branches out."

"I don't think you're going to find very many followers. Not many people want to join a cult that denies all possession." Greg laughed uneasily, but soon quieted when Jeff walked past him to the front door.

"Well? Come on. I want to show you how I've hacked at the chaos and brought it under supervision. I want to show you what can be done when you simplify your life, when all the extraneous is ruthlessly cut away down to the very roots where the trouble lies."

Jeff took his friend to Mrs. Whipshaw's freezer first thing. They walked together through the scrupulously cleaned empty apartment to the spare bedroom.

When the stunned, horrified remonstration began, it was a beast of a battle to get Greg subdued enough to shut his mouth.

To shut his mouth forever.

Less than a week passed after Greg's visit before Jeff wandered through the silenced apartment house in the middle of the night saying good-bye to his perfectly balanced world.

People had come to inquire. Mrs. Whipshaw's son screamed that he'd be back with the police. He would see his mother, goddamnit, if he had to bring in the National Guard to do it. She never would have left town without telling him, he claimed from the bottom of the apartment steps. Don't tell him she would.

The boyfriend of one of the Danju sisters left without a squawk, but as he went to his car, he kept squinting suspiciously over his shoulder.

Two law school students stopped by to ask why their friend had not been to classes. Sick? They hadn't heard from him. Too sick to call them? Contagious? Wasn't that funny, though, he always seemed in such good health.

Yes, it was time to go. As much as he hated to. He had invested a ridiculous amount of time in creating order, in simplifying the complex. It was a shame, terribly unjust, that he must flee what was an almost perfect creation.

Yet ... yet ... An apartment house in the center of a seedy district inside of an abhorrently chaotic big city was no real place for him, anyway. He needed his own Walden Pond. He needed to escape to the wilds, sequester himself away from the mad, clattering, bruising world.

With the money Greg and the apartment dwellers had on their persons or in their possession, Jeff took a bus from Houston to the dry West Texas town of Midland. Once there, he hired a taxi driver to take him into the desert.

"Where?"

"Where no one lives," Jeff said, waving money in the man's face.

"Are you nuts? How are you gonna get back? No phones out there, buddy. Nothing but snakes and tumbleweeds, sand and cactus. You can't go out there."

"A friend's meeting me later in his car, if it's any of your business. I'll come back with him. Now will you drive?"

He drove. For two hours. Blabbering all the way, bitching about the heat, the absurdity of this, the kooks he ran into, what a job.

Jeff ignored him in favor of reading, for the dozenth time, from *Walden*. He knew exactly what he was doing. He knew now where the bone glistened most cleanly. It was not in the woods where Thoreau had hidden away himself. It was not in the mountains where shady towering presences safeguarded the timorous. It was not in the lush valleys where Nature rioted and the senses were overwhelmed.

It was in the plain open desert, the place man had not yet desecrated with his two-bit palaces and his glittering signs and his bubbling, stinking tarmac laid end to end, forever and amen.

It was here, in the steaming heart of untrodden, forgotten land, that Jeff Castain knew he would find the ultimate simplification. He wanted that more than breath itself.

"This buddy of yours don't show up in time, you could have a sunstroke out here without water. I tell ya, this is the craziest thing I've ever seen," the cabby complained. "I don't like it none-a-bit. I ain't gonna be responsible for you dying out here, you know, a hundred-five in the shade, if there *was* any shade. I been trying to talk you outta this, ain't that right?"

Jeff failed to answer except to say, "Pull over here. This is where I get out."

Even before the taxi made a U-turn on the infrequently traveled two-lane highway, Jeff was already heading off across the hard packed sands. He moved west toward the lowering sun, Thoreau's book clutched tightly in hand.

Heat mirages blinked on and off in the distance like defective pale blue neon tubes. A lone vulture rode the high currents, a dot in the scalding blue sky. Here was soul. Here was where eternity sat down to shake hands with creatures courageous enough to come unfettered.

Jeff Castain looked back only once to make certain he was losing sight of the long black strip of highway. To make sure he was leaving civilization behind. He thought now it had never belonged to him. That world was under rule of someone else. Someone other. Alien.

He lost all sense of time when day segued into night into day into night. He stumbled and dropped the book; picked it up, surprised to see his hands blistered black, but never mind, never mind.

Finally his tongue swelled in his mouth and hung over his cracked lips like a fat gray slug. His lungs, a fiery bellows, labored to keep him going. His eyes had swollen to slits, blocking the blazing red disk of sun. His skin—his clothes at some past time discarded—seeped clear fluid from pustules that he split apart between pinched fingers.

Each passing second he could feel the loosening of the hold the world had on the flesh. He was a dragon whose scales fell clattering at his feet. Each faltering, dragging step he managed to take brought him ever nearer the crux of reality. Ever closer to the bone.

He yearned. He begged. He prayed. In the end, he

raged. "Didn't I sacrifice enough?" He yelled across the endless sand. "Didn't I scrape past all the filth?"

He pulled on his sack of skin until he tore off pieces and had ripped an ear from his skull. He went to his knees and screamed soundlessly.

At last he could hear a velvety voice hissing across the still air as it approached. He was almost home, it said.

He bowed his head in relief and wept bloody tears.

Come, it said. Nearer, it said. Where life is simple, life is true. Where no one knows you, no one cares, and nothing can get you back again.

Come now. Where you belong, it said.

Ever closer.

Come with me.

Where life is sweetest.

Near the bone.

Near the white, white
bone . . .

Slasher

F. Paul Wilson

I saved the rage.

I let them bury my grief with Jessica. It cocooned her in her coffin, cushioned her, pillowed her head. There it would stay, doing what little it could to protect her from the cold, the damp, the conqueror worm.

But I saved the rage. I nurtured it. I honed it until its edge was fine and tough and sharp. Sharp enough to cut one day through the darkness encrusting my soul.

Martha was on the far side of the grave, supported by her mother and father and two brothers—Jessie's grandparents and uncles. I stood alone on my side. A few friends from the office were there, standing behind me, but they weren't really with me. I was alone, in every sense of the word.

I stared at the top of the tiny coffin that had remained closed during the wake and the funeral mass because of the mutilated state of the little body within. I watched it disappear by tiny increments beneath a growing tangle of color as sobbing mourners each took a turn at tossing a flower on it. Jessica, my Jessica. Only five years old, cut to ribbons by some filthy rotten stinking lousy—

"Bastard!"

The grating voice wrenched my gaze away from the coffin. I knew that voice. Oh, how I knew that voice. I looked up and met Martha's hate-filled eyes. Her face was pale and drawn, her cheeks were black with eyeliner that had flowed with her tears. Her blond hair was masked by her black hat and veil.

"It's your fault! She's dead because of you! You had

her only every other weekend and you couldn't even pay attention to her! It should be *you* in there!"

"Easy, Martha," one of her brothers told her in a low voice. "You'll only upset yourself more."

But I could see it in his eyes, too—in everybody's eyes. They all agreed with her. Even I agreed with her.

"No!" she screamed, shaking off her brother's hand and pointing at me. "You were a lousy husband and a lousier father. And now Jessie's dead because of you! *You!"*

Then she broke down into uncontrollable sobbing and was led off by her parents and brothers. Embarrassed, the rest of the mourners began to drift away, leaving me alone with my dead Jessie. Alone with my rage. Alone with my guilt.

I hadn't been the best father in the world. But who could be? Either you don't give them enough love or you overindulge them. You can't seem to win. But I do admit that there were too many times when something else seemed more important than being with Jessie, some deal, some account that needed attention right away, so Jessie could wait. I'd make it up to her later—that was the promise. I'd play catch-up next week. But there wouldn't be any later. No more next weeks for Jessica Santos. No catching up on the hugs and the playing and the I-love-yous.

If only . . .

If only I hadn't left her on the curb to go get her that goddam ice cream cone.

We'd been watching the Fourth of July fireworks down at the harborfront. Jessie was thrilled and fascinated by the bright flashes blooming and booming in the sky. She'd wanted an ice cream, and being a divorced daddy who didn't get to see her very often, I couldn't say no. So I carried her back to the pushcart vendor near the entrance to Crosby's Marina. She couldn't see the fireworks from the end of the line so I let her stand back by the curb to watch while I queued up. While she kept her eyes on the sky, I kept an eye on her all the time I was on line. I wasn't worried about someone grabbing her—the thought never entered my mind. I just didn't want her wandering into the street for an even better view. The only time I looked away was when I placed the order and paid the guy.

When I turned around, a cone in each hand, Jessie was gone.

No one had seen anything. For two days the police and a horde of volunteers combed all of Monroe and most of northern Nassau County. They found her—what was left of her—on the edge of old man Haskins's marshes.

A manhunt was still on for the killer, but with each passing day the trail got colder.

So now I stood by my Jessica's grave under the obscenely bright sun, sweating in my dark suit as I fought my guilt and nurtured my hate, praying for the day they caught the scum who had slashed my Jessica to ribbons. I renewed the vow I had made before—the guy was never going to get to trial. I would find a way to get to him while he was out on bail, or even in jail, if it came to that, and I would do to him what he'd done to my Jessica. And then I would dare the courts to find a jury that would convict me.

When everyone was gone, I said my final good-bye to Jessie. I'd wanted to erect a huge angelic monument to her, but Tall Oaks didn't allow that sort of thing. A little plaque would have to suffice. It didn't seem right.

As I turned to go, I noticed a man leaning against a tree a hundred feet or so away. He was watching me. As I started down the grassy slope, he began walking too. Our paths intersected at my car.

"Mr. Santos?" he said.

I turned. He was a big man, six-two at least, mid-forties, maybe two-fifty, with most of it settled around his gut. He wore a white shirt under a rumpled gray suit. His thinning brown hair was slick with sweat. I looked at him but said nothing. If he was another reporter—

"I'm Gerald Caskie, FBI. Can we talk a minute?"

"You found him?" I said, my spirits readying for a leap. I stepped closer and grabbed two fistfuls of his suit jacket. "You've got him?"

He pulled his jacket free of my grasp.

"We can talk in my car. It's cooler."

I followed about fifty yards along the curving asphalt

path to where a monotone Ford two-door sedan waited in the shade of one of the cemetery's eponymous trees. The motor was running. He indicated the passenger side. I joined him in the front seat of the Ford. The air conditioner was blasting. It was freezing inside.

"That's better," he said, adjusting one of the vents to blow directly on his face.

"All right," I said, unable to contain my impatience any longer. "We're here. Tell me: Do you have him?"

He looked at me with basset-hound brown eyes.

"What I'm about to tell you is off the record, agreed?"

"What are you—?"

"Agreed? You must never reveal what I'm about to tell you. Do I have your word as a man that what I tell you will never go beyond this car?"

"No. I have to know what it's about, first."

He shifted in his seat and put the Ford in gear.

"Forget it. I'll drive you back to your car."

"No. Wait. All right. I promise. But enough with the games, already."

He threw the gearshift back into park.

"This isn't a game, Mr. Santos. I could lose my job, even be brought up on criminal charges for what I'm going to tell you. And if you do try to spill it, I'll deny we've ever met."

"What is it, goddam it?"

"We know who killed your daughter."

The words hit me like a sledge to the gut. I felt almost sick with relief.

"Have you got him? Have you arrested him?"

"No. And we won't be. Not for some time to come."

It took a while for the words to sink in, probably because my mind didn't want to accept them. But when it did, I was ready to go for his throat. I reined in my fury, however. I didn't want to get hit with assault and battery on a federal officer. At least not yet.

"You'd better explain that," I said in a voice barely above a whisper.

"The killer is presently a protected witness in an immensely important federal trial. Can't be touched until all the testimony is in and we get our conviction."

"Why the hell not? My daughter's death has nothing to do with your trial!"

"The killer's a psycho—that's obvious. Think how a child-killing charge will taint the testimony. The jury will throw it out. We've got to wait."

"How long?"

"Less than a year if we lose the case. If we get a conviction, we'll have to wait out all the appeals. So we could be looking at five years, maybe more."

Cool as it was in the car, I felt a different kind of cold seep through me.

"Who is he?"

"Forget it. I can't tell you that."

I couldn't help it—I went for his throat.

"Tell me, goddam it!"

He pushed me off. He was a lot bigger than I—I'm just a bantam-weight accountant, one-fifty soaking wet.

"Back off, Santos! No way I'm going to give you a name. You'll have it in all the papers within hours."

I folded. I crumpled. I turned away and pressed my head against the cool of the side window. I thought I was going to cry, but I didn't. I'd left all my tears with Jessie.

"Why did you tell me any of this if you're not going to tell me his name?"

"Because I know you're hurting," he said in a soft voice. "I saw what you did to that reporter on TV."

Right. The reporter. Mel Padner. My claim to fame. As I walked out of the morgue after identifying Jessica's tattered body, I was greeted by an array of cameras and reporters. Most of them kept a respectful distance, but not Padner. He stuck a mike in my face and asked me how I felt about my daughter's death. I had the microphone halfway down his throat before they pulled me off him. His own station never ran the footage, but all the others did, including CNN. I was still getting cards and telegrams telling me how I should have shoved it up Padner's other end instead.

"And this is supposed to make me feel better?" I said to Caskie.

"I thought it would. Because otherwise the weeks and months would go on and on with no one finding the killer, and you'd sink deeper and deeper into depression.

At least I know I would. I've got a daughter myself, and if anything ever happened to her like . . . well, if anything happened to her, that's the way I'd feel. I just thought I'd try to give you some peace of mind. I thought you'd be able to hang in there better knowing that we already have the killer in a custody of sorts, and that, as one father to another, justice will be done."

I turned and stared at him. It's a comment on our age, I suppose, that decency from a stranger is so shocking.

"Thanks," I said. "Maybe that will make a difference later when I think about it some. Right now all I'm thinking is how I want to take the biggest, sharpest carving knife I can find and chop this guy into hamburger."

He raised his right fist with the thumb stuck in the air.

"I hear you, Mr. Santos."

"Call me Pete."

"I'm Gerry. And if the government didn't need the testimony so desperately, I might be tempted to do it myself."

We shook hands, then I got out of the car and walked around to his side. He rolled the window down.

"Thanks again," I said. "You didn't have to do this."

"Yes, I did."

"Sure you won't tell me his name?"

He smiled. "These are some *bad* dudes we want to put away with this trial. But don't you worry. Once all the legal proceedings are over, justice will be done." Again, the thumbs-up sign. "We'll see to it that she gets what's coming to her."

And then he drove away, leaving me standing on the path, gaping.

Her?

It wasn't working.

The day after Jessica's body was found, I went back to my apartment—Martha got the house, so I've been living in a two-bedroom box at the Soundview condos—and trashed the place. All except Jessica's room. The second bedroom had been reserved exclusively for Jessie. I went in there and with a black magic marker drew the outline of a man on one of her walls. Then I took the biggest carving knife I could find and attacked that figure. I slashed at the wallboard, driving the blade through it again and again until I was exhausted. Only then was I able to get some sleep.

I'd done that every night since Jessica's death, but tonight it wasn't working.

Caskie's last words were driving me crazy.

My little Jessica had been slashed to ribbons by a woman? A *woman*? I couldn't believe it. It gnawed at my insides like some monstrous parasite. I couldn't work, couldn't eat, couldn't sleep. The FBI knew who'd killed my Jessica and they weren't telling. I had to know, too. I needed a name. A face. Somewhere to focus this rage that was coloring my blood and poisoning every cell in my body.

A woman! Caskie must have been mistaken. Jessica had been—I retched every time I thought of it—sodomized. A woman couldn't do that.

I lasted two days—and two nights—of heartlessly attacking the male figure outlined on her wall. Then I acted.

First thing in the morning, I took a trip to the nearest FBI office. It was on Queens Boulevard in Rego Park. I knew I'd given agent Caskie my word, but ... my daughter ... her killer ... no one could expect me to hold to that promise. No one!

I was in the lobby of the FBI building, searching the directory, when I heard a voice to my left.

"What the hell are you doing here?"

I turned. It was Caskie. I stepped toward him with my hand extended.

"Just the man I was looking—"

"Don't talk to me!" he hissed, staring across the lobby. "Get out of here!"

"No way, Caskie. Your people know who killed my daughter and they're going to tell me, or I'm going to the papers."

"You trying to ruin me?"

"No. I don't want that. But if I have to, I will."

He was silent for a moment, then he made a noise like a cross between a sigh and a growl.

"Shit! Meet me outside. Around the corner in the alley. Ten minutes."

He walked away without waiting for my reply.

*   *   *

The alley was long and narrow, blocked at the far end by a ten-foot cyclone fence. I waited near its mouth, keeping to the shady side. Mid-morning and already it was getting hot. Caskie showed up a few minutes later. He walked by as if he hadn't noticed me, but he spoke out of the corner of his mouth.

"Follow me. I don't want to be seen with you."

I followed. He led me all the way back to the rear of the building. When we rounded a rancid-smelling dumpster, he turned, grabbed me by the front of my shirt, and threw me against the wall. I was caught by surprise. The impact knocked the wind out of me.

"What the fuck do you think you're doing here?" he said through clenched teeth.

I was ready to take a shot at his jaw but the fury in his eyes made me hesitate. He looked ready to kill.

"I told you," I said. "I want to know who killed my daughter. And I'm going to find out."

"No way, Santos."

I looked him in the eye.

"What're you going to do? Kill me?"

He seemed to be considering it, and that made me a little nervous. But then his shoulders slumped.

"I'm so fucking *stupid*!" he said. "I should have minded my own business and let you stew for a year or two. But no, I had to try to be Mr. Goodguy."

I felt for him. Actually, I felt like a shit, but I wasn't going to let that stop me.

"Hey, look," I said. "I appreciate what you tried to do, but it just didn't work the way you thought it would. Instead of easing my mind, it's done just the opposite. It's made me crazy."

Caskie's expression was as bleak as his voice.

"What do you want, Santos?"

"First off, I want to know why you said the killer was a 'she' the other day?"

"When did I say that? I never said that."

"Oh, yes, you did. As you drove off. And don't tell me I misunderstood you, because I didn't. You said, 'We'll see to it that *she* gets what's coming to *her*.' So how could Jessie's killer have been a woman if they're tracing the killer through DNA analysis of the semen they found in ...." My stomach lurched.

Caskie's smile was grim and sour.

"You think the Bureau can't get a local coroner to change his report for matters of security? Wake up, Santos. That was put in there to make sure no one ever has the slightest doubt that they're looking for a male."

I wanted to kill him. Here I'd spent nearly a week believing Jessica had been raped before she was slashed up. And it had never happened. But I kept calm.

"I want her name."

"No way."

"Then I go to the *Times,* the *Post,* and the *News*! Right now!"

I turned and began walking up the alley. I'd gone about ten feet when he spoke.

"Ciullo. Regina Ciullo."

I turned.

"Who is she?"

"Bruno Papillardi's ex-girlfriend."

That rocked me. Bruno Papillardi. New York City's number-one crime boss. His racketeering trial had been in the papers for months.

"Is she that important to the case?"

"The way the judge is tossing out our evidence left and right, it looks like she's going to be the *whole* case. She may be a psycho, but she's not dumb. She made recordings while she and Bruno were in bed together. Seems that when all the grunting and groaning is done, Bruno tends to brag. There's one particularly juicy night where he talks about how he personally offed a Teamsters local boss who wouldn't play ball. With Regina Ciullo's testimony, we might be able to nail him for more than racketeering. We might get him for murder-one."

I didn't care about Papillardi. I cared about only one person.

"But Jessica ... why?"

Caskie shook his head.

"I don't know. I'm not a shrink. But I know your daughter wasn't the first. Regina Ciullo's done at least two others over the past two years. The others were just never found."

"Then how do you—?"

"She told us. She gave us the slip on the Fourth. She returned the following morning around three. We found the knife in the backseat of the car. We made the connection, put the pressure on her, and she told us. We'd always known she was weird but ..." He shuddered. "We never realized ..."

I wanted to run from the alley, but I had to see this through.

"So you can see our dilemma," Caskie went on. "We can't turn her in. At least not yet. Papillardi's people are combing the whole Northeast for her. If she's arrested she won't survive her first night in jail. And if by some miracle she does, her lawyer will immediately enter an insanity plea, which will destroy the value of her testimony against Papillardi."

I swallowed. My throat was gritty.

"Where are you keeping her?"

"Are you kidding? I tell you so you can go out there and try to do a Rambo number on her? No way."

"I don't want to kill her."

"That's not what you said the other day at the cemetery."

I smiled. It must have been a hideous grimace because I saw Caskie flinch.

"I was upset then. A little crazy. I couldn't stick a knife in someone. Besides, I already have enough information now to kill her. If I want her dead, I can call Papillardi and tell him she's in Monroe. He'll do the rest. But I don't want that. I just want to know what she looks like. I want to see a picture of her. And I want to know where she lives so I can drive by every once in a while and make sure she's still there. If I can do that, I can survive the wait."

He was studying me. I hoped I'd been convincing. I prayed he'd buy it. But actually, I hadn't left him much choice.

"She's staying on Shore Drive in Monroe."

I couldn't restrain myself.

"In my hometown? You brought a child killer to my home town?"

"We didn't know about her then. But believe me, she won't get out of our sight again. She's hurt her last kid."

Damn right! I thought.

"I want to see her file."

"I can't get that—"

"You will," I said, turning. "And by tonight. Or I'll be on the phone. Bring it to my apartment."

I didn't give him my address. I was sure he already had it.

Back in my apartment, I took the magic marker and enhanced the drawing on Jessica's wall with a few details. I added a skirt. And long flowing hair styled in a flip. Then I picked up the knife and went to work with renewed vigor.

Caskie showed up around ten P.M., smelling like a leaky brewery, a buff folder under his arm. He brushed by me and tossed the folder onto the living-room table.

"I'm dead!" he said, pulling off his wilted suit jacket and hurling it across the room. "Two more years till my pension and now I might as well kiss it all good-bye!"

"What's the matter?"

"*That's* what's the matter!" he said, pointing at the folder. "When that turns up missing, the Bureau will trace it to me and put my ass in a sling! Nice guys really do finish fucking last!"

"Just a minute, now," I said, approaching him but staying out of reach. He looked *very* upset. "Hold it down. If you return it first thing tomorrow morning, who's going to know it was ever missing?"

He stared at me, a blank look on his face.

"I thought you wanted it."

"I want to *look* at it. That's all. Like I told you: just to know where she lives and what she looks like. If the killer's got a name and a place and a face, I can stay sane until the Papillardi trial is over."

As I was speaking, my body had been gravitating toward the folder. I wasn't aware of my legs moving, but by the time I'd finished, I was standing over it. I reached down and flipped the cover open. An eight-by-ten black-and-white closeup of a woman's face stared back at me.

"That's . . . that's her?"

"Yeah. That's Regina Ciullo."

"She's so ordinary."

Caskie snickered.

"You think someone with Bruno Papillardi's bucks and pull is gonna waste his time with someone 'ordinary'? No way. Good-looking babes are falling all over that guy. But Ciullo's weirdness is one of a kind. She's *anything* but ordinary. That's what attracted him." His voice turned serious. "You really mean that about not wanting to take the file?"

"Of course."

I picked up the photo and stared at it. Her irises were dark, the lashes long. Her hair was wavy and long, and very black. Despite strategic angling of the camera, her nose appeared somewhat on the large side. Her lips were full and pouty. She looked thirty-five or so.

Caskie peered over my shoulder.

"That picture's a few years old, when she was going under the stage name of Bloody Mary. Doesn't show any of her body, which is incredible."

" 'Stage name'?"

"Yeah. She used to be a dancer in a specialty club down in SoHo called The Manacle. She'd do a strip while letting a white rat crawl all over her body, and when she was down to the buff, she'd slice its throat and squeeze its blood down her front as she finished her dance." Caskie's expression was sour. "A real sicko, but she sure as hell got to Papillardi. One show and he was hot for her ass. Say, you got any beer?"

I pointed the way to the kitchen as I continued to stare at the photo.

"In the fridge."

This was the killer of dear Jessica. Regina Ciullo. When she tired of slashing rats she went out and found a child. I felt my pulse quicken, my palms become moist. The photo trembled in my grasp, as if she knew I'd be coming for her.

"Where on Shore Drive is she staying?"

Caskie popped the top on a can of Bud as he returned to the living room.

"The Jensen place."

"Jensen! How'd you get her in there?"

The beer can paused inches from his lips.

"You know them?"

"I just know they're rich."

He took a long gulp.

"They are. And they're hardly ever home—at least in this home—except in the spring. They're on a world cruise now. And since Mr. Jensen is a friend of the present administration, and a personal friend of the Bureau's director, he's allowed us to stash her in his mansion. It's a perfect cover. She's posing as Mr. Jensen's niece." He shook his head slowly. "What a place. That's the way to live, I tell you."

The woman who murdered my daughter was living in luxury out on Shore Drive, guarded by the FBI. I wanted to scream. But I didn't. I closed the file and handed it back to Caskie.

"I'll keep the picture," I said. "The rest is all yours."

He snatched the folder away from me.

"You mean it?

"Of course. You'll never hear from me again . . . *unless,* of course, Papillardi is convicted and she isn't indicted. *Then* you'll hear from me. Believe me, you'll hear from me."

I had put on a performance of Barrymore caliber. And Caskie bought it. He smiled like a death-row prisoner who'd just got a last-minute reprieve.

"Don't worry about that, Santos. As soon as Papillardi's case is through, we're on her. Don't you worry about that!" He turned at the door and gave me another of his thumbs-up gestures. "You can take that to the bank!"

And then he was gone.

For a while I stood there in the living room and stared at the picture of Regina Ciullo. Then I took it into Jessica's room and tacked it over the head of the latest outline on the wall. Then I stabbed the figure so hard, so fast, and so many times that there was a football-sized hole in the wall in less than a minute.

A week later the walls of Jessica's room were so swiss-cheesed with holes that there was no space left for new outlines.

Time for the real thing.

I'd been driving by the Jensen place regularly, some-times three times a day. I always kept the photo on the seat beside me, for quick reference in case I saw some-one who resembled Regina Ciullo. I was sure I'd know her anywhere, but it's good to be prepared.

The houses on Shore Drive all qualified as mansions—all huge, all waterfront, facing Connecticut across the Long Island Sound. Although there was always a car or two in the driveway behind the electric steel gate—a Bentley or a Jag or a Porsche Carrera—I never saw anybody.

Until Thursday. I was in the midst of cruising past when I saw the front gate begin to slide open. I almost slammed on the brakes, then had the presence of mind to keep moving. But slowly.

And who pulls out but the bitch herself, the slasher of my daughter, slayer of the last thing in my life that held any real meaning. She was driving the Mercedes. Speeding. She passed me doing at least fifty and still accelerating. On a residential street. The bitch didn't care. The top was down. No question about it. It was her. And she was alone.

Had she given her FBI guardians the slip again? Was she on her way to find another innocent, helpless, trust-ing child to slaughter?

Not if I could help it.

I followed her to the local Gristedes, trailed her as she dawdled along the cosmetics aisle, touching, feeling, sniffing. Probably looking for the means to whore herself up. As ordinary as the photo had been, it had done her a service. In the light of day she was extremely plain. She needed all the help she could get. And her body. Caskie had described it as "incredible." It was anything but that from what I could see. I guess there's no ac-counting for tastes.

I caught up to her in the housewares aisle. That was where they sold the knives. When I saw a stainless steel carving set displayed on a shelf I got dizzy. Visions of Jessica's mutilated body lying on that cold, steel gurney in the morgue flashed before me. A knife like that had ripped her up. I saw Martha's face, the expressions on her brothers' faces—*Your fault! Your fault!*

That did it.

I ripped the biggest knife from the set and spun her around.

"Remember Jessica Santos?" I screamed.

Shock on her face. Sure! No one was supposed to know.

I pretended she was one of the outlines on Jessica's wall. A deep thrust to the abdomen, feeling the knife point hesitate against the fabric of her dress, and then rip through cloth and skin, into the tender innards. She screamed but I didn't let that stop me. I tugged the blade free and plunged it in again and again, each time screaming, "This is for Jessica! This is for Jessica!"

Somebody pulled me free of her and I didn't resist. She'd been slashed like Jessica. The damage was irreparable. I knew my duty was done, knew I'd avenged my daughter.

But as I looked into her dying eyes, so hurt, so shocked, so bewildered, I had the first inkling that I had made a monstrous mistake.

I slammed my fist on the table.

"Call the FBI! Check it out with them!"

They'd had me in this interrogation room for hours. Against the advice of my lawyer—who wanted me to plead insanity—I'd given them a full statement. I wasn't going to hide anything. This was an open-and-shut case of a man taking justifiable revenge against his daughter's murderer. I wasn't going to be coy about it. I did it and that was that. Now they could do their damnedest to convict me. All I needed was the FBI file to prove that she was the killer.

"We *have* called the FBI," said Captain Hall, chief of the Monroe police department. He adjusted his belt around his ample gut for the hundredth time since he'd stuck me in here. "And there's no such agent as Caskie assigned anywhere in New York."

"It's a deep-cover thing! That woman posing as a Jensen is Regina Ciullo, a federal witness against Bruno Papillardi!"

"Who told you that?" Captain Hall said.

"Agent Caskie."

"The agent who doesn't exist. How convenient. When did you meet him?"

I described my encounters with Caskie, from the cemetery to my apartment.

"So you were never in his office—if he ever had one. Did anyone see you with him?"

I thought about that. The funeral had been over and everyone was gone when I'd met him in the cemetery. We'd stood side by side for less than a minute in the foyer of the FBI building, and then we'd been together in the alley and my apartment. A cold lump was growing in my gut.

"No. No one that I recall. But what about the picture? It's got to have Caskie's fingerprints on it!"

"We've searched your car three times now, Mr. Santos. No picture. Maybe you *should* plead insane. Maybe this FBI agent is all in your mind."

"I'm not crazy!"

Captain Hall's face got hard as he leaned toward me.

"Well, then, maybe you should be. I know you've had a terrible thing happen to your family, but I've known Marla Jensen since she was a girl, back when she was still Marla Wainwright. That was poor Marla you sliced up. And what's more, we think we've *found* the killer. The *real* killer."

He had to be wrong! Please God, he had to be! If I did that to the wrong woman—

"No! You got to listen to me!"

A disgusted growl rumbled from Captain Hall's throat.

"Enough of this bullshit. Get him out of here."

"No, wait! Please!"

"Out!"

Two uniformed cops yanked me out of the chair and dragged me into the hall. As they led me upstairs to a holding cell, I spotted Caskie walking in with two other cops.

"Thank God!" I shouted. "Where have you been?"

His face was drawn and haggard. He almost looked as if he had been crying. And he looked *different*. He looked trimmer and he held himself straighter. The rumpled suit was gone, replaced by white duck slacks, a white linen shirt, open at the collar, and a blue blazer with an emblem on the pocket. He looked like a wealthy yachtsman. He stared at me without the slightest hint of recognition.

One of the cops with him whispered in his ear and suddenly Caskie was bounding toward me, face white with rage, arms outstretched, fingers curved like an eagle's talons, ready to tear me to pieces. The cops managed to haul him back before he reached me.

"What's the matter with him?" I said to anyone who'd listen as my two cops hustled me up the stairs.

My attorney answered from behind me.

"That's Harold Jensen, the husband of the woman you cut up."

I felt my knees buckle.

"Her husband?"

"Yeah. I heard around the club that she started divorce proceedings against him, but I guess that's moot now. Her death leaves him sole heir to the entire Wainwright fortune."

With my insides tying themselves in a thousand tight little knots, I glanced back at the man I'd known as Caskie. He was being ushered through the door that led to the morgue. But on the threshold he turned and stole a look at me. As our eyes met, he winked and gave me a secret little thumbs-up.

(Thanks to Joe R. Lansdale on this one.)

To Die For

Ed Naha

Jon Shulman had it all. A transplanted New Yorker who had majored in business, he was now king of the Hollywood hill. Mid-thirties. Hundred-dollar haircuts. Banana Republic outfits. Terminally hip with a flaming red Porsche.

He was a major mover and shaker at Pinnacle Studios.

Although he didn't know his ass from his elbow when it came to people or even stories *concerning* people, he somehow instinctively knew how to make money. Lots of it.

He had skyrocketed to the top within the last three years spewing out movies that just seemed to attract big dollars. *Thanksgiving Carve-Up, Honey: I Slashed the Kids, The Dead Parents' Trap*. Now, he had both Streep and Streisand vying for the lead in *Ghost Mom*. Fuggim. He'd screw them both and hire Midler. People knew him as an unorthodox go-getter. A maverick in the Biz. Why should he disappoint them?

Shulman's chrome and glass office overlooked the best of Burbank. Sometimes, he could even see the freeway through the smog. The short young executive leaned back in his chair, reading the past weekend's grosses in *Daily Variety*. He glanced at the top of his glass desk. In the middle of his stacks of script coverages (he didn't have time to actually read the scripts himself) and high-tech toys sat a portrait of his wife, Melissa, and his son, Bobby.

He smiled to himself, pushing his back deeper into his plush leather office chair. Nice family. He didn't have too much time for them, with his work and his two mistresses but, damn, if they didn't photograph well.

Outside, the sun was setting behind a solid wall of airshit in Burbank. The evening sky was glowing light brown. It was time to go home.

Shulman took his private elevator down to the parking level of his building and, climbing into his Porsche, headed west to Malibu; car phone firmly in hand for the entire drive. There were still deals to be made. Product to be packaged.

As he angled his car homeward, the wind blowing through his laminated, golden hair, he felt a deep pang within what passed for his soul.

"I want," his essence seemed to murmur. "I want *more*."

Shulman chuckled out loud.

He could get all the *more* he desired, these days.

Pulling up into his driveway, the Pacific Ocean crashing meaninglessly onto his front yard, Shulman took a few minutes to prepare himself for his family. Melissa had turned out to be a major drag. She was pretty enough. In fact, she looked ten years younger than her real age. Of course, Shulman paid to keep her that way.

The woman *lived* at Jane Fonda's workout spa on Robertson Boulevard. She had great tits and great buns. Most of the time, however, the woman was totally zoned out. Nose candy. Helped her through the day. Shulman sighed. What the hell, he could afford it. He never took her out in public, anyway. If she was going to be an embarrassment, let her embarrass the maid. Shulman didn't need any extra pressure in his life. His work supplied that quite nicely.

As for Bobby, aged nine? A major pain in the butt. The kid was into ecology and heavy metal, hated school, and, more often than not, had his head buried behind those stupid Nintendo video games that parents who didn't have enough time for their kids bought their kids to keep them occupied.

No wonder Shulman drank at night. His wife was a zombie and his kid a video-voidoid.

The car safely parked inside the garage, Shulman ambled toward the sprawling ranch house along the Pa-

cific Coast Highway. He knew the routine. He'd give
Melissa a peck on the cheek. Say something banal to
Bobby. Have the cook of the week make him a stiff one.
He'd pick at his dinner and divide his attention between
the titles of the scripts he had approved and a list of
whatever smutty films were on cable tonight.

God, how he loved smut.

Beautiful, glistening women screaming out their pas-
sions while they fondled soap in a shower.

Why couldn't real life be like that?

"Dad," Bobby said, interrupting Shulman's reverie.

"Mmmm?"

"My principal wants to see you."

"Can't he see your mother?"

"He's seen Mom. He wants to see *you*."

Shulman grimaced. He wasn't into this domestic stuff.
Bush league. "Okay," he sighed. "Have his people call
my people."

By nine o'clock, Melissa was out cold and Bobby was
upstairs in his bedroom, equipped with a totally awesome video arcade. The little bugger would play until he
dropped off into sleep.

Jon walked into his videotape-laden den and sank into
an immense, and very expensive, black leather couch.
Life was okay, he theorized, but it just didn't quite give
him the buzz he wanted. He flicked on the remote control to his five-foot-square TV. God bless cable, he
thought. Instead of thirteen meaningless channels to flip
through, Jon now had forty or more.

Guzzling another drink, he pressed his left thumb
down on the "change channel" button and, religiously,
flicked through the various, stagnant offerings on the
tube. Reruns of *The Beverly Hillbillies*. *The Best of Mor-
ton Downey, Jr. Surfing Sluts.* He made a note to come
back to that one later. What station had that been on?
HBO? The Playboy Channel? Made no difference. He'd
find it on the next loop.

He continued to plunge through the channels.

"Yuppie larva!" a bronzed announcer enthused. "Have
it all? Want more? This is the commercial for you!"

The announcer winked at the camera, a lush, tropical
paradise behind him.

Jon eased his thumb off the remote, casually interested. He hadn't seen *this* one before.

The commercial announcer, who resembled a slightly muscular Ken doll, continued his spiel. "For *one night* only, Really Rich Toys is offering the *ultimate* in television viewing."

The camera panned back to reveal that the announcer was standing before a wall-sized TV screen. Several scantily clad native girls walked out onto the screen and began doing a dance that hovered somewhere between aerobics and the Kama Sutra.

"Yes, powermongers," the announcer continued, "it's a *one-of-a-kind offer*! A wall-sized, high-definition TV unit! Designed by the rich *for* the rich. Look at this! Can you see any difference on your home screens between *me,* in real life, and these delightful ladies in videoland?"

The announcer turned toward the wall unit. He puckered his lips and leaned forward. One of the dancing girls reached for him and, astonishingly, seemed to grab the man's lips and give him a deep kiss. Tongue and all.

Shulman was getting excited.

The announcer turned toward his viewer. "Yes, my friends, the Really Rich Toys Wall Screen TV puts *you* in the picture!"

One of the women on the wall unit behind him seemingly stroked his hair. The announcer chuckled. "Hey, cut it out!"

"A trick of the eye?" the announcer grinned. "Maybe. But, then again, you'll never know until you *own* one. And, videophiles, we guarantee you that this system, priced at only twenty thousand dollars, will provide you with the type of television viewing you've always dreamed of. I mean, anyone who is *any*one in France already has one and, believe me, the French know what *living* is all about, right?

"*But* . . . it's only being sold for the next twenty-four hours. It's a discreet treat for the elite! Jot down the number that will appear on your screen. If you're tired of real life, try escaping with Really Rich Toys' latest advance in TV tech. Feel like you're part of the big picture."

The announcer flicked a remote. Suddenly, the city of Atlanta was burning, torched by Yankee troops behind him. Rhett Butler would be there soon.

"Whooo," the announcer joked. "It's getting hot in here. But if you like your entertainment in a big way, you'll be hot to trot for this giant advancement. Remember, Really Rich Toy collectors. This big-screen action is to die for! Give us a call. Give us your all. We offer a free, ninety-day warranty. The boob-tube is no longer for boobs! Although you can watch those, too, bigger than life! Until tomorrow night, this is Lance Hobie wishing you pleasant dreams and more toys!"

A phone number appeared on Jon's screen. He jotted it down. Then, without warning, the channel faded from his TV. Jon grabbed his remote and scanned the stations. *Surfing Sluts* returned to the airwaves. Jon frowned as two barely legal-aged girls straddled their surfboards sans swimsuits. Boring, Shulman thought. It wasn't *big* enough for him. It didn't excite him. He wanted *more*. He moved to the den phone and dialed.

"Really Rich Toys," an operator announced.

Shulman smiled. "Hello," he said. "I'd like to order one of your items."

Three weeks later, Jon supervised the delivery of his Brobdingnagian boob tube. Two men who resembled Laurel and Hardy in coveralls lugged the massive, delicate object toward Shulman's home. "Careful there," Jon admonished. "It's breakable."

"So are my nuts," one of the deliverers wheezed.

Jon beamed as the pair of sweating men waddled toward the house.

At that moment, Bobby trotted out of the house. "Dad?"

"What is it, son?" Shulman sighed.

"You still haven't seen my principal."

"Tell him to call the office."

"You haven't returned his calls."

"Then, have Mom call him."

"He wants to see *you*! He said that if you don't show up at school, he's going to show up here. He wants to know what kind of parental supervision I'm getting."

"The best that money can buy. Look at that, son. Isn't that something?" Jon beamed at the massive package being dragged into the house.

"What is it?"

"Only the *ultimate* in TV," Jon enthused.

"I don't get it," Bobby said, casually pushing a skateboard into the rosebushes.

"Watch the flowers, will you?" Shulman admonished.

"Yes, sir."

"That, son, is the biggest high-definition television screen in the *world*."

"Can I watch it when you hook it up?"

"Afraid not, son."

"Awwww."

"But you can have my *old* screen," Shulman said, puffing up his sparrow's chest. "You can have the five-footer."

Bobby was pleased but somehow disappointed. "I can't use the new one *ever*?"

"No, son," Shulman beamed. "This screen is for adults only."

"Can Mom have an opinion about this?" Bobby countered.

Jon smirked. "When was the last time Mom could muster an opinion?"

Bobby sagged under the weight of the truth. "Good point."

He grabbed his skateboard and took off down the congested highway.

Secretly, he hoped he had been adopted. That would explain a *lot*.

That night, after the installation and a few stiff drinks, Jon sat before his wall-sized TV unit. "Do it to me," he whispered, half-soused, picking up the remote control. He flicked the "on" button and he found himself whisked away into a world called television.

The universe before him blinked to life. Three buxom women were doing aerobics on a local cable channel. One of them was particularly buxom.

"God," Jon sighed. "I'd love to have *that* one."

The black-haired, spandex-encased exerciser bumped

and grinded away as a drunken Jon Shulman approached the screen.

"I want to have you," he muttered.

The three woman continued to work out.

Jon continued to shamble forward. "I *want* you," he whispered. "I want you *now!*"

Jon felt himself falling forward. He plunged *into* the screen. He felt the warmth of the screen embrace him. He smelled the sweet sweat of the exerciser. Jon leaped toward her. The woman screamed as she hit the ground. Jon found himself ripping off her clothes. He undid his pants.

The woman screamed as the show continued, Jon now upon her. He plunged into her terrified body. The woman writhed beneath him. Shulman found himself cackling like a madman, finding a rhythm in her protesting movements. Jon bellowed and then withdrew with a smile on his face. He lurched backward from the exercise show and tumbled back into his own den.

"I *did* it," he babbled. "Goddamn! This is great! I can do whatever I want to whomever I want!"

He sank down onto the couch, pulling up his pants, and watched the aerobics show slowly unravel before him.

His victim began screaming, slowly climbing off the studio floor. Her two fellow fitness freaks turned, startled, and ran forward to help the sobbing woman. Jon flicked the channel. Sylvester was chasing Tweetie around Granny's house. Jon chose not to get involved. He checked his *TV Guide*. A rerun of *Charlie's Angels* was due in an hour. He had always wanted Farrah Fawcett to give him head. And now, he knew, she *would*. Money was wonderful.

It was all that mattered.

"Goddamn," he wheezed. "Science. Man! It's wonderful!"

Behind Shulman, in the half-opened doorway leading to the den, little Bobby stood, mesmerized. Was that a bitchin' video tube or what?

Melissa Shulman teetered down the staircase from her bedroom. It was noon. Her husband had taken a week's sick leave, telling the studio his wife was in bad shape.

Melissa, her red hair cascading down onto her shoulders, managed to elicit a snarl. "Hey!" she called, to no one in particular. "Hey! What the hell is happening in this house?"

"Nothing out of the ordinary, dear," Jon smiled, slithering out of his den (after having Ursula Andress in *Dr. No,* Marilyn Monroe in *Some Like It Hot,* and Brigitte Bardot in *And God Created Woman*). "I just decided to spend a little quality time with my family."

Melissa, half zoned-out, nodded dully. "Great. Fine. Have you met with Bobby's principal?"

"Uh, no," Shulman replied. "I thought I'd let Bobby settle that on his own."

"He had all 'F's' last semester, you know," Melissa slurred.

"He didn't tell me *that*!"

"How could he?" Melissa smirked. "You've been glued to that TV for the last week."

"Just another toy," Jon shrugged.

Melissa stiffened. She turned and marched back up to the second floor. "I know. I know," she whispered, sadly.

Shulman watched his wife shamble back toward her bedroom. Nothing more than a worthless zombie. He slowly walked back into his den. "This is my world. This is where I *belong*."

He picked up a copy of *TV Guide*. He perused the pages, sipping from a gin and tonic. "Goddamn. I can have *any* woman I want."

Young Bobby marched home, yet another note from the principal in his hand. He knew what would happen as soon as he delivered it. His father would shrug it off. His mother would cry. He hated to see her unhappy. He hadn't seen her happy since his father had become successful. He said a silent prayer that his principal just wouldn't show up at the house. Bummer. Father a major asshole. Mother permanently living in the Twilight Zone.

He entered the house. Shulman was in the den.

In his headquarters, Jon watched Humphrey Bogart lead Ingrid Bergman toward the plane leaving Casablanca. Shulman sneered as Bogart's Rick turned Bergman loose to her husband.

"I'm saying it because it's true," the trenchcoat-encased Bogart stated. "Inside of us we both know you belong with Victor. You're part of his work, the thing that keeps him going. If that plane leaves the ground and you're not with him, you'll regret it."

Bergman's Ilsa, her tear-stained face turned toward the camera, shook her head no.

Shulman leered. "Now *that's* a high-class fuck," he said. He leaped into the screen, snatching Ilsa from Rick.

Bogart was stunned. "What the hell?"

"I want you!" Shulman yelled to a startled Ilsa. "I want you *now*!!!"

Ilsa screeched and Rick stood immobile in the fog, the plane revving up its engines behind him. "What the hell is going on here?" Rick yelled. "This isn't part of the deal!"

Shulman dragged Ilsa away into the rising damp, to a grassy area near the landing strip. He was going to *have* her. He was going to *have* her in any way he wanted.

Meanwhile, in Malibu, young Bobby entered his father's den. The room was empty. He glanced at the screen, the letter from his principal still in his hand. He saw an actor who looked a little like his father in an old black-and-white movie. The actor was slapping a woman around. Bobby looked this way and that for any sign of his territorial dad.

"This is stupid," Bobby said, grabbing the remote. "I hate black-and-white movies."

"No!" the character resembling his father yelled from the screen. "No!"

The actor scrambled away from the sobbing woman and began to run toward the camera.

"No!!"

Tommy flicked the remote. He scanned the channels. TV on a big screen was no less boring than TV on a small screen. Bobby came to a stop and smiled. A *Friday the 13th* film was on. Bobby eased himself back into his father's couch and watched evil Freddy, the master of the dream world, slither out of a shroud of fog, his metal fingers dripping with blood.

"And now, as for you ..." the scarred slasher Freddy snarled.

Freddy's next victim, a very familiar looking actor, reached out toward his audience.

"For the love of God, son! Change the channel! Change the goddamned channel! It's me! It's me!!!"

Bobby stared at the big screen. He had never seen this scene before.

"Correction," Freddy beamed. "It *was* you!"

Freddy extended his Ripper's hand and slashed the victim over and over and over. The figure spurted blood in gorgeous technicolor and fell out of frame.

Bobby watched, fascinated, as Freddy leaped out of frame as well. Slice. Dice. Slash. Gash.

"It's Daddy, Bobby!" a feeble voice called. "It's Daddy."

Bobby gulped. There was something weird about this movie.

Suddenly, the mutilated face of his father appeared on the screen, emitting one last, dying breath.

"Bobby!!!"

Bobby sat there, frozen. Oh, boy. Was he in big trouble now. Compared to this, his report card was small beer.

Bobby flicked off the TV screen and considered his options.

Michael McGann, the principal of Our Lady of Perpetual Sorrows Junior High School, pounded on the door of the Shulman house.

A very pleased, very defiant Bobby Shulman answered the door.

The fat, gray-bearded schoolmaster gazed down upon him. "I suppose you know why I'm here?"

"I guess so," Bobby noted.

"I want to see your *father* about your appalling grades."

"Right," Bobby nodded.

Bobby turned to the interior of the house. "Maaaa! The principal's here!"

Within seconds, a beaming and decidedly straight Melissa was at the door. "So nice to see you again, Mr.

McGann," she said, brushing back her long red hair. "May I speak with you?"

"I'm afraid not, Mrs. Shulman. We've been through all this before; spoken about Bobby on a half-dozen occasions, with no results. This time, I'm here to see the boy's *father*."

Melissa and Bobby exchanged glances.

Bobby shrugged. "No problem."

Bobby turned toward the innards of the house. "Hey, Dad?"

The principal peered into the house as the door to the den opened. McGann's jaw dropped open as a trench-coated, square-jawed man, cigarette dangling from his lip marched up to the front door.

"Whaddya want?" Bobby's father asked.

"I'm Mr. McGann, Bobby's principal."

"I'm Rick," the father said, extending a hand. "Now, whaddya want?"

Bogart, McGann thought to himself. It's Bogart in the flesh. "I . . . I . . ."

"If it's about the report card," Rick said, exhaling a cloud of smoke into the principal's face, "don't sweat it. Little Bobby here has promised me that he'll do his best from now on. We have an agreement, see? A favor for a favor."

"Yes," the principal said, growing nervous as Rick slowly slid his left hand into a trench-coat pocket. McGann backed toward his car. "I understand. I understand *exactly*. I trust your faith in Bobby will be rewarded."

Rick took another drag from his cigarette. "A deal's a deal. That's all it amounts to."

The principal scuttled into his car and drove away. Melissa grinned at Rick. "Dinner will be ready in ten minutes," she said, disappearing into the house.

"Thanks, babe," Rick said with a nod.

Bobby looked up at Rick. "Thanks, Dad. You saved my life."

Rick wrapped a protective arm around his son and shrugged. "No problem, squirt. Now, tell me about my new car. How fast will it go?"

"The Porsche? A hundred, a hundred and twenty miles an hour."

Rick whistled through his teeth. He grinned through the cigarette smoke. "You know, Bobby? I think this could be the beginning of a beautiful friendship."

Rick and his son eased the front door shut behind them.

And walked into the house and toward the future.

Mistaken Identity

T. L. Parkinson

November moved forward like a spider crawling, black X's marking the days. Two more left, and then the month would be finished, the first November without Paul.

Francine shook the letter in front of the calendar, as though the calendar could see. The lines and dates and her own sometimes faint, sometimes fierce marks blurring through tears, made a smudgy black mess. Moments before it had simply been a month.

The letter, of course, was from Paul.

The mailman crunched down the gravel driveway. She remembered the odd smile he had given her. He knew she was alone. Did he think less of her?

Francine opened the letter. Cool silky paper; elegant, careful handwriting—definitely Paul. Each character, each imagined stroke of his pen, tore away a little of the scar tissue about her heart, allowing bright sharp pain to rise.

Feeling suddenly off balance, she sat down. The room spun about, the letter at the center. She began to read.

> Dear Francine, I have so much to say to you that I can't say it, so I have to write it. I can't stand thinking of you in that cold house alone, while I'm here, away from you. Even though it had to be. I feel so guilty I could burst. I know how sad you must be and how you hide it.

Francine paused, choking back anger and more tears,

walking into the bedroom with the letter held stiffly at her side, like a gun that has just shot someone.

She sat on the bed and waited for the strength to continue. She hated to cry. It was like throwing up—something you had to do when you swallowed something bad, that reminded you of the bad things always, the mistake. I am tired, she thought, of hating myself for loving the wrong man.

"Maybe I should keep this to myself," the letter continued, "but I think I have found happiness, here, finally . . ."

Francine went to the window, opened it. The cold was bracing; a cold burning in her lungs. Outside, it was dark though it was really the middle of the day; clouds unfurled like bolts of black cloth.

There was an odd scraping sound, like boots, coming around the house. She continued to read, trying to ignore it.

Sorry, sorry, sorry. The words merged, melted. Mark? Was that his lover's name?

She beat the air with the letter, as if to fan away the pain. There was a tentative footstep, the cracking of ice, a panicked rush across the recently frozen surface of the pool.

A neighborhood boy, wanting to catch a glimpse of the mysterious swimming pool? She turned to see.

He was there, filling her sight, certainly not a boy, a man and a big man at that, leaping through the window.

Pinned beneath him on the floor, her hands clutched the letter.

Ink merged with sweat and the words ran.

Retreating footsteps, a door gently closing, cold thin wind across her face.

At first she couldn't move. She had no desire to. This stillness could not be violated; she imagined that with the faintest movement something would burst through, a flood of pain, and she would drown.

She counted the ticking of the clock, until the numbers got too big to remember and she lost count; then would start again, at zero. She had always, since a child, started counting at zero, not at one. When her teachers had chastised her, she had changed her outward behavior, but inside she still did it the same.

A steady cold breeze moved across her naked body. She thought she should shut the window; she could hear the furnace humming away against the cold. Such a waste.

But it was not the cold that made her move. Nor was it the waste and futility of the running furnace, when she had so little money to spare.

It was the hand, bursting through her glasslike stillness, slapping her into painful awareness, bringing on a rush of pain that was red like a muddy river and as wild as that river before it tumbled over a waterfall.

She moaned, turned on her side.

"Not again," she said to the man, to the hand, no longer there.

And felt the tiny trickle of blood down her groin, a warm line at first almost pleasant, then terrifying when she realized what it was.

She felt weak and knew she should call for help. She slept the night and woke in a wet bed, barely strong enough to get dressed.

She should call a friend; but she had no words, no explanations, no reasons.

She took a taxi to her family doctor. He lived on the outskirts of town, underneath bare elms nestled between gun-metal gray hills, scoured now of vegetation. The ride cost twelve dollars; she paid the cab driver numbly, refusing to meet his eye.

"You all right, lady?" he asked in his cab-driver voice, leaning darkly over the torn plastic seat.

"No," she said, and got out.

She had packed her groin with cotton; the blood had dried and now pulled at her skin. Also, there were bruises on her milk-white arms, dark spots in circles like clusters of grapes.

She knocked on the door.

"Dr. Junkerman," she said, "I have had an accident." She hobbled in. He led her immediately into his office.

Luminous gray hair, thoughtful calm eyes, he touched her bare arms—she had let her gray cloth coat slip from her shoulders, like a child displaying yet ashamed of a wound. Although he did not recoil from the bruised flesh, as Francine thought he might, thought he should, he touched her tentatively. His eyes seemed emotionless.

It is impersonal, Francine thought, looking at the ceiling, imagining the sky; life is impersonal. What am I doing here?

She was directed, by a soft movement of his graying hands, to a worn leather chair next to a window—his eyes are looking at me with concern, yet there is an accusation behind.

The curtains were dark red, dirty velvet, and had an inner curtain of white, transparent, light-colored. The curtains were not completely closed; a diagonal of light cut the mahogany desk in half, across the leather-bordered paper blotter.

Dr. Junkerman sat down carefully, opened his vest, picked up a fountain pen (as thick as a cigar), and cleared his throat. "Francine, now tell me what has happened."

"I fell," she said. "I fell when I was in the shower, and hurt myself here." She pointed to her groin, where she could feel the dark dry stain.

"You fell—how?"

"I fell on the faucet. I slipped on the soap. I've always been clumsy."

"The bruises on your arm—?"

She stared at him blankly. She had to think fast. She had fallen, a neighborhood boy had helped her up too roughly; she had always bruised easily. But no, she could not tell the doctor that. How would she explain the presence of the boy in the house when she was in the shower? The doctor would think the worst: that she drew these twisted men to her, that it was her fault.

Instead, she pretended she didn't hear the question. She stared at the back of a gold clock on the desk. She stilled her breathing, trying to will invisibility.

The doctor leaned back in his chair and quietly waited. Francine had known him for years. He had been a dear friend of Paul's father, Paul who had left her two years ago, so that things like this could happen.

After a time, the doctor looked at his watch; his

cheeks were turning splotchy red. This happened slowly, over several hundred seconds.

"Francine," he said, his voice deepening like a wind passing over a ravine, "now tell me what's happened to you."

"Nothing, absolutely nothing. I mean—I told you what happened." She felt flustered; she was coming unglued. Would she have to go through it again, in front of someone who had known her since she was a baby? She shriveled at the thought.

"Come over and lie down on the table." He motioned to the shiny steel table, the only modern-looking thing in the office. "I want to examine you. And then maybe you'll tell me about it—trust me enough to tell."

Francine did as she was told, but she thought it was unlikely she would trust him enough to tell—or trust herself enough to hear the words spoken.

All winter long the skies had been smoke colored, the land sepia tinted, and no snow. The ground kept freezing deeper and deeper; walking on it was like walking on rock, deep gray twisted rock on which nothing had ever grown.

Francine thought it would be much nicer if it would snow. Snow blanketed the earth, hiding stone. Snow hid the footprints that led inside.

She walked slowly, trying not to consider Dr. Junkerman's suggestion. He had given her a mild painkiller and cleaned her wounds. She had promised to come back in two days and talk to him some more. She did not think she would go.

She had been lucky, he said. The physical part would heal in time; as for the other, well that was up to her. This was a matter for the police; he would not report it himself because it would do no good. The words had to come from her.

She walked up the curving driveway to the tract house. The grass in the postage-stamp yard was frozen stiff, blue colored; she hated to walk on it. It crunched like breaking bones.

Up the slight incline to the door, carefully, because the sidewalk, which she had forgotten to salt down, was slippery; and her legs must ache, though she could not feel it because of the drug. The pain was there, some-where; she must pay attention.

She took out her key, smiled weakly at her foolish-ness; now remembering. She had not locked the door.

Bursting through into the faintly greasy smelling, unlit interior, she thought: Wouldn't it be strange if the per-son I surprised was me, waiting inside untouched by anything.

But no one was inside.

She lay on top of the covers. The TV station had gone off. A red and blue snowstorm filled the room. Francine felt a tingle on her flesh as the dots danced over her; the feeling was hot, like snow was sometimes when she closed her eyes and forgot what was touching her. She used to fool herself like that when she was a child: The snow is hot, I'm burning up.

She picked up a book but couldn't follow the lines of print; her eyes kept unfocusing and joining the random patterns the TV snow was making.

After a time she started to see a face in the air, in the middle of the room.

The face grew a body, a hard angled body, broad shouldered, narrow hipped. Soon he was full, complete; just standing there, just being. So certain, so full of him-self. He walked slowly toward her, the lamplight glinting from his shiny dry skin, his face tilted down so that she could see only shadows, dark pools, a steadily burning fire beneath.

He looked at her, a hard passionate look. She was shaking, afraid, and she backed into the pillows. He came forward anyway, confidently, as though he knew what she really wanted. He would show her; she would listen.

He reached down with arms hard veined but covered with soft dark hair, and picked her up. Then carefully, slowly, he laid her back down, as though he wanted to show her the proper position for her to accept him.

Then he slid on top of her. He smelled like Dial soap and sweat and something else—an animal smell. She buried her head in his imaginary shoulder, smelled his imaginary smell.

Her racing heart slowed to his slow steady beat; her fear left her. She felt ravished, overpowered. She started to cry a little, and he wiped away her tears, with his soft-hard arm.

The bedroom was now black and gray, snail colored. French provincial bed, throw rug (green in the day), picture of her parents and herself on the bureau.

There in the small pool of light from the pink-shaded lamp, the surface of the picture shimmered, like sunlight on water. Francine walked over to it.

Mother, stern, straight-backed, loving; Francine, next to her, staring at her new shoes (white patent leather; she had waded in deep water the next day, ruining them). Father behind them, a circle of arms, one on Francine's shoulder, the other on her mother's; such long arms. His eyes looked empty, like caves, because (he had said) the photographer had not been any good.

Francine kept the picture, however, because it scared her; and because Father didn't like to have his picture taken, so this was the only one. He had often said, joking, that he believed like the Indians that pictures captured your soul.

When she looked at the eyes, Francine suspected another reason. The emptiness there, the lack of warmth or any feeling, was all too apparent. She remembered his shaking hands, his nighttime pacing, the strange way his face changed from one expression to another, like channels switching. She had to look quick or she missed it.

And his hands: small, feminine fingers shaking like windblown leaves.

She shivered, set the picture down, walked to the window. A frost forest had grown there, day after day thickening. If I were a sleeping princess, she thought, a prince would have a hard time getting through all that yellow cold.

In the night when the wind was high the wind clicked and snapped the glass in the weak aluminum frame, the sound like something suddenly freezing and then being thrust into a fire.

She turned out the light, made her way blindly to the

bed. The cobalt blue air seemed to spill into her, then harden.

As she lowered herself to the mattress she recoiled slightly, then forced herself to relax. She had slept here with Paul for three and a half years. She pressed her face into the linen.

She could still smell Paul's distinctive odor, like vinegar and raked leaves and wind from the lake.

But no, that was impossible. She was fooling herself again.

She said a children's prayer three times, until she began to forget.

". . . and if I die before I wake, I pray the Lord my soul to take . . ."

As she fell asleep, she pieced together a face, out of somewhere, ruddy, square jawed, nose and forehead a single straight line, clear gray eyes.

He had come for her once, shattering her loneliness. Would he return?

She woke at 3:00 A.M. and then again at 4:00. It wasn't completely dark; the cloudy sky cast a pearly light day and night. It seemed the division between the two, this winter, had gotten lost. This was the land of the midnight sun.

She sat in the stiff-backed chair that had been Paul's favorite (he had begged her to let him take it, so that he and Mark his new lover could have it in their home). She smiled nervously, there in the pearly dark, as she remembered her stiff-lipped refusal, and his stiff-lipped disappointment as he had marched out of the house without the chair.

Her toes were numb and she wiggled them. Blue-gray in the night light, they didn't feel quite real—cold and dry and hard—as if they belonged to someone else.

The pain in her groin had diminished over the past couple of days, and her arms were beginning to turn skin color again (oddly, the bruises had never hurt; she wondered if she weren't missing some nerves there).

She rubbed her feet, then got up and went to the window. She put her hand on the marbled frost, which

was now inside as well as out. When her palm felt cold
and dead, a spot had cleared so that she could look out.

Paul had excavated the yard to within three feet of its
borders, and built a big cement swimming pool two and
a half years ago. Francine had tried to talk him out of
it; she had preferred the little mowed lawn with the
chain-link fence, the view of the other neighbors' yards,
watching the kids climb fences, chasing each other with
plastic guns, seeing new kittens come out from under
the houses, and then go back again when the kids
treated them cruelly, pitching them about like baseballs.
She found it unnerving, after the pool was built and the
redwood fence around it, not to be able to connect the
now eerie squeaking of chains with children swinging on
their swingsets.

She wondered how deep the ice was. She had not
emptied the pool this winter, hoping the pressure of the
ice would crack the cement and give her an excuse to
have it filled in with dirt next spring.

She imagined an earthquake, a knockout punch, and
then the cement walls would somehow cave in, forcing
the ice upward in a single glacial movement. Perhaps the
house itself would be leveled.

Until then, she thought, now wide awake, a crawly
tingle moving down her spine, then up again, now resting
at the base of her neck like an insect, the pool is a sort
of path for people to walk across.

Once, someone had walked across it, when the ice was
new. Stumbled across it in a panic, not knowing me, not
knowing what he was doing. He wanted me so badly he
did not pay attention. His blood was boiling.

When she thought of Paul's soft gentle hands, the
fluttering birdlike fingers of her father, she felt a surge
of desire.

Next time will be different. Like I wanted last night,
and the night before, and the night before that. Don't
ask; make me know what I want, what I am. Be inside
me, fill and complete me.

She had been reading the papers since his visit to her.
She had been the first, at least as far as she could tell
from the news. It had been three weeks now. The rapist

was terrorizing other women, hurting them badly, killing three. Two more were in critical condition.

One night after long imagining about what he was really like, what the other women had done wrong, how they had struggled and angered him, a thought struck Francine, like lightning, all black and silver-white:

"What man?" she had asked under her breath for Dr. Junkerman's sake, although he was going deaf and probably didn't hear.

Outside, in the gray wind, the other part of her answered: "The man I will change, who will change me: my one true love."

"Dear, you'd better be more careful," Mrs. Arthur said. She had come over to say hello this dry winter day. The door had been opened a crack, and she had pushed her way in, uninvited.

She was middle-aged, overweight, frightened looking; her husband had died last year of a stroke. She had tried to get closer to Francine, since they were now both alone, but Francine had kept her at a distance, treating her graciously but not generously.

"Oh, I'm not worried," Francine said, although her voice shook a little. She walked over and closed the door, but deliberately did not lock it. She gave Mrs. Arthur a look of stubborn triumph.

Mrs. Arthur shifted her weight from one varicosed leg to another; she wore cheap nylons which made her legs look like fading street maps. Francine frowned, tried to look away.

Mrs. Arthur apparently noticed Francine's distasteful look. "You are a young woman, still," Mrs. Arthur said petulantly, "and he's drawn to young women. Especially pretty *pale* ones who live alone."

He must care for me a little, if he did not kill me.

If I am good, he will come back to me and help me get rid of all this dry pain—if I do what I am told.

I will be the best little girl in the world.

Reading the papers, she waited for the footsteps across the pool.

She waited in bed. When she thought she heard the

shuffle shuffle shuffle of his thick black rubber boots, she would look out and see Mrs. Arthur, her next-door neighbor, struggling with her groceries or something, looking over her shoulder as if pursued.

She waited in the living room. Hearing a cracking sound like boots trampling frozen grass, she would rush to the window to see the house next door where the Nortons had lived (and the young son had died), the black skeleton of the burned house slowly giving out, another scaled dark beam crashing to the scorched earth.

She was nearly well now. Dr. Junkerman had said so when she had returned, although she had not planned to; she wanted to set his mind to rest. She had not told him anything, but hinted that she might look for professional counseling "when she could face it." He had said he understood her shyness and humiliation, it was completely normal. He told her to keep her windows and doors tightly locked, because sometimes these crazy men returned to the scene of the crime.

Francine congratulated herself on not crying out that night, several weeks ago. If Mrs. Arthur had heard, and found out, then what awful pity and friendship would she have had to endure?

No, this was better; to live alone and wait.

"I've been reading the papers, too," Francine retorted, "but I don't honestly think he'd show his face around here. Why would he come to a dumpy little 'burb like this? I'd think he'd go to some lovely house and force his way in, break through a glass door on a balcony maybe, find a woman in an expensive silk nightgown—that sort of thing." Francine tried to rescue herself—her tone had become obviously dreamy—but too late.

Mrs. Arthur's voice took on a worried tone. "You have been spending too much time alone, since that horrible husband of yours—" she couldn't seem to bring herself to say it "—left you for—"

"I know what he did!" The words erupted from Francine. "I don't need to be reminded."

Mrs. Arthur looked sympathetic, motherly. Francine was white with rage. Mrs. Arthur gathered up her parcels, walked slowly on swollen ankles to the door. She stood on the blue flagstones, in front of the colorless wooden door with the porthole window.

She opened the door. "You've got my number, don't you, if you need something? Or if you don't have time to dial, holler. I've got my ears open. I can hear a pin drop a block away."

When the door had closed and silence returned, and the need to fill that silence flew about the room and through her like a trapped bird, she thought:

I hope not.

And then, suddenly jealous: I don't want anyone to hear him but me.

Each tick of the clock was a footstep. Nearer and nearer he came. His arms were hot against her back, the lips on hers frantic, tasting like salt and blood.

Exhausted, satisfied, she lay against his heaving chest, watching the sweat trace a silver line down the firm belly; she could see the heart beating furiously in his ribcage, threatening to burst through.

She had drawn a map, figured out a pattern, cutting the articles from the newspaper and keeping a scrapbook. She had cleared out the pictures of high school friends, old boyfriends, Paul and their friends, to make room. She tried peeling off the plastic daisies on the cover, but they were stuck tight.

Only two pages were now filled; the rest of the scrapbook was shiny and black and empty, lonely looking. But it was a beginning.

He was busily looking for her. The city was in a panic, the press was having a field day, the police had doubled their patrols, some of the officers dressing like women to try to trap him.

He was confused, frightened, though strong, strong as a house, as a mountain. He could get in anywhere. Follow the voice of my heart, Francine thought, and you will find the one you're looking for.

When he was finished with his journey, he would return. And find her waiting, at the end of the path.

Francine had a small income from a trust fund, and the monthly checks from Paul, which arrived on the third of each month (unless the third were a Sunday, in which case it would arrive a day early); Paul was more dependable now than he had ever been. He even called one day to check on her, since a recent attack had been in Forest Hills, a suburb only a couple of miles away from the cracker-tin house with the thin walls that was now legally hers.

Really, if he is so worried, Francine thought, hanging up the phone, he would be over here at night, protecting me. Anything could crash through these paper walls; I'm surprised they keep the wind out.

But the wind was not kept out entirely. She would lie in bed, or stare dreamily at the ceiling with blinded eyes, and imagine it, call to it.

And the wind would answer her call, puffing under the floorboards, roaring through the eaves, sending the mailbox into shuddering concussions like the beating of a panicked heart.

She woke one powdery blue Monday morning, her head stuffy, her eyes red from not crying. She felt emptied, parched, like something a strong wind could pick up, tear apart, send flying in many directions.

She brushed her teeth; did not answer the phone, which rang three times; quickly removed the paper from the front porch (the blast of cold almost knocked her off her feet).

Nothing in the paper about him. Nothing in herself about him. She searched. A hollow man-shape was what she found. She felt almost sad, suddenly, and a single tear fell down a dry cheek.

She wiped it away angrily.

How long must she wait?

She made pancakes for breakfast, which she used to make only on Sundays for Paul. She set the table for two, and did not eat. She thought about Paul's sad blue eyes, like broken china, his strong tan hands, the timid way they had held her, cradled her as though he were afraid he might hurt her.

She picked up the iron skillet and threw it against the wall. It bounced off the pink refrigerator and smashed against the window that looked out at the black burned house.

Francine felt immediately guilty and went to the window.

Where was the burned house?

There was a brownish stain on the earth, a few bricks, and a pane of broken glass where the black skeleton of the house had been.

She shook her head. Was she losing her mind?

But no, she thought, examining a small chip in the refrigerator and putting the skillet in the dishwater to soak, they must have leveled the house in the last couple of days. She had been inside for two days, really inside. Thinking. The sound had not gotten in. Was that possible?

She touched her ears, rubbed her fingers together like doctors do when they test hearing; yes, she could still hear. She squinted against the hard gray light; she could still see.

Francine walked into the bedroom.

It was so quiet, like nothing would ever again move through this house; she felt like a ghost in a house long after all the people had died: a dead quiet.

"No," she shouted to the ceiling, to the floor, to the walls. The sound bounced back, hollowly. "I can't stand it. Come back to me, please. I can't wait anymore."

The clouds had lifted, and the sky was clear black, filled with stars. She lay under the down covers in her robe. She had left the bedroom window open and the wind filled the room, shaking the lampshade, throwing shadows like the shadows of flames. Her body was sweaty and hot and her face cold and still.

At 4:23 A.M. (and she was looking at the clock, counting each tick, each imagined footstep) the footsteps became real, finally, after long days and nights of counting.

Like a hollow outline, the sound was filled out. She could almost guess the depth of the ice by the sound, different than before, when he had rushed across, perhaps afraid the ice would give way. The pool must be frozen halfway to the bottom, but the cement walls had not cracked, the ice had not yet risen up.

The footsteps across the ice were long, two single treads, like a stubborn child's.

She started to get up. Suddenly, she was filled with doubt. Her damp body got tangled in the covers and stopped her. Maybe she should lock the window, phone the police. Maybe she wasn't so special after all.

Hands reached over the windowsill, irregular white fingers, hair on the knuckles.

Too late. He was in the room and then on the bed in a single movement.

He ripped off the bedclothes, then her robe.

"Hello," she said, trying to sound tender, but failing; she had rehearsed it too well. "I've been waiting."

He didn't seem to hear her. He tore her nightgown, pulled it over her head until she choked.

She could only see his square dark head bobbing and long curved neck. She kept carefully still. One frantic hand grabbed her wrists and held her arms over her head. The other clamped down over her mouth.

"No," she mumbled against the hand. "I won't scream."

The violence of his thrusting made the mattress shriek, and the lamp spilled over.

The bulb flickered, came on.

Suddenly, Francine was filled with fear. It rose in her like a wall of ice, up and out in a single movement. She had opened her eyes all the way, lowered them to his face, which was hidden in its own shadow. He released her arms; he held something sharp against her throat, cold and hot, like snow.

He raised his face from her chest, where he had been butting his head like a bull.

No eyes, no ears, just smooth featureless skin. The man without a face.

She had waited for nothing.

Her tender smile was for nothing; she let it sink into a frown, then a grimace of pain. The softly whispered words, which he could not hear: now a sharp intake of breath.

I am not me, she thought. This is happening to someone else: a stranger. She stared at the ceiling, found a water crack, spidery and dark, and concentrated.

A river streamed from her rattling eyes to the crack. The pressure of the water widened the crack, and then there was a hole in the ceiling big enough to escape through.

She struggled, she swam up the river. Her arms hurt but she kept going.

She watched from above, from the raging waters which were as hot as tears. Her body on the bed was limp, tossed about, an empty suit of clothes he seemed to be trying to fit into.

"Hold still, lady," the down-below man said. "You're disturbing me."

Francine woke from wherever she had been. She gathered the bedclothes to her streaming body.

She stood unsteadily, balancing herself against the wooden bedpost. She tried to move forward, teetered wildly, her eyes filling with tears. One minute, she thought, I will move in one more minute.

A minute later she took a step, and then another. When she reached the window, she heard a terrible crashing sound, like something breaking.

She looked out the window. The ice in the pool had cracked through a wall. There was a black gash snaking along the top of the cement; the ice kept pushing and then began to push itself out of the pool.

Francine closed the window, locked it. Then she went to the phone and dialed.

"Mrs. Arthur," she said, the sobs matching the pounding of her heart, "this is Francine. Can you come over? Something's happened."

Dead Things Don't Move

Lawrence Watt-Evans

The house stood alone at the end of the road, a thousand feet or more from its nearest neighbor, and the big graceful oak trees that had shaded it from the summer sun all day also hid most of it from view. It was a perfect target.

At least, Sid said it was a perfect target. Jack had his doubts.

"So what're you *worried* about?" Sid asked. "There's just the one broad living there, I'm sure of it." He stubbed out his cigarette in the van's overflowing ashtray, ignoring the hot ashes that drifted to the floor.

"I dunno," Jack said, "I just don't like it. How c'n you be so damned sure she's alone?"

Sid sighed, and leaned forward over the steering wheel. "Look, I *told* you," he said. "There's just one name on the mailbox, and it says 'Mudgett,' and I looked up Mudgett in the phone book, and the only one on this road is *Carol* Mudgett, Carol with one R, so it's a woman. If there was a man there, or anybody else, don't you figure he'd have *his* name on the mailbox, too? Of if his name's Mudgett, wouldn't he be in the phone book?"

"I wouldn't be too damn sure," Jack muttered.

"Well, damn it, if you really gotta know, I've been watching the place for three days, and I haven't seen anybody go *near* the place except the one broad and a couple of the neighborhood kids. I even fired off the twelve-gauge, just to see if anybody'd notice, and nobody did—not even Carol goddamn Mudgett. Now, quit *worrying,* will you?"

Jack slumped down in his seat and didn't answer.

The van pulled off the road onto the shoulder and slowed to a stop; Sid turned off the engine and yanked the key from the ignition in one quick gesture, then reached forward and flicked off the headlights.

Darkness engulfed both men; there were no street-lights this far from town. The only light came from an upstairs front window of the house, filtered through the leaves of one of the oaks.

They sat in silence for a moment, contemplating that light; Sid stared out the van's window at it, Jack peering around him.

"You got the gun?" Sid demanded, turning away from the light.

"Of course I got it," Jack answered, annoyed. "I've had it on my goddamn lap for the last five miles."

" 'S it loaded?"

" 'Course it's loaded."

"Check it."

Jack started to protest, then thought better of it. "Put on the light," he said.

Sid reached up and switched on the overhead light; the darkness vanished, then seemed to seep back around the edges as their eyes readjusted.

Jack broke open the gun and held it up. "See? Shells in both barrels, all set to go."

"Good." Jack slammed the breech shut, and Sid turned off the light. The darkness surged back around them.

"I need a cigarette," Sid said into the night.

"No, you don't. Come on, let's get this over with," Jack replied. He opened his door and climbed out onto the gravel, the gun nestled under his arm.

The driver's door opened as Jack rounded the front of the van, and Sid stepped out.

"Gimme the gun," he said.

"Take it," Jack said, relieved; he thrust it out in both hands. Sid accepted it, weighed it carefully, and held it ready.

"Come on," he said.

Jack followed him up the crumbling concrete walk, stumbling once on the broken surface in the dark. The steps creaked, first under Sid's weight, and then under his.

"Be a shame if she didn't have anything worth stealing after all this," Jack whispered.

Sid smiled. "Oh, there's always *something*. Worst comes to worst, we can always hock her refrigerator or something."

The porch was narrow; Jack couldn't stand comfortably behind his partner unless he stayed on the steps, so they stood side by side, Jack glancing nervously back at the van perched up by the roadside, while Sid pressed the doorbell button.

They didn't hear it ring; all they heard was the sound of insects chirping in the tall grass. A few seconds passed, and Jack said, "Try it again."

"No, I think I hear footsteps," Sid said.

Jack had not heard any footsteps. He started to say so, but before he could get out the first word the porch light came on. The night was pressed back down the steps and over the railing, and Jack could see that the paint on the old narrow clapboards beside the door had faded and begun to peel.

There was no screen or storm door; when the door opened and the woman leaned out, there was nothing to block Sid's actions. He thrust the shotgun under the woman's chin and pulled the trigger.

That instant seemed to freeze as Jack watched. He saw very clearly every detail of the woman's face. She had a long nose and faded red hair, and was younger than he had expected. Her expression was vaguely worried, and Jack thought she had been starting to speak. Her eyes were shaded by the doorframe and he couldn't make out their color; the hallway behind her was unlit. Her lips were pale—no lipstick, Jack thought. Why should she be wearing any? She hadn't expected company.

She looked like she might have been a nice person, Jack thought; a bit old for him, though, in her late thirties at least, but younger than he had expected. He had been thinking of her as a little old widow, living alone out here, and had been worried, he realized, that she might look like his mother.

She didn't.

The roar of the gun drowned out the crickets and everything else, and the flash was blinding. Jack blinked, twice.

The woman's face was gone, fallen out of his line of sight; he heard the thump of her body hitting first the wall, and then the floor, as she tumbled backward into the dark. He smelled gunsmoke.

"So much for Carol goddamn Mudgett," Sid said. "I think the damn recoil just about broke my wrist." He kicked the door wide open and stepped over the corpse's legs into the hallway. "Come on," he called.

Jack didn't move; he stared at the legs. They stretched across the doorway, full in the light of the bare bulb hanging from the porch roof. They were bare to just above the knee; the woman had been wearing an old blue dress, shapeless and baggy, and the skirt had bunched up as she fell.

They were still a woman's legs, just as they had been. They looked as if their owner might awaken at any moment and reach down to tug her skirt back into place. The blue dress was visible up to the waist; the woman's upper body lay back in the shadow behind the doorframe.

Then Sid found a wall switch, and light poured into the hallway from an adjoining room.

"Oh, my God," Jack said.

Blood had sprayed in a broad, wet stripe down the dirty wallpaper, from eye level down to the floor, and bits of hair, bone, and tissue clung to it. At the baseboard lay the woman's body; her head had rolled forward onto her breast at an angle that would have been utterly impossible had it still been fully attached. Her neck consisted of two blood-drenched strands of ragged flesh; the shotgun had drilled a two-inch hole through the front of her throat and ripped the back of her neck and the base of her skull completely apart. Blood was pooled on the hardwood floor, dripping from where her neck should have been. One pale hand was flung out, the other folded across her breasts, where her almost-severed head stared blindly at the splayed fingers.

"Oh, my God," Jack said again.

"What's wrong with you?" Sid asked from the other room; he came to the door and peered back.

"Jeez, she does look bad, doesn't she? I didn't get a good look at her before," he said.

Jack didn't answer, and Sid cast him a worried look.

"Hey, c'mon, don't stand there staring; you'll be sick. Get in here and give me a hand."

Jack looked up and tried to swallow.

"C'mon, you knew we were going to kill her," Sid said.

"Yeah, but . . . I mean, my *God,* Sid! What'd you *do*?"

"I shot her, dummy. One barrel, like we said, in case we run into trouble."

"I didn't know it would do *that*!"

"Well, hell, neither did I, but dead is dead. What difference does it make? At least it musta been fast. Now, get in here and give me a hand, willya?"

Jack refused to look at the corpse again. He stepped over the spread legs and hurried across the hallway into the room where Sid waited.

"I think we're gonna do all right," Sid told him, smiling. "Take a look!"

Jack looked. The room was a relic—a relic worth a fortune in antiques. An octagonal clock hung on one wall, ticking loudly with each swing of its gleaming brass pendulum. Dresden china was packed on the mantel like the crowd on the rail at the track, and the mantel itself was an elaborate Victorian construction of carved oak and beveled mirrors. An honest-to-God velveteen settee stood in one corner between matching cherry end tables, one holding a bell-jar anniversary clock, the other a huge old music box and a stack of punched copper disks for the box to play.

"It might be hard to sell," he said, not really believing it.

"The hell it will be! We drive up to New York, go to an antique dealer, tell him that our dear sainted mother passed away last month and we need to sell her things to settle her medical bills. We'll get a thousand bucks, easy, for a vanload of this stuff!"

"Yeah, I guess," Jack said. He couldn't work up any

real enthusiasm with the image of the dead woman in the front hall still fresh in his mind.

"We'll need the blankets and stuff to wrap everything," Sid said.

Jack remembered the corpse lying across the threshold and said, "You get 'em; I'll look around some." He headed toward a door at the back of the room, wanting to get farther away from the body.

"Okay," Sid agreed. He turned back toward the hall, and then froze.

Jack did not notice; he had no intention of looking in that direction.

"Jack," Sid called in a loud whisper, "something moved."

"What?" Without thinking, Jack turned around, and saw the bloody smear on the hallway wall, framed in the rectangle of light from the parlor. He looked quickly away, before he could see anything worse. "Jesus, Sid, what're you talking about? There's nobody here but us and that woman, and she's dead."

"I know," Sid said, still whispering, "but I swear, I saw something move out there in the hall. Honest to God, Jack." He stared into the shadows.

"My God, Sid, you blew her head off! She's dead; dead things don't move!" Memories of stories he had heard or read as a child, of horribly mutilated corpses pursuing bloody poetic vengeance, flooded his mind.

"I didn't say *she* moved, I said *something* moved. I don't know what it was."

"Well, so what? Maybe she's got rats." Jack immediately regretted that suggestion as he imagined what rats might do to the body after he and Sid left. "You got the gun; go take a look if you think you saw something. I'm gonna look at the rest of the house." He turned away again.

Sid was not visibly reassured, but he said, "Yeah, you're right; I got the gun." He broke it open, checked the remaining live shell, then snapped it shut. "I'll go look."

"You do that. You just yell if you need me," Jack answered. He fumbled around the far side of the door to the next room, and finally found the light switch.

The switch worked an old hanging lamp with a stained-glass shade; more money, Jack knew. It hung above an oval table strewn with tatted doilies, and lit a glittering collection of china and glassware in matching cabinets along the far wall. Jack went to investigate what looked like Wedgwood.

Sid, too, was investigating. He inched toward the hallway, his gaze fixed on the red ruin of his victim's head. He knew that she was dead. He knew that as Jack had said, dead things don't move. Still, he was certain that he had seen something move, and what else could it have been? The hallway was almost unfurnished; a braided rug lay on the floor, a hat rack stood at the foot of the stairs, and the corpse was sprawled by the open door, but otherwise, it was empty.

Still staring at the body, the gun clutched tightly in both hands, he stepped through the doorway.

Immediately, before he consciously felt anything, he knew he had made a mistake. He knew that he should have turned on the hall light, should have looked carefully around the corner. He hadn't; he had been too busy watching the corpse. That was his mistake. Dead things don't move; that meant he had seen something alive.

That something, whatever it was, had gotten him; he felt a sudden sharp coldness exploding into his side, beneath his left arm, and sensed something warm running down inside his shirt, and then the pain hit him. He sucked in air, but couldn't find the strength to scream.

"You killed my mother," a voice hissed. Sid looked down and saw a small hand pulling the butcher knife from his side, and then driving it in again. The pain turned to blackness, the gun fell from his hands, and he toppled forward.

In the dining room, Jack heard the crash. "Sid?" he called.

No one answered.

"Sid?" He called more loudly this time, a note of desperation creeping into his voice.

Still no one answered.

"God, Sid, if you're pulling a joke, I swear I'm gonna kill you. You hear me, Sid?"

The house was silent, save for the ticking of the clock in the parlor.

Jack stood in the dining room for a long moment, waiting for some new sound, waiting for something to happen. He could hear the crickets, very faintly, chirping outside the window; he could see nothing but darkness and his own reflected image when he looked at the glass. China gleamed, white and cold, in the light from the lamp; he noticed that one of the little squares of yellow glass in the shade was cracked across.

"Sid?"

Nothing answered.

He had to do something, he knew that. His first thought was to get out, to run, to get away as fast as he possibly could. He would forget about Sid and about the antiques and just leave.

Sid had the keys to the van; without them, he would have to walk, five miles back to town, alone in the dark.

Worse, the corpse lay in the front door. He would have to get past it. Sid had vanished when he went into the front hall to see if the dead thing had moved. To get out of the house, Jack would need to do the same thing.

He couldn't do it; he knew that immediately. He would have to find some other way out of the house.

There would have to be a back door, but to reach it he would have to explore new, still-dark rooms. That did not appeal to him.

He looked at the window. It was certainly large enough to climb through, but he could see immediately that it couldn't be opened; he would have to break it. He could tell by the doubling of his reflection that there was a storm window on the outside, and those could, he knew, be almost unbreakable.

There were other windows, though. He would find a way out. He started back toward the parlor.

"Don't move," a voice said, a small, high-pitched voice, neither man nor woman; visions of freaks and monsters whirled through Jack's mind. He froze.

The voice came from his left. Very slowly, keeping his hands well out from his sides and open flat, he started to turn, to see who had spoken.

Another doorway, one he had not paid attention to,

connected the dining room to the hall, and standing in
that doorway was a young girl, perhaps nine or ten years
old. She was wearing an old flannel nightgown, white
with pink flowers. Her face was flushed and speckled
with chickenpox. Her feet were bare. Her hands, and
the front of her gown, were smeared with fresh blood.

She held Sid's shotgun awkwardly in both hands.

"I told you not to move," she said conversationally,
"and you're moving, but I know how to fix that."

She raised the shotgun and pointed it at Jack's face.

"Dead things don't move," she said as she pulled
the trigger.

The Man Who
Collected Knives

John Gregory Betancourt

"Jason? Are you listening to me?"

He stood at the kitchen counter chopping vegetables that last fateful day, *snick-snick-snick*ing the butcher knife through onions and green peppers, half-dreaming himself away in a bubble of time. *Escape.* Yes, escape. He felt the room darkening, dropping out of focus. He longed for his freedom.

And the glittery sharp blade of the knife did it. Like always when he immersed himself in his work, when he held a blade of some kind, its edge pulled him like a moth to flame.

He drew a deep breath and abruptly stood someplace else, someplace far away. A hot, dry wind blew in his face. A sky black with clouds glowered overhead. Jagged rocks crunched underfoot as he took a hesitant step.

"I'm here," the creature said.

Jason turned, smiling for the first time.

"Jason? You bastard, *listen* to me! *Jason!*"

It had started innocently enough, in the summer of 1971, when Jason's father gave him a Boy Scout knife for his thirteenth birthday. He had stared at it hesitantly before pulling it from its box. Mother had never let him have one before—they were too dangerous, she said.

"You're almost a man, and a man needs a good

knife," Pa had told him, grinning and winking. "Treat her well and she'll last a lifetime."

"She?" he asked slowly.

"Every knife has a personality. Take this one here." Pa unfolded the parts one at a time—how could there be so many?—two bright steel blades, an awl, a bottle opener, and even a magnifying glass. Perhaps it was the magnifying glass that did it, pushed him from mere childish interest to awed fascination.

"*This* knife," Pa went on, "can do just about anything, from starting a fire to skinning a skunk."

"Pa!"

"It's true!" And Pa had laughed and folded all the parts away and pressed it back into his hand. "Just don't tell your mother I gave it to you, okay? It'll be our secret, man to man."

"Cool," he said solemnly.

Throughout June and July and August he carried it always, carving his initials into every tree he met until a ten-block radius of their house bore his mark. But the knife didn't last a lifetime; it didn't last the summer before it fell to pieces—the parts inside worn out from the countless times he'd opened and closed them.

Then Jason started saving his allowance for real hunting knives, not kids' toys like the one his father had given him. He bought his first real Bowie knife that October, and the strong steel blade fascinated him—certainly better at carving wood than his scout knife had been. A few months later he found a set of meat cleavers on sale at Wal-Mart, an impulse buy that left him broke for a month. That Christmas he found his grandfather's old army sword in the attic and took it to hang on his wall.

His mania grew through high school. Ginsu knives from television ads. Bayonets from flea markets. Dirks and daggers and cutlasses and épées and scythes and Japanese throwing stars—

When he graduated, his parents bundled him off to the far-distant University of Pennsylvania, hoping a change of friends and environment might broaden his interests. Instead it served to focus them. The college fencing team found him an eager student. History courses provided information on ancient arms he might never have encountered otherwise.

He also met Joanne Bleiler there. She had like interests in history (though it was politics that drew her), and they found themselves paired in a little study group that led to a romance that led to marriage in their senior year.

But their interests were perhaps a bit too far apart. While Joanne joined a law firm as a clerk, pushing, always pushing, he found himself left behind. Alone, most evenings, with nothing but his collection of knives.

Then the creature came to him. Small and gray and vaguely batlike, with silvery eyes and needle-sharp teeth, it seemed disturbingly familiar. Perhaps it had always been there, he thought, just waiting to be heard. Or perhaps need brought it to him.

Whatever, the creature came whispering soft words, saying how bright and beautiful his blades were (why did Joanne never see that?), urging him to buy more, telling him everything he wanted, everything he needed to hear. He listened. Perhaps that was his greatest mistake.

And as Joanne grew more shrill and insistent, he fled to the creature for comfort and understanding. It always knew what to say. It always made him feel good.

Now, in their little apartment, as Jason chopped vegetables for dinner and his mind floated on some other plane talking to a thing that could not possibly exist but somehow *did,* his wife's voice broke through the perfection of the moment. It felt like fingernails scratching on slate.

"Jason!"

He sighed. He blinked. The alien landscape faded. The creature with eyes like steel faded, too.

"Yes?" he said, looking at her for the first time that night.

"At last." She struck her classic Angry Woman pose: hands on hips, feet set, neck tense. "Sometimes," she said, "I wonder if you're all here, Jason. And sometimes I know you're not. What do you think this is?" She held

out her hand. In it, crumpled but still recognizable, lay
his paycheck.

"Money, dear," he said. He went back to chopping.
"We've gone over this before."

"Only twenty-two dollars! Where's the rest?"

"I took it in merchandise. I got a bayonette. It's the
best I've ever seen, with two figures etched on—"

"How could you?" she cried. She waved one hand at
the racks of cutlery over the cabinets, at the knives
under the counters, at the axes by the door, at the guillotine in the corner. The guillotine was his prize. He'd
built it himself, and the blade (he had a letter of prove-
nance saying so) had actually snicked off several aristo-
cratic heads in those wondrous days of *La Revolution*.
"Enough is enough!" she cried.

"It makes sense," he insisted. "Weapons hold their
value. They're an excellent investment."

"Try pearls," Joanne said bitterly.

She turned and stalked from the room. A second later,
Jason heard the front door slam.

He winced. And turned back to his knives. And in a
moment stood on that barren plane with his only friend
in the universe.

When Joanne's father, a prominent local lawyer, filed
the divorce papers two weeks later, Jason felt the loss
more keenly than he wanted to admit. His wife's leaving
left a hole, like a missing tooth, and as he probed the
edges he felt a dull unfocused pain. Realizing she wasn't
coming back, he cried himself to sleep for the first time
in his life.

The creature came in a dream to comfort him.
"Relax," it said. "You don't need her. Now your apartment has more room for weapons."

Giggling, it told him where to go, what to buy. He sat
up and began taking mental notes, distracted for the
moment from his grief.

The next day, a bankrupt jewelry store sold him display cases. And The Velvet Handcuff Novelty Shoppe
provided padded hooks for his walls and ceilings. Under
the creature's guidance, he set up a private museum.
Sabers filled one wall of the living room, axes another,

Swiss army knives a third. In his bedroom, great swords hung over the bed, blades polished until they shone like mirrors. He lay there naked, late one night, with the lights on, and just stared at the reflections.

"So beautiful," the creature told him, "so beautiful."

He smiled to himself. And the creature told him he was happy. But still he felt the hole in his life where Joanne had been.

The jump from collecting to *using* those blades came not long after that. He'd worked late at the antique shop cataloguing a new shipment from Canada, and as part of his commission he took a pair of matched dueling knives, both with intricately worked ivory handles. By the time he finished for the evening, midnight had come and gone.

He might have made it home all right if it hadn't been drizzling. Because of the cold and the wet, the streets lay deserted, and the night had an eerie quality. Jason stuck the knives in his overcoat's pocket and huddled under his umbrella as he trudged homeward.

He started down the subway steps, same as always, same as he'd done a thousand times before on a thousand nights just like this one. But then footsteps echoed behind him. The lightbulb overhead suddenly *crunch*ed and went out, little bits of hot glass raining down in the darkness.

Run! something inside him cried, and he dropped his umbrella and fled in terror down the steps. *Mugger— wolf pack—*

Time seemed to stretch. Thunder rumbled, lightning flickered. He glanced over his shoulder, saw a black kid of maybe fifteen laughing hysterically, his hair slick with water, his eyes wild.

Then it was dark again and Jason slipped and fell, rolling, feeling nothing in the rush of the moment but certain somewhere inside that he hurt.

"Watcha got, man?" The kid stood over him—how had he moved so fast?—and started pawing Jason's pockets.

Jason grabbed for his billfold, but instead came up with one of the knives. How it got in his hand, he didn't know. The whole scene was moving too fast for him to follow, too fast for him to comprehend.

"Now!" the creature cried.

Without thinking, he stabbed up, into the black kid's belly. The blade slit cloth and skin and muscle with ease.

The kid stopped laughing. For a horrible second they just stared at each other in a flash of lightning, both surprised, both too shocked to move. Then the kid began to scream, like a hurt animal, like nothing Jason had ever heard before.

"Excellent," the creature whispered. "Now go—go— *gooooo!"*

Jason surged to his feet and ran. A train was just pulling up when he reached the tracks, and he staggered into it. An empty car, thank God.

A whistle blew. The doors hissed shut and the train lurched forward. After a minute, Jason realized he still held the knife. He stared at it in amazement for a few seconds, then quickly stuck it back into his pocket.

I should feel something nasty, he thought. *Shame or horror or regret, at least.*

But he didn't. He felt something else, something he tried to repress, but couldn't quite. Was it . . . pleasure?

He leaned back, pressing fists to his eyes, somehow appalled. The smell of blood, the kid's blood, hung on his clothes like a cloying perfume. *How could I enjoy it?*

He sobbed helplessly.

He didn't remember walking home or going to bed. When he woke the next morning, he still had his coat on, and the knife, its blade stained a muddy red-brown, lay in his pocket.

At first he threw it away. But the creature murmured incessantly about what a prize it was, what a *trophy,* completely unique in his collection. He covered his ears and still its voice came through, nagging him, prodding him, whispering, whispering, whispering.

Finally, screaming for silence, he rose and fished the knife from the trash can. Held it in a trembling hand. Admired it, the curve of the blade, the way dried blood picked out the delicate scrimshaw work on its ivory hilt of (how had he missed it before?) a dragon devouring its own tail.

After breakfast, he carved a new notch in its handle. The physical act of crediting his kill gave him a rush like nothing he had ever felt before, better than drugs, better than sex. He didn't need a letter to prove *this* blade had tasted blood!

And, deep inside, at the back of his consciousness, the creature urged him on.

The next night Jason made sure he worked late at the store. *Payday*. Same as always, he took most of his salary in hard, cold steel, this time a cavalry saber, circa 1860. Engraved on its side were the letters CSA. Perhaps it had fought the Civil War at some southern gentleman's side. Later perhaps it had carried civilization west, helping defeat the hordes of Indians who waited behind every rock and tree to ambush innocent settlers.

His boss had brought the saber back from Illinois along with a truckload of other antiques. It had been love at first sight, and the worn leather grip had fit his hand like a glove. It had been meant for him, he knew.

"Feels good, doesn't it?"

Nodding, he hefted the saber. Eight little nocks in the hilt; eight deaths attributed to its might. If only Joanne could see it, share it with him, he thought. Then life would be perfect.

Slowly, he tested the blade with his thumb. Dull as a butter knife. ("Can't have that, not with such a fine weapon," the creature said, and he agreed.) Such a waste, otherwise.

Taking a whetstone from his desk, he began to work the saber's edge back toward razor sharpness. *Shhhhhht, shhhhhht*. The touch of the steel made his hands tingle. Finally finished, he wrapped brown paper around it, but loosely, so it could be drawn. Turning off the lights, he set the alarms and locked the doors.

Then, trembling, he stood in the doorway for an instant, just watching his breath mist the air. This felt like a turning point in his life, as though he stood on the brink of something tremendous, something great and good and powerful, like knowing God or being the first man to walk on the moon. It felt like that, only more so, because it was happening to *him* and not some stranger on TV.

He could feel the sword's weight. When he eased his hand into the paper and touched its hilt, an electric thrill ran through him. *Ecstasy.*

"You can win her heart again!" the creature inside him cried. "She'll see reason. She *loves* you."

"But—"

"Trust me," it said. "*Do* it! Doitdoitdo*it*!"

He hugged the saber to him and cast his lot.

Two blocks' walk and he came to the subway. He fed the machine his token, then pushed through to stand impatiently waiting. Why did it seem to take forever *tonight*, when for the first time it truly mattered?

Finally a train came. He boarded with a couple of old black men, then sat alone at the opposite end of the car with the saber across his knees. As they rode the tunnel, he watched graffitied walls flow away behind.

At last he reached the right stop. Her parents' house lay two blocks away. She was staying with them till she got herself on her feet again—that's what her father had told him the one time he'd gotten up enough nerve to call. He'd just hung up, been too scared to ask to speak to her. But now, tonight, it would all be different.

He climbed the subway steps. Stood breathing the cool night air. Turned and walked slowly and purposefully toward the right house.

In his mind he rehearsed what he'd say to her. Something debonair, he thought, something romantic. She liked romance.

When he rang the bell, she answered. Her eyes widened when she saw him, and she started to close the door.

He blocked it with his foot. "Joanne—"

"I have nothing to say to you," she said. "Go away or I'll call the police!"

"I—I'm sorry," he said. "I miss you. I just wanted you to know that. And . . ."

"What?" she said. She opened the door a bit more.

"I'm sorry." Her eyes, he saw, brimmed with tears.

She missed him! She still loved him! "May I come in?" he asked. "Please?"

She moved back. He entered. The TV blared from the living room, showing the end of some swashbuckler. Tyrone Power swung, sword in hand, across the deck of a burning pirate ship.

"Are your parents here?" he asked.

"They went to a play."

"Good," he said. "I wanted—I *needed*—to talk to you. Alone. I love you, Joanne."

She bit her lip and said nothing.

"Look," he said. "I brought you something." He began to unwrap the cavalry saber. As soon as she saw it, he thought, she'd know what it meant to him, to *them*, and then she'd come back and everything would be perfect. The saber would do it. The creature had promised.

But when she saw what he held, she flinched back. "Get out!" she screamed. "I'm *sick* of you and your swords! *Get out!*"

He stepped forward and she hit him. He blinked in surprise. She hit him again and again, flailing wildly, shrieking and screaming—

"Now!" the creature inside him commanded.

And he swept the saber *up,* backhanded, cleanly severing her head. Blood sprayed across the far wall in a huge, silent, beautiful arc. Her body slumped, twitching. Her head bounced a dozen feet, then fetched up against another cardboard box and stopped, grinning back at him with an impossibly happy expression.

He grinned too, and hacked again and again, stabbing, chopping, *killing* until blood flowed like water underfoot and the creature inside him roared its approval, roared its joy.

And then her chest lay open and he saw her heart. It pulsed briefly, then lay still.

He knelt and hugged her to him. Her heart came out in his hands and he cradled it to his face, softly whispering of his love.

The Roadside Scalpel

Thomas F. Monteleone

The bastard's house looked just about the way Doctor Frederick Wilhelm had figured it would: a squat little Cape Cod with tiny little rooms and unit air conditioners sticking out of every window. The lawn needed cutting and nasty-looking weeds choked what was left of the flower beds. A beat-up, boxy-looking Ford hulked in the driveway like the dinosaur it was. No way Raczkowski would replace his wreck with anything new—he was a used-car kind of guy.

Wilhelm smiled at his small joke, and moved stealthily from the neighboring house's shrubbery, across the unkempt crabgrass and clover, to crouch next to a rusting Sears Roebuck utility shed. Moonlight blued everything in pastel half-glows. Frederick wondered how visible he would be to anyone idly glancing in his general direction.

Probably not very. People usually weren't looking out their windows at 3:00 A.M. But if they were, they most likely were sitting in the bathroom trying to purge a raging gastrointestinal system and not looking for a Midnight Skulker.

A *skulker.*

Is that what he was? No, not exactly.

He allowed himself a little smile, then inched around the shed to the rear of the house carrying a classic Gladstone bag by his side. He had little trouble negotiating a cellarway and steps leading down to a basement door. Silent. Like a snake in the woods. Actually, he was surprising himself a little. I'm pretty damn good at this.

When the basement doorknob turned in his hand, he

nodded as though expecting it. An article he'd read in *Newsweek* reported more than forty percent of all homes in America were left unlocked on a regular basis. And besides, Raczkowski had seemed like the type who wouldn't be real careful.

With a gentle surge forward against the wooden door, Frederick let himself into the dark clutter of the basement. An assortment of smells greeted him: sawdust, soap detergent, paint thinner, WD-40, all overlayed by a general mustiness. He used a penlight to carve a narrow path through the shadowed junk—cardboard boxes, Hefty bags of old clothes, garden tools, patio furniture, abandoned appliances, broken toys. It was like many of our basements and attics, he observed casually. One of those places where we stash the pieces of our lives we can't live with anymore, but somehow cannot consign to the oblivion of the trash man.

He moved to the stairs. Old. Wooden. No railing, which was again typical. Frederick moved up to the plywood door, turned the cheap brass knob. Again, there was no resistance and he was suddenly in a cramped hall, illuminated only by seeping moonlight through venetian blinds in the living room. It was a space punctuated by empty Bud cans, the carcass boxes of home-delivered pizzas, empty cheese doodle bags, and overflowing ashtrays. The coffee table in front of a red velvet Mediterranean couch was the removable hard top from a Chinese red '55 T-Bird. Cute. Real cute.

Is this what Raczkowski was doing with his money? What an asshole . . .

Unable to resist his curiosity, Frederick checked out the kitchen and was pleased to find it as filthy and disarrayed as he'd hoped. Butter melting in its wrapper on the countertop, Dunkin' Donuts moldering in their boxes, a sinkful of dishes crusted with hard fragments and probably crawling with bacteria. Anyone who lived in such squalor deserved whatever misfortune might come their way.

Frederick smiled. And tonight, that misfortune is *me*.

Turning from the kitchen, he crossed the living room and ascended the shag-carpeted stairs. His Reeboks carried him up in total silence. So quietly, in fact, he could hear the sinusoidal breathing of Donald Raczkowski before reaching the second-floor landing. The sound was a medium-pitched fluting, symptomatic of a deviated septum, and like a beacon it directed Frederick to the left, to stand in the doorway of a bedroom that reeked of unemptied ashtrays, unlaundered bedclothes, and a particularly foul blend of semen and cheap after-shave.

Just enough ambient light filtered through the chintz curtains to detail the body sprawled stomach down on the bed. Being the overweight, unsightly mess he was, Raczkowski had no bed partner—just as Frederick had expected.

Moving quickly, just as he'd practiced it hundreds of times, he knelt by the bed, reaching into his bag for the prepared syringe. Smoothly, with the soft, expert touch of many years of practice, Frederick injected forty cc's of Xylothal into the blubber of Raczkowski's bicep. The large man grunted awake from the puncture-prick, started to raise up his sour bulk on one elbow, but his eyes rolled back as the drug reached his cortical area.

Another grunt and he fell into the fouled bedsheets on his back. Just barely conscious, he looked glassily at Frederick, who waited for recognition to flicker like a dime-store flashlight behind Raczkowski's eyes.

"Good evening, Donald. It's Doctor Wilhelm."

The large man grunted weakly. Ah. Recognition at last.

A slight dilation of the pupils. Fear? One could only hope.

"I've come to get something that's rightfully mine," said Frederick. "Your left arm . . ."

Ah, yes. The eyes definitely widened on that last phrase. He knows. He remembers. Good.

Xylothal was an interesting drug. It had the ability to keep a patient on the edge of consciousness, with no loss of sensory input, for many hours at a time, while simultaneously damping down entirely voluntary motor centers. In other words, Raczkowski would retain full awareness of his surroundings without being able to move a muscle, and he would still feel pain.

That was the important part. The man would need to feel pain all along the spectrum, from mild discomfort to mind-ripping agony. The man needed to be paid back for all the anguish and torture he'd inflicted upon Doctor Frederick Wilhelm.

As he reached into the Gladstone for his scalpel case, Frederick's mind rewound some choice memories, replayed them faster than real time . . .

. . . And once again the rain-black skin of the Interstate was slithering beneath his Cadillac Seville. He'd been driving back from a much-deserved golf vacation in Myrtle Beach, South Carolina. Frederick was tapping out a rhythm on the steering wheel as his Alpine car-stereo played a CD called *Digital Duke,* and Ellington had never sounded sweeter. Frederick Wilhelm, orthopedic surgeon, at the age of forty-five had achieved and acquired everything a man could hope for: faithful devoted wife, healthy kids going to the best schools, investment real estate and a fat stock portfolio, the standard finely appointed house, and a mistress who would diddle him six ways to Sunday for just a taste of the good life. Sure, he was overextended, and sure he spent more than he could immediately pay for, but didn't we all do that? Whether you made a hundred bucks a week, or a hundred thousand every month . . .

And it hadn't come easy. No way. The third son of a construction worker in East Lansing, Michigan, Frederick had worked his ass off to pay his way through college and medical school. Not like a lot of those shits he studied and interned with. The guys from the Northeastern prep schools and the family estates where they had stables as well as garages.

No way. Freddie Wilhelm had *earned* everything that had come his way. And nobody would ever take it away from him.

It was that kind of determination and willful attitude that had served Frederick so well. And it didn't mean he was ruthless or heartless or anything of the sort. If that were true, he would have never stopped when he'd seen the accident.

In the wet murk beyond his wiper blades, he saw the tangle of metal on the side of the Interstate. A four-by-four had sluiced off the road to mix it up with one of the stanchions that support the big green exit signs. It must have happened recently, because Frederick saw no other cars or movement of any kind.

Without hesitation, he braked down to the shoulder and slowly approached the twisted mess that had been an old Ford Bronco. He'd always kept an emergency kit in his trunk, and being a doctor, he'd kept it stocked with a sophisticated array of drugs, instruments, and supplies. Grabbing the leather case from the rear of his car, he moved quickly to the wreck.

The driver's side door had been pinched off and the cab had accordioned inward. The vehicle must have flipped on its side and slid into the upright support at high speed. The lone occupant, a flabby man in a red plaid shirt, had been thrown halfway through the shattered windshield.

Leaning into what was left of the cab, Frederick winced at the mixture of odors—coppery fresh blood and bad rye whiskey. Everything had been stained a black-red and he feared he was too late to help the driver. Anybody losing this much blood was severely injured. He had to act quickly. Being too cautious meant lost time, and then it would be too late.

As he struggled with the man's bulk, getting him the rest of the way out of the cab, the worst of his injuries became clear—his left arm was practically severed at the shoulder and the main brachial artery was pumping out blood like a ruptured hydrant. Frederick worked quickly, with the cold efficiency that came from twenty years' experience. Rather than just stanch the wound and lose the arm, he attempted miracle surgery in the cold rain. It may have been an act of hubris or heroism—motivation never crossed his mind. It simply occurred to him that his skills might save the man's arm as well as his life.

It wasn't the prettiest sight, but by the time the paramedics arrived and the victim was hurtling off to the nearest county hospital, the arm, no longer dying, had been reattached and throbbed with the pink glow of flesh. Frederick gave his name and address to the highway police, drove to the nearest motel where he changed out of his ruined clothes, and resumed his trip home. As he cranked up the CD, he found himself smiling, feeling good about himself. He'd done one of those good things—he'd saved a man's life and perhaps his occupation when he preserved the severed limb.

Funny, he'd thought: he never even got the guy's name.

But he learned it about six months later when he was slapped with Donald Raczkowski's malpractice suit. The legal brief charged him with administering medical attention without the patient's permission, and causing Raczkowski to lose more than fifty percent of the utility in his left arm, further resulting in the loss of Raczkowski's employment in the local pickling plant. The only job the scumbag had ever been able to keep.

Sure, it was a bullshit case. But in a backward, bullshit state where they'd never got around to passing any "Good Samaritan" laws, it was also a case that would stick.

Frederick wouldn't have really cared if he'd kept up his malpractice insurance premiums, but Christ, with Anthony in his third year at Princeton, and Jennifer Louise accepted at Stanford, he'd been a little short, and he figured he had to rob Peter to pay Paul for a little while. When his insurance carrier claimed default and Donald Raczkowski claimed victory, things went very badly for Frederick.

Very badly and post haste.

The settlement required the liquidation of almost every asset Frederick had ever acquired. The houses, the cars, the boat, and of course the entire stock portfolio. But it didn't stop there. When he tried to sell some of Tina's jewelry and furs, she decided she'd suffered enough indignity and took off for her parents' home in Shaker Heights—*with* her jewelry. Telling the kids they'd have to complete their educations at the local state diploma factory drove a stake through the heart of whatever had been left of their fibrillating relationships. In addition, his colleagues considered his malpractice conviction the equivalent of a kiss on the cheek after a Mafioso dinner. Not only did every doctor in the country stop referring patients to his office, but they also stopped talking to him as well. When his country club refused to offer him a membership renewal, Frederick really wasn't

all that surprised. But perhaps the final and most telling
blow was the hasty departure of Shawna, his young,
long-legged mistress, who really didn't need to tell him
she'd loved Frederick's money a lot more than the
man himself.

For a while, Frederick continued to believe in his own
self-worth. He attempted to retain his dignity, rebuild
his shattered practice, and remove the tarnish from his
reputation. Living in a small suburban apartment complex colored with grim, blue-collar workers and legions
of screaming, chocolate-mouthed kids on Big-Wheels,
Frederick continued to plummet into the abyss of his
private desperation. The growing reality that things
would never be as they once had been began to crush
him down like the great heel of a socialist government.

Every day became a monumental struggle. To pay the
bills, to be civil and polite, and finally to even be a competent physician.

When not scrounging up local industrial accident
cases, and the occasional neighborhood broken arm,
Frederick spent his time alone. Assuredly, he would
never see his wife again, unless it were over the shoulder
of her divorce attorney; his children were both embarrassed and outraged at his failure to protect himself and
properly educate them. Shawna of the long, tanned legs
and high breasts had, by this time, wrapped her per-
fumed flesh around a new sugar-doc; and there were
certainly no more Sunday afternoon ballgames or golf
foursomes in his future.

Alone.

Either in his spartanly appointed office, for which the
rent seemed eternally due, or in his meager apartment
populated by yard-sale furniture and a yeoman-class
television. Alone, with thoughts that grew increasingly
torturous. He grew to realize it was probably bearable
to live only the skeleton of a *real* life—if you've never
known any better—but impossible if you've ever been
on top.

Campbell's tomato soup instead of a rich bouilla-
baisse? Montgomery Ward's after Abercrombie and
Fitch? A Ford Fiesta where a Mercedes once purred?
And didn't you just know off-the-rack permanent press

slacks didn't have the feel and fit of custom-tailored worsted wool? But it wasn't just the money, Frederick knew. It was the entire mind-set, the *ambience*, the way a man's trappings served to define him. The way a man perceived himself.

Frederick slipped gradually down the chute to madness. The worst part of the journey was his almost total awareness of what was happening to him. Reality became increasingly plastic and mutable, all according to the whims of his tortured psyche, and even though he *knew* it was happening, he couldn't do a goddamned thing about it.

But then, there *was* something to be done, wasn't there?

Not a rectifying, restorative act, to be sure, but a sweet enough substitute for any man exceeding the posted limits on the Oblivion Expressway.

Frederick accepted his mission with a semi-stoical smile—if there can be such a thing. Revenge is that special chord played out in the mind that has worked through the whole sliding scale of emotional responses and found them wanting. And revenge, Frederick discovered, became his raison d'etre.

In several weeks he'd transformed himself from ruined orthopedic specialist to a far more romantic amalgam: tactician, private investigator, commando, and most importantly, avenging angel. He watched his prey from close range, studied his habits, made his plans, and when the time was just right, reached for his Gladstone bag . . .

. . . and unleashed the instrument of his revenge. Even in the feeble light of the bedroom, the scalpel shone with a preternatural brightness. As Frederick bandied it gracefully, like a conductor with his baton, before Raczkowski's bugging eyes, it seemed to grow brighter and shinier still.

Such a tiny little blade, thought Frederick. Ever since medical school, he had been amazed at how efficient a cutting tool it was. Laying its flat surface on the flabby skin of Donald's shoulder, Frederick let his former patient feel the cold kiss of the steel. He let the moment linger, like a foul odor that won't go away, in Donald's mind. The anticipation of the first cut would be worse than the actuality, wouldn't it?

Yes, of course it would.

Then with a simple, confident turn of his wrist, a subtle downward pressure, the little blade was plunging effortlessly through Raczkowski's doughy, mole-blighted flesh. Blood seeped at first, but as the capillaries gave way to heavier plumbing, things began to get a little messy. Raczkowski tried to scream, but the Xylothal wouldn't allow it.

Frederick smiled. A big, burly asshole like Raczkowski making these wimpy, gaspy little kitten mewlings was kind of funny.

Pausing, Frederick peered down at his ex-patient with an expression most psychiatrists would describe as *flat*. Now what was he going to do about the major arteries and veins? Of course—just tie them off crudely, seepage be damned. That would hold things at least until he finished sawing through all those tough tendons and ligaments.

He smiled and went back to his work, moving the blade with renewed confidence, trying to retrace the scar marks of his previous work. Raczkowski's pain levels were red-lining now. Even under the hammer-lock of the Xylothal, the man was managing to give the suggestion of writhing on the blood-soaked bed. If eyes could bulge voluntarily from a skull, his would have long since left their sockets.

The pain must have been exquisite, thought Frederick.

At last, all remaining gristle had been separated, the final shreds of connective fascia flensed away, and Frederick's work was completed. Raczkowski was beginning to hemorrhage badly, beginning the long slide into terminal shock. Frederick left him to leak away in the cruel moonlight.

He paused to wrap the arm in a Hefty bag, then wash up before slipping into the comfort of the darkness. Within minutes, Frederick was motoring down the Interstate. It had started to drizzle but he didn't care. When he was several miles along, he hurled the bagged arm out the window. It landed on the highway's shoulder and he chuckled at the ironic appropriateness.

Oddly enough, though, the great sense of vindication he'd expected remained absent. Oh, of course he was pleased Raczkowski had received suitable punishment for his gross ingratitude, but there was not the expected feeling of *completion,* of a mission finally ended.

Worse (or perhaps, *better*), Frederick discovered something new about himself. In a truly transcendent moment, while slicing through the last remnants of what had been a human arm, he'd realized he *liked* what he was doing. How odd his life had taken such turns until it now lay at the antipodes of all to which he'd ever aspired.

White Healer turned Dark Destroyer.

He smiled. There was a curious but fulfilling symmetry to it all. Yes, he thought as he gripped the wheel and peered out into the murky predawn, maybe somebody out there needs me.

Maybe they need a Good Samaritan . . .

The Pharaoh's Crown

Christopher Fahy

"I've seen them last almost forever," Dr. Waxman said as some drool escaped Parker's mouth and ran down his chin. "On the other hand, I've seen them give out in two days." Parker gagged. "Suction," Dr. Waxman said, and the hygienist set to work with her hose.

When the roar had stopped, Parker said, "Well what happens then?"

"If the endo crumbles?"

"Yes."

"We give it another try. If it doesn't work, we lose the tooth."

We, Parker thought. "So what would you recommend?"

"We cap it," Dr. Waxman said. "Gold crown."

"That sounds like big bucks."

Dr. Waxman looked pained. "It's not inexpensive, but think of the advantages. You can practically chew on stones. Once you've gone through the hassle of a root canal, doesn't it make good sense to protect your investment?"

Investment, Parker thought. He was starting to drool again. "Well . . ." he said.

The following week he had an impression made, and two weeks after that the crown was set in place. At home in his condo he checked the job in the mirror. He'd never liked gold teeth, and now he owned one—at considerable cost. It glowed far back near the hinge of his jaw, out of sight of the masses, the casual observer, the public. Thank God for that. He hated to call attention to himself. His ex-wife Gloria had called him the shyest man in the world. As if she had known all the men in the world, he thought with a sour sniff. There must have been a *few* she'd overlooked.

He closed his mouth, bit down. The metal clicked against the opposing molar. It felt too high—and weird, as if his tooth were trapped, imprisoned, suffocating.

He mixed himself a gin and tonic and sat on his couch, his hide-a-bed, one of the only pieces of furniture left from his Gloria days. That hotshot lawyer of hers had damn near wiped him out. She was to blame and he was wiped out; wasn't that some kick in the head? She had been on this very same hide-a-bed when he'd caught her, had come home early from work and found her with Adam Howard. Again he pictured her brazenly strutting across the floor in nothing but white silk stockings and lacy blue garter belt—items he'd never laid eyes on before—casually smoking as Howard had groped for his clothes. He went hot as he thought of that smirk on her hateful face. And the gall of her calling him "drab"! If he saw her again he would kill her, he swore he would!

He drank. Gin tingled against the tender gum surrounding the golden crown. The nub of tooth under there was dead, no worry about a sudden jolt from that. He could chew on the ice with impunity if he wanted. And King Mohteb was pleased.

He swallowed a shred of lime and thought: What? Who? King . . . who? He stared out the window, frowning. New buildings were going up by the river, tall concrete slabs; they looked ominous now in the dying light. Far off, on the water, the windows of one of the boats caught the sun and flashed red. Parker's heart sped up, he felt hot again, and he thought: that dental work sure does a number on you. Something about how you have to lie back like that. Saps all your strength. I'll hit the sack early tonight.

He had horrible dreams. His new tooth was glowing, ablaze. His breath was a dragon's breath, searing all in his path. King Mohteb grinned down from his throne as the fire spun into a circle, turned into the sun. The slabs ran red. Stone burned.

In the morning his mouth felt fine. The redness around the crown had faded away. When he brushed his teeth—no pain.

He was working hard on the Marshall report when the noises began. The fluorescents again, he thought. He hated fluorescents, especially the one in the ceiling above his desk, which would randomly flicker and buzz like a heavy bee. Sometimes a rap with his knuckle would quiet the thing, and Parker was ready to climb on his chair and bop the plastic panel diffusing the "cool white" tubes, when he noticed an odd undulation in the buzzing sound.

It wasn't the light, it was voices—a number of voices, low, in unison, a chant. Parker frowned, feeling slightly dizzy. "Hey Janet," he said to his closest coworker, "do you hear anything?"

"Like what?" Janet said with a squint, her eyes tiny behind her strong glasses.

"A buzzing, sort of," Parker said.

"I don't think so." She cocked her head. "No, nothing. Do you?"

"I thought I did for a minute. Thanks."

Parker stared at the Marshall report. He could still hear the voices, the rhythmical rise and fall, soft and low and yet urgent. His gum began to tingle and he poked it with his tongue. The crown felt warm and was vibrating ever so slightly like . . . like a radio speaker.

Parker opened his mouth and closed it again. Again, again. The noise was coming from his crown.

"Every so often a filling will pick up radio waves," Dr. Waxman said. "It's quite uncommon, but it does occur."

"It's occurring to me," Parker said.

"What stations can you get?" Waxman asked with a jolly grin. "It's hell for a classical music fan to be stuck with rock and roll."

Parker wasn't amused. "Look, I want you to stop it, it's driving me nuts."

"Chances are it will just go away," Waxman said.

"You had that endo for weeks without hearing voices, and it's probably temporary."

"The voices started when I got the crown."

"The crown isn't to blame. It isn't gold that picks up radio waves, it's silver."

"If it doesn't stop, I'll want the whole thing done over," Parker said. "I can't go around with voices in my mouth."

Dr. Waxman shrugged. "The job may not turn out as well next time. These root canals . . ."

"Om-ah-wat-toh-meh-ley-tep-cha . . . Amon, Amon, Amon . . ."

Parker held his head. The voices had persisted all afternoon, and now with three stiff gin and tonics under his belt and the sun long gone, they continued to drone.

He'd discovered a pattern to them. Certain syllables were repeated, especially that "Amon, Amon." The sounds were a language, not random noise as he'd thought at the start. But *what* language? Just his luck to pick up some *foreign* radio station, a broadcast in some tongue he'd never heard. He always got the bone in the burger, the cherry pit in the pie. As Gloria had told him once, he could fall in a basket of roses and come up smelling like dung. Oh she'd been a supportive bitch, all right!

"Meh-lah-mah-tep-osh-beh-rah-tah . . . Amon . . ."

Parker slapped headphones over his ears and turned up the sound: The *1812* Overture: Crash! Boom! Blam! He drank and stared out at the river. And somewhere below the noise he could still hear "Im-leh-tak-met . . ."

This night's dream sent him jolting straight up in his bed, wide awake, his hand clutching his chest.

He had been in a dusty, arid land, a land of relentless sun. The sun had been a gold ball in his mouth, a ball surrounded by now too-familiar syllables: "Pah-leh-moh-ket . . ." He retreated from light and searing wind, was in dark chambers, smelled sharp incense, lifted the hem of his robe and was handed the sword. He tested its edge with his fingertip. Its very touch drew blood. He smiled, and the sun fell out of his mouth, rolled to the altar.

The female sacrifice was naked, pleading, pale. King Mohteb glared from his golden throne. Parker ascended the steps to the slab. He raised the blade. Quick expert motion. The scream filled the air with red.

"It's still there," Parker said to the phone. "Three days now. It never stops."

"I'm still pretty sure it will," Dr. Waxman said. "If you want me to look again ..."

"I don't want you to *look,* I want you to take out the crown."

"The crown isn't the problem, I told you that."

"Well, take out the whole damn *tooth* then, I don't care."

"Mr. Parker, it wouldn't be wise ... You just invested—"

"Hey! I can't sleep! I can just about *think*! I want an appointment! Now!"

"Very well," Dr. Waxman said. "I can see you on Friday at three. That will give you some time to reconsider."

Reconsider, right, Parker thought as he hung up the phone. It would give him some time to go looney, go totally nuts! To turn into the raving maniac that Gloria claimed he was when he finally caught on to her game. He'd bet the dregs of his checking account that she was behind all this. Still twisting the knife!

He stared out the window. The walls of the new construction protruded like giant gravestones, like monstrous teeth. It looked like the necropolis out there, the Valley of Tombs. King Mohteb ...

He slapped his hands to his temples. "Stop it! Stop!" he cried out loud.

Blood, so much blood, he could taste it in his mouth. He awoke to a slanting gold sword blade of sun and turned the alarm clock off. The buzzer died. The chant began. He groaned and sat up in the bed. How long had he slept? Two hours? Three? He would die if this didn't stop, he would literally *die*. In the back of his mouth the golden crown felt hot.

In the living room he snapped on the TV set. Amon.

A coup in South America. Amon. The weather would be steaming hot. Amon. The Sox had lost again. Amon, Amon. He closed his eyes, saw red. The economic indicators rose. Amon. "And here's an interesting thing about gold, Steve, something I'll bet you didn't know. It's been recycled so many times throughout the centuries that nearly every wedding ring, every bar in the vaults at Fort Knox contains traces of gold from the bracelets, crowns, and amulets of the ancient Egyptian pharaohs."

"Out," Parker said.
"Just the crown," Dr. Waxman said.
"Just the crown."
Dr. Waxman sighed. "It seems such a shame."
"If this works, you can make another crown. I'll be glad to pay. I just don't want *this* crown."
"I did such a nice job."
"Out," Parker said.

The voices were gone. They were gone! Parker laughed with glee as he drove. Nothing to it. A two-minute hammer and chisel job, some silver amalgam to build up the stub, and that was it. It *had* been the crown all along.

At home he made himself an extra stiff drink to celebrate. When he looked out the window the buildings seemed fine again, were mere buildings, not teeth, not tombs. When he sat on the couch he heard traffic, and that was all. He laughed again. He drank. He bit on the ice and he heard something crack. When he opened his mouth and leaned forward, the shards of his broken root canal tumbled into his waiting palm.

"Yes, that's how it goes sometimes when they're unprotected," Dr. Waxman said. "Sometimes you lose the tooth. Now I'd like you to count from one to seven backward." Parker looked at the tube in his arm. "Sev—" he said, then slid into the cool, dark vault.

The taste of blood. The white light of the gods shone down.

"Don't rinse till the gums stop bleeding," three hazy

Dr. Waxmans said in a voice that blurred to other voices, a familiar drone. Parker narrowed his eyes and nodded slowly, just once. The cotton was gone from his cheeks but his mouth still felt fuzzy and full. Dr. Waxman was pale, unfocused, but Parker's mind was clear. The voices called him, each syllable diamond bright. He'd been gone so long, so very long, and now it was time to return.

"Take it easy, now," Dr. Waxman grinned.

Take it easy. Parker tossed his head back and laughed. Dr. Waxman frowned.

The taste of blood. Outside he hailed a cab. "To the airport," he said.

The guide was a low-caste clown, an incompetent peasant. "Then, after thousands of years of glory, this city was sacked by the Assyrians," he said with a casual wave at the columns that lay in the blistering sand. A gust of dusty wind swirled up, and a woman with wrinkled jowls and purplish spun-sugar hair began to cough. "That happened in 661 B.C. The Romans sacked the city in 29 B.C., and once-glorious Thebes was reduced to a few scattered villages."

Parker squinted and thought: You fool! The great god Amon lives! He looked up at the sun and grinned.

The fools never missed him. From his hiding place in the cliffs he watched the bus depart. Before its dust dispersed on the horizon, the voices began again.

Parker turned in their direction, to the cleft in the stone, and entered the cool of the crypt. The smell of incense filled the gray light. The chant grew strong.

At the corridor's first turn, he donned his robe. He acknowledged the priests with a silent nod. At the second turn, they gave him his sword. It was cool and gleaming, perfectly balanced. He tested its edge with his fingertip. It drew bright blood.

As he entered the vault, the row of priests fell to their knees. On his golden throne, King Mohteb stared with burning, shadowed eyes. Gloria, naked, bound to the altar, struggled in vain, bruising her skin on the stone. As Parker approached, she screamed.

Parker raised his blade. His eyes were suns, and the good taste of blood filled his mouth.

Slit

Richard Laymon

The library would be closing in five minutes. Charles knew that the last of the students had already left. He was alone with Lynn.

He saw no point in heading off into the stacks to shelve books, so he lingered beside the circulation desk, arranging volumes in the cart and sneaking glances at her.

She sat on a high stool behind the desk. Her empty loafers were on the floor. Her feet, in white socks, curled over a wooden rung of the stool. Charles could see one smooth calf, the crease behind her knee, and a few inches of bare thigh. Her legs were parted as far as the straight denim skirt would allow. The skirt's hem looked so tight against the side of her thigh that Charles wondered if it might leave a red mark on her skin.

She was leaning forward, elbows resting on the desktop, hands on cheeks, head down as she looked through *Kirkus*. Her white blouse, tucked into the skirt, was taut against her back. Charles could see the bumps of her spine, the soft curves of her ribs, the pink hue of her skin through the fabric, the slim bands of her bra.

He squatted down and placed some books on the lower shelf of the cart. This angle allowed him to see Lynn's right breast. It was there beyond the underside of her arm, a sweet mound cupped by the tight blouse, its front hovering just above the edge of the desk.

It would look so much better without the bra. The seams, the pattern, the stiffness. All in the way.

Charles pictured himself slicing through its straps.

Lynn reached out, turned a page, flinched and blurted, "Ow! Damn!" She jerked her hand up. She held it rigid in front of her face, fingers spread and hooked. A gleaming dot of blood bloomed on the pad of her index finger.

Charles felt his mouth go dry. His heart thudded. Heat rushed through his groin. He moaned.

She glanced over at him. Her face was red, her teeth bared. Her eyes returned to her hand. She looked as if she didn't know what to do with it. She shook it a couple of times like a cat with a wet paw, then pressed the bleeding fingertip between her lips.

"A paper cut?" he asked.

She nodded.

"I hate those things," he said.

A cut. A slit.

He stayed crouched, hard and aching.

Lynn took the finger away from her mouth. It left some blood on her lips. She scowled at the wound, then gave Charles a tight, twisted smile. "It's not that they hurt so much, you know? They're just so . . ." She shuddered. "They're like fingernails skreeking on a blackboard." She licked the blood from her lips, then returned the finger to her mouth.

"Would you like a bandage?" Charles asked.

"Do you have one?"

"Oh, sure. I'm always prepared."

"Like a Boy Scout, huh?"

"Yeah." Rising from his crouch, he hoped that the books on the cart's top shelf were high enough. They were. Their tops reached up past his stomach.

He turned away from Lynn and hurried into the office behind the circulation desk. There he took a bandage from the tin inside his briefcase. He adjusted the front of his pants to make the bulge of his erection less apparent. But it still showed. He took his corduroy jacket off the back of a nearby chair, put it on, and fastened the middle button. He looked down. The front of the jacket nicely concealed his secret.

When he came out, he found that Lynn had turned around on her stool to face him. "It's stopped bleeding," she said.

"Yeah, but paper cuts. You rub them the wrong way and flip back the skin and ..."

"Yuck. I guess I will take a bandage. Would you like to do the honors?" She held her hand toward Charles.

"Sure," he said. Trembling, he stripped the wrapper off the adhesive strip. He moved closer to Lynn, halting when the wet end of her finger was inches from his chest. He stared down at the slit—a crescent across the finger's pad, rather like the gills of a tiny fish, pink under a thin white flap. The edge of the flap was away from him.

"Do you think I'll live?"

"Sure." His voice came out husky. He felt terribly tight and hard.

"Are you okay?" she asked.

"Yeah. Cuts make me nervous."

"You aren't gonna faint or anything, are you?"

"Hope not." He fumbled with the bandage, peeling the shiny papers away from its sides. He let them fall. They drifted down like petals plucked from a flower, and settled on her skirt.

Pinching the sticky ends of the bandage, he lowered the gauze center toward Lynn's cut.

He wanted to hurt her.

No! Don't!

He wanted to grab her finger and rub his thumb back, flipping up the little edge of skin, making her jerk and cry out.

Not Lynn! Don't!

As fast as he could, he pressed the bandage to her cut and flipped the adhesive ends around her finger. He whirled away and rushed for the office.

"Charles?" she called. "Charles, are you all right?"

He didn't answer. He dropped onto his swivel chair, hunched over and grabbed his knees.

It's over, he told himself. You didn't do it. Lynn can't even suspect ...

He heard her quiet footsteps behind him. She put a hand on his shoulder. "What's wrong?" she asked.

"Just ... cuts. They upset me."

Her hand squeezed him through the corduroy. "If I'd known ... What is it, a phobia or something?"

"I guess so. Maybe."

In a lighter tone, she said, "That probably explains why you carry bandages around, huh?"

"Yeah."

She patted his shoulder. "Maybe you'll feel better if you get some fresh air," she said. "Why don't you go ahead and take off? I'll close up the library."

"Okay. Thanks."

He waited until she was gone, then carried his briefcase outside. The night was dank and misty.

Feverish with memories of Lynn's cut, he lingered near the library entrance. Soon the upper windows went dark. He pictured her up there, alone in the stacks, lowering her bandaged finger from the switch panel, starting down the stairwell.

His Swiss Army knife was a heavy lump against his thigh. He slipped his hand down into his pants pocket. He caressed the smooth plastic handle.

And savored thoughts of slitting her.

Just wait for her to come out . . .

No!

He turned from the library and walked quickly away.

In his apartment three blocks from campus, Charles went to bed. But he didn't sleep. His mind swirled with images of Lynn.

Don't think about her, he told himself.

You can't do her.

But it would be *so* nice.

But you can't.

Lynn was a graduate student. Like Charles, she earned a small stipend by working part time at the Whitmore Library. Everyone knew they worked the same hours. Too much suspicion would be focused on him.

Besides, he really liked her.

But damn it . . . !

Forget about her.

He tried to forget about her. He tried to think only about the others. How they yelped or screamed. How their faces looked. How their skin split apart. How blood spilled out like scarlet creeks overflowing banks of ripped flesh, spreading and running, forming new streams that slid along velvety fields, that settled to create shimmering pools in the hollows of the body, that flowed down slopes.

So many faces. So many bodies flinching with surprise or thrashing in agony. So many flooding slits.

All belonged to strangers.

Except for the face and body and cut of his mother. Struggling to stop the confusing flood of images, fighting to keep his mind off Lynn, he concentrated on his mother. Her voice through the door. *Honey, would you be a dear and get me a Band-Aid?* He saw himself enter the steamy bathroom, reach high into the medicine cabinet for the tin of bandages, take out one and step to the tub where she reclined. The water was murky. Patches of white suds floated on its surface. From her chest rose shiny wet islands, wonderfully round and smooth, each topped by a ruddier kind of skin that jutted up in the center. Looking at the islands made Charles feel strange and squirmy.

His mother held a razor in one hand. Her left leg was out of the water, its foot propped on the rim of the tub under one of the faucet handles. The cut was midway between her knee and the place where the water rippled around the wider part of her leg. *I'm afraid I nicked myself shaving,* she said.

Charles nodded. He gazed at the wound. He watched the strands of red slide down her gleaming skin. They made the bathwater pink between her legs. She had a hairy place down there. He couldn't see her dingus. He stared, trying to find it even though he knew he shouldn't be looking at that place. But he couldn't help himself. He felt sick and tight.

You din't cut it off, did you?

Cut off what, honey?

You know, your dingus.

She laughed softly. *Oh, darling, mommies don't have dinguses. Here.* And then she took gentle hold of his hand and guided it down into the pink, hot water. She slid it against her body. Against a cut—no, not just a cut—a huge, open gash with slippery edges. He tried to jerk his hand away, but she tightened her grip and kept it there. *Go on, feel it,* she said.

But doesn't it hurt? he asked.

Not at all.

It was almost as long as his hand. Warm and slick inside. And very deep. She squirmed a little as his fingers explored.

Her voice had a funny sound to it when she said, *I'm made this way. All mommies are.* She released his hand, but he kept it there. *That's enough, now, honey. You'd better put that Band-Aid on my leg before I bleed to death.*

Then Charles had the bandage ready. As he lowered it toward the small bleeding cut on her leg, she said, *You aren't gonna faint or anything, are you?* But it wasn't his mother's voice. He turned his head. The woman sprawled in the tub was Lynn.

At dawn, groggy and restless, Charles climbed out of bed. He didn't know whether he had slept at all. Maybe a little. If so, his sleep had been a turmoil of dreams so vivid that they might have been memories or hallucinations.

He felt better after a long shower. Returning to his bedroom, he sat down and stared at the alarm clock. A quarter till six. That gave him just more than ten hours before returning to work at the library. And seeing Lynn again.

He saw her naked beneath him, writhing as he slit into her creamy skin.

"No!" he blurted, and stomped his foot on the floor.

There were ways to prevent it. Tricks. He'd worked out *lots* of tricks over the years to feed his urges—to ease the needs, to keep some control.

Weller Hall seemed huge and empty. Charles knew that it wasn't empty. But he saw no one as he eased the door shut and made his way to the staircase. Those few students and professors unlucky enough to be burdened with "eight-o'clocks" were already snug in the classrooms, probably yawning and rubbing their eyes and wishing they were still in bed.

He climbed four creaky stairs, then stopped. He listened. Beyond the sounds of his own rough breathing and heartbeat, he heard a distant voice. Probably Dr.

Chitwood. Dr. Shithead to the students who had to suffer through his mandatory (this being a university of Methodist origin) History of Christianity class. Known as Heist of Christ. Not only mandatory, but boring, and forever scheduled for 8:00 A.M.

It was one of only three classes taking place in Weller Hall on Monday, Wednesday, and Friday at such an ungodly hour. Chitwood's room was right at the top of the stairs.

Grinning, Charles pulled out his knife. He pried it open and dug into the smooth, worn wood of the banister. He carved a neat, two-inch slot down the rail's top. He scraped it clean of splinters. Crouching, he ran his thumb over a grimy stair. He rubbed his thumb against the pale cut on the handrail, darkening it with dirt, camouflaging it.

Using needle-nosed pliers, he snugged an injector blade into the slot.

He straightened up and admired his work.

The edge of the blade protruded just a little bit above the surface of the rail. It was hardly visible at all.

Shivering with excitement, Charles hurried outside. He waited on a bench and watched the entrance to Weller Hall.

This'll be great, he thought. It was always great.

But he'd never done it on campus before. He began to worry about that. He even considered returning to the stairway and pulling out the blade. He could walk into town and set up the trap somewhere else, somewhere safer.

He didn't want to do that, though. Too often, the trick ended up wasted on somebody old and ugly. He couldn't take a chance on that happening. He needed to slit a coed, a fresh young woman. One like Lynn.

The minutes dragged by. When people began wandering into the building, Charles feared that he might miss the event. He waited a while longer, fidgeting. Then he rose from the bench, trotted up the concrete steps, and rushed inside.

A few students were wandering the corridor, lingering near doorways, entering classrooms. Nobody on the stairs. He strolled to the far side of the hall. He removed a paperback copy of *Finnegans Wake* from his briefcase, opened the book, leaned back against the wall, and pretended to read.

From here, he had a good view of the stairway.

The book trembled in his hands.

He held his breath when a couple of girls walked past him and turned toward the stairway. They looked like freshmen. They acted like freshmen, the way they talked so loudly and laughed and gestured.

The girl on the razor's side of the stairs held books to her chest with her left arm. Her right arm swung free. At the first stair, she rested her hand on the banister. It slid up the rail as she began to climb.

Her shiny blond hair swayed against her back. She wore a sleeveless sweatshirt. Her arms were slender and dusky. Her white shorts were very tight. Charles could see the outline of her panties. Skimpy things.

His heart slammed.

As she stepped from the third stair to the fourth, she jerked her hand off the railing.

Got her!

But she didn't flinch or cry out. She simply chopped her hand through the air. Some kind of damn gesture to accompany whatever inane point she was making to her friend.

She was almost to the landing before her hand returned to the banister.

Charles sighed. He felt robbed.

It's not over yet, he told himself.

She'd been so perfect, though. Pretty and blond and slender like Lynn. A few years younger, but otherwise just right.

I couldn't have seen the look on her face, anyway, he consoled himself.

From above came a thunder of footfalls.

Charles perked up. Heist of Christ was out, the students stampeding to escape. In seconds, the first of them rounded the landing and rushed down the lower flight. Trembling with excitement, Charles watched those near the banister. A boy in the lead. Luckily, his arm was busy clamping books to his hip. Behind him came a lithe brunette, breasts jiggling the front of her T-shirt. But she carried a book bag by its straps and didn't bother with the rail.

Coming down behind her was a fat guy in a sweatsuit. But behind *him* was a real beauty with flowing golden hair, her shoulders bare, her torso hugged by a bright yellow tube top. Her hand was on the banister!

Yes!

"Ow! Shit!"

The fat guy.

No!

He jerked his hand off the railing and halted so abruptly that the blonde nearly crashed into him. He lifted his hand to his crimson, stunned face. Blood dripped off, streaking the front of his sweatshirt. "Fuckin' A! Looka this! Jeeeeez!"

Kids started to crowd around him.

Before long, someone would find the razor.

Releasing a long sigh, Charles closed his book. He tucked it under one arm, picked up his briefcase, and strolled up the corridor.

Later that morning, after his seminar in Twentieth-Century Irish Literature, Charles sat on a park bench along one of the campus walkways. The bench was fairly well hidden by hedges at both ends and an oak to the rear.

He took two X-Acto blades from his briefcase. Each was about an inch in length, V-shaped, with fine sharp edges. At the blunt end of each blade was a tab that could be slid into one of the several handles that were part of the kit. Charles hadn't brought the handles with him.

With the blades cupped in one hand, he pretended to read Joyce. He watched the walkway. People kept coming by.

Patience, he told himself.

Before he could find time to plant the blades, a couple roosted on the bench across from him. They had bags from the Burger King a block from campus. Charles waited while they ate and gabbed. He waited while they snuggled and kissed. Finally, they wandered away, the guy with his hand down a back pocket of the girl's short denim skirt.

He checked the walkway. Clear at last!

Working quickly, he planted one blade upright in a green-painted slat beside his right thigh. He scooted away from it, then dug a place for the other blade on a slat of the backrest. After checking again for witnesses, he inserted the blade.

Then he roamed across the walkway and settled down on the bench where the sweethearts had wasted so much of his time. They'd left a fry behind. He brushed it to the ground. He opened *Finnegans Wake* and waited.

People came by. A lot of people. Alone, in pairs, in small groups. Students, instructors, professors, administrators, groundskeepers. Male and female. Slender, lovely girls. Plain girls. Slobs.

Into the afternoon, Charles waited.

Nobody sat on the bench.

Nobody.

Still, Charles waited. Over and over again in his mind, beautiful young women sat down on the bench. Their faces twisted and went scarlet. They leaped up, shrieking. They hurried away, blood from gashed buttocks spreading across the seats of shorts and skirts and jeans, blood from ripped backs staining blouses, T-shirts, flowing down the bare skin of those who wore tube tops or other varieties of low-backed garments.

In his best fantasy, it was Lynn who sat on the bench. Wearing a white bikini.

He often returned to that one while he waited.

Lynn stopped in front of him.

He gazed up at her, puzzled. She wasn't wearing a bikini. She wore a white cotton polo shirt, pink shorts that reached almost to her knees, and white socks and sneakers. Her huge leather shoulder bag hung against her hip.

"Hi, Charles," she said. "How's it going?"

He shrugged. He tried to smile. He was reasonably certain this was Lynn, not a figment of his imagination.

"Ready to head on over to the salt mines?" she asked.

He glanced at his wristwatch. Ten till four. Impossible! He couldn't have been sitting here *that* long.

"I guess it's time," he muttered.

Lynn tilted her head to one side. "Are you all right?"

"I didn't get much sleep last night."

"I had kind of a restless night myself. So, are you coming?"

"Sure. Yeah. I guess so." He put his book away, lifted his briefcase, and rose from the bench. With a last glimpse at the other bench, he started walking with Lynn.

It's Fate, he thought. He'd *tried* to direct his need away from Lynn, but his efforts had failed. They were meant to fail. He was being guided by forces beyond his control, forces that had ordained Lynn to bleed for him.

"Check out my finger," she said as they walked along. She raised it in front of his face.

The bandage was gone. Charles saw a tiny curve of white fringe on the pad of her finger. His heart thudded. "It looks good," he said.

"Almost as good as new." She smiled as her upper arm brushed against him. She lowered the hand to her side. "If it weren't for your first aid, no telling what might've happened. Who knows? I might've bled to death."

Charles knew she was joking. But his heart pounded even harder. Heat spread through his groin. "From a paper cut?"

"Of course. Happens all the time. It's the leading cause of death among librarians and editors. Honest to God." She looked at him. "You *do* know how to smile, don't you?"

"Sure," he muttered.

"Let's see one."

He tried.

"Miserable," she said. "You know, you'd be a pretty handsome fellow if you'd smile once in a while."

He gazed at her. He pictured how her face would look with bright red blood streaming from it. He imagined himself licking the blood from her cheeks and lips.

"That's more of a leer than a smile, actually," Lynn said. "But it'll do. You just need more practice."

*   *   *

Even after all the books were shelved, Charles stayed in the second-floor stacks.

If he went downstairs, he would see Lynn. She would be sitting on her stool behind the circulation desk, checking books in and out, or maybe wandering the floor, cheerfully offering suggestions to students in need of assistance.

As long as I don't see her, he told himself, nothing will happen.

A few students came up. Some searched for books while others slipped into carrels along the far wall and studied. There were girls, but he paid them no attention. It would be Lynn, or no one.

He ducked into a carrel, himself. For some unknown reason, it had been placed in a corner away from the lights. That suited him well. He felt snug and hidden.

He folded his arms on the desktop and put his head down. Maybe I'll sleep, he thought.

He closed his eyes. He pictured Lynn suspended from the ceiling beam, wrists tied, arms stretched high, feet off the floor. He had no rope, though. Too bad. Go back to his apartment and get some? The emergency exits had alarms. He couldn't leave the library without passing Lynn's desk.

Maybe use my belt instead?

That had worked before. He'd put a loop around the girl's hands and nailed the other end high on a wall.

No hammer. No nails.

A rope would be better, anyway. Even though he didn't have one, he liked the image of Lynn hanging helpless. He knew she was wearing a polo shirt. In his mind, however, she wore a regular blouse. With buttons. And he saw himself slicing off the buttons, one by one.

Charles flinched awake when someone stroked the back of his head. He jerked upright in his chair. Lynn was standing close beside him, frowning down with concern on her shadowy face.

"You really zonked out," she said. Her voice was little more than a whisper in the silence.

"I'm sorry. I didn't . . ."

"That's okay." Her hand stayed on the back of his

head, caressing his hair. "I was a little worried about you, though. You just disappeared."

"I was shelving books up here. I felt so tired . . ."

"No problem." A smile tilted the corners of her mouth. "I thought maybe you were trying to avoid me. You've been acting so strange ever since last night."

"I've been *feeling* pretty strange."

"Are you still upset because I cut myself?"

"In a way, I guess." He stood up. The chair made a loud squawk as it was scooted away by the backs of his knees. The noise made him cringe.

"I haven't been quite myself, either," Lynn said.

He turned to face her. "Really?"

"Really." Gazing into his eyes, she took hold of his hands. "The way you acted last night . . . You were so sweet, getting me the bandage and everything, putting it on my finger even though you have that phobia about cuts. I just suddenly realized . . . how really special you are, Charles."

"Me?"

"Yeah, you." She lifted her hands to his face. Gently caressing his cheeks, she eased against him. She tilted back her head. She pressed her mouth against his lips. After a slow, soft kiss, she looked up into his eyes. "We're all alone," she whispered. "I've already locked up for the night."

All he could say was "Oh." He was trembling. His heart was punching, his breath ragged. His groin was tight and the way Lynn pressed against him, he knew she must be able to feel his erection.

She stepped back to make a space between their bodies. Her hands roamed over his chest. "I was awake all night," she said. "Thinking about you."

"I was awake thinking about you, too."

"You were?" He heard a tremor in her voice.

"Yes."

"Oh, man." She made a soft, nervous laugh. "I should've cut myself a long time ago."

Her trembling fingers unbuttoned his shirt. She spread it open. She kissed his chest.

With one hand, Charles stroked her back. With the other, he dug into the pocket of his pants. He squeezed the plastic handle of his knife.

Staring into his eyes, Lynn plucked at the bottom of her polo shirt. She pulled it free of her shorts, drew it over her head and dropped it to the floor.

Charles felt as if his breath had been sucked from his lungs. He struggled for air.

Lynn fumbled at the waist of her shorts. The garment slipped down her legs. She stepped out of it, nudged it away with her sneaker.

The plastic knife handle felt greasy with sweat.

"Do you like how I look?" Lynn whispered.

Charles nodded. "You look . . . so beautiful."

So beautiful. Slender and smooth, naked except for her skimpy white bra and panties, her white socks and sneakers.

She had a calm, dreamy look on her face. A hint of a smile. Arching her back, she reached both arms up behind her.

"Don't," Charles murmured.

Her eyebrows lifted. "I was just going to unhook . . ."

"I know. Let me?"

Her smile brightened. "Sure."

Charles pulled out his knife. As he opened the blade, he watched Lynn—ready to grab her if she should try to flee.

Her smile went crooked. She stood motionless, eyes on the knife. "You're kidding, right?"

"I have to."

She lifted her gaze to his face. She seemed to be studying him. Then she shrugged one shoulder. "Go ahead, Charles."

"Huh?"

"If you have to, you have to. I'll buy a new one."

"Oh."

She put her hands on his hips. He felt them shaking slightly. They squeezed him when he cut through each of the shoulder straps. Then he slid his blade under the narrow band between the cups of her bra. She closed her eyes. Her mouth hung open. He heard her raspy breathing. He tugged, severing the band.

The bra fell away.

Lynn opened her eyes. A smile fluttered on her face. "This is pretty kinky," she said, her voice husky.

She shivered when he rubbed the blade's blunt edge down the top of her left breast. In the faint glow of the

nearest fluorescent light, he saw the smooth skin go peb-
bly with goosebumps. Her nipple grew. He pressed it
down with the flat of the blade, and watched it spring
up again. Lynn groaned.

She tugged open his belt. She unfastened the button at
the waist of his pants, jerked his zipper down, feverishly
yanked his pants and underwear down his thighs.

Can't be happening this way, Charles thought. Never
had anything like this happened. He wondered if he
might be asleep, dreaming.

But he knew that he was very much awake.

Lynn's fingers curled around him.

"Do my panties," she whispered. "With the knife."

He cut them at the sides. The flimsy fabric drooped,
but the panties didn't fall. They clung between her legs
until she reached down. A small pull, and they drifted
toward the floor.

"This is so weird," she gasped. "I've never . . . nothing
like this."

Her soft, encircling fingers slid on him. Up, and down.

The knife shook as Charles moved it toward her chest.
Just above her left breast, he pressed the point against
her skin. Gently.

"Careful there," she whispered. "You don't want to
cut me."

"I do, actually."

Her hand slipped away. She stood up very straight,
searching his eyes. "You're kidding, aren't you?"

"No."

"But you *hate* cuts."

"I'm sorry. As a matter of fact, I love them. They . . .
they do something to me."

"You mean like they turn you on?"

"Yes."

"But that's crazy!"

"I guess so. I'm awfully sorry, Lynn."

"Hold on, now."

"I *have* to do it. I have to cut you up."

"Oh, my God."

He shook his head. "You're so beautiful, and . . . I
guess I love you."

"Charles. No."

He stared at the knife point denting her skin. A slit all the way down to the tip of her breast ...

Lynn grabbed his hand, twisted it. As Charles yelped, the elbow of her other arm crashed against his cheek. Stumbling backward, he heard his knife clatter on the floor. His pants tripped him. He slammed the side of the study carrel and fell.

Lynn scurried, crouched, came up holding the knife.

Charles got to his knees. He gazed up at her. So beautiful. Scowling at him, naked except for her white socks and sneakers. The blade of the knife in her hand gleamed.

"Oh, Charles," she murmured.

Tears stung his eyes. He hunched over, clasped his face with both hands, and wept.

"Charles?"

"I'm sorry," he blurted. "God, I'm so sorry! I don't know why I ... I'm sorry!"

"Charles." Her voice held a note of command.

He rubbed tears from his eyes and lifted his head.

Lynn stared down at him. She nodded slightly. A corner of her mouth was trembling.

She flicked her wrist. She flinched and grimaced as the blade cut a tiny slit. She closed the knife and lowered it to her side.

Charles watched the thin ribbon of blood. It started just below her collarbone and trickled down. It ran along the top of her breast, split in two, and one strand began a new course down the pale round side while another made its slow way closer to her nipple.

"Come here," Lynn whispered.

Charles was embarrassed horribly the next day in the pharmacy.

Lynn was giggling.

She plopped three boxes of condoms down on the counter. The clerk, a young man, glanced from her to Charles. He looked amused.

"You got something against safe sex?" Lynn asked.

The clerk blushed. "No. Huh-uh."

Charles wanted to curl up and die.

"Ring these up, too, while you're at it." Onto the counter, Lynn tossed three tins of Band-Aids.

Rubies and Pearls

Rick Hautala

At first there was pain ... an incredible, searing pain that made every nerve in his body burn like an overheating wire. But then, with an audible snap, as if a cheap electrical fuse had blown, the pain stopped, and he was instantly, miraculously beyond the pain ... or above it, floating like a rain-laden cloud, drifting through the cold, black void of the night sky.

But even then he suspected that the void was internal, deep inside his own mind.

What the shit? ... Am I dying?

The thought was sharp and clear, but, curiously, it held no terror for him. His name was Alex St. Pierre, but throughout the state of Maine and the rest of the country, he was better known as the "Stillwater Slasher." He had seen plenty of death in his thirty-eight years. Hell, nearly twenty times, now, he had stared death straight in the face, watching with a dizzying mixture of glee and curiosity as, one by one, his victims—all eighteen of them—died slowly in his arms, their life-blood seeping from the long, curved slash he had carved into their throats, running from ear to ear.

He had watched, fascinated, as the blood, looking like small, rounded rubies, had beaded up all along the edge of the cut, and then—all eighteen times—he had drawn his knife along the slit a second time, running the blade in deeper so the blood would gush down the young woman's throat until it looked like she was wearing a scarlet turtleneck sweater. And then, once she was lying still, maybe not quite dead yet, but certainly beyond resistance, the glow of life dimming in her eyes, he had unbuckled his belt, dropped his pants to his ankles, and, kneeling beside her, had masturbated onto the dying woman's blood-smeared throat.

"Rubies," he had whispered tenderly, like a lover to all eighteen of them. "The drops of your blood ... are a necklace ... of rubies." Then, just as he reached his climax, his mind spinning with ecstasy, all eighteen times he had leaned close to the woman's senseless ear and, gasping with exhilaration, had whispered, "And my cum ... is a necklace ... of pearls."

Later, after he had regained his strength, he would clean himself up and take the body down to the Stillwater River, where he'd dump it in, not caring if it sank or floated down to the Penobscot and then made it all the way to the ocean.

But after nearly four years, in which he averaged four victims a year, one for each season, the police had finally caught up with him, and for the past two months he had been a prisoner in the Maine State Prison, awaiting trial. That's where he was when the blood vessel in his brain had popped, and they had to rush him under heavy guard to the emergency room at Mid-Coast Medical.

He had only a vague recollection of the timeless ambulance ride to hospital. Once or twice he wished he could have mustered enough strength to put up a fight, maybe use this situation to try to make a break, but he knew there were at least three armed guards in the ambulance along with the medical team. Besides, he was strapped securely to the stretcher.

Nearly every sound he heard, even the caterwauling wail of the siren, seemed muffled with distance, as though his head were packed with cotton. Only one sound had any clarity. That was the heavy thumping deep inside his head. He hadn't realized it was his own pulse until it started to flutter and slow. Then, from far off in the distance, he heard a wild commotion of disembodied voices, shouting frantically back and forth. He sensed a flurry of activity around him and felt his limp body being jostled about, but it didn't affect him. Nothing affected him. He felt curiously detached from everything when he opened his eyes and found that he was looking down from the ceiling as a platoon of doctors worked on the motionless figure lying on the operating table. After a timeless beat, he realized that he was looking down at his own lifeless body.

Well, son of a bitch! . . . I must be dead! he thought, but surprisingly, the thought still held no terror for him.

In life, he had known death as a friend, almost as intimately as a lover. He had seen it drop like a shimmering gauze curtain over the eyes of eighteen young women and countless cats and dogs that he had tortured and then killed when he was young. He had seen death extinguish the glow of life, making the facial expression of each woman go suddenly slack and frozen, casting her skin with a weird, gray pallor. He had studied it, trying to understand it, to experience it, but until now, he had never truly tasted of death's sharp sting.

And the surprise was, there wasn't any sting.

There had been no panic, no pain, no struggle whatsoever.

That surprised him because he was positive he had seen extreme pain and agony and fear in the eyes of all eighteen of his victims. He had been thrilled as he watched each of them try so desperately to cling onto life, but it had slipped away like fine sand, sifting between their fingers.

So why did he feel none of that now?

There was only a curious, almost giddy sensation of flying, of floating high above the pain and agony of what he thought death should be.

For another timeless beat, he hovered above the scene in the operating room, watching as the medical team fought to save him. His mind felt clear and focused, honed as razor sharp as it had been on those eighteen glorious nights when he had taken his victims. He could see everything the doctors and nurses were doing and hear everything anyone said. He noticed funny little details, like what shoes they were wearing and on which wrist they wore their watches. But he found that he didn't care. He almost laughed at their pathetic efforts to revive him. It was funny because he didn't need them . . . he didn't *want* them to succeed.

No, this was just fine with him.

Finally, however, he became aware of a subtle shifting behind him. Although it took no physical effort, and he had no sense of motion, he turned and saw a bright tunnel that receded into the distance like a long, luminous telescope. The tunnel was filled with a soft glow of lemon light that drew him toward it like comforting, beckoning arms.

Didn't I hear something about death being like this on "Geraldo" or something just a little while ago? But—hey, I thought that was all bullshit!

He was filled with a curious flutter of excitement and expectation as, floating weightlessly, he was drawn inexorably toward the inward spiraling tunnel of light. At the far end, the light seemed to brighten, shifting subtly from yellow to a pure, white radiance. He didn't even consider resisting the euphoric rush as he drifted like a dandelion puff along the softly pulsating walls of the tunnel. And then, up ahead, he could dimly make out the hazy silhouettes of people who appeared to be moving toward him, blowing like drifting snow. As they drew closer to him and his vision cleared, he saw that their arms were uplifted as though in greeting.

Son of a bitch! This is just like what those nut cases on "Geraldo" said it would be!

He remembered how all of the people on the show that day who claimed to have died and then come back described the overpowering sensation of warmth and well-being, of flying, and of seeing friends and relatives who had died before coming to greet them.

Swept along through the tunnel, he heard the soft whispering rush of wind in his ears and felt a gradually strengthening blast of embracing heat wash over him. With the bright, pulsating light behind them, the figures were still indistinguishable, but he smiled to himself as he watched them draw closer, their arms held out to him.

And then, just as suddenly as the realization that he had died had hit him, everything changed. The yellow light quickly blended to a hurtful, stinging red pulse that throbbed like a frantic, racing heartbeat. Hard, grinding thunder rumbled all around him, deafening, and the tunnel seemed to collapse inward on him, squeezing him. With their arms raised high over their heads, the figures swept toward him, and in a moment of blinding intensity, he saw and counted all eighteen women.

Jesus God! No!

Something punched hard against the inside of his chest as he glanced from one blank face to another. Cold, unblinking eyes stared at him, glowing as they bored into him with the acid of their eternal hatred. Their thin hands hooked into claws that twitched and trembled as they swung at him, slicing the air with whistling hisses. Dangling around each woman's throat, glowing dully in the eerie light, was a large necklace of alternating rubies and pearls. The gems made harsh grating noises that sounded like a dreamer grinding his teeth in his sleep as they swung back and forth with the savage motions of the women.

Panic as deep, cold, and stinging as the cut of a razor blade sliced through him as he stared at the eighteen women. Their eyes were glazed with death as they stared straight back at him. He withered beneath their steady gaze as they formed a circle around him and, filling the steadily narrowing tunnel with high, squealing laughter, clawed at him.

No! Oh, Jesus, please! No!

He twisted and turned to avoid their icy touches, but every time their hands passed through him, he felt a sting of numbing, sharp pain. In the back of his mind, he realized that he didn't have a body, but this pain was worse. Every nerve, every fiber of his being vibrated with agony. The women's howling screams rebounded inside the tunnel, wavering with maddening intensity. For a timeless instant, he imagined that he was nothing more than a thick column of heavy, black smoke that was being ripped apart by fierce, cold winds.

But then, with an incredible burst of energy, he somehow managed to propel himself away from the women. His mind echoed with their high, receding laughter and his own agonized wail as he fell, spiraling in a fast-turning, backward spin. Blackness and icy terror embraced him as he struggled futilely to stop the headlong, dizzying rush.

And then—abruptly—it was over.

With a roaring intake of breath, he opened his eyes

and looked up at the glaring light suspended above the operating table. Through his watery vision, he saw the knot of figures huddled around him. For a flashing, panicky instant, he thought they were still the eighteen women, but then he recognized the pairs of concerned eyes peering at him over the edges of green surgical masks.

"Oh, Christ! Oh, *Christ!* I ... I'm not dead," he said, his voice nothing more than a trembling gasp.

"No, sir, you're not," said a stern voice that resonated all too close to his ear, all too real. "But for a minute there, we thought we'd lost you."

"Wish we had," said a faint, feminine voice.

"Please," he whispered. "Please don't let me die!"

His hands felt like they were being controlled by someone else as he reached up and fumbled to grab onto something—an arm, he thought—and squeezed tightly. "Please! Oh, Jesus, *please!* You can't let me die! I saw them ... They ... they're waiting for me over there!"

"Huh? Who's waiting for you? Where?"

"Jesus Christ! *They* are! *They are!*"

A torrent of chills washed through him like a flood of ice water.

"They are, goddamnit! And they ... they're all wearing their ruby and pearl necklaces!"

Old Blood

Gary Brandner

McCoy braced himself on the flying bridge of the deep-water cruiser and peered ahead into the hanging mist of Puget Sound. Up there somewhere, he fervently hoped, was Blackthorne Island, smallest and bleakest of the San Juan group. He strove to hold on to happy thoughts, but it was not easy while bouncing across the choppy gray water with the taciturn Captain Aaronson at the helm and two people in the cabin who would clearly prefer to be somewhere else.

"Is that the island up ahead?" he asked, realizing as he spoke that he sounded like a kid in the backseat: *Are we there yet?*

"Nope," explained Captain Aaronson.

"Ah, hah," said McCoy, as though he were enlightened. "Guess I'll go below."

The captain's answering grunt gave no indication that he appreciated McCoy's salty term.

Tracy Mannering and Dr. Henry Bischoff sat across from each other on narrow bunks in the compact cabin. Tracy had a trim, athletic figure, long legs, and green eyes that glittered now with exasperation. Dr. Bischoff, a wiry little man with a sharp nose and pale eyes magnified by thick lenses, sat scowling at his hands.

"Everybody having fun?" said McCoy.

"I don't know why you couldn't have done this on Catalina," Tracy said. "It would have been closer to budget."

"You're talking like a studio accountant."

"Dennis, I *am* a studio accountant."

"And a lovely one," said McCoy.

"That's getting close to sexual harassment."

"I know, I'm working up to it."

Dr. Bischoff cleared his throat noisily. "This may be a lark for you two, but I honestly don't know why I have to be here."

"Because the studio wants you here," McCoy said. "As technical adviser on *Old Blood,* I guess they thought you'd add a touch of authenticity to the kick-off party."

"Authenticity!" Bischoff spat out the word. "This publicity stunt has all the authenticity of an Abbott and Costello movie."

"Well, it doesn't have to be—" McCoy began.

"In the first place, why hold it on an island? Everyone knows Vlad Dracul, Count Dracula if you prefer, lived in Transylvania in the northwest part of what is now Romania. Transylvania is a mountainous area. There is no significant body of water within three hundred miles. Hence, no island."

McCoy spoke with as much patience as he could muster. "Dr. Bischoff, who cares? This is a party. It's sole purpose is to promote a motion picture. We used Count Dracula instead of Count Fred because he's a household name, and in the public domain. The people are coming tonight to have fun. They don't care whether he lived in the Carpathian Mountains or Canoga Park."

"And it's not even a castle," Dr. Bischoff grumbled. "This . . . this hotel. Dracula did not live in a hotel."

McCoy made one more try. "Dr. Bischoff . . . Henry . . . the Blackthorne Hotel was available. They are tearing it down next month to build a fish cannery or something. We got it cheap." He glanced at Tracy Mannering. "I know that word rings a bell with accounting."

Tracy rolled her eyes. "My boss thinks increased box office for *Old Blood* will pay for this. I have my doubts."

"Hey, *Fang* magazine is picking up part of it. Their fans are paying two hundred dollars a head to spend a night with Dracula, and there are ninety-some reservations. We can't lose."

"We'll see," Tracy said.

Dr. Bischoff lapsed into a muttered monologue about lack of respect for history.

McCoy sighed and went back up to join the silent Captain Aaronson.

Ten minutes later the cruiser pulled alongside the dock on Blackthorne Island. The wind threw icy spray across the deck. McCoy shielded his eyes to look up the slope from the water's edge to the Blackthorne Hotel. The old Victorian building, a mass of weathered cupolas and gables, seemed to lean menacingly toward him, darker than the angry clouds behind it. A pale light shone through the mist from the ground-floor windows. The upper floors were dark.

A mutter of thunder sounded in the distance.

Tracy came out of the cabin clutching her collar close around her throat. "Oh, great, we're going to have a storm."

McCoy forced a grin. "Think of what we'll save in special effects."

Dr. Bischoff joined them and they stepped gingerly out of the boat onto the wooden dock. Captain Aaronson watched them from the cockpit with folded arms.

"Aren't you coming with us, Captain?" McCoy called.

"Nope. I'm fine right here."

"Well, suit yourself."

Tracy looked up at the looming hotel as they approached. "I hope it doesn't fall down tonight."

"Don't worry they built things solid back in the Twenties."

"Maybe, but this one's been closed for ten years."

Thunder rumbled closer. Tracy pulled her lightweight California jacket closer. "When do the *Fang* fans get here?"

"A ferry's bringing them at sunset." McCoy looked up at the glowering black clouds. "Officially that's in about an hour. Comes back to pick them up tomorrow."

He pulled open the heavy oak door and the three of them walked inside, subdued by the size of the cavernous lobby. A crackling blaze in the huge fireplace did little to dispel the chill. Studio lights had been brought in to brighten the place, but crannies of the vaulted ceiling remained in shadow.

"Cheery place," Tracy observed.

"Hey, it's supposed to be Dracula's home."

Dr. Bischoff snorted. "If Count Dracula walked the earth today do you imagine he would choose an archaic setting like this? More likely he would choose a modern townhouse. Or a suburban tract home."

"Doctor, what we're shooting for here is a spooky ambience, not boring reality."

"And I suppose you will have your actor—What is his name? Randolph?—dressed in that impossible formal attire affected by Bela Lugosi in the 1931 movie."

"As a matter of fact, yes."

"I thought as much. Do you take the vampire for a fool? Do you think he would dress in a manner that would stand out so blatantly from his surroundings?"

McCoy was saved further argument by Tracy's interruption. "Isn't the owner supposed to meet us here?"

"That was the plan." McCoy looked off toward the ornate staircase that climbed from the rear of the lobby into the gloom of the upper story. "Olin Zachary has lived in his own wing since the hotel closed. I don't think he's too happy about the party, but the deal was made with the people who bought him out."

"So where is he?"

"I guess he'll show when he's ready. We really don't need him for anything."

While Dr. Bischoff wandered off to examine the old books in the hotel's reading room, McCoy and Tracy Mannering made a tour of the first floor. A registration desk stretched along one wall. Young studio employees waited there to pass out identification tags and schedules of the night's activities to the arriving guests. Beyond the desk, toward the rear of the lobby, an archway led to the cocktail lounge, rechristened for the night as Evil Spirits. Two scarlet-jacketed bartenders stood at parade rest behind a polished mahogany bar. Rows of sparkling glasses were racked overhead, ranks of bottles stood along the back wall. On the opposite side of the lobby was the entrance to the dining room. The long tables in there were draped with white linen and set for the occasion with heavy black china and blood-red napkins. In place of flowers, the centerpieces featured bare twisted branches on which roosted stuffed owls and bats. A second large room off the lobby held booths set up for vendors of books, masks, coffee mugs, T-shirts, posters, and any other items that could carry the movie's logo.

McCoy and Tracy climbed to the second floor, where musty hallways branched left, right, and straight ahead. Rooms along two of the halls had been prepared for tonight's guests. The third, leading left from the top of the stairs, was dark. A chain that stretched from wall to wall bore a sign that read:

PRIVATE
DO NOT ENTER

"Mr. Zachary, I presume." Tracy guessed.

McCoy peered into the shadows. "I should really talk to the man before we get under way." He hefted the chain, then let it drop. "Ah, it can wait. He won't be going anywhere."

They picked a room several doors from the stairway and went in to look around. The ceiling was high, the paneling dark, the furniture cold and formal.

Tracy shivered. "It is not the Holiday Inn."

A blue-white flash of lightning outside momentarily washed out the shadows and froze them like figures in a tableau. A second later the explosive thunderclap flung Tracy into McCoy's arms.

He held her to his chest. She stayed there a second or two longer than was necessary before stepping back.

"Don't get any ideas," she said. "I've always been afraid of storms."

McCoy spread his hands innocently. "Not an idea in my head, I promise. But if it gets worse, you know where to find me."

"Oh, it'll get worse," Tracy said, watching the branch of a tall Douglas fir beat against the window. "Everything gets worse."

Another sound floated through the gathering darkness. A low mournful bleat. Tracy looked at him.

"That'll be the ferry," McCoy explained. "In a few minutes we'll be up to our armpits in horror fans."

"Which reminds me," Tracy said, "shouldn't there be some kind of security?"

"Taken care of. I hired a man named Berger from Seattle. He's supposed to be very good."

"So where is he?"

"Maybe he came on the ferry. Let's go meet the boat."

The ferry, *City of Anacortes*, in stark contrast to the hotel, was brightly lit, rocking with music and laughter. It docked on the opposite side of the pier from Captain Aaronson's cruiser and disgorged its cargo of young horror fans garishly dressed as ghouls, monsters, zombies, demons, and other assorted creatures of the night. Among the females, Vampira costumes allowing ample cleavage were most popular.

Freddy Krueger stalked down the gangplank and up the slope to where McCoy and Tracy stood. He pulled off his latex face and grinned at them, Freddy no more, but a goggle-eyed young man with a sparse blond beard. He stuck out a hand.

"Mr. McCoy? I'm Kevin Quilty, editor of *Fang*. Did you order up this weather?"

Lightning forked into the ocean somewhere off shore and thunder crashed around them. Tracy edged closer to McCoy.

"I'd take credit for it if I could, but this one's on Mother Nature."

"It's perfect, just perfect." Quilty pulled his Freddy Krueger face back on and hurried to direct his partying ghouls up the hill.

"Looks like a fun bunch," Tracy said, and shuddered.

"Darling, these are the people who will shell out seven dollars apiece to see *Old Blood* and keep you and me employed."

They fell in behind a couple from *Night of the Living Dead* and followed them to the hotel. Before they reached the door a hand dropped on McCoy's shoulder. He spun around with a little cry.

A tall, powerfully built man with sandy hair and moustache smiled at him. "I didn't mean to startle you. I'm Leo Berger. Security."

McCoy recovered and shook his hand. "We were wondering where you were." He looked over the man's shoulder. "You're not all alone?"

Berger smiled more broadly. "Don't worry, Mr. McCoy, I have people here. They're dressed to blend in with the guests. I think that's better than having us stand around in uniform looking grim."

"Makes sense. I don't expect any trouble, but you want to be ready, just in case."

A woman in a blue smock with a smudge of rouge on her forehead came down the stairs and looked uncertainly around the lobby. She spotted McCoy and hurried over.

"Mr. McCoy? I'm Stella. Makeup."

"Yes, Stella, what's the problem?"

"It's Mr. Randolph. He doesn't want to do it."

"Do what?"

"He doesn't want to be Dracula."

"Well, for . . ." McCoy let out an exasperated breath. "I'll go talk to him. Want to come along, Tracy?"

She took a look at the costumed horror fans rapidly filling the dark old lobby. "I think I will. Down here I feel underdressed."

Jay Randolph was forty-four years old and convinced he should be ranked with DeNiro and Nicholson instead of playing vampires for the Clearasil crowd. It was, however, preferable to being unemployed. He sat scowling into the dressing-table mirror as McCoy and Tracy entered.

"Wow, Jay, you look great!" McCoy said, rubbing his hands with bogus enthusiasm.

"I look like Bela Lugosi on a bad day," the actor said without turning to face them.

"Dracula is *supposed* to look like Bela Lugosi."

"That's not what the old guy with the pointy nose said."

"Dr. Bischoff was here?"

"Bad enough having the old fart poking around on the set, does he have to follow me?"

"Studio's orders," McCoy said.

"Well, it's too much. I decided the hell with it. I did my bit in the stupid movie. I'll do interviews, I'll do talk shows, but I won't wear this ridiculous Halloween makeup."

"Jay, do it for me this one last time. I mean, what would a Dracula party be without Dracula. You're the star. You're what all these people paid their two hundred dollars to see."

"Two hundred dollars? Apiece?"

"Not counting airfare."

"Well . . ."

McCoy laid a hand gently on the evening-caped shoulder of the actor. "I knew you wouldn't let us down, Jay."

He and Tracy left the actor's room and walked back down to the lobby. There Jason, the hockey-masked slasher from *Friday the 13th,* was talking excitedly to Leo Berger. The rigid plastic mask thoroughly garbled his speech. Berger shook his head in confusion.

Jason removed the hockey mask to reveal a chubby-faced youth with a nervous blink. "She went to find the ladies' room when we came in, and I haven't seen her since."

"Who are we talking about, son?" Berger said.

"My date. Her name is Nicole. She's dressed like the Bride of Frankenstein."

"Shouldn't be hard to spot, son. Let's have a look around." Berger winked at McCoy and Tracy and walked off with his hand on the shoulder of the unmasked Jason.

As the security chief guided the fan away, the Creature from the Black Lagoon flapped up to McCoy in swim fins and demanded, "Why isn't the *Fang* booth open?"

McCoy looked over at the dealer's room, where the vendors appeared to be doing a brisk business in horror paraphernalia. Conspicuously shuttered was the large central booth bearing the *Fang* magazine logo.

"Beats me," said McCoy. "Kevin Quilty is supposed to be running it."

"Well, I haven't seen him," the Creature complained, and he flapped off toward the registration desk.

"I don't like the way this is starting out," Tracy said. To punctuate her thought a clap of thunder exploded like a bomb, freezing the milling monsters for a second. After a brief silence the lobby came alive again with excited chatter.

"Shall we see if the bar is functioning?" McCoy said.

"Sounds good to me." Tracy took his arm and together they made their way through the ghoulish guests to the cocktail lounge.

On a small stage a rock band called Splatter was testing the decibel limits of the room. The bar was doing a brisk business, with Zombies and Bloody Marys naturally popular. Also available were Deadman's Daiquiri, Gravedigger Gimlet, and Monster Martini. McCoy settled for a non-alliterative bourbon on the rocks. Tracy took a vodka and tonic. They carried the drinks to a relatively quiet alcove with two tall chairs flanking a narrow window. Outside wind-driven rain lashed the glass. A crackle of lightning threw the bleak landscape into momentary relief. Thunder boomed.

"It's going to be a long night," Tracy predicted.

"Mr. McCoy?"

He turned at the new voice to see a normally dressed young man with *Registration* lettered over his name tag.

"The *Fang* fans are getting upset. They want their booth opened and nobody can find Kevin Quilty."

"Has anyone called his room?"

"The in-house lines aren't connected."

"Okay, give me the room number and I'll go up and check."

Tracy winced as the band raised the sound level another notch. "I'll go with you."

The room assigned to the young editor lay halfway along the dim hallway that angled to the right from the stairs. McCoy knocked, waited, knocked again.

"Nobody here, let's go."

"Aren't you going to try the door?" Tracy said.

"What for?"

"They always do that in movies."

McCoy sighed. He grasped the heavy knob and turned it. The door swung inward. Tracy gave him a smug look, and they entered.

A single lamp threw angular shadows up the walls to the dark recesses of the ceiling. A suitcase lay open on the narrow bed. Inside were neatly stacked copies of the current *Fang*. The covers featured a bloody skull with a rat disappearing into an eye socket.

In a high-backed armchair sat Kevin Quilty. His head was canted to one side, his lips parted, his eyes fixed on some point in space. The flesh of his face was a sick tallow color.

"Oh, shit," said McCoy, and crossed the room to the chair. He touched the young man's wrist and quickly drew his hand back.

"He's dead, of course," said Dr. Bischoff, striding into the room past Tracy Mannering. He brushed by McCoy and leaned over Quilty, putting his face close to the sallow flesh.

"Yes, he's been sucked dry," the doctor said.

McCoy recovered his voice. "What is that supposed to mean?"

Bischoff placed two fingers under the young man's chin and raised his head. "Observe the throat."

Tracy came forward with McCoy. They leaned down to look, and quickly straightened. Two inches below Quilty's earlobe was a ragged wound in the flesh, crusted around the edges with dried blood.

"Unquestionably the work of a vampire," Bischoff announced.

McCoy snapped upright. "Doctor, we're not playing anymore. Drop the fairy tales."

"Fairy tales?" Dr. Bischoff's face darkened. "Mr. McCoy, vampires are not make-believe. Count Dracula is not a legend. These creatures existed in antiquity, they exist today. This man is the victim of a vampire."

"He's the victim of somebody, for sure. I'm calling the police."

They were met at the top of the stairs by Leo Berger. "I found the missing Bride of Frankenstein," he began, "she—"

"We've got bigger trouble than that," McCoy interrupted.

Berger raised his brows.

"I'll show you," Bischoff said.

Berger hesitated a moment, then followed the doctor back along the hall. McCoy and Tracy continued down the stairs to the registration desk.

"Did you find Quilty?" asked the young man there.

"We found him. He's, uh, indisposed. Put a CLOSED sign on the *Fang* booth."

The young man waited a moment for further explanation, then moved off toward the dealers' room when he saw none would be offered.

"What are we going to tell the fans?" Tracy asked.

"Nothing. Not until we have to. The last thing we want is a bunch of costumed crazies running around hunting vampires."

He reached under the desk for the telephone, put the receiver to his ear and spun the dial.

"Shit."

"Let me guess," Tracy said. "The phone is dead."

"Dead as Kevin Quilty."

"What do we do now?"

"I'll tell the caterer to serve dinner early. Get the fans' minds off the dealers' room. We'll keep Quilty on ice, so to speak, until the ferry comes back in the morning."

There was some grumbling when the early dinner was announced, but McCoy silenced the complaints by announcing there would be free wine.

He left Tracy at the studio table and turned away.

"Aren't you eating?"

"I've got to find Olin Zachary. Maybe he has another phone line out of here."

While the dining room filled and the free-flowing wine raised spirits, McCoy returned to the shadows upstairs. He saw at once that the chain closing off the owner's private wing was unhooked and lying across the floor. The sign forbidding entrance lay face-down on the maroon carpet. He stepped over the chain and walked into the dark.

"Help me!"

The voice, faint and female, stopped McCoy in midstride. He cocked his head, listening.

"Please. In here."

The door on his right was open about a handsbreadth.

Soft light flickered through the gap. From inside came a low whimpering. McCoy pushed the door fully open and went in.

A guttering candle sent shadows dancing about the room. Against the far wall a slim blond in a gauzy costume stood hugging herself. She held out her arms to McCoy and stumbled forward. He crossed the room in swift strides and caught her as she was about to fall. She was light in his arms as a sack of feathers.

For a long moment McCoy let the girl cling to him. Then he pulled his head back for a look at her. And gasped.

The face that turned up to him was no schoolgirl. The eyes were red rimmed in dark pockets. The lips were full and purple against waxy white flesh. They peeled back to reveal vicious canine teeth. McCoy cried out and pushed at the girl's shoulders. The frail body did not budge. With impossible strength she grasped his shoulder with one hand, the fingers digging into a nerve there until his arm was paralyzed. Her other hand clamped on the nape of his neck. Powerless, he felt his head drawn down until the girl's breath moistened his throat.

"Stop it! Let him be!" The command came from somewhere behind him.

The pressure of the girl's grip eased. The terrible face withdrew as the eyes dilated in their deep sockets. McCoy strained to turn his head toward the new voice. Silhouetted in the doorway was Dr. Bischoff. His short legs were spread and braced, one arm outthrust toward them. In his right hand he clutched a white ceramic crucifix.

The girl released her hold and McCoy staggered backward. The shoulder where she had gripped him throbbed with his rapid heartbeat. Dr. Bischoff advanced, holding the crucifix before him like a sword. The girl hissed in fury. She swiped once at him with a clawed hand, but continued to retreat.

"Be damned!" he swore, lunging with the crucifix toward her face.

Squealing, the girl whirled and crashed through the window. The night storm blew in through the shattered glass. Stunned, McCoy stumbled forward and stared down through the rain. Below him the ground was wet, dark ... and empty. Nothing ... no one lay there. Breathing hard he turned to face the doctor.

"Wh-what was that?"

"That, Mr. McCoy, was a vampire."

"Not a fan who got carried away?"

Bischoff snorted. "Is that what you think?"

McCoy shook his head dumbly. "You win." He pointed with a shaking hand at the crucifix. "And that ... that works? Like in the stories?"

"Sometimes. You are fortunate that this one was relatively young and inexperienced. An older, wiser vampire cannot be deterred by icons."

McCoy's pulse began to subside. "Well, at least you got rid of her."

"There will be others," Bischoff said.

"Why do you say that?"

"There always are. The vampire does not travel alone."

With a groan McCoy left the room and hurried back downstairs. He stood in the archway between the lobby and the dining room until he caught Tracy Mannering's eye and beckoned her to him.

"Jesus, are you all right?" she said when he had told her of the encounter with the blond vampire.

"Thanks to Dr. Bischoff."

"Did you find Olin Zachary?"

"I forgot about him."

"Then you don't know if there's another telephone."

"No. I doubt it. I think we've been purposefully cut off from the mainland."

"Who would do that?"

"You don't want to know."

Tracy stared at him a moment before she spoke. "What about the boat? It should have a radio we can use to call the mainland for help."

"You're right!" McCoy exclaimed. "I'll check with Captain Aaronson. See if you can find Berger. We've got to protect these people, and at the same time stave off a panic."

"How are we going to do that?"

"Hell, I don't know. Leave it to Berger, he's the professional."

"All this is going to make Jay Randolph's Dracula impersonation look a little sick."

McCoy smacked his forehead. "Jesus, I forgot about Jay. We sure don't want any pretend vampires tonight. I'll stop by his room and tell him he can bag the act."

Jay Randolph lay stretched full length on the bed in full Dracula costume and makeup, arms crossed on his chest. McCoy grasped his upper arm and gave it a gentle shake. The actor's head rolled toward him, the shadowed eyes glassy in the white-painted face. McCoy jumped back when he saw the ragged hole in his throat.

He ran out of the room and down the stairs and out the front door. Oblivious to the windblown rain, he stumbled and slid down the muddy slope to the dock. At the bottom he skidded to a stop, his heart frozen for an instant. The cabin cruiser was gone.

Wait, there was the boat! He could just make out the flying bridge on the far side of the pier. The tide must have gone out. Sure, that was it. McCoy breathed again and hurried toward the end of the pier. He made his way carefully across the slippery boards to the cleat where the bow line of the cruiser was secured. He looked down and groaned into the storm. The flying bridge was all of the boat that remained above water. And lashed to the helm, his body flopping in the storm, was Captain Aaronson. A ghastly reference to the skipper of the doomed vessel in Stoker's *Dracula*.

The dead arm of the captain, jerked by the wind, seemed to beckon McCoy down into the roiling sea. With a shouted curse that was lost in the howl of the storm he turned and scrambled back up to the hotel.

At least in the lobby he found a semblance of order. The horror fans were straggling up the stairs, a bizarre parade of decaying corpses, Vampiras, alien monsters, horned demons, malevolent ghosts. Leo Berger stood at the bottom, directing the parade with quiet authority. McCoy, trailing a path of puddled rainwater, located Tracy standing near the registration desk. His expression announced bad news.

"What?" she said.

"Aaronson's dead and the boat's on the bottom. Where's Dr. Bischoff?"

"Around somewhere, why?"

"I'm afraid we're going to need him."

They found the doctor standing at one of the tall windows, peering out into the turbulent night. He nodded sagely when McCoy told him about the fate of the boat captain.

"He wants us kept here."

"He?"

"The master vampire. He controls the others. He is the one we must find."

"What then? Kill him? Stake through the heart?"

Dr. Bischoff looked at him pityingly. "Would that it were so easy. You do not kill a vampire at night. The darkness is his ally."

"Then why do we want to find him?"

"Once we identify the master, we can isolate him. Protect ourselves. Otherwise, we are at his mercy."

The fans marched on up the stairs in their grotesque masks and makeup, innocent kids costumed to celebrate what they did not understand.

"If only we could get a message out," Tracy said.

McCoy looked at her. "I never did find Olin Zachary to ask about another line."

"I suggest we do so," said Dr. Bischoff, "without delay."

The three of them, trying not to show their growing desperation, edged past the procession on the stairs. Berger was on the second-floor landing now, directing the fans to their rooms. McCoy led Tracy and Bischoff over the fallen chain and down the unlighted hallway where Olin Zachary had his living quarters. He could not suppress a shudder as he passed the room where the female vampire had attacked him.

"Mr. Zachary!" he called. Tracy and Dr. Bischoff joined him in shouting the hotel owner's name.

"In here." The hoarse answer came from a room near the end of the hallway.

The door stood halfway open. A pale light glimmered within. McCoy entered cautiously, followed by Tracy and Dr. Bischoff. A tall, lean man in a crimson dressing gown stood across the room with his back to the window. His face was pale in the light of the single lamp, his eyes shadowed pools.

"Mr. Zachary?"

The man nodded once, but said nothing.

McCoy turned his head while keeping his eyes on the hotel owner. "Doctor, take a look at this guy. Could he be—?"

As he spoke a throaty laugh came from the lean man. As McCoy and his friends stared, the dry body of Olin Zachary was flung aside like an empty husk. Behind him stood one of the young women costumed as Vampira. Her lips opened to reveal long, deadly teeth.

Behind them the door slammed. Two more females barred their escape—the slim blond in gauze and a witch, who pulled off her hag's mask to reveal a more terrible face beneath.

McCoy grasped Tracy's arm and pulled her close as he moved beside Bischoff. "The cross, Doctor, get it out!"

Bischoff fumbled in a coat pocket and came up with the white crucifix.

"Get back," he commanded. "All of you!"

The Vampira who had manipulated Olin Zachary's body hissed at them and took a step forward. Behind them the other two also advanced. They laughed. An obscene, mocking sound.

"What's the matter?" McCoy demanded. "Why isn't it working?"

"They are too strong. The power of the cross cannot cope with the three of them."

With a sudden coordinated movement the vampires were upon them. McCoy was borne to the floor as though he were a child. He saw the others go down at the same time. The vampire's lips touched his throat.

"Stop!"

The powerful voice boomed like a cannon in the room. Instantly the pressure pinning McCoy to the floor was eased. He sat up and saw the vampires rise slowly from their fallen victims.

"Back!"

Obediently, their mouths working hungrily, the females backed away.

McCoy reached for Tracy, found her hand. "Are you all right?"

"I-I think so," she answered, her voice shaking.

"Dr. Bischoff?"

"Yes. I was not bitten."

"How did you stop them?"

"I didn't," said the doctor.

"It was *I*," said the booming voice.

McCoy scrambled to his feet and saw for the first time that the door was open. Standing there was Leo Berger, one hand still gripping the ornate knob. The female vampires stood motionless, watchful.

"Berger, thank God. But how . . . ?"

He slowly closed the door behind him. "I told you I had my people here." He swept his hand to indicate the three females. "These are my people."

As McCoy, Tracy, and Dr. Bischoff watched, frozen, the security chief pulled off the sandy wig and false moustache. He straightened to his full height and smiled.

"The real Leo Berger floats facedown beneath the pier. As for me . . . I think you know my name."

Baring his teeth, the master vampire came toward them.

Heroes

Richard T. Chizmar

1

I've always watched him. Secretly. From the time I was a child. Watched the way his eyebrows danced when he laughed. The way he lit his pipe or handled a tool, like a magician wielding a magic wand. The way he walked the family dog; bending to talk with it or ruffle its fur, but only when he was sure no one was watching. The way he read the newspaper or one of his tattered old paperbacks, peering over the worn pages every few minutes to keep me in check. The way his eyes twinkled when he called me "son." I've always watched him.

2

The detective's name was Crawford and when he disappeared into the crowd, I wondered for what had to be the tenth time tonight if I was truly insane for trusting him.

It was Thursday, December 21, and Baltimore-Washington International Airport was suffering under the strain of thousands of holiday travelers. A river of lonely businessmen and women, sweatshirt-clad college students, and entire families flowed by North Gate 23, blocking my view of the exit tunnel. I remained sitting on one of the orange-padded seats in the waiting area while Crawford tried to get close enough to look out the airport windows. Our man was due on an 8:30 P.M. flight from

Paris—a private charter—so the computer screens all around me offered no news of its arrival.

I stared at the clock on the far wall. It was almost time. Months of research and planning were about to come to an end. My stomach felt like it was bubbling over and I was tempted to duck into the bathroom. Instead, afraid to leave my seat, I popped another Tums and waited for it to dissolve under my tongue.

Crawford reappeared, trailing behind an overweight couple who were moving with the grace and speed of a pair of hermit crabs. I could see by the expression on his face that the news was not good. I'd hired Ben Crawford, a Philadelphia-based private detective, two months earlier. He'd been the only one of the half-dozen detectives who'd been recommended to me who was willing to take my case. A fifty-thousand-dollar certified check—half payment in advance—had sealed the deal.

We made an odd pair. I stood over six feet tall but tipped the scales at only one-sixty. Crawford, on the other hand, could best be described as a human stump; only five-four, he weighed in with one hundred and seventy pounds of compressed muscle. His arms and legs strained against his clothing, and like many other muscular men of his size, he more waddled than walked. Despite my edginess, I smiled and almost laughed aloud at the sight before me: the waddling detective and Mr. and Mrs. Hermit Crab.

"What's so damn funny?" he asked, moving his coat from the chair next to me and sitting down.

"What . . . oh, nothing. Nervous tension, I guess."

He checked his watch. "The plane just landed. It'll be another ten minutes or so."

I nodded, my throat suddenly dry, my stomach tightening another notch.

Now it was Crawford's turn to smirk. "Hey, take it easy, you're white as a sheet. Don't worry, he'll be on that plane." He glanced at his watch again. "Another couple of hours and it'll all be over. Trust me."

I nodded again. I trusted him all right. I had no other choice.

3

Twenty years ago, when I was seventeen and still in high school, each student in our Senior English class was assigned to write a paper about the person he or she most admired. The class was a large one and the list of heroes was long and impressive: Martin Luther King, Abraham Lincoln, John F. Kennedy, Joe Namath, Willie Mays, John Glenn, and dozens of other famous figures. I was the only student who chose to write about his father. A nine-page tribute. My father cried at the kitchen table when he read it. Stood up and hugged me real close. I'll never forget that day. Never.

4

Our man was the only passenger in the tunnel. A shadow. Moving slow. Carrying no luggage.

Even in the dim light, I could see that he was a striking man. Tall. Elegant. Draped in a fine black overcoat, dark slacks, and shiny, zippered boots. His face contrasted sharply with his slicked, black hair and his dark apparel. Deathly pale flesh appeared almost luminous in the airport lights, and sharp, high cheekbones seemed to hide his eyes under his forehead. Eyes as dark as midnight.

"Jesus," I whispered.

"Yeah, I know," Crawford said, leaning close enough that I could feel his breath. "He's something, ain't he?"

Before I could answer, the detective stepped past me and met our visitor at the side of the walkway, away from the swelling crowd. I stumbled blindly after him, not wanting to be separated.

"It's a pleasure to see you again, sir," Crawford said.

Neither man offered forth a hand, and I noticed that our visitor's hands were covered by black leather gloves. He nodded and smiled. A quick flash of teeth. Like a shark. A chill swept across my spine.

"As promised, I am here." His voice was mesmerizing, his words soft and melodic like music. I wanted to hear more.

"Yes, you certainly are," Crawford said, sounding infinitely more civilized than I had ever heard him. "I trust your trip was satisfactory."

"Indeed, it was quite comfortable. But, my friend, I long for the journey home, so may we continue on quickly?"

"Yes, yes, of course." Crawford eased me forward, his fingers digging into my arm. "This is—"

"Mr. Francis Wallace," he interrupted, smiling again. I felt a wave of nausea rush forward and began to sway. The detective's fingers tightened on my arm again. "I have crossed an entire ocean to make his acquaintance."

"I . . . I really must thank you for coming here," I said. I looked helplessly at Crawford. "I'm not sure I believed him until I saw you walking up the tunnel. I was so terribly afraid that I had been wrong all this time."

"It is not necessary to thank me, Mr. Wallace. I have thought about this moment many times since your friend's visit to my home. I admit, initially, I was wary, hesitant to come. But yours is such a strange story, such a strange reason for my journey. My decision to come here was much easier than your decision to seek me, I trust."

A pack of giggling children skittered past us, brushing the man's coat. He cringed and turned to Crawford. "I am ready to proceed now."

The detective led us through the busy airport, outside into the bitter December air, to his rental car in the upper-level parking lot. The traffic on the interstate was moderate. We drove north in silence.

5

It was my father who stood at my side on my wedding day, and I by his, eight months later, when Mother passed away. Barely a year later, and it was my father again, his arms around me, who broke the news to me that my precious Jennifer had been killed in an accident. It was the worst of times, but still we had each other.

6

The house I grew up in was dark, the street deserted. The rental car was parked in the driveway, its ticking engine the only sound in the night. I sat on the front porch, Crawford on my left side, smoking a cigarette. Snow flurries danced around us, drifting to the ground and melting. I played with the zipper on my coat for a long time before I looked up.

He was staring at me.

"You okay?" he asked, his breath visible in the chill air.

"I don't know." I took a deep breath and looked over my shoulder at the front door, which our visitor had disappeared into just minutes earlier. "I planned this for so long ... thought about it for so long, but I don't know. I'm still not sure it's right."

He shook his head. "Listen to me, I gotta admit that I thought you were a genuine nutcase when you hired me. Offered me a hundred thousand to go find this guy and convince him of your little plan. Hell, I only signed on because I was short on cash and long on bills."

He stood up and inhaled on his cigarette. Began pacing the walkway. "I mean, I thought he was a fantasy, something made up for the movies and books. But the more you showed me about this guy—the papers, the files, the photos; all dated over hundreds of years—and the more time I spent around this house, getting to know you and your old man ... the more I understood. You've gone to an awful lot of trouble, Wallace, an awful lot. Now, you don't know me very well; not well at all, in fact. But if you're asking for my opinion, my view of all this, I think you did good. I think you did damn good."

A soft thud sounded from the house and I jerked around.

Crawford kneeled at my side, pointed a finger at me. "You did good, Wallace. Trust me."

"Oh, God, I hope so."

7

I don't watch my father anymore. It hurts too much.

Ten months ago, on a Friday night, he forgot my name. I had just returned from the grocery store with the week's supplies—he was no longer able to drive himself—when he called me into the den. The television was on the wrong channel and he couldn't figure out how to work the remote control. He looked me straight in the eyes and said, "Charlie, could you please turn on HBO?" I laughed, thinking he was acting the smart-ass, one of his favorite pastimes.

But later at dinner, he asked, "Charlie, pass me the salt and pepper."

I looked at him; there was no humor in his voice, no mischief in his eyes. "Dad," I said, scared, "who is Charlie?"

A confused expression creased his face. "What the hell kind of question is that?"

"Just tell me who Charlie is, Dad."

He laughed. "Hell, you are. Don't you even remember your own name? We served in the war together, Charlie. You were my wing man, for Christsakes."

It came to me then. Charlie Banks—my father's best friend, dead over fifteen years now.

It was a long night, but the next morning, everything was back to normal. I was his son again, Charlie Banks completely forgotten.

But I could see the signs then. No longer able to drive, arthritis, failing eyesight and hearing, advancing stages of senility . . . the list continued to grow as every month passed.

As did my own depression and anxiety. I remember someone once said that there is nothing sadder, nothing more heartbreaking, than watching your hero die.

They were right.

It was during that time I decided I couldn't let that happen.

8

The snow was falling harder now. The narrow streets were covered, neighborhood yards of dead grass just beginning to glisten a beautiful white.

I was standing by the rental car, nervously running my bare hand over the cold metal. The two of them stood huddled together on the porch, Crawford's cigarette aglow. The man had emerged from the house several minutes ago, but the detective had insisted on talking to him first. Alone. I'd trusted him this far, so I'd agreed.

Five minutes later, twenty minutes before midnight, they finished talking and walked to the driveway.

Crawford pulled me aside and said, "Your dad was sleeping like a baby. Just as we planned. There was no pain, no surprise."

I closed my eyes, nodded my head. "Thank you," I whispered. "Thank you so much."

"It's been my pleasure," the detective said, reaching for my hand. "And I mean that. Now, don't worry about anything. I'm going to get our friend back to the airport and back on that plane. You get inside." He waved at me from the car. "I'll be in touch."

Before he joined Crawford, the man laid a hand on each of my shoulders, touched a single gloved finger to my face. "Immortality is a rare and wonderful thing, Mr. Wallace. But it is not without its failings. It will not always be easy. Cherish this gift, protect it, as I know you will, and you and your father will be truly rewarded."

Tears streamed down my cheeks. I opened my mouth to thank him, but the words did not come.

He held a finger to his lips. "Say nothing. I must go."

I watched the car back out of the driveway, pull away into the night, its brake lights fading to tiny red sparks in the falling snow. I looked at the second-floor window—my father's bedroom—then at the front door. A snowflake drifted to my lips, and I opened my mouth, tasted it like I had done so many times as a child. I looked skyward and caught another on my tongue. Then, I started across the lawn, his words still in my head.

Immortality is a rare and wonderful thing.

God, I hoped so.

Valentine

Daniel Ransom and Rex Miller

1

Pretusky is his name, and you're right, he's a cop. At forty-three, after eighteen years on the force, twelve of them as a homicide detective, he's got that look, that feel about him. It's that look and that feel that caused his wife to seek solace in the arms of a dentist (no fooling) named David Randolph. At least their two kids were grown and off in college when the divorce came down.

This is the night of April twenty-third, just as dusk falls on the city, following a chill two-hour rain. The sky is a beautiful, melancholy indigo, perfect for the lovers who hurry along these streets as they exit the nearby trendy restaurants on their way to their BMWs, blissed-out New Age music seeming to roll from every door. Back in the fifties, Pretusky remembers this neighborhood had been mostly hamburger joints, or variations thereof, and the music had run to Elvis and Chuck Berry and Fats Domino.

Pretusky is standing outside a phone booth, the booth a monument to how mindlessly violent the city has become. The glass panels have been smashed, the phone book has been ripped out, the shelf beneath the phone has been severely dented as if by a giant angry hand, and the telephone receiver has become coated with saliva, palm sweat and God knows what else. The metal floor of the booth reeks of piss, vomit, and even dog shit. If AIDS could ever be transmitted by a phone booth, this would be the one where you could catch it.

Despite his overcoat, Pretusky shivers. It is cold. He wishes two things: a) that he hadn't given up cigarettes because in chilly weather like this those old Pall Malls are pretty good friends, and b) he wishes the fucking phone would ring. He said he'd call at six-thirty. It's now nearly seven.

So he waits some more. He has no choice.

2

An hour ago, when she came in, the doorman took special note of her. As what kind of able-bodied heterosexual male would not?

Tall with a face that suggests both eroticism and vulnerability, wearing the designer jeans-and-full-length fur coat so popular among rich women these days. She also wears mid-calf boots and carries a gaily wrapped buff blue package with a big blue ribbon on top. Not even her dark glasses lend a jarring note; on her, even at dusk this way, they seem natural. Just part of the uniform. The doorman feels his cock swelling in his pants. He wishes he could get this hard for his old lady out there on Long Island watching her soaps and wrestling matches . . .

The woman—who this evening is calling herself Ella Task in case anyone should ask—takes the penthouse elevator all the way to the thirty-eighth floor.

When the doors part, a chunky man in an expensive suit nods to her and walks forward and without any hint of apology, begins patting her down.

"What's in the package?"

"Just a present for him."

"All right," he says, obviously figuring he doesn't want to honk off Renotti too much by hassling his latest girlfriend.

When he's finished, he stands upright and points to the door behind him. "He's waiting for you," the bodyguard says.

She nods and moves gracefully past him, knowing his

eyes are watching her and envying the hell out of Renotti, the man she is visiting this evening.

The penthouse is exquisite. Really. Renotti may be nothing more than a mobster—albeit a very successful mobster—but he has the taste and judgment to hire good people to build him a tasteful life-style.

The living room floor is sunken, with groupings of furnishings arranged at angles to permit easy conversation. A fireplace that takes up much of one wall throws soft light across the marble floor. The framed reproductions run to Chagall and Renoir.

Not even a two-thousand-dollar silk smoking jacket can soften Renotti's hood look. He's just one of those street guys—short, beefy, nose flattened from too many fights, hands and knuckles a primate would envy. So he looks faintly comic in the wine-jacket-and-brandy-snifter role, trying hard to give the impression that he just had lunch with Cary Grant and later will be taking in an opera.

Plus, he has not exactly learned the language of love. As she drops her fur coat on the couch, he takes in the magnificent swell of her simple white blouse and says, "That blouse really flatters your tits, honey."

She smiles. He doesn't seem to see the rue in her smile. He's not that sophisticated. "Thank you," she says.

"How about some brandy?"

"Fine."

He looks at her one more time. "Goddamn, baby, you really get my heart started, you know that?"

The smile again, soft and mysterious.

"Brandy," he says, and then strolls away in his two-thousand-dollar silk smoking jacket.

3

As everybody knows, homicide detectives rely a lot on informers. Have to. Informers are the only people who really know what's going on in the criminal world. But informers are not always easy to get along with. They make demands. They play a lot of games to make themselves important. And they insist on their own ground rules.

Take Carney. Sonofabitch has done two turns in stir and could well take a third and final tumble any day now, yet when he works with Pretusky, he treats Pretusky as if he's some kind of low-born employee. Do this. Do that.

Carney is why Pretusky is standing out here in front of this phone booth freezing his modest little balls off.

Because, if Carney is telling the truth, tonight Pretusky may be able to finally lay his tired human eyes on the woman known only as Valentine.

Eight months and four bodies ago, prominent local mob figures started dying. Violently. Always left behind was a heart shaped valentine, usually set right in the center of the dead man's chest.

Pretusky, reliable homicide cop that he is, is one of many cops assigned to the case. Even though the dead guys are mobsters, the mayor feels that it's bad press for the city to turn into a morgue this way (as if it weren't already a morgue, what with more than three hundred homicides already this year).

So for the past seven months, Pretusky has spent most of his work hours on the so-called Valentine case, talking to every informer, every low-life rumor peddler in the city. Fortunately, Carney had to come back from a California trip to see his dying brother.

Carney used to be on the fringes of the mob himself. He claims that he knows a) who this woman, this Valentine, probably is, and b) what it is these four mobsters had in common and why she wanted to kill them.

Today he called and even went one better. "I think I know who she's going to hit tonight and it's gotta be tonight because he leaves for Europe in the morning." Then he gives Pretusky these god-damn James Bond instructions to wait at this phone booth until he calls. Pretusky knows better than to complain about the instructions. Carney is a real cloak-and-dagger freak.

So now he waits. And thinks about Valentine. Because, much as he hates to admit it—this isn't good for his macho insensitive-male cop image—because Pretusky, lonely Pretusky, has started having fantasies about this Valentine. He already knows she's beautiful. He already knows that despite the fact she's killing people, she's heavily into true and lasting justice. And he already knows that in some strange way he's got this thing for her. Not sexual fantasies, either. It's more innocent, more like *Laura*, Pretusky's favorite movie in which homicide detective Dana Andrews falls in love with the portrait of a supposedly dead woman. Romantic. The joyful way Pretusky hasn't felt since his one and only year in college when he used to dance his future wife around in the shadowy gymnasium while listening to Johnny Mathis records.

Pretusky wants to meet Valentine not to arrest her but just to keep her from getting killed. He's scared for her. She's playing with the most vicious pigs in society. And nobody can get away with what she's doing forever.

He starts shivering again and looks back into the reeking phone booth. God damn Carney and his god-damn cloak-and-dagger.

C'mon, phone, *ring*.

4

"How's the brandy?" Renotti says.

"Very good."

"You look like you're getting a little sleepy."

The smile. "A little dizzy, I guess. As I've told you, I'm really not much of a drinker."

He pounces, which is his style. Not to seduce, not even to respectfully ply her with endearments, but to pounce.

She's been expecting this and knows that she'll have to go along with it.

He gloms onto her right breast even before he manages to jam his tongue into her mouth.

Ah, romance.

5

The phone rings.

Pretusky looks like a track star getting into the booth.

"Hello," he half-shouts, trying not to notice how

sticky the receiver is, trying not to think of what could possibly have made the receiver this gummy.

"Arnie?"

"Arnie? Who the hell are you calling, pal?"

"Arnie Silverman, who the hell do you think I'm calling?"

"Jesus," Pretusky says, and slams the phone.

He goes back outside and starts clapping his hands together to stay warm and listening to all that New Age music floating up the street.

He keeps trying to think of a reason for liking Kenny G. He can't come up with a single one.

6

Renotti kind of shimmies his hand, eel-like, up her inner thigh.

Touchdown.

She can hear the cheering crowd playing in his head.

Renotti. The greatest ass bandit of all time.

"I love pussy," he says.

Another line that should go down (you should forgive the expression) in Great Seduction Lines of All Time.

I love pussy.

Gee, Mr. Renotti, I just can't wait to jump into bed with you.

"You ready for the bedroom?"

"Yes," she says. She tries real hard to make her voice breathy, the way Marilyn always used to when she was giving in to Clark Gable or Robert Mitchum or somebody else. Valentine isn't old enough to remember Marilyn but she's a tireless and respectful watcher of old movies.

"I'll tell Rudy that we're not to be disturbed."

He winks at her and playfully pats her cheek with a hand that must weigh in the vicinity of two thousand pounds, thanks to all the rings.

That Renotti, he sure knows how to move.

She hasn't been here but twenty-two minutes and he's already loading her up on the bedroom express.

What a mover, what a shaker.

Renotti goes to tell Rudy whatever the fuck it is guys like Renotti always go to tell guys like Rudy.

7

The phone rings.

Even though he's half-expecting this'll be another call for the infamous Arnie Silverman, Pretusky dives inside the booth.

"Hello."

"Hey, man, how's the gumshoe business?"

"You always get that wrong, Carney. Gumshoes are private investigators."

"Oh, like Mike Hammer?"

"Yeah, like Mike Hammer. And cops are flatfoots."

"Oh, yeah, flatfoots. I gotta remember that."

It is not likely that Carney will be winning any kind of Nobel Prize this year. At least not in the category of smarts.

"Renotti."

"What about him?"

"You know the name?"

"Of course I know the name."

"He's the one who'll get iced tonight."

"How do you know?"

"Trust me. I know." Carney's playing cloak-and-dagger again.

"Do you know where I can find Renotti?"

"He's got a secret penthouse."

"Where?"

Long pause and then Carney says, "I need a favor."

"God, Carney, I want to get there before anything happens. What's the fucking address?"

"I need the favor first."

Pretusky sighs, knowing he'll have to play along. "What's the favor?"

"Well, the other night I was out with this chick see and—"

"Shit, Carney, did you beat her up?" Nobody said that paid informants were nice guys and Carney sure proved that. He had this thing about beating up women before he bedded them. No broken bones, no skull fractures, nothing like that, but he sure wasn't shy about handing out black eyes and busted teeth.

"Not really beat her up. But she's yowling about pressing charges. You know how broads are."

"Yeah, those inconsiderate bitches. You'd think they'd be more appreciative when a guy pushes them around."

"So I was just wonderin' if you could put in a word for me downtown—you know, if this bitch actually presses charges—help me get the charges dropped. I don't want to go back to stir, Pretusky. Last time I was there I had a real sore asshole."

"I'll do what I can. Now I need the address."

"You'll really help me out?"

"I'll do what I can, Carney. Now give me the fucking address, all right?"

So Carney finally gives him the fucking address.

8

She's on the bed. Her buff blue present is on the floor next to the bed.

Renotti's got one hand in her bra, the other hand stuffed down her pants.

"You got a nice tight pussy, babe," he says.

He's been doing this ever since they hit the bedroom, giving her a kind of play-by-play description of her own body as his greasy paws violate every inch of her. What a charmer.

He starts ripping her designer jeans off.

Not sliding, not scooching, *ripping*.

And at the same time his little pee-pee pops out thanks to him unzipping himself with almost blinding and unerring speed.

The bedroom is huge, with a vast circular waterbed in the center. Half the east wall is a big screen TV, half the west wall is a dry bar, and the north wall is this huge window with a small door built right into the glass itself. The door leads to a veranda that offers a stunning view of the city thirty-eight floors below.

He's just about to guide himself into her when she says, "Do you remember a man named Robert Frazier?"

Renotti looks dumb, which for him is not exactly an accomplishment.

"He was my father," she says, tears sudden in her eyes and voice. "He was my father and you killed him."

Rudy checked every part of her except her boots and that was a terrible mistake because now from one of her mid-calf leather boots, she extracts an ivory-handled stiletto with a long, gleaming blade.

She stabs him at the top of the spine, ripping downward to cause maximum damage. Then she stabs him in the back of the head, pushing him off her and rolling him over so she can stab him in the heart.

She gets him dead on. Dead on.

He has time enough to scream. Scream very loudly.

From the back pocket of her jeans—which she's now pulling up and fastening—she takes her calling card, the small heart-shaped valentine, and tosses it on top of his bloody wriggling chest.

He is in grotesque death throes, sobbing, fouling himself, shaking, his whole system on red alert.

She hears Rudy come running through the penthouse, shouting for Renotti.

Not getting any response, Rudy starts doing what all good Rudies start doing in such a situation.

Emptying his god-damn gun into the locked bedroom door.

She realizes she may be only seconds from her own death.

9

Pretusky appears to be setting some land-speed records on his way to Renotti's penthouse.

When he pulls up in front, he leaves the red emergency light he popped up there earlier flashing into the night.

He has just started out of his car when he hears shouting from the sidewalk as two pedestrians look up and point.

10

The buff blue box contained the mountain climbing gear she has used at various times in her life, variations on the pitons, snap links, and chocks normally used.

She rushes out the door built into the glass and starts her way down the building.

Rudy is still trying to get through the bedroom door . . .

11

Pretusky is thrilled. That's the only word for it. He has no doubt who this is, scaling down the walls this way.

And he'll be waiting when she touches the ground.

He'll whisk her into his car and . . .

Then he'll see what happens . . .

12

Rudy runs into the bedroom. Sees the bloody form of his boss on the bed.

Fucking bitch.

The veranda door is open. The wind is numbingly cold.

He rushes through the door. Peers down.

Bitch is halfway down already.

Crowd gathered there.

Cop car with whirling cherry.

No way he can fire at her from here.

He rushes back through the penthouse. To the elevator. Presses DOWN . . . and *keeps* pressing DOWN.

13

By now, the crowd has tripled in size. Pretusky is pushed forward.

Valentine has maybe seventeen, eighteen floors to go.

Pretusky is very anxious . . .

14

Rudy hits the ground floor, virtually dives through the opening elevator doors and runs across the lobby in the center of which he collides with the doorman.

"Stupid bastard!" Rudy shouts, knocking the doorman to the floor.

Rudy doesn't look back, he just runs outside.

15

Eight floors or so.

Pretusky is at the front of the crowd, flashing his badge, saying back, back as if he's trying to quell wild animals.

Which, in a sense, he is.

He wants to give Valentine plenty of room ...

In only a few minutes, he will be talking to her in the privacy and safety of his car ...

This woman who has possessed his thoughts these past eight months ...

16

Rudy finds a good spot at the back of the crowd.

His weapon of choice is a Walther PPK. She's got five floors to go.

When she gets to four—

The Walther is not especially wonderful at long distances but—

She reaches the fourth floor, self-confident as a cat.

The crowd is applauding her.

It's a frigging circus here.

Rudy opens fire, the sounds the Walther makes are loud even above the din of the crowd—

He can see immediately, the way she jerked there, that he hit her—

17

Pretusky hears the gunfire in disbelief.

In a kind of slow motion, he turns, and starts pulling out his own weapon.

The crowd, in their kind of horrified slow motion, begins to scatter, screaming as the gunshots continue.

But like an Old West lawman, Pretusky stands stock

still, having found his target now, and just keeps firing
and firing and firing—

18

Sonofabitch.

Fuckin' cop.

He killed me, Rudy thinks as the bullets strike home,
lungs, heart, liver.

Sonofabitch.

Fuckin' cop.

Rudy (slow-mo again here) starts falling forward to
the pavement as the cop (what is the sonofabitch, insane
or something, just keeps firing and firing and firing) and
images are flashing across Rudy's mind, his First Com-
munion and his old dog Sandy and his first mob hit
and his—

But he's dying. He's god-damn dying.

Sonofabitch.

Fuckin' cop.

19

When Pretusky turns back to the building, satisfied that
the gunman is no longer a problem, he looks up and
finds that—

—she's gone.

Somehow, despite the fact that she was wounded, she
managed to finish her descent and flee.

Crazed, Pretusky runs first eastward for maybe half a
block, and then westward but—

—nothing, no sign of her whatsoever.

He runs back to the building where the rope still
dangles.

There is a small pool of blood on the concrete.

She was wounded all right.

But where could she have gone?

20

Sleep takes many hours of bourbon and relaxation. Trying to get her out of his mind. But he can't. Too many

months he's thought of her. Yearned to meet and know her.

Sleep comes sometime around dawn when Pretusky finally nods off staring at a framed photograph of his two kids on the bureau. Good kids; God, he loves them . . .

He isn't sure what time it is when the phone wakes him.

"Detective Pretusky?"

"Yeah."

"I just wanted you to know that I'm all right."

Then he sits straight up in bed because he's figured out who this is.

"Where are you?" he says. "I'd like to meet you."

"Someday maybe. When my work is done."

"I—" And then he stops himself. God, was he really going to say it, was he really going to say *I love you*?

"I was concerned about you," Pretusky said.

"Rudy was paid far too much. He's not that good a shot."

"So all this—it keeps going on?"

"For now. Till it's finished."

"But—"

"You sound tired, Pretusky. Why don't you get some sleep?"

He knew she was going to hang up so he said, quickly quickly, "I think about you a lot."

"Believe it or not, I saw your photo in the paper a few months ago—how you were stalking me and all— and I started thinking about you, too. You've got a very nice face, Detective Pretusky. Very nice. Kind. And there's so little kindness in the world."

He started to say something but before he could speak, she said, "I'll call you again sometime, Detective Pretusky. But for now I've got to go."

She hung up.

21

For the next week, every night, all Pretusky did was sit in the easy chair watching TV and waiting for her to call.

She never does call.

But he knows she will someday; someday soon.

The Ecology of Reptiles

John Coyne

From the air it appeared that all the vegetation had been scraped together into a thicket behind the village, stretching a few thousand yards down to the edge of the Baro River at the western edge of Ethiopia. A dozen women of the village were washing clothes among the rocks and children were running along the shore, throwing pebbles at a crocodile that cruised beyond their range.

Four foreign relief workers had camped at the river for the weekend and one of them, an Englishman, Roger Sample, was telling the others about crocodiles, lecturing them in textbook fashion about the ecology of reptiles.

Roger was tall and thin and had deceiving looks. From certain angles, and in certain lights, his profile was strikingly handsome, but full faced, his features were in disproportion. His nose was too small, his lips too thick, and his eyes were set too close together, as if at birth his face had been pinched.

Roger's wife, Hetty, who was from Nice, and who had left the group for a smooth patch of sand, was very unlike her husband. She was small and stout with no startling features, no figure whatsoever. Nevertheless, she was sensuous and in some ways resembled Simone Signoret.

And unlike her husband, people were attracted to her. She had a gracious manner, and went out of her way to make others comfortable.

All of the campers, for one reason or the other, had come on the trip because of her.

It was a trip, however, planned by Mark Mayer, an American CARE employee, and his lover, Paula Lance.

Mark had sent out the invitations, had them hand delivered by his houseboy, inviting them to a "Beach Party in the Heart of Africa."

Mark, who had been sitting with Roger in the noonday sun, now stood and walked up the patch of hot sand to join Hetty in the shade of the acacia trees.

The year in Africa had been hard on Mark, leaving him pale and underweight. Hetty, watching him approach, was swept with a wave of compassion, seeing his gauntness, and wanted to gather him in her arms and hold him close, to comfort him like a child. But instead she looked away, looked out at the muddy Baro River, and let the emotion melt away.

After a moment she realized she had been watching the crocodile, watching it slip and slide in the mucky water, drifting a hundred yards, then with a violent slap turning to go upstream. It was the only crocodile she had ever seen in Africa and she watched it as if it were on film.

"Have you decided?" Mark asked.

"We're breaking up." The hot day flashed before her like photographs.

"Good."

She reached out to touch him and be reassured, but he unexpectedly moved, leaving her to make an empty gesture.

On the very first Saturday afternoon that they had made love Mark had whispered that he loved her. His words had angered her. She had turned away, noticing his new digital Seiko watch and the time, 3:09, then looked across the room and out the window. She could see a bit of the African sky. It was a brilliant March day with a breeze tossing the white curtains cooling the Ras Hotel room. Her husband had flown up to Lalibela that morning to inspect a UNICEF resettlement camp and she was glad he had good weather. She could picture him tramping along in the sun, pushing ahead of all the others, speaking out in Amharic, making his presence known. She had begun to cry.

Paula Lance was also American and a nurse with Catholic Relief. She was assigned to a regional hospital in Debre Marcus, caring for patients suffering from malnutrition. She had never been out of the United States until she flew to Africa, and all of it, the harsh living and primitive conditions, the famine and wholesale poverty, had stunned her so, that even now, eight months after arriving in the country, she was afraid to go anywhere by herself.

She had met Mark Mayer four months after she arrived in Addis Ababa, at the ambassador's July Fourth party. She had been on her way in the hospital's Land Rover, where she knew the driver had a small pistol tucked away under the seat in case they were attacked on the road. She had hoped she was drunk enough to kill herself. Instead, Mark had taken her down in the bushes behind the tennis court and demanded she give him a blow job. He had saved her life, she had told him afterward, making her feel valued.

Now, obediently, she listened to Roger talk about crocodiles and how they were territorial and flesh eaters, though she had stopped paying attention to what he was telling her, and was thinking only that she wouldn't be able to wash her hair in the Baro, not with a twelve-foot crocodile yards from shore. She was also too afraid to ask either of the men why they had chosen such a place for their campsite.

Paula had not been in the country long enough to have the harsh life and the high plateau climate wear her down, and she could obtain enough cosmetics at the American commissary and from the small Italian beauty salons near the Ethiopian Hotel. She really only saw glimpses of the countryside, of the hot desert and the lowlands of the escarpment, when she went off with Mark on weekend trips. She hated to camp. She had only one wish and that was to be out of Africa, away from this place. She knew she would leave Mark if it meant she could go home again to Virginia.

Hetty, squinting into the sun, saw that her husband had been abandoned in the heat. Paula had come up the shore and into the shade and stretched out on her sleeping bag, away from where Mark had fallen asleep beside Hetty. Paula had not said anything to her, Hetty realized, when she came to the shade of the acacia and saw Mark there, beside her.

It was quiet on the bank of the Baro. Hetty panned the shoreline and stopped again to look at Roger. He sat with his back to her, scooping sand with one hand, aimlessly, like a bored child. She put her book aside and stood, being careful not to wake Mark.

"The croc is gone?" Hetty asked, walking down to her husband, and shading her eyes to search the surface of the river.

"He's been gone for hours, if it matters to you." Roger kept up with the sand.

"Don't be a sonovabitch, Roger."

"Why the fuck not?"

"You'll get sunstroke staying out in the sun," she advised.

"As if you gave a shit."

"You didn't have to come."

"Yes? And let that bloody American bang the both of you all weekend long?"

Hetty's feet turning in the sand crunched in his ears, and then receded. He strained to follow the sound, like listening for an echo, until all he heard was the rush of water, birds shrieking in the trees, and then muffled sounds of the jungle racing to the edge of the bank.

The trees across the narrow stretch of water seemed to teeter against the river. The thick branches pulsed before his eyes like his own heartbeat, palm leaves spread themselves a hundred yards, then shivered, and expanded. In his ears, the sound of the river grew and gushed. He heard Tississat Falls a thousand miles away in the east, and he turned toward the two tents, pockets of darkness in the blaze. He tried to raise his arm in a faulty gesture, then tumbled face forward, teeth biting into the coarse sand. His body twisted on top of him and before he fell, like a crippled bird; his stomach retched an early-morning breakfast of bacon and hard rolls, coffee and melon, onto his face and shirt.

When they reached him sandbugs had already converged on his vomit.

"Put him on the cot and take off his shirt," Hetty ordered. "Get that canteen of water and douse his forehead." She glanced at Mark. A wedge of fear was caught in his eyes and she looked away, ashamed for him.

"We should have warned him about the sun," Paula said.

"He's been in Africa long enough," Hetty answered, peeling off his shirt. "It's his own damn fault." She felt suddenly very tired of having to care for her husband.

Paula, startled by Hetty's anger, went for the canteen. Paula wanted to suggest that they go into the village. The airlines clerk spoke some English, and Mark had told her there was a white missionary at the leprosarium across the Baro, but she was afraid to suggest what to do. She never really knew what to do, not even in the relief hospital in Debre Marcus. She was just thankful people gave her orders, told her what to do for them.

She went into the tent to find her cigarettes and would have liked to hide there a while, but the heavy canvas was airless, and she had to step outside again to breathe.

Her slight body and heavy breasts were hidden in sloppy clothes, a pair of Mark's jeans cut off above her knees, and his old workshirt that she had tied in a knot at the waist because she thought it made her look something like Marilyn Monroe. She loved to wear Mark's clothes. It made her think that she really belonged to him. Her hair had lost most of its color since she had come to Africa, but she was afraid to let any of the hairdressers touch it. Now it had returned to its natural dirty brown, a color she had not seen since she was in junior high. At home in Virginia, she loved to do her hair and put on her makeup in the morning. Now she couldn't bear to look at herself.

Roger had come around. His hand reached for his forehead and he moaned, complaining of a headache. Hetty was kneeling by the cot, mopping his face slowly and efficiently, as if she had always cared for the sick. Paula looked away. She finished one cigarette and lit another from the butt. She was suddenly worried that she hadn't brought enough cigarettes for the weekend. Maybe they'd go home early, now that Roger was sick. That gave her hope, and then she remembered she was told to get the canteen and went rushing to where they had parked the F.A.O. Land Rover, hating Hetty for being so competent. It made her feel small and useless.

"What's eating you?" Hetty asked. She had followed after Mark when he took his cup of tea and walked away from the tents.

"Feeling crowded, that's all."

"You know you have an unique ability to make me feel like shit."

He set the cup on a rock and felt in the pockets of his bush jacket for his cigarettes, letting the remark wither away.

"Can't you be nice? Can't any one of you be nice?" A gush of tears swelled to her throat and she swallowed quickly to keep from crying.

"What do you want, for chrissake?" He turned on her.

"I'd like you to talk to me. Roger gets stupidly sick and you walk off, leaving me to help him. And then Paula . . .!" Hetty could hear her voice whine and it angered her more. It made her feel rotten, depending on others. She prided herself on being resilient, and she spun away from Mark and walked off.

There was always an edge of coolness about Mark, like early-morning frost. It was as though he awoke in a rage, angry with the world.

She hadn't realized this at first. He had been witty and entertaining when they met, and such a change from all the European relief workers. She had lingered over a cappuccino with him, thrilled by the chance meeting at the Ras Makonnon Bar. Then one week later, while she was pulling her VW out onto Menelik Avenue, he had stopped her; he waved from his Land Rover, and pointing toward the Hilton Hotel asked if she had time for a drink.

"Where's my wife?" Roger demanded, sitting up in his cot.

"Would you like some tea?" Paula offered at once, nervous about being alone with him.

"Where is she?" Roger was enjoying the sound of his demands. It made him feel better.

"She's gone for a walk," Mark shouted from the shoreline.

Roger laid back on the cot. He knew Hetty was sleeping with Mark. She had come home after meeting him and insisted that he be invited for dinner, then a week later, Hetty had met Mark again in Addis, and there was more talk about the "witty American." He knew then, and when he pressed her about inviting Mark for dinner, she had made excuses.

"I shouldn't have come along," Paula was saying to Hetty. "It's not my kind of thing, you know." She smiled apologetically. They were sitting together two hundred yards downriver from the campsite.

"Oh, Paula, it's not so . . ."

"I'm uncomfortable, you know, all over. I feel dirty. And my hair!"

"In another hour it will be cooler. We can go swimming. I saw a lagoon earlier . . . just the two of us girls." Hetty smiled, trying to be encouraging. In twenty minutes the sun would be down. There would be no lingering sunset that close to the equator and Paula, she knew, would be happy with a warm fire and something to eat.

"I'm not going swimming! There's a crocodile. I saw it."

"They're territorial; Roger said so. It'll never leave that stretch of the river."

Paula's throat tightened, listening to Hetty's little speech of encouragement. Hetty always had them ready, like mini-sermons, but before she could say more, Paula asked in a rush of words, "Are you sleeping with Mark?"

"Paula! What a thing . . ."

"Everyone says so."

"That doesn't give you . . . Do I pry into your life?"

"Yes, you do!" Paula turned to stare at Hetty. Her eyes were red and puffy from the hot weather and her anger. "You're always interfering," she went on, "telling me what to do."

"Paula, you're upset. I've only tried to be . . ."

"Who asked you?"

Hetty stared back at Paula, then without saying more, she stood. It was time to organize dinner. She forced herself to plan. These people were not dependable. She had to do everything herself, she realized.

Roger, abandoned in the shade, watched his wife prepare dinner. She ran their house in the village that way, relentless in her organizing. It had been a dark, unattractive house when they arrived in Ethiopia, but she had needed only two weeks to make it like their suburban London home. She had it whitewashed, made curtains and pillows herself, put down Dessie rugs, hired the help and trained them. She had planted a flower garden and several yards of vegetables.

Roger had watched with fright and fascination. She had made a portrait of· the place for all the Ethiopians to see and marvel at, for the other relief workers to envy. But he hated the house and what she had done with it. It reminded him of London.

After dinner, he would often go back to his office in the resettlement camp where books and papers were left in piles on the floor, in a disarray that Hetty would never allow. He loved his own squalor. It made him feel comfortable.

Hetty insisted Mark get the same room at the Ras Hotel: a corner room with windows that overlooked the garden and interior courtyard. The third-floor room also caught the soft afternoon light and the breeze from Mount Entoto. She would check in early, leaving him drinking in the bar. She wanted to be alone and take a bath, to fill the tub and pour in bubble soap she had purchased in Athens on the way down to Africa. It was French and expensive, even at the duty-free shop, but she loved the scent. She'd slide deep into the water and listen to Addis Ababa outside. She felt as if she were far away from the famine and poverty of Africa. She felt safe, as if she were home again in Nice and listening to the sea.

Hetty showered, washed and set her hair, and then, sitting naked on the bed, did her nails and dried them quickly, wandering about the room barefoot on the hardwood, her arms waving. She combed her hair out next, then stripped the blanket off the bed and slipped between the sheets. Mark would find her sleeping when he came into the room. It was the way she wanted him to find her.

Hetty had stopped sleeping with her husband. One morning she set up a bed in the extra room, and put up curtains and bright furnishings. Nothing was said between them, but both welcomed her decision. They no longer had to worry about each other. When she went off on Saturday morning to the city, he'd bring the maid into his room. They'd get drunk and the girl—giggling and encouraged by Roger—would dress up in Hetty's underwear and prance half-naked about the house.

"Mark, what do you feel about me?" Hetty woke him in the hotel room with her question.

"I'm very fond of you ... you know that."

"Never mind." She turned away, ashamed of her question, and of his answer, and watched the windows until it was light enough for her to get out of bed and take another bath before Sunday breakfast.

Every week Hetty made out her shopping list and boarded the bus in the dark dawn. Roger would not give her the government Land Rover, saying it might be needed, nor let her drive his VW, so she squeezed onto the local bus with the peasants, their chickens and goats, all bundled and tied up beneath the seats. The bus was full of rancid smells, human and animal odors, and she would always get sick before she reached the city.

Hetty always planned on doing the shopping quickly and returning home that night, telling herself she would not go to the bar and let herself be used by Mark. But she would go anyway, hoping that Mark was not waiting for her.

But he was always waiting, drinking a cup of cappuccino and reading his mail. She was jealous of his mail. Her letters were shared with Roger. Even her mother wrote them both, "Dear Hetty & Roger." Her friends from Paris knew them as a couple. She knew no one alone, except for Mark.

And Mark did not share his mail. It was read and

digested in silence, then the thin airmail stationery was folded back into the light blue envelopes and put away. Only then, when he had ordered another cappuccino, would he turn his attention to her.

Tell me why do I make love to you? Why do I strip naked and perfume my breasts, comb my hair, and go to you in those coarse hotel sheets? Why do I let you insult me with your silence? You are not even nice to me. We meet like this in the bar and you treat me with abuse. Why can't you be kind to me? Don't I deserve better?

Late on Sunday afternoons, after he had made love to Hetty, Mark would drive four hours north back into Gojjam Province, and spend the night with Paula in the town of Debre Marcus.

"How's Hetty?" The question was predictable. Mark found himself waiting for it, just to have it out of the way.

"She's fine."

"Are you still sleeping with her?"

"I'm not sleeping with Hetty, now or ever."

"Room 211. Ras Hotel. Everyone knows."

"What the shit do I care?"

"I know you're fucking her."

"And I'm fucking you, too." He sat up, determined to have it over with. "What does it matter?"

"It matters. She's a friend of mine."

"Bullshit! You can't stand Hetty. No one likes her, not even her husband."

"I like her," Paula answered meekly, trying to make an argument. Then she turned away from him. Her body made a shallow mound, like the outline of a grave, in the narrow bed.

"None of you women like Hetty because she has more class and style than the whole lot of you. Goddamn bunch of leeches!" Mark had heard a thousand remarks about Hetty: the other relief workers always watched for her failings. Then he was disgusted at himself for leaving Hetty, for treating her so poorly, for driving out of Addis Ababa and racing up the northern road just so he could sleep with Paula. He got out of Paula's bed and put on his trousers and stepped out into the cold night, needing to get away from the woman. She cried after him, telling him that she was sorry for making such a fool of herself.

"My wife, she thinks a goddamn camping trip is a great way to spend a weekend," Roger complained. He was feeling better. His headache was gone and he had been able to keep down his food. "You know where we are? We're two thousand yards from the Sudan, that's where. There are warring tribes over there. The Nuer cross the Baro and steal cows from the Anuak. They kill strangers; did you know that, Paula? They cut off their tits and balls. How about that?" He grunted and giggled.

"Roger, don't! It only frightens me. Please don't tell me anything about this place."

For a moment he was quiet, and then he asked, "You up for a beer? This village must have one bar. Let's go celebrate."

"What?" she asked, missing the point.

"Us!" he told her, laughing again.

Holding Roger's hand and walking through the woods, Paula got excited. She was not interested in Roger, but she liked the idea of Mark and Hetty turning around on the shore and calling to them through the darkness and finding them gone. It made her feel bitchy and free of Mark.

Roger stopped then in the dark woods and kissed her. It was a sloppy kiss, a fumbling of arms. Paula let him play a moment with her breasts, and hated herself for letting him do it, but she couldn't stop him. She was afraid he'd get mad and leave her there in the middle of the jungle. Mark would not have done this, forced himself on her. He would have waited, gone into the village and drunk beer, let her get an edge on, and then on the way back, he would have taken her down to the Baro, and there on the warm sand, he would have made love to her with the water lapping at their legs.

"What's the matter?" Roger dropped his hands.

"Nothing's the matter. You've startled me, that's all. Let's go get drunk. I feel like getting drunk."

"They must have gone into the village," Mark said, coming down to the river's edge. "Do you want to go too?"

Hetty shook her head. She wanted to be left alone and not to have to contend with him, but he dropped down next to her and put his hand on her thigh.

"Leave me alone, please."

"Aren't you a little bitch tonight?" He stood again and went up the bank to the campsite, and from there through the woods, to the village beyond the thicket, leaving Hetty sobbing to herself.

They would go back late after dinner to the Ras Hotel. A luxurious dinner at the Hilton with cocktails, boeuf bourguignon or galantine of salmon, wine and later liquor. Hetty would get herself drunk so she wouldn't think of all the starving children in the famine camps less than two hundred miles from Addis Ababa.

In their hotel room he would roll dope and they'd smoke a joint, sitting crosslegged on the wide bed. Mark, intent on his task, would speak only occasionally, then just a few mumbled syllables. She would light an incense candle and its fragrance mixed with the grass and took them away from Africa, from the sounds of sporadic gunfire in the streets and from the memory of the famine camps, filled with silent children, too hungry to cry.

Hetty would get off the bed and remove her dress, taking her time, knowing he liked to watch. She moved slowly, barefooted on the hardwood floor. She took off her blouse and felt each of her weighty breasts, the rubbery nipples tensing. She kept moving, unwrapped her skirt and let it slip into a dark corner. Her panties were a patch of white. She stripped them off with a quick tug and turned to let him study her. Her eyes were brown and watery, complacent as a tamed animal.

It was not a compelling body. Her breasts did not soar, her ass was not tucked tight. Yet she knew she was sensual for she had heard the sharp, almost painful intakes of breath men experienced when seeing her naked.

She moved to the edge of the bed and placed both her hands around his head and pulled him forward. Outside their room a noisy couple of foreigners went past, speaking in French, and she felt a shiver of vulnerability at her nakedness. Then she brought Mark's wet lips to her crotch and forgot about everyone else, the couple, her husband, the starving children of Africa.

The next morning they ate breakfast in silence, like airline companions being careful not to touch. They sat at one of the small tables near the open doors. A rose had been picked from the garden and placed in a thin glass vase on their table. Water still clung to the red petals. They could see the garden, lush with vegetation, growing in abundance, and above the trees of the court-yard she saw the windows of their room thrown open, and their bedcovers slung over the ledges of the win-dows, airing, as if they had been contaminated during the night.

Paula and Roger, in the barren village, were drinking gin in large tumblers without ice. There was no electric-ity or refrigeration and the bar had no tonic. They sat against the wall at a table made from packing crates, rough hewn and slapped together.

On the table was a blunt candle, waxed to the boards. A half-dozen other candles were lit around the small room and on the counter was a kerosene lamp. Its yel-lowish glow lit up a row of bottles on a shelf behind the counter. The gin they were drinking was homemade and poured into a Gordon bottle. Someone had amended the label to read, "A Type of Gordon's Gin."

Paula had acquired a taste for gin. It was a sharp, cutting alcohol that burned her throat. She could get drunk on it without a next-morning blinding headache and nausea. Instead, she awoke with, at the base of her throat like an irritating itch, the need for another shot, taken neat in her bathroom. The gin purged her and left her trembling.

Then the nag was gone and she recovered, cleared her eyes with drops, brushed her teeth, gargled, combed her thin hair, and with the practice gained from a thousand mornings, pulled her face into order, never once letting her eyes catch her face fully in the mirror.

Now in the comfort of the dark bar she relished the drink, positioned herself for a long night. Roger had quickly finished one glass, banged for another. She nursed hers. She let the alcohol work slowly. It was only the first taste that was truly enjoyable.

Afterward, she just kept drinking, kept pushing herself to catch again those few moments of equanimity.

But the moments always escaped her and she'd become loud and clumsy and then maudlin, weeping herself to sleep toward morning in the little house where she lived alone. She pushed those occurrences from her mind. She had only three more months in Africa. That thought made her feel warm and safe. She sipped the gin to celebrate, watching Roger with a smile. Perhaps she should sleep with him. It didn't seem like a bad idea now, in the candlelight.

Paula had told herself she would not sleep with Mark again, but on Sunday she found herself listening for his Land Rover, and when it roared into the yard announcing his arrival, all her breath escaped, as if he had physically assaulted her.

She sat up quickly and lit a cigarette, listened to his feet grate across the gravel yard and to the door. Mark did not knock. The front door shoved open and he came inside with arrogant self-possession, as if he owned the house, everything in it; owned her. She hated him for that assumption. He stood in the middle of the room and said nothing. He dominated the small house as he shoved his gloves into the pockets of his bush jacket and coldly stared down at her.

He made love to her in the living room, disregarding her protests. His eyes did not flinch from her face, but held her, like a threat.

"My wife is sleeping with Mark," Roger announced.

"He's a son of a bitch," Paula answered.

"I'll get him," Roger nodded knowingly, then sat back against the barroom wall. "And I'll get her."

"How?"

Roger gestured that he had everything under control. He looked pleased, saying, "They're down there right now on the river making love, you can bet your sweet ass on that."

Paula stared into the dim candlelight, too confused by drinking to understand what he was saying.

Roger leaned forward over the crate table and whispered, "Let me tell you something else about the ecology of reptiles."

Hetty could follow them into the village, she knew, but Roger and Mark had taken both flashlights and she was afraid of getting lost in the thicket. She heard noises, rustling in the bush, the crunch of sand on the bank. She peered into the dark, her eyes aching from the smoke of the camp fire.

She had to keep busy to hold off the fear. She would make more coffee and clean up the cups. She took the pot and walked down the bank to the river's edge. Halfway to the water she stumbled in the dark. "Oh, damn," she swore, falling to the warm sand, and thinking she had had too much to drink.

"Crocs sleep on the bank at night, you know that?" Roger said, grinning over the glass of gin. "They come up from the Baro and burrow into the warm sand at the river's edge."

Paula stared at him, trying to catch the drift of his remarks. She was like that. People told her she was a good listener, but she never listened. It was too much work, especially after she'd had a few drinks.

"And you know how they kill you?" he asked.

Paula shook her head.

"They drown the victims. They seize something, someone, in those jaws and pull them into the deep water, drown them. Then in the river itself, on shelves up under the banks, they have secret dry beds. They leave their catch, you see, on the dry shelves and come back later to eat their prey. How about that?"

Paula sat up and tried to clear her mind. Roger was telling her something, but he wouldn't just say it straight out.

"They wanted a little party all by themselves. Well, let them." He sat back, downing the last of his gin.

"Does Hetty know?" Paula asked, beginning to understand him. "I mean, does Hetty know that crocodiles sleep on the bank?" Asking him, she realized that Hetty didn't know anything at all. "Roger!" she said, starting to cry.

"Paula, it's all right; Paula, it is." He reached for her, to pull her into a drunken embrace, but she slipped off the stool and then ran from the dung-hut bar and into the dark night.

She remembered the path, where it went into the thick vegetation, but once in the trees, she did not know what she was doing and she stumbled forward, crying hysterically, but kept running. She would see the camp fire soon. She remembered how it had been blazing when they left the dark shore. She had turned back after Roger's fumbling kiss and wished she were sitting close to the fire, being warmed by the heat. His hands had been cold on her breasts.

She stumbled and fell forward and was caught by Mark.

She screamed then.

"Jesus H. Christ, Paula!"

She kept screaming. She could hear herself screaming and wanted to stop and tell Mark that the crocodile had come ashore and would find Hetty sitting there by the fire, but she couldn't stop screaming. It made her feel immensely better, screaming out in the dark night.

Mark hit her. He slapped her once when she wouldn't stop screaming, then hit her a second time. She fell against him, sobbing and clutching his body.

"What the fuck are you talking about?" He had her by both shoulders and had pulled her face up to his.

In the black night, she could not even see his face.

"The crocodile! Roger says the crocodiles come on shore at night."

"Jesus!" Mark let go of Paula and spinning around, ran back down the sandy path to the shoreline. Paula could hear his soft, sliding footsteps fade away.

"Don't," she whispered, not wanting to be left behind, and she stumbled after him, tried to keep up. She could see only the wavering spot of his flashlight. She kept running, terrified of being alone.

When she came out onto the shore, she realized she had taken the wrong path. There was no camp fire, no parked Land Rover in the grove of acacia trees, no camp fire blazing, signaling her home.

"Mark!" Her panic took the strength out of her voice. "Mark!" she said again, whispering, and then, "Oh, dear mother of God, please help me."

She should never have come to Africa, she thought. It was all a terrible, stupid mistake. What was she doing here, with these people, in this strange place? She started to run again, ran along the shore in what she thought was the right direction, and then through the palm trees, the scrub brush, and the thin thorny acacias, she saw the tiny blaze. It seemed miles ahead of her, flickering like a firefly, but its light melted her fear, and she felt safe. She slowed, exhausted by her effort, and the ground moved under her.

She was hit by the fierce wedge of a crocodile's tail and knocked sideways into the water. The blow killed her outright, and in swift silence a half-dozen crocodiles slipped into the warm river and went after her meat, tearing her limb from limb.

Mark had one flashlight, but he couldn't find Hetty. He reached the Baro's edge and went slowly along the shore. The thin beam was helpless against the enormous black night. It frightened him to see how feebly the flashlight lit the surroundings.

He was hearing every sound in the dark, all of the jungle, and the rushing river. He was hearing as he had never heard in the day. The forest, the river, the whole world of the game park. There were crocodiles here, he knew, and also hippos and lions. Mark had not said anything to the women. They would not have come if they had known the campsite was in the middle of the game reserve.

It was not the wildlife that worried Mark, but the Nuer from the Sudan who he had heard crossed the Baro at nightfall and stole whatever loose cattle they could find, driving them back across the river under the safety of darkness. The missionaries had told him to camp close to the village, warned him about tribal raiding, but he had kept quiet and let Roger pick the site for the campsite, this cluster of acacia close to the water.

"We don't want to walk too far for water," Roger had chimed, like a Boy Scout.

"Hetty!" Mark shouted.

Behind him, in the deep night of the woods, something moved.

"Hetty?" he asked again, his voice cracking. He could hear his own fear. He stepped back, away from the trees and underbrush. There was more movement and the swaying of thick palm leaves. Mark stumbled in the sand, but quickly regained his footing, flashed the thin light back and forth, trying to see beyond its pale beam.

"Hetty? Jesus Christ, where are you?" He felt that there were people in the woods: the natives from across the river. He had seen a group of them earlier selling handicrafts. They were tall and slim, with the passive eyes of the dead, like those he had seen in a hundred thousand starving children farther north. They would kill him, he guessed, simply for his flashlight and the dimming batteries. All that they had been waiting for was nightfall.

He felt the wetness of the Baro River. He had stepped backward into the soft sandy shores. The water was warm, and he remembered that the missionaries had told him there was a soda spring nearby where the water bubbled up from the roots of trees. It was something of a tourist attraction, the missionaries had joked.

Now, through the thick growth of trees, he saw more shadows, huge shadows, coming closer, coming down to the water's edge.

"Christ!" he said out loud, realizing it wasn't tribesmen at all, but elephants. They moved slowly like a leather wall, and in the night breeze he smelled their bodies.

He shouted out, trying to frighten away the herd, and a bull elephant roared back in warning.

Mark tripped and fell. He would swim across the river, he thought next. It was, he knew, narrow there at the campsite, and he could spend the night at the missionary complex on the opposite shore. He dove into the mucky water at once and swam for his life.

A crocodile caught him when he was less than twenty yards from the opposite shore. It seized his ankle and pulled him under the tide of water in a swift and sudden plunge. He had no time at all to scream for help.

Roger, coming from the bar, had heard elephants, and circled through the trees to where the Land Rover was parked. He would be safe in the Land Rover, safe until morning, or whenever the elephants finished drinking from the river.

He turned on the flashlight and aimed it at the darkness. The light picked out the water in the thicket. It surprised him, seeing how dark it had become. Earlier, there had been an ocean of stars, but now, after midnight, the sky had closed over. If it rained, they would have a hard time getting the heavy vehicle off the bank, he thought next. There was always something going wrong in Ethiopia. Nothing ever went right. Not the land. Not the people. Not even them, foreigners coming to help. The whole damn country was cursed.

The high-beam lights of the Land Rover popped on and blinded him where he stood on the sand. He raised his arm to cover his eyes.

"Mark! For fuck sake!" He stumbled in the soft earth, trying to see, and then he heard the elephants roar, and he turned toward the herd.

The half-dozen beasts were still at the shore. Several of the bulls had moved onto the shallow reaches of the river. He saw a hippo farther out in the swift river, and a dozen small hartebeests and reed bucks. It looked like a peaceful kingdom, there at the river's edge, all lit by the bright beams of the Land Rover.

He grinned, feeling safe. It was that goddamn Paula getting him so excited. He shouldn't have told her about the crocodiles just to amuse himself with her fear.

Shit, what a stupid American.

The Land Rover moved.

"Mark, for godsake." He tried to walk in the soft sand, but his legs, tired from the hike to the village, and his body, tired from too many days in Africa, too much to drink, wouldn't let him run. He waved his arms, seeing the big machine coming, still coming toward him, down the slight slope, forcing him ahead. "You'll hurt someone, you bloody fool!" He was trying to shout over the roar of the heavy engine, waving at the blinding headlights.

The elephants roared, hearing the beast of machinery behind them, and they spun away from the sound, moving in their slow and graceful dance, swinging their ten tons of weight, their giant and deadly tusks. The reed bucks and hartebeests bolted, and one small roan, stumbling into the Baro, was caught by a submerged crocodile and dragged into the depths of the river.

Caught between the charging elephants, the river, and the Land Rover, Roger raced for the trees, ran to the safety of the dense underbrush, knowing that there would be a low hanging branch that he could grab and swing out of harm's way. He almost made it. The lumbering elephants caught him before he reached the safety of the trees. The heavy club foot of the queen mother kicked him off his feet and a dozen others, all frightened by the beast of the Land Rover, trampled him to death in the soft sand.

Hetty kept driving, following the riverbank for another two hundred yards to where she had earlier found the narrow road into the thick vegetation. She swung right and drove through the village, lit only by candlelights and a few lanterns. She thought a moment of stopping, of telling the locals that there had been an accident at the edge of the Baro River, but she thought better of it and kept driving north out of Illubador Province. In the morning there would be nothing left at the river's edge. The campsite would be stripped by the roaming tribes from the Sudan who, Roger had once told her, crossed the Baro after dark and scavenged the landscape. They would take away all the sleeping bags, tents, and utensils, and in the morning no one would know they had even been there, a camping party from Addis Ababa. As for her husband, lifeless on the soft shore, the crocodiles would have him. It was the way of nature, the only ecology of reptiles.

She kept driving. In eighteen hours she would reach Jimma, and another day's drive would get her to the capital. She would drive for a hundred kilometers and then sleep a few hours to be ready for the long haul in the heat of the next day.

Hetty reached down and rubbed her knees, felt where she had bruised herself tripping over the boulder. It was nothing to complain about. To come away from a camping weekend with only a minor bruise was nothing at all. She thought about the bath that awaited her at the Ras Hotel. The luxury of it, the simple pleasure of the warm water, made her smile as she downshifted the heavy Land Rover and, picking up speed on the dry road, raced across the lowlands of Africa, raced for the warm water that would clean her body, cleanse her of this night, and of all the reptiles of Africa.